RIP THE ANGELS
FROM HEAVEN

ALSO BY DAVID KRUGLER

The Dead Don't Bleed

RIP THE ANGELS FROM HEAVEN

A NOVEL

DAVID KRUGLER

PEGASUS CRIME

NEW YORK LONDON

RIP THE ANGELS FROM HEAVEN

Pegasus Books, Ltd.
148 W 37th Street, 13th Floor
New York, NY 10018

First Pegasus Books cloth edition July 2018

Interior design by Maria Fernandez

Library of Congress Cataloging-in-Publication Data is available.

ISBN: 978-1-68177-778-8

10 9 8 7 6 5 4 3 2 1

Printed in the United States of America
Distributed by W. W. Norton & Company

To my parents, John and Dee

RIP THE ANGELS FROM HEAVEN

PART 1

Transgressions

Washington, D.C.
July 6–12, 1945

BP/5730A

Sabotage, Espionage, and Countersubversion (B-7)
NAVY DEPARTMENT

SECRET   Washington, 25, D.C.   12 May 1945

From: Lieutenant (j.g.) Ellis Voigt
To: Commander Burton Paslett
Subject: Summary findings death Lieutenant (j.g.) Logan Skerrill

MISSION

1. Investigation of April 25, 1945 murder Lt. (j.g.) Skerrill led myself and
    Lt. (j.g.) Terrance Daley to H & H Clipping Service, 1321 K Street,
    Washington, D.C. N.W. Suspicion H & H a Soviet spy front led me
    to adopt cover identity as dishonorably discharged Shipfitter Second
    Class Ted Barston, known communist sympathizer. Purpose: infiltrate
    H & H to determine if Skerrill a Soviet agent.
2. Clipping service owner Henry Himmel hired me, posing as Ted
    Barston, as deliveryman. Regular deliveries included receipt of coded
    messages from Soviet couriers, confirming espionage activity said
    clipping service and Skerrill's active part in espionage. Coded mes-
    sages copied for O.N.I. Content believed to relate to top-secret Army
    weapons project New Mexico.

3. Investigation proved clipping service employee Philip Greene, known communist, killed Lt. Skerrill at Himmel's order. Motive: Skerrill was a double agent who had confessed his treason to the F.B.I. Rather than arrest Skerrill, F.B.I. kept him in Soviet cell to investigate scope of espionage. Greene killed Skerrill before he could expose cell.

4. Tail of Himmel led to F Street restaurant where he met with unknown male subject claiming to be from Army weapons project New Mexico. Subject delivered package with schematic or diagram of suspected significance.

5. Tail of Himmel after receiving package failed. Himmel now missing along with package. Identity New Mexico subject still unknown.

RECOMMENDATIONS

1. Capture of Himmel and package urgent.

2. Identification of New Mexico subject also urgent. He may try to again deliver copy of weapons project schematic to Soviet agents. Security of weapons project at grave risk until Himmel and New Mexico subject are captured.

CHAPTER 1

THE ROOM, LIKE EVERY OTHER ONE I'D BEEN QUESTIONED IN, WAS DIM, empty, industrial. Concrete columns supporting a latticed ceiling. Concrete floor with drains. Rows of worktables and sturdy metal shelves, all bare. Faint smell of machine oil. Narrow band of grimy windows on the exterior wall. War contracts had required the tool and die plant previously located here to move to a bigger building outside the city, making this abandoned factory the perfect place for an interrogation. Even in daytime, there wouldn't be much sunlight. Of course, it wasn't daytime—it never was.

"Tell us again," the Russian asked. Face like a shovel blade, flat and hard. Broad nose, square chin, angular cheekbones, creased forehead. Black hair razed short, scalp visible. He was dressed decently—light gray summer weave suit, white dress shirt, and blue and white tie with diagonal stripes—but he was uncomfortable, tugging his cuffs, rolling his shoulders.

New to this? I wondered. Or maybe just the clothes were new. Maybe the N.K.V.D. had ordered its American agents to dress better. To try to fit in.

"Himmel asked me to meet him on F Street," I said. "Outside the Automat at seven-thirty." The third time I'd given this answer, but I said it plainly and clearly. No sigh, no protest, no impatience—I knew better. Those tired tricks didn't play with the Soviet secret police. When it came to interrogations, the commies were all business, even if they were operating in a foreign land.

"Why?"

"He wanted to know what my C.O. had made of the documents I'd copied." Slightly different phrasing this time.

"Made of?"

"Sorry. What Commander Paslett thought the documents were. What they meant."

"What did you say?"

"I said I didn't know because I hadn't briefed the commander yet."

"Did you tell Himmel this on F Street?"

A new question. The two times before, he'd asked where we'd gone after meeting outside the Automat.

"No," I answered. "We were sitting on the bench beside the statue of General Hancock, at Seventh and Pennsylvania."

"How did you get there?"

"We walked."

"The streets, please."

So I told him, again. Every corner, every turn, every street name. I'd lived in Washington, D.C., for more than three years—I didn't need a map to tell someone the most direct route from the Automat to that statue.

For the first time, his partner said something. Loudly, swiftly, in Russian. He was thin and pasty, with a beak of a nose and a jutting Adam's apple. He also looked uncomfortable in his suit. Shovel-face looked away from me as he replied. They knew I didn't understand their language, they could have been swapping lines from *Eugene Onegin* for all I knew.

"Why did you go there?" Shovel-face asked me.

"To the statue? It's a good place to talk without being overheard."

"Did you pick this place?"

"Yes."

"What else did you speak about?"

"The F.B.I."

"Explain."

"Himmel wanted to know more about how they'd questioned me when they'd picked me up."

"What did you tell him?"

"That the Bureau knew he was operating a spy ring out of his clipping service. That the agents knew I was working as the courier. And that the Bureau didn't believe I was who I said I was."

My syntax tripped up the quiet Russian, but Shovel-face followed me. "The F.B.I. did not believe your cover story," he said.

"Right."

"What did Himmel say after you told him this?"

"Nothing."

"Nothing?"

"He just thanked me and left."

"What time was this?"

"A little past eight o'clock."

"How did he leave?"

"He walked south on Seventh Street to Pennsylvania Avenue."

"Did he tell you where he was going?"

"No. And I didn't ask."

"Where did you go?"

"I went home." *Just like I told you already.*

More rapid-fire Russian from the quiet one. Shovel-face furrowed his brow in impatience, raised his hand to cut him off. "Da, da"—I caught. At least I understood that. *Yes, yes.* Which meant the quiet one was reminding his partner to tell me to—

"Keep reading the newspaper, Lieutenant Voigt," Shovel-face said. He meant the classifieds in the *Evening Star*, the Lost and Found section. *Lost: woman's silver ring set with red gemstone, band engraved R.L. to E.B., reward offered, call Brentwood 3816* was my summons to this industrial building in Southwest Washington.

"I will," I answered.

He ticked his head at the door. *Russian for So long, see you tomorrow,* I thought. I got up, strode to the rear, and wrenched open the heavy steel door. Pushed it shut and walked quickly out of the alley.

My story was good, it was tight, a close weave of facts and lies. The man in question, whom I'd known as Henry Himmel, had met me outside the Automat self-serve diner on the night of May 9, 1945—the day after the Germans surrendered. We'd talked about the work I'd done for him, but not in the way I'd just told my N.K.V.D. interrogators. And we hadn't done our talking on the park bench. Himmel and I had taken a taxi to the Jefferson Memorial, my idea. The memorial was closed for renovations, it had been secluded, quiet, absent passersby, that is, witnesses. I couldn't tell the Russians any of this, of course—then they'd have all the more reason to believe I was the last person to see Himmel alive. The way this operation was set up, Shovel-face and his sidekick had to believe I was one hundred percent on their side, a Benedict Arnold, a traitor. And to sell my treachery to the Reds, I had to go it alone, I couldn't give them any inkling I had no intention of actually helping them.

That's why I wasn't telling them the whole truth about what had happened at the Automat. The problem with my story was the kid, the eager-to-help teenager who'd been working in the Automat kitchen that night. He had let us in, I'd sworn him to secrecy after he saw the Office of Naval Intelligence identification card. The kid didn't know why I was there, but he'd gotten a good, long look at me and Filbert Donniker, the communications technician I'd brought with me. He'd seen us set up the portable listening rig, he'd watched me put the headset on and listen to Himmel's conversation with the scientist from New Mexico. I should've sent the kid on an errand, should've pushed him out the door, but that was easy to see now. In the Automat, I'd needed to get the rig up and running, needed to get Filbert out on the floor, posing as a beat-down old man so he could get the microphone close to Himmel and the scientist. Letting the kid hang around—well, I'd had no choice.

Had the Russians found him? My gut said no. If they had, I wouldn't be sitting on a paint-splattered chair in an unused factory, calmly telling my tale to two N.K.V.D. agents. If they'd found the kid, I'd still be telling my story, only under much more stressful circumstances. One rumor was the N.K.V.D. liked to start with an ice pick. Probably a legend, wafting out of Mexico because of the way they did Trotsky, but I sure didn't want to find out.

Maybe my story wasn't so good, wasn't so tight, after all. Not unless I found the kid before the Russians did.

CHAPTER 2

WHAT HAPPENED WAS, I GOT ASSIGNED TO WORK UNDERCOVER. I WAS detailed to B-7 in the Office of Naval Intelligence—the Sabotage, Espionage, and Countersubversion section. In late April 1945, a fellow officer, Lieutenant (j.g.) Logan Skerrill, was murdered in an alley close to the Washington Navy Yard, and my C.O., Commander Burton Paslett, wrested the case from the Metropolitan Police Department and gave it to me and my partner Terrance Daley. Our investigation led us to H & H Clipping Service, owned and managed by Henry Himmel. Turned out *Himmel* was a pseudonym for a Russian who ran a spy ring out of the business. Paslett had given me a cover, Ted Barston, a dishonorably discharged shipfitter. The real Ted Barston was a doper who'd died of an overdose in the brig. He'd had no wife, no family, no people to claim his meager personal effects. The O.N.I. had sealed the records of his death, in effect keeping him alive to use as an alias. Posing as Barston, I'd gotten a job as a deliveryman at H & H. By getting in tight with the receptionist, I learned that Logan Skerrill had been hauling his ashes with the accounts manager, Nadine Silva. She was Red to her marrow—so was Skerrill. The good lieutenant had compromised the O.N.I. but good, giving Himmel details of every case he'd worked on, including a mission to deliver an escaped German physicist to a hush-hush weapons project in New Mexico.

The good news, or so it had appeared, was that Himmel began using me as a courier. During my regular deliveries—the clipping service was for real and had dozens of legitimate clients—I sometimes received sealed envelopes I was supposed to discreetly deliver to Himmel. I did, but not before copying the contents for Paslett. Within a few days, I'd intercepted a schematic from the National Bureau of Standards and a coded postcard about the New Mexico project. Before I could get anything more, two agents from the F.B.I. swept me off the street and interrogated me, just as I'd told the N.K.V.D. agents. The Bureau boys didn't know I was actually a naval intelligence officer. To protect my cover, I didn't enlighten them, even after they worked me over—they wanted "Ted Barston" to tell all about the espionage running through the clipping service. Paslett sure as hell hadn't told J. Edgar we were investigating the spy ring, so how had the Bureau stumbled upon it?

Took me a bit, but I discovered that Skerrill had gone to the Bureau, confessed to being a spy, and volunteered to be an F.B.I. source. This dangerous game had signed his death warrant—once Himmel found out the fair-haired lieutenant was two-timing him, he'd ordered a hit. A gun I obtained from the apartment of another clipping service employee, a loyal commie named Philip Greene, matched a bullet taken from Skerrill's body. Greene was in jail right now, no bail, but he wasn't awaiting trial for murdering Skerrill; J. Edgar had pulled strings to transfer Greene to federal custody on espionage charges.

Which Himmel had wanted to happen all along. The morning after my confab with Himmel at the Jefferson Memorial, Commander Paslett informed me that what I'd brought in—the schematic, the coded postcard—was malarkey, all of it useless, feints to throw O.N.I. and the Bureau off the trail. Himmel had made me the moment I walked into the clipping service, he'd played all of us. While we were slathering over the decoys and the Bureau was following me, Himmel was setting up receipt of the real McCoy: a diagram from the New Mexico weapons project.

That's why he'd gone to the Automat, to meet a scientist who'd come all the way from New Mexico to deliver a sealed envelope and these instructions, which he had had Himmel memorize: *To diffuse the Uranium-235, use uranium hexafluoride and a metal filter with submicroscopic perforations, do not use a mass spectrometer.* I picked this up thanks to Filbert Donniker, the O.N.I.'s radio and electrical expert. His portable listening rig, the one we had set up in the Automat's kitchen, allowed me to eavesdrop. Filbert wore a microphone disguised to look like a pen jutting from his shirt pocket. It had good range, so he didn't have to sit close to Himmel and his contact. Only I could hear their conversation through the headset and, just like Himmel, I memorized the instructions about the uranium. It was all Greek to me, but Paslett and I did know this much: Army was building some kind of bomb down there in the desert. After the scientist left and Filbert returned to the Navy Building, I confronted Himmel outside the Automat and persuaded him to go with me to the Jefferson Memorial.

Now Himmel was missing and the N.K.V.D. wanted to find him in the worst way. The Russians knew he'd received the diagram, they knew the egghead from New Mexico had told Himmel something awfully important about that bomb project. And they knew I was involved, they just weren't sure how. If I wanted to keep the Russians from getting the information they needed to build their own bomb, I had to convince them I was telling the truth about that night, had to keep them from learning where Himmel and I had gone for real. I also needed to track down the scientist who'd turned over the diagram before he passed on another copy to the Russians.

First things first, I told myself as I walked away from the factory. Selling my lie to the N.K.V.D. required finding that kid from the Automat. The Russians weren't just grilling me, they were methodically retracing every step Himmel had made on the night of May 9. Pretty soon it was going to occur to them they should show my photograph to Automat employees. If the kid still worked there, he'd have a pretty hard time acting like he'd never seen me before. Even if he tried not to, he'd flash a tell. A gulp, a blink, a stutter, something. (Takes a lot of practice to become an effortless liar.) If the kid—hell, I'd never even asked his name—still worked at the Automat, and if Shovel-face and his partner came around, he was in danger. I needed to check on him, figure out a way to keep his existence a secret from the Russians, do whatever it took to keep him safe. *Tomorrow,* I told myself, *I'll find him tomorrow . . .*

RATTLED BY THE RUSSIANS, I WENT INTO THE FIRST TAVERN I SAW ON Fourth Street. Corner one-story brick heap, rusty Pabst sign swinging from a truss. Men shoulder-to-shoulder at a long bar, shot glasses and beer bottles lined up like sentinels. Cloud of blue smoke, buzz of idle chatter, barkeep wringing out a towel—same scene you'd find in a hundred and one other joints. I claimed an empty stool at the bar's end, facing the door. The barkeep padded over, looked me up and down. I circled my finger in the direction of the nearest beer bottle and shot glass, he nodded. Returning with a Natty Bo and the rye, he swept up my dollar with a meaty fist. Silent transactions, my favorite.

I sipped the whiskey, took a long draw of cold beer, lit a Lucky. Inhaled like a pearl diver about to go under—the Russians, damn them, hadn't smoked during my interrogation, which meant I hadn't been able to light up either. Put me about four cigarettes behind for the day, I figured. Told myself I'd pay down that debt, go one more round, then get some chow— I'd been too nervous to eat before my "appointment" at that abandoned factory. It was my duty to keep the Russians at bay, to protect our New Mexico weapons project, whatever it was, but going in by myself, without backup, had shaken me hard. What if Shovel-face had decided he didn't like my answers, what if he had orders to "take care of" that troublesome naval intelligence officer who kept turning up like a bad penny?

Too many what-ifs, not enough whiskey. I finished my shot, squinted through my cigarette smoke, surveyed the scene. Rickety tables filled the floor between the bar and the plaster wall. His and her washrooms, a pay phone, rear exit. No booths, no jukebox, no dance floor—this tavern wasn't laid out for romance or atmosphere.

Which is why the couple at a table along the far wall caught my eye. Young, smartly dressed, attractive. Her: ginger-brown hair, bangs cut high and straight, tight curls tucked behind her ears. Apple cheeks, demure nose, full lips. Slender, her shapely legs crossed under a belted maroon dress with white trim and sharp collars. First thought: she's the girl the girl next door confides in. Him: blond, tan, square-jawed, narrow-set eyes. Athletic build, biceps filling out the short sleeves of his blue and white sport shirt.

Sharp-creased chinos, polished two-tone wingtips. First thought: runner-up high school tennis champ. Two fish out of water, why were they bending elbows in a watering hole for working stiffs?

Fighting, apparently. I couldn't hear them, but their expressions were loud and clear. His lips pursed tight, eyes blazing. Her gaze on the fly-specked window above them, her mouth fixed in a scowl. She started to say something, broke it off with a terse shake of her head, eyes returning to the window. I couldn't read lips, but it wasn't hard to figure out what he was saying. *What, what?* She didn't answer, he angrily swilled his beer, wiped his mouth with the back of his hand. Now she said something, probably a crack about his manners. He smirked, started giving her more what-for. She caught me looking; I smiled and mouthed the words *good luck*. She grinned, he whipped his head around to glare at me, but I'd already turned my attention back to my business: beer, another shot, cigarettes.

I was busy trying not to think about the snafu my undercover work had gotten me into when I felt a tap on my shoulder. I turned: the girl. Champ was nowhere to be seen.

"Thanks," she said. Rich, expressive voice, light drawl. Upper South, I guessed.

"For?"

"Encouraging me to dump him."

"Did I?"

"Isn't that what you said? *Dump him*?"

"Sure did," I decided to say.

"Do you often give out sage advice in bars?"

"Ever since my advice column got cancelled."

"Well, I took it."

"Yeah? How'd he take it?"

A shrug. "Ah'm sure one of his other girlfriends will soften the blow."

"That kind, huh?"

A laugh. "Yeah, that kind."

I asked, "A drink to celebrate your independence?"

"S'long as it's not here."

"Bad memories, huh?"

Another laugh. "How'd you know?"

14

I finished off my second shot, dropped a tip, we left.

"This your neighborhood?" she asked.

"Nope. Yours?"

She shook her head. "Our feud started at a party, and being the decent folk we are, we came here so as not to cause a scene."

"I know a quiet place the other side of the Mall," I said.

"A quiet place in Washington? Didn't know one existed."

"They don't advertise."

"Off the beaten track?"

"Could say that."

"Sounds nice."

"They pour more than rye, too."

A grin. "Yes, you don't seem like a shot and a beer kinda joe."

"No?"

"Ah'm thinking manhattans."

I shook my head.

"A gin man, then."

"Good guess. Gibsons."

"How's your barman's highball?"

"He adds a kiss of ginger ale to the club soda."

She clapped her hands in delight. "A man who knows his drinks, Ah'm so pleased."

I didn't ask if she meant me or the barman. She opened her tiny black clutch and pulled out a gold cigarette case. I tapped out a Lucky from my crumpled pack, struck a match, lit us up. Cool evening, breeze riffling leaves. She had a cream-colored shawl wrapped around her shoulders, pulled it tighter. We were walking north on Fourth Street, past dilapidated row houses and more taverns like the one we'd just left. Close to the Mall, dull government offices had sprouted like weeds. Social Security, Railroad Retirement Board, the Federal Warehouse.

We kept up the chitchat as we crossed the green expanse, crowded with "tempos" to house war agencies. Her name was Mara. She didn't volunteer her family name, I didn't ask. Hailed from Greensboro, North Carolina, had washed up in D.C. in '43. Worked as a steno at "one of those alphabet soup agencies," no further details offered. I kept my story short, too, and true. Grew up in Chicago, enlisted in the Navy right out of high school, finagled a commission before Pearl, arrived in D.C. in '42.

The place I was taking her was just off Third and Indiana, about a block from the Federal Court House. Basement space, rear entry, no sign, just a solid wooden door with a glazed window at the bottom of the stone steps. Wasn't a speakeasy—you didn't have to use a special knock or other Prohibition-era nonsense to get in—but it sure helped if a regular brought you in your first time and vouched for you. An assistant U.S. attorney I'd helped out a couple of years earlier had initiated me—the lawyers, clerks, and judges who worked in nearby Judiciary Square regarded the place as a kind of gentlemen's club. Downie's, the attorney had called it. I didn't make a habit of drinking there, but I liked to show my face now and again so I wasn't forgotten.

"Gibson, sir?" the bartender Frederick asked as soon as we were seated at the upholstered bar with a glimmering top.

"Please. And a highball for the lady."

He nodded respectfully and turned to his work. Frederick was an elderly Negro, his hair snowy white. A trim, short man, he dressed impeccably. That night, a bespoke suit, dark blue, an off-white oxford shirt pressed and starched, silver cuff links, a tie with a gray and silver pattern. Looked just like the lawyers who frequented the place. Hell, for all I knew, Frederick was a lawyer—maybe there was more money in cocktails than in whatever legal work the D.C. big shots left for the colored bar.

Mara looked around at the dark oak paneling, the polished light sconces, the plush chairs in the lounge. "Far cry from the last place," she commented.

Asking what I was doing down in Southwest D.C.? I wondered. "Night and day, sure," I said.

"Do you bring all your dates here?" Smiling playfully.

"Only my wife."

"You don't strike me as the settled-down type." Still smiling, knowing I was joking.

"These days, is anyone?"

"Well, the war's almost over."

"So what date did you pick?"

"What d'you mean?"

"In your office pool. For when the Japs cry uncle." At the Navy Building, I had twenty on August 4.

"Now, Ellis, what makes you think Ah'm the gambling sort?"

You're here, aren't you? Instead, "I'm blessed with modest powers of clairvoyance."

"Modest? That mean you're too shy to use those powers?"

"Oh no. Palm, please."

She extended her right hand, fingers limp, as if for a gentleman's kiss. I turned her palm up, and, cupping her knuckles with my left hand, traced my right forefinger across the horizontal creases on her palm. Kept my touch light, felt a quiver in her wrist.

"So what's my fortune?"

"That I don't know."

"So what can you tell me?"

"That you are a gambling kinda gal and you picked July twenty-seventh for the Japs' surrender."

She laughed. "Close—July twenty-second."

"Like I said, 'modest powers.'"

Frederick set our drinks down, we clinked glasses. "To bright futures"— Mara's toast. I thought she might ask what I did for the Navy, but she kept the conversation frivolous. How'd I like D.C., had I seen *The Valley of Decision* yet? She prattled about the party she'd been to with Champ, told me how nice her landlady was. Another girl, another night, I would've made a play halfway through our drinks, but I decided to hold back, see if she'd take the turn herself.

Which she did by asking, "So do you billet with your fellow officers, Ellis?"

I shook my head. "Got my own place."

She arced a perfectly plucked eyebrow—in the wartime boomtown, your own place was as uncommon as a hosiery sale or copper pipes. "How'd you swing that?"

I rubbed my temples. "I used my modest powers of clairvoyance. Which are also telling me nightcaps await us there."

Not one of my better lines, but considering the day I'd had, I was long gone past slick.

CHAPTER 3

BACK IN MY BASEMENT FLAT, I MIXED TWO MARTINIS IN THE KITCHEN and brought them to the living room, where Mara sat in the lone upholstered chair. I didn't have a sofa, so I brought in a chair from the kitchen. When she toasted to "bright futures" again, I leaned close and said, softly, "Starting now," and set my drink down.

I kept the kiss slow, gentle, long—she liked that. Her breath quickened, she shifted closer. I lifted the glass out of her hand and set it on the floor, sloshing gin everywhere. Ran my hand over her neck, her back. We kindled the kiss for a long minute, but it's pretty uncomfortable to neck with the arms of chairs between the two of you. Taking her hand, I stood and led her down the hallway. Pretty Spartan, my bedroom—just a thin double mattress on a wooden frame, a lamp atop an upturned apple crate, a wooden chair, and a battered chest of drawers—but if Mara was boarding, then chances were she was hot-cotting in a bunk bed.

We stood at the foot of the bed, keeping the kiss alive, her hands clutching my back. I let my hands drift down her back, to just above her hips. Mara was a fine kisser, no masher. When my fingers sought out the buckle on her belt, she gently but firmly pulled a step away.

"If you'll allow me?" Smiling, she unbelted the dress, gracefully pulled it over her head, and expertly folded it. She set it on the seat of the wooden chair and reached behind her back to unfasten her brassiere, a blue lacy number that must've cost a fortune. The matching panties came off next. She also folded her undergarments, placed them atop the dress. A man didn't have to be a Casanova to catch this cue—I was busy undressing, too, though my clothes didn't end up folded and stacked. Now she only had on her patent leather pumps—an awful nice look for the right kind of girl, and Mara was the right kind of girl. Hourglass figure, flat stomach, firm breasts with brown-red nipples. She stepped out of the pumps, I pulled the covers back.

Afterward, Mara didn't exactly skedaddle, but she didn't linger, either. We shared a cigarette and the usual cooing.

"Ah'd better get dressed before I get sleepy," she said.

"You don't have to leave," I said.

"Ah'd love to stay, but it's a busy day for me tomorrow."

"Sure."

She slid off the mattress and stood, still unabashed, but gave me a shy, awkward look as she picked up her clothes. "Your bathroom is . . . ?"

"First door on the right," beckoning.

I smoked another cigarette, glanced at my crumpled clothes on the floor, and wondered how she'd say good-bye.

"Ah wouldn't say no to another highball some night," that's how. Standing in the doorway, the belt of her dress perfectly straight, fresh lipstick reflecting the dim light of the bedside lamp.

"That sure would be nice, Mara." I got out of bed and pulled on my shorts, hoping I wouldn't step on the condom I'd dropped somewhere in the vicinity of my clothes.

"You can leave messages for me at this number." She extended a slip of paper with her name and a telephone number printed in neat block letters. I palmed it and walked her to the door, treating myself to a long look at the sway and switch of her hips under the snug fabric of her dress.

"Maybe an evening next week?" I proposed.

"Maybe. My social calendar fills up fast." Giving me that playful smile she'd first tried out at the tavern on Fourth Street.

"Then I won't wait long to call," I said.

"That's good to hear."

At the threshold I leaned close to kiss her cheek, mindful of the lipstick. She turned to smile once more as I shut the door.

I picked up my unfinished martini, took it to the kitchen, and dropped in two ice cubes. Back in the living room I sprawled out in the upholstered chair and went over the evening so far, since the moment I left the factory. Figured the Russians were watching me close. A shadow was a cinch, I hadn't even bothered checking window reflections to see who was trailing me. But had they gone one step further, had they planted Mara in the closest tavern to the factory, figuring I'd need a drink or three to steady my nerves? That kind of gutbucket didn't front B-girls, and it sure as hell didn't draw lookers on the make. Was Mara on the Russians' string, a party member or pinko eager to help the cause? If so, the scene with her squeeze was staged, Champ another Red starring in the one-act breakup so I wouldn't get suspicious. The more I thought about the scene, the more it felt like a setup. Mara had glided from Champ to my bed in all of two hours. Maybe some girls pounced that fast, but not a well-bred deb like her, not for a lieutenant junior grade like me. Another clue: the note with her number. High-class Southern girls went to finishing schools where they perfected their cursive, but Mara had block-printed. Sound tradecraft, that—never leave a handwriting sample. Finally, the way she'd made love. She hadn't been frigid, but she'd let me know what she wanted and when without saying a word. There was a word for her bedroom manner, but I couldn't think of it until I remembered how she'd undressed: fastidious. Like she'd been ordered to make it with a stranger but to ensure it looked like a genuine quickie, not a setup. Staying in control, keeping everything neat and clean, that's how she'd gotten herself through it. Right down to the husky but brief cry of pleasure at the end. Had she faked it? Of course—the whole night was faked, now I was certain. The Russians were pushing the pedal, speeding up. Mara was a plant, a roper. Next time I brought her home, she wouldn't leave after our roll in the hay. Dutifully following her instructions from the N.K.V.D., she'd offer to make us drinks and dope mine. Then the Russians would give my flat a real wringing, toss it from top to bottom while I snored, naked and flat on my back. Finding the pawnshop ticket I'd hidden in the kitchen wouldn't take long, and this operation would fail awful fast once they redeemed that hock.

I drained my martini, the ice cubes clinking, and looked regretfully at the spilled gin on the floor from Mara's drink. That had been the last of my booze, and I needed another drink.

THE NEXT MORNING WAS SATURDAY, BUT I WAS ON DUTY AT 7:00 A.M. at the Navy Building, the Mall tempo that housed the O.N.I. I decided against telling my C.O., Commander Paslett, about my go-around with Shovel-face and his pal. Better to wait until I knew what to do about the kid from the Automat. As it was, I had one day left on a punishment detail for a mistake I'd made while undercover as Ted Barston: just before picking up an envelope for Himmel as his courier, I'd sent a telegram, as Ellis Voigt, to my gal, Liv, setting up a date. The F.B.I. agents had found out and told Commander Paslett. He'd filed a spec, a specification of an offense, which I hadn't disputed. I could have been—I should have been—demoted, but Paslett liked me, he'd secretly been proud of how I'd stood up to the drubbing from the Bureau while I was posing as Barston. So for two months I had to answer the telephone number we give out to the public. Only Sundays off. Say Joe Q. Citizen thinks his boss is bribing a naval procurement officer, or Mary Do-Gooder's machinist boyfriend is stealing dies from his shop at the Navy Yard. They could call that number to make a report without leaving their names. The nutter line, we called it, because ninety-nine of one hundred calls were stinko. By my third day, I'd taken close to sixty calls from raving loons, grudgers looking to settle scores with coworkers and bosses, Miss Lonelyhearts desperate to talk, and a few jokers who thought I could bust their landlords for rent gouging. But every time I felt like beating my head against the desk, I reminded myself that the spec offered good cover for the game I was playing with the Russians.

The morning was slow, just two calls, both useless. To keep from watching the clock, I read every story in the *Times-Herald*. Twice. Worked the crossword, read my horoscope. It wasn't encouraging. Plenty of activity in the building—O.N.I., like all intelligence agencies, worked round-the-clock—but no one popped in to even say hello. My partner, Terrance Daley, sometimes dropped by to chew the fat, but he was off that day. I sorely missed knowing what was going on in the Navy Building and being a part of it. Occasionally I caught rumors, including a juicy one that the new president was going to disband a rival agency, the Office of Strategic Services, or O.S.S., and give some of its duties to O.N.I., but mostly I kept my head down and waited out the long hours on the nutter desk.

At noon I let the switchboard know I was taking my lunch break and raced out of the building. Driscoe's, on Seventeenth, was my greasy spoon as of late. Decent hash, strong coffee, didn't skimp on the sandwich meat. I'd just tucked into a cheeseburger, the news murmuring on the Philco at the end of the counter, when I caught the reflection of Agent Clayton Slater, of the F.B.I., in the coffeemaker as he entered. Because of the urn's curve, his face was oval, nose huge and eyes bulging. Good look for him, I decided. Slater and his partner Reid were the two agents who had detained me while I was undercover. They'd roughed me up, they'd ratted me out to Paslett about the telegram to my gal, they'd wanted me court-martialed. Last night the N.K.V.D., today the Bureau—how come my horoscope never gave me a heads-up?

Slater slid into the stool next to me and helped himself to a French fry.

"Any good calls this morning, Voigt?"

"Other than from your wife, no."

"Aw, s'that all you got? Last time I saw you, you were a fountain of sarcasm."

I slid my platter away so he couldn't take another fry. "Ted Barston was a lot funnier than me."

"That's for sure. But then, you're a lot luckier than Ted, aren't you?"

Instead of the bait, I took a huge bite of my cheeseburger and chewed noisily.

"Two months on the nutter line for breaking cover, that's barely a slap on the wrist," Slater went on, as if I had replied. "Not to mention the fact that Ted's dead and you're not. Like I said, lucky."

"Say what you came to say, then beat it."

"Philip Greene is telling us quite a tale."

"So?" Greene was the commie charged with killing Skerrill, the naval lieutenant who'd been working for both the Russians and the Bureau. I'd found the murder weapon at Greene's flat, I'd had him arrested, I'd interrogated him, all before the Bureau took him into custody.

"Greene says he didn't kill Skerrill."

"Well, I hope you've released him posthaste—we can't have innocent men cluttering our prisons now, can we?"

"Greene says he knows who killed Skerrill for real."

I shrugged, worked on my cheeseburger.

"We laughed, we patted him on the head for being a funny boy. Greene says but listen."

"D'you tell him the Bureau only listens through bugs?"

"So we listen. Said commie stooge makes his case, point by point. All of a sudden, we're not laughing anymore."

"That's too bad. You Bureau boys need more laughter in your lives."

But Slater was just warming up. "Said commie stooge has no proof, he's got no evidence. But he tells us: dig, and dig deep. So that's what we're doing, Voigt: we're digging, and digging deep." He studied me closely, like a salesman who'd finished his pitch.

Hell if I was going to take the bait, no way I was going to ask: *Golly, whose name did Greene give you?* Instead I said, "Listen up, buttercup, I don't give a rat's ass what name said commie stooge coughed up, because Greene did Skerrill on Himmel's orders. And yeah, Greene pulled the trigger, but Skerrill's blood is all over the Bureau's hands, got it? Cause if you and your toadie boss hadn't tried to run him as a source, no hit woulda been ordered. You shoulda arrested him the second he came to you, we shoulda been interrogating him from the get-go. But no, you Hooverites got cute, and it got a sworn officer of the U.S. Navy killed. He was a traitor, sure, but he didn't deserve to bleed to death in a crummy alley—and that's all on you." I wagged a fry for emphasis. Fortuitously, I'd dragged it through catsup first and a dab splattered on his tie.

Slater plucked a napkin from the dispenser and dipped it in my water glass to wipe off his tie. "Nice try, Voigt, but you boo-hooing for the late great Logan Skerrill—well, that just doesn't cut it, does it?" And with that, he left.

I pushed my platter aside. I'd eaten too fast, now I had indigestion. I lit a Lucky to calm my stomach and my nerves. Slater had wanted me to ask for the name Greene had given, but I hadn't played along. So he'd found a different way to tell me. *You boo-hooing for the late great Logan Skerrill—well, that just doesn't cut it, does it?*

Because the name Greene had coughed up as Skerrill's killer was mine.

CHAPTER 4

F IRST THE N.K.V.D., NOW THE BUREAU. THE RUSSIANS SUSPECTING I
was lying about Himmel, that was bad, but the F.B.I. suspecting I'd
killed Skerrill—that was worse. The Russians wanted to know what had
happened to Himmel because they were chasing the dope on the weapons
project in New Mexico. The Reds needed me as much as they distrusted
me, but if the Bureau was convinced I had turned, gone Benedict Arnold,
it would stop at nothing to prove I was guilty of treason. Hell, Hoover had
a thick file on Eleanor Roosevelt—how much consideration would I get as
a lowly officer? Didn't matter a lick that my undercover work had busted
up Himmel's spy ring, Slater was out to get me, for sure.

As mammoth as my problems were, making sure the kid from the
Automat was safe was my first concern, but I couldn't do anything until I
was free to leave my desk. The afternoon dripped by like a leaky faucet.
I stared at the telephone, willing it to ring—at least nutters prattling on

would speed up the clock. No such luck; I had to sweat out the afternoon in silence.

At four o'clock I stubbed my umpteenth Lucky of the day, donned my hat, and skedaddled. *The kid, the kid*, I kept telling myself, practically muttering the words like a mantra. I had to make sure he was safe. A lot of time had passed since that night at the Automat, probably the kid didn't work there anymore. That thought cheered me. Who would remember who had worked in the kitchen a particular night months ago? I doubted Shovel-face and his sidekick would do more than ask an employee or two a couple of questions. I didn't see how they could get at the Automat's old timesheets, didn't think they'd even try. And if the kid still worked at the Automat, I could take him aside, coach him, convince him if the two Russians came around, he'd need to avoid them at all costs, even if it meant ditching a shift. No way I could turn him into an Olympian liar, one capable of fooling veteran Soviet agents.

Instinct told me to keep my head down, my appearance nondescript, so I changed into civvies: gray trousers, white oxford, no tie. The Automat was hopping, a dozen people lined up to get nickels from the cashier, a girl who looked no older than fourteen. One nice thing you can say about war, it opens up lots of jobs for teens.

When I reached the register, I said, "I'm looking for a kid who works in the kitchen, about your age, maybe a little older, has acne?"

She pulled a face. "Ugh. You mean Kenny."

"Right, Kenny."

"He didn't show up for his shift."

My stomach tensed. "When was he due in?"

She shrugged. "Dunno. Two, I guess? God, I hope this gets him fired, he's such a—"

"Listen, where's your manager, I gotta talk to him."

"No manager here."

"Who can I talk to?"

"You could try the office." She scribbled the number on a scrap of paper and handed it over.

"It's open on Saturdays?"

"Til five."

I glanced at my watch: 4:43. I thanked her and left. Could be lots of reasons Kenny hadn't shown up, I told myself. Maybe his bike got a flat. Maybe his mother was sick. Maybe he found a better job and hadn't bothered to call in to quit. I fired up a cigarette to calm my nerves—didn't help.

I crossed F Street and entered the Peoples Drug Store, beelined for the telephone booths in the back. Dropped my nickel, called the number.

"Horn and Hardart, how may I help you?" a perky female voice asked.

"This is Sergeant First Class George Litton, U.S. Army," I said officiously. "I'm trying to get ahold'a one of your employees at the F Street Automat."

"What's his name?"

"I only have his Christian name, ma'am, it's Kenny, he's about seventeen, works in the kitchen."

"He's not in trouble, is he?"

"Oh no, ma'am, he came into a recruiting station but forgot to give us his last name. Need to get it and his address so we can talk to him some more."

"Okay. Can you hold for a moment?"

"Sure."

She was back on the line within two minutes. "Okay, Sergeant, Kenny's family name is Newhurst, and he lives at 134 Randolph Place, Northwest."

"Okay, thanks." I hung up, left the drugstore, flagged a hack. I could ring the Newhursts, but what good would that do? A stranger calls, asks about their son—they'd clam up tight. I needed to find Kenny pronto, and there was still a chance he was home. He might have mixed up his schedule, or maybe he broke his arm climbing a tree and was getting a cast at the hospital. And if he wasn't home—my mouth went dry just thinking about what that might mean—I needed to know when his folks had last seen him.

Randolph Place was just two blocks long, lined with three-story row houses with high front porches, bay windows, and mansard roofs. The Newhursts had whitewashed their front steps; petunias and tulips brightened a tiny flower bed. I came up the steps, knocked on the screen door. The other door was open, a news announcer's voice on an unseen radio.

"Just a moment," a woman called. A moment later, she came thumping down the stairs and peered at me through the screen. Slender, late thirties, a redhead, her fashionable permanent framing a pretty face. She smiled uncertainly, giving the stranger on her threshold the benefit of the doubt. "Yes?" she asked.

"Missus Newhurst?"

"Yes."

"My name is William Brady, I work for your son's employer, Horn and Hardart. May I talk to you and your husband?" I cursed myself for being such a coward, but I couldn't use my real name without compromising the investigation of the Russians.

"Please, come in."

I followed her into the parlor.

"Lyle's not home, he's at the golf course," she said, beckoning for me to sit in an upholstered armchair. "May I offer you something to drink? Iced tea?"

"No, thank you."

"If you're sure?"

I nodded and she settled into the sofa, directly across from me. She wore white Capri pants and a light blue blouse with short sleeves. Light touch with the makeup, just a press of lipstick and a dab of mascara. Magazines were fanned like a winning hand of poker on the coffee table between us, the cut glass ashtray was spotless. The radio, still on, was prewar but looked brand new, an Admiral housed in a walnut cabinet. On the wall, framed pictures of the Newhursts on outings with their son.

"What did you want to speak with me about, Mister Brady?"

"Missus Newhurst, did your son leave to go to work today?"

"Of course. He isn't there?" Trace of alarm.

"No, ma'am, he didn't come in. How does he get to the Automat?"

"He takes the Sixth Street trolley. I don't understand, Kenny's never late, he's never missed a shift."

"Yes, he's a model employee."

She nodded, barely hearing me as the logical question hit her: Why hadn't someone from the Automat called at two to ask where Kenny was?

"The thing is, Missus Newhurst, Kenny wasn't supposed to come to the Automat today at two—I'd arranged for him to meet me at our company office."

"Why?"

"Kenny called yesterday to tell us about theft at the F Street location. I asked him to meet me to tell me about it."

"Theft? What kind of theft?"

"Some employees are skimming the registers. Who it is we don't know, we're hoping Kenny could tell us."

The color drained from her face. "My God, it's past five, he's been missing over three hours, I should call the police."

I silently berated myself again. We had no time for the cops—I needed to get out of there to look for Kenny.

"Now, there's no need to panic, Missus Newhurst. What I think is, Kenny's just a little nervous, that's all. He did the right thing, of course, by telling us about the theft, but the schoolyard code is awful strong. I'm sure he's just having second thoughts about talking to me. He's probably at the park with friends or at a movie."

"That's not like Kenny at all," she said firmly. "He wouldn't not go to work or miss a meeting with a boss and just go off with his friends."

"Tell you what, Missus Newhurst, why don't we wait for Kenny to come home and take it from there? Maybe you could call some of his friends, see if he's with them. In the meantime, I'll—"

"Did you change Kenny's shift?" she interrupted with urgency.

"What do you mean?"

"Did you tell the Automat he'd be in later, after your meeting—like three or four o'clock?"

"Well, yes—I mean, I had my secretary change his start time so we wouldn't tip anyone off about what he was doing."

"Maybe he's there now. Maybe you're right, he had second thoughts about talking to you, but he still went to work. Yes, I'm sure that's it." She stood and strode to the telephone stand in the hallway.

Keep it simple, always. I'd broken this ironclad rule with my hastily spun lies about theft and "William Brady." Now I was flailing to protect a worthless cover story. As Kenny's mother flipped through the directory, I said, "It's best if you don't mention I'm here, Missus Newhurst—we don't want the thieves to put two and two together."

She didn't acknowledge me and began dialing. "Yes, hello, this is Georgette Newhurst, Kenny's mother—is he there?" She sucked in her breath at the answer. "When was he due in?" At this answer, she looked sharply at me. "I see. Well, when he comes in, have him call home imme- diately." She enunciated her telephone number and asked the clerk to repeat it back before hanging up.

"They said he was due in at two, Mister Brady."

"Only the kitchen staff know Kenny was due in at four, Missus Newhurst, and the telephone's in the office on F Street. Whoever answered wouldn't know about his changed shift."

"How could they not? Why isn't Kenny there?"

I had to get out of there—too late, I realized I should never have come. I'd whipped Georgette into frenzied fear, and I'd squandered precious time. Believing that Kenny was at home had been a subconscious attempt to dodge the consequences of my actions. But if I acted *immediately*, I might not be too late.

Standing, I said, "I'm gonna drive straight to my office and see if Kenny came in while I was here. You call his friends, like I said, okay, Missus Newhurst? I'm sure one of us will find out where he is. I'll call you when I get there, okay?"

She nodded uncertainly. "You'll call as soon as you can?"

"Absolutely, Missus Newhurst." Hoping lightning wouldn't strike me dead for this last lie.

"All right, I'll call his friends."

"Yes, you do that, I'll show myself out." I clipped down the front steps and walked briskly away without looking back. If I'd been the praying sort, I would have begged God to give me back the lost time so I could ensure that everything the Newhursts had—a lovely home, a good son, happy lives—would remain theirs.

CHAPTER 5

IT TOOK AN ETERNITY, IT SEEMED, TO FLAG A HACK. I TOLD HIM TO drop me off at Tenth and E, SW. To my relief, he didn't try to strike up a conversation. I tried to distract myself by looking at the businesses lining Sixth Street. An array of cafeterias, launderers, and cobblers with colorful signs rolled by, but I kept seeing Kenny's mother's anxious face. By now, she'd called her son's friends—none had seen Kenny. She'd called her husband's golf club and left a message for him to come home immediately. She'd called the Automat again, this time telling whoever answered that "William Brady" of Horn and Hardart was also looking for Kenny. And when she'd heard "Who's William Brady?" she'd hung up, dialed zero, and cried at the operator to call the police. Georgette Newhurst seemed pretty sharp, she'd remember my face, my voice, my story; she'd tell all to the cops. They'd take her seriously, too. A teenage boy missing for three hours was an eye-roller, but a possible kidnapping? City detectives were likely on their way to 134 Randolph Place.

But I couldn't worry about all that at the moment. *Find Kenny, fix this*, I told myself. The hack turned onto E Street and stopped at the curb. I paid him, watched him drive off, and crossed the street. The empty factory where I'd been questioned the night before was located in a wedge-shaped lot between Ninth Avenue and Maine Avenue, which ran along the Washington Channel. Bringing Kenny to this location was risky—it was daylight, someone might see them entering the building; the Harbor Patrol Station was just blocks away—but N.K.V.D. agents were like stray cats, they had habits, they had hideaways, and once they found a protected nook, they came back. The sun beat down, but tough questions sweated me as much as the heat. Had they posted a guard? Could I get close enough to observe? How was I going to look in—the windows were high, narrow, dirty. What if the Russians had taken Kenny elsewhere?

I approached from the north. The night before, I'd knocked on the south entrance, per the coded instructions in the classifieds. Shovel-face had let me in, leading me through a small front office to the shop floor. Built to fit the triangular lot, the factory was widest at the rear. There had to be a loading dock, a coal bin lid, another door. But if the owners hadn't locked down every ingress when they left, the Russians probably had.

The alley behind the factory was cobbled and weed choked. A brick warehouse abutted the alley, but its dock was empty, bays shuttered; work had stopped for the day. No sign of a sentry, so I trod lightly up a set of grated steps to the factory dock and surveyed my options. None looked promising. The loading doors were behemoths, ten feet high and sheathed in riveted metal panels—even if they were unlatched, they'd heave and creak at the first tug. I tried the handle of a regular-sized wooden door on the left side, but it was locked. No windows on this side.

Then I remembered the vents on the roof. During my interrogation, I'd noticed a row of fans set into circular casings with tin-plated, pointed rain guards. Could I see through those shafts if I could find a way onto the roof? I wasn't so lucky as to spot a ladder on the warehouse dock, but a wooden pallet I retrieved from the alley made a nice substitute. I leaned it against the west wall, clambered up, and pulled myself up using an eave bracket. The roof was flat and tar-papered. I unlaced my brogans and took them off. In a crouch, I crept toward the rear fan, which offered a decent sight line to the factory floor.

What I saw turned my stomach. Kenny was lashed tight to the same chair I'd sat on. Shovel-face stood in front, his partner behind. The boy's nose was bleeding, his right eye was swollen shut.

"What did the old man look like?" Shovel-face demanded.

"Jes' an old man, told you," Kenny said thickly, sobbing, his shoulders heaving. "Please stop."

Shovel-face slapped him across the cheek. "Was he thin, was he fat, tall or short? If you tell us, we will let you go. Otherwise . . ."

I backed away and ran across the roof as lightly as I could. Scrambled down the pallet, panting on the dock as I pulled on my shoes, my hands shaking. How was I going to get Kenny out of there? I was alone, without a weapon, no time to call for help.

I raced from the dock to the factory's front door, its small window papered over. Yanked on the handle—locked. Pounding on the metal door I shouted, "Police! Open up, you're trespassing, come out now!" I moved to the side and planted my feet, hoping that Shovel-face would want to talk his way out, that he'd say he was the new owner or was an inspector—as long as he unbolted the lock and cracked the door. The moment he did, I'd hurtle in, leading with my shoulder. Knock him down, seize his weapon. Shoot him, then his partner. Untie Kenny, get him out of there. Odds I could pull it off, ten to one. But I had no choice except to try.

When there was no response, I pounded again. "Open up or we'll arrest you!" I crouched and set my shoulder. *Open the goddamned door you ugly stupid commie sonofa—*

Pop, pop, pop—three shots hit the door, one shattering the window. Glass fragments burst past me. Instinctively I hit the ground and rolled away from the door. So much for tricking my way in. Now what? I looked up at the narrow band of windows set high on the exterior wall. *Get a rock, bust out the glass, climb in—*

Pop. Just one shot, muted. It didn't hit the door. *Oh Jesus, please, no.* From the rear, a metallic creak, then a thud—the two Russians running away through the rear. I shot my right hand through the hole in the broken window, strained to turn the bolt, and wrenched the door open. Shards lacerated my forearm, blood beaded—I felt nothing. I ran through the small front office and onto the shop floor. Kenny was slumped in the chair, chin on his chest. Blood seeped from a wound just below his rib cage on his left side. I heard a gasp—he was still alive. Racing forward, I gently lifted his chin, looked into his glazed eyes.

"Kenny, can you hear me?"

His lips trembled, but no words came out; his eyelids drooped. I needed to compress the wound, but with what? I fumbled with the rope that bound the boy to the chair. I ripped my fingernails pulling at the knots, finally loosening them enough to free him. I ripped his shirt off, popping off the buttons, and hurriedly folded it into a square. Pressing the cloth to the wound with my left hand, I eased him to the floor and crouched over him.

"Stay with me buddy, you're gonna be okay, you're gonna be okay." I pressed the compress tighter, blood—his and mine, from my cuts—staining my hands.

Kenny moaned. In my panic, heart pounding and breathing rushed, a sharp warning rose out of my jumbled thoughts: *If you stay, he dies.* I whipped off my belt, cinched it around his torso to hold the compress tight. Was the bleeding slowing down? I lifted Kenny back into the chair and gently lifted his chin.

"Look at me, buddy, look at me."

He was in shock, but for a moment his gaze locked on mine. Did I see recognition in his eyes, or was it only pain?

"Kenny, I'm going to get you to help, okay? It's not far, but I need you to do something, all right? Nod if you understand."

Tick of his head.

"Put your arms around my chest when I pick you up and hold your hands together, like this." I held up my laced fingers, as if praying. "Can you do that?"

Another nod, and a yelp of pain.

"Okay Kenny, we're getting outta here." I crouched, backed into the chair, started to rise. "Put your arms around me now!"

He reached around my chest, groped weakly, locked his hands together.

"That's it, that's it." Taking a deep breath, I stood as quickly as possible, hooking my forearms under his knees like we were contestants in a piggyback race at a picnic. Only this was no game. I was going to carry him to the Harbor Patrol Station, where he could get real first aid and the fastest possible trip to a hospital. All my scheming to conceal my identity on the telephone and to Kenny's mother—useless! And selfish, so selfish. As someone who went undercover, I was trained to carry out my investigations and protect my identity at all costs. God knows, I'd committed awful acts to do that in the past, but hazarding this boy's life to bust up the Reds' spy ring was despicable, monstrous, the worst thing I'd ever done in my life. Why hadn't I realized the Russians would go after him? I should have known the N.K.V.D. wouldn't just grill me, that its agents would go after anyone who had knowledge of what had happened that night. Even the earnest, amiable kid in the white apron and crooked paper hat from the Automat. That very morning, I'd realized I had to find Kenny, needed to protect him somehow, some way—why hadn't I seen the danger sooner? Just one day earlier, even a few hours . . . if only, if only I had acted sooner.

Bent-backed, I started running, Kenny clinging to me. Burst out the door the Russians had shot at, blinking in the sun, already huffing. The back of my shirt quickly became damp—I hoped it was just my sweat and not Kenny's blood. My belt buckle chafed against my spine, but that meant the compress was holding tight. I felt Kenny's breath on my neck, heard his whimpers of pain. No way to stop the jostling, I had to run as fast as I could.

"D'hell?!" A portly man ahead on the sidewalk was slowing his pace, gaping at me. A working stiff, his overalls splattered with paint.

"This boy's been shot," I shouted at him. "Help me!"

"Shot, for real?" He stopped, eyes wide, cigarette drooping from his lip.

"Go in front of us, clear the way!"

"Whaaa—" he stammered.

"Move, goddammit!" I yelled.

That got him going. He dropped the cigarette, started trotting, turning his head awkwardly.

"Do you want—should I, should we carry him together?"

"No, we just, we just gotta get him to the police station, they can take . . ." My voice, strained by Kenny's weight and the running, trailed off.

"Okay, gotcha." He too was huffing but he kept going.

A motorist on Maine slowed his car, craned his head out the open window.

"What's going on here?"

"This boy's been shot!" shouted my good Samaritan.

"You kiddin' me?" The driver started blathering useless questions while the Samaritan repeatedly said, "I don't know nothing." And I kept running, muttering, "Almost there, Kenny, almost there."

With the Samaritan still in front, we burst into the Harbor Patrol Station. Beads of sweat stinging my eyes, I blurrily saw the desk sergeant leap to his feet. He raced over to me, his cop's intuition taking over.

"How bad's he hurt?"

"Shot in the side, I've got cloth on the wound but—"

"Follow me," the cop cut me off. "You, come with us," pointing at the Samaritan.

We trailed the cop as he ran down a corridor behind his desk. "Get Ramsay," he shouted at an approaching Harbor Patrol officer who took in the scene wordlessly and swiftly reversed directions.

"In here," the desk cop said, flinging open a door. A map room, lined with wooden cabinets for harbor charts. In the center, a broad table.

"Put him down," the cop said, not bothering to pull off a sheaf of charts on the table.

As carefully as possible, I brought Kenny to the table, my back turned, and the cop helped me gently lay him on his back. Kenny still yelped with pain.

"It hurts so bad," he whimpered.

"I know, kid, I know," the cop said.

"Mother of God," the Samaritan whispered.

A middle-aged cop hurtled into the room with a first aid kit. RAMSAY, CHIEF ENGINEER his nameplate read.

"Whadda we got?"

"Gunshot," the desk cop said. I was finally able to read his nameplate: BENDER.

Ramsay looked into Kenny's eyes as he opened his kit. "What's your name, kid, when were you born?"

"Kenny, Kenny Newhurst . . . February 17, 1928," he whispered through gritted teeth.

"Call an ambulance," Ramsay said to Bender, who nodded. Ramsay said to Kenny, "Okay, we're going to get you fixed up, all right, Kenny? You don't have to talk anymore, just try to breathe normal, okay? Squeeze my hand if you understand." He took his hand and said "Good boy" at his grip.

Bender pointed at the Samaritan and me. "Don't you two leave this room, understand?"

I nodded briskly; "Yessir," the Samaritan answered. Bender hurried out, closing the door behind him.

Ramsay scissored through my belt and gently pulled it free of Kenny's torso. He peeled off the compress I'd put on. He swabbed the wound area with an alcohol-soaked pad, expertly wiping away dried blood as he took Kenny's pulse.

"How bad is it?" the Samaritan asked in a hushed voice.

"Nothing I didn't see in the last war," Ramsay said matter-of-factly. "I don't think the bullet hit any organs, and he hasn't lost much blood." Looking at Kenny, he said, "You'll pull through, kid, and we're gonna do something about the pain real quick."

"Anything we can do to help?" I asked. *He'll pull through!* I was so relieved, so happy, I almost shouted, *He's not gonna die, he's not gonna die!*

"Just keep staying outta my way."

Bender returned, again shutting the door behind him.

"Ambulance is on its way, three minutes tops."

"Great," Ramsay murmured, concentrating on the syringe he was preparing.

Bender turned his attention to the Samaritan and me, eyeing us over. That veteran law stare, eyes boring down, searching for distinctive features, recording all details of our appearances. Making judgments about our likely occupations and backgrounds, taking guesses about how we knew each other. And this experienced cop, a trim joe with a crew cut and a deep suntan from his time out on the water, didn't like what he saw, not at all. As he worked through the possibilities of how we'd come to bring in a boy with a gunshot wound, his mouth tightened, his expression hardened—only for an instant, but I could tell what he was thinking. Were we diddlers or worse, kiddie snatchers with unspeakable urges? He was coloring in the scene, seeing us cruising hardscrabble neighborhoods looking for boys, biding our time, then making quick grabs by brandishing a revolver. This time, something had gone wrong, the weapon had discharged accidentally. Why we'd bring in the boy instead of fleeing, he hadn't worked out, but that's what interrogations were for, right? The Samaritan and I were Suspects 1 and 2 in this boy's shooting, and neither of us was leaving this station house for a long, long time.

I couldn't spare the time to convince Bender of the truth. *What did the old man look like?* Shovel-face had demanded of Kenny. *Jes' an old man*, he had whimpered. The Russians had beaten up poor Kenny to get every detail of what he had seen that night in May at the Automat when Himmel met with his spy. Although Kenny couldn't remember what the old man looked like, Shovel-face and his partner now knew I'd been holding back on them. That I hadn't gone to the Automat alone, that this old man had accompanied me and he'd brought along listening equipment that we'd set up in the kitchen. It wouldn't take the Russians long to figure out who the old man was: Filbert Donniker, O.N.I.'s resident gadgets man. I'd coaxed Donniker to come with me to the Automat, I'd dragged him into this unholy mess along with Kenny. What the Russians had just done to Kenny was a rehearsal compared to what they'd do to Donniker if I didn't get to him first.

Which meant I had to get out of the Harbor Patrol Station pronto.

CHAPTER 6

OFFICER BENDER WAITED TO CONFRONT THE SAMARITAN AND ME UNTIL after the ambulance orderlies had taken Kenny out. That gave me an opening. Figure Bender would isolate us, question us separately to see how our stories matched up. Figure he'd hit us each hard, no good-cop-bad-cop nonsense for him. The Samaritan had nothing to hide, he'd tell all. Bender wouldn't believe him, he'd call him a liar and worse, but after the cops checked out the Samaritan's story, they'd let him go. The man had done nothing wrong, he had nothing to hide. Meanwhile I'd be sweating my interrogation. I couldn't improvise a fake identity, no way I could knit all the necessary lies together as Bender peppered me with questions. Who are you, where do you live, where do you work—the seasoned cop would smell fish from the get-go. What I had to do, I was going to hate myself for doing, but I didn't have a choice. The Samaritan had been minding his own business, walking down the street when he stumbled across me and

Kenny. He hadn't hesitated to help save Kenny's life, and being treated as a low-life criminal would be his only reward.

"So, stranger, you gonna tell us what the hell happened to that boy?" I said sternly, pointing an accusing finger at the Samaritan.

The poor man blanched, the color ran from his face like water down a drain; his eyes widened with terror and confusion. What a shitheel I was! Tried to tell myself I was doing this for Donniker, for the case, but that didn't wash my shame and guilt away, not a bit.

"D'hell, whaa, I, uh, I, I . . . th-th-that's not—"

Bender cut off his stammering. "You two don't know each other?" he asked with suspicion.

"No, no! I don't know him from Adam!" the Samaritan cried, finally finding words. He was trembling. "For chrissake, I was walking down the street, that fella came running outta nowhere, he's got the boy on his back, he's starts shouting how he's been shot, I gotta help, so that's what I did, s'all I did, I helped 'em get here!"

A full-on cop glare from Bender. "Awright you two, we're gonna get this sorted out. C'mon." He flung the door open and waited for us to pass by him to enter the hall. Solid cop instincts, making us go first (never leave a suspect behind your back), but he should have brought another cop with him.

I followed the Samaritan, who stopped uncertainly in the corridor. I stepped behind him, leaving myself a path toward the rear of the station. When Bender came out, I knocked the Samaritan's right leg from under him and shouldered him into the startled cop. Both men went down, a tangle of limbs and curses. I shot down the corridor and out the door. The good news: No one was in my way. Bad news: I'd just trapped myself on the Harbor Patrol's dock on the Washington Channel. No time to make a break for Maine Avenue—Bender would be out the door in seconds, a bevy of cops behind him.

I dropped, rolled, and lowered myself into the murky water, gripping the side of the dock, peering into the darkness. I needed a cable, a ring, a cleat—anything to hold onto. Had to get my hands off the dock, had to find a way to remain perfectly still. Two pilings supported the dock, but no handholds. I let go of the dock, dropping full into the water, and reached for one of the pilings. No choice but to bear-hug it, my legs clasped and arms wrapped, hands gripping my arms to keep from slipping. The rough wood of the pilings scraped the cuts I'd gotten breaking the window at the factory, but I ignored the pain. Couldn't avoid splashing as I positioned myself, but the cops were making more than enough noise to cover me. Boots thumping, planks clattering as two officers ran onto the dock, excited shouts all around. "D'fuck he go?!"—"Hit the street! Hit the street!"—"Check the boat."

The Harbor Patrol's boat was moored at the end of the dock, and it took the cops a good five minutes to search it. I stayed as still as possible, oily water lapping at my chest, my arms aching.

When the cops were back on the dock, one asked, "Maybe he's in the water?"

My heart jumped into my throat, but the cops didn't peer beneath the planks—they must have scanned the channel.

"Well, he ain't swimming for it."

"What if he gets over to the Potomac?" He meant the Potomac River Line, which operated passenger boats on the channel and river. Its dock was on the north side of the patrol station.

"Shit, he might mix in with the crowd." The boots thundered overhead as they hurried away.

I waited a beat, took a deep breath, let go of the piling, and went underwater. Squinting in the dark water, I breast-stroked toward the patrol boat's stern and grasped the ladder next to the rudder. I slowly broke the surface, scanning the scene. My visibility was limited, but the dock looked empty—the search had already fanned out. I scrambled up the ladder and dropped to the boat's deck, beneath the gunwales. Crawling to the cabin, I sounded like a rainstorm: drops pattered from my drenched clothing, my shoes squished. I immediately went down into the hold so I couldn't be spotted through the cabin portals.

How long did I have? I couldn't risk hiding aboard, because the cops could return any moment to recheck the boat. I needed to get out of my wet clothes pronto, needed to disembark. That meant, of course, I had to walk right back toward the station house. A change of appearance wouldn't help if I crossed paths with Bender, Ramsay, or the Samaritan.

First things first. I emptied my pockets, stripped off my shoes and clothes. Found a blanket in a locker and dried myself. Naked, I continued to search the hold, checking the other lockers, pulling out drawers and opening cabinets. I was hoping to find a Harbor Patrol overcoat—no such luck, I had to settle for a stained, frayed jumper. But a battered metal toolbox stamped PROPERTY OF M.P.D. gave me an idea. I donned the jumper, vigorously toweled my hair with the blanket to dry it, and pulled on a pair of rubber boots I'd also found. A work cap and a pair of reading glasses finished my disguise, such as it was. After removing the tools from the box, I rolled my wet clothes into the blanket and stuffed it into the box, adding my wallet, keys, and other pocket items. My ruined cigarettes and matches went into the bilge. Dabbed my face with grease from a wrench and took a moment to study the engine. Then I grabbed the toolbox and came out of the hold.

I trod onto the deck, my posture hunched to make me look shorter. Two cops were now on the esplanade, arguing about who was going to get his feet wet. Sounded like someone—Bender, probably—had finally thought to check beneath all nearby docks. I'd never seen them before, but if they were the same two who had searched the patrol boat a little while ago, I was screwed.

"You lost the toss, so wade in, friend," one was saying.

"Funny how I always lose the toss when you flip," his partner answered.

They stopped squabbling as I strode toward them.

"Where's Ramsay?" I called out, remembering that his nameplate had identified him as the chief engineer.

"Ramsay, dunno"—"Who're you?" they said at the same time.

"Frank Morgan, Central Garage, Ramsay called me in. Tells me you got a bad gasket, all's I gotta do is replace it, okay, but what he doesn't tell is, you also need a new manifold, so I gotta take apart the whole damn engine—twenty-minute job, my ass—say, what time is it anyway?"

The unhappy cop glanced at his watch. "Quarter past six, but—"

"You been aboard all this time?" the coin-flipping cop exclaimed.

"How d'hell am I gonna fix your engine if I'm not on the boat?"

"Anyone come aboard, we got this guy—what did Bender say he looked like?"

"Tall, black hair," the unhappy cop said. "Didn't say anything about glasses." Now both of them were studying me.

"Jesus, d'same question your pals asked me—'anyone come aboard?'"

"Our pals?"

"You're all Harbor Patrol, aren't you? They came flying aboard, ass over tea kettle, tearing that boat apart, asking me over and over, 'Sure you haven't seen this guy, you sure'—hell, I'm not blind or deaf! Nobody was on that boat but me."

I thought for sure the coin-flipping cop was going to tell me to take my cap off, but to my great relief his partner had a different idea.

"You said you're from the Central Garage?"

"Yeah, so what—I can fix a boat engine the same as a—"

"Where's that located?"

I knew the answer—some of my Navy cases had required help from the city government—but I had to stay in character.

"What, you don't think I know where I work?"

"Where is it?" he persisted, his voice low but firm.

"Why're you busting my balls—the garage's in the old Ford Building on Pennsylvania, goddammit!" If this didn't clinch it, my goose was cooked—someone who had seen me inside the Harbor Patrol Station was bound to come out any minute.

The unhappy cop eyed me over again, his gaze lingering on the toolbox I was holding tight. *Please, please don't let him recognize it!*

"Awright, okay, simmer down, we got an escaped prisoner, we gotta be careful."

I shrugged. "I'm just a grease monkey, whadda I know?"

"We better get going," his partner said.

"Yeah, I know," he sighed. "You need to see Ramsay, you're gonna hafta wait—he's out in a car looking for this guy."

"That's okay, his engine's fixed, he doesn't need to see me."

They stepped aside so I could pass; I checked the urge to say good luck. Frank Morgan was kind of a self-absorbed guy, plus he was in an awful hurry to be someplace else.

CHAPTER 7

FILBERT DONNIKER LIVED EAST OF UNION STATION, IN A NARROW, BRICK two-story close to the convent of the Little Sisters of the Poor. I had no choice but to keep wearing the dirty jumper, since my clothes were still soaking wet. Which meant I needed to hang onto the toolbox. But looking like a grimy mechanic was good cover, no one gave me more than a passing glance. Once clear of the Harbor Patrol Station, I had to take two buses to get to Donniker's. I'd fooled two cops, but I might not be so fortunate with an alert taxi driver who'd received an A.P.B. from the police.

The ride seemed to take forever, and I resisted looking at my Harvel 1302 (thankfully waterproof) to see the time—I'd get there when I got there. My hope was, Shovel-face and his partner were first looking high and low for *me*. Only when I didn't turn up would they attempt to learn who the old man was. I hoped. Worrying about Kenny Newhurst further

agitated me. Ramsay, the cop who'd given him first aid, had seemed opti-
mistic about the boy's chances, but maybe he'd been putting on a front,
maybe he hadn't wanted to admit in the presence of civilians the boy was
going to die. *Donniker's gotta have a phone, we'll call the hospital and ask*, I
told myself. If Donniker was home, if he was safe.

I disembarked at Union Station, in front of the Columbus Fountain,
and hurried to Second Street. My arm ached from carrying the toolbox,
the rubber boots were blistering my feet. I thundered up Donniker's steps
and pounded on the door before a terrifying thought hit me: *What if the
Russians are already here?*

The door eased open, and to my enormous relief, Donniker scowled at
me. He was of an indeterminate age, old, but how old, no one was sure—he
might have been fifty-six or eighty-two. His knuckles were knobby, but his
hands were agile and quick; he had a full head of hair that had settled on
a steel-gray hue; his gaunt frame belied strength and stamina.

"Voigt! D'hell you dressed like that?"

"They shot the kid," I said bluntly.

"Who shot who?"

"Kenny, his name is Kenny Newhurst, the kitchen boy at the Automat,
the one who let us in that night we used your listening rig. Two N.K.V.D.
goons shot him before I could stop them."

"Jesus Christ. You better come in."

I followed him into a parlor that looked like a Victorian museum taken
over by a radio repair shop. Atop a walnut credenza, the shells of Admiral,
R.C.A., and Monarch sets surrounded a tarnished silver tea set. Vacuum
tubes brimmed from cups and bowls in a glass china hutch. Brightly colored wires—green, yellow, orange, red—festooned a coat rack with carved
hooks; metal antennae were stacked atop a dusty Victrola. All of the curtains were pulled tight, the overhead light dim. We didn't sit.

"What happened?"

"The Russians found him."

"What Russians?"

"The fella we set up on back in May, his name is Henry Himmel—he
works for the Russians. That undercover work I was doing, that was to
watch Himmel."

"Who was the joe this Himmel was meeting with?"

"Some kinda scientist. He passed on something awful important to Himmel."

"Spies." He spit the word out like a sour grape. "Why'd they go after the kid?"

"Himmel went missing that night, with whatever that scientist gave him. The Russians wanna find him real bad. So they're retracing his every step, that led them to the boy. I went to check on him today but he never showed up for work."

"And they shot him, just like that? Where?"

"Empty factory down by the docks. They had Kenny tied to a chair. Had already beaten him up pretty bad."

"If you could see 'em, how come you—"

"I was up on the roof, all by myself! Looking through a vent. Got down as fast as I could, but the door was locked, and when I pounded, they shot at me through the door, and then, then . . ." I didn't finish, my legs shaky, stomach queasy.

"Jesus, Voigt, you better sit down." Filbert strode over and took me by the elbow, guided me to a chair, took the toolbox from my hand, and set it down.

"Can I—could you get me a glass of water?" I asked in a hoarse whisper.

"Water, hell." He went over to a bar cart and lifted a liquor bottle out of a snarl of wires and clips, like a magician lifting a rabbit from a top hat. Two glasses also appeared; he poured generously. "Drink this."

I took a long draught. Whiskey, but unlike any I'd ever had, caramel-colored, with an earthy scent and a smoky taste. It burned my throat, but I immediately felt better.

"What were you doing there alone?" Filbert asked.

"Looking for the kid, I told you."

"But if you thought the Russians had him, how come you didn't get Daley or somebody—"

"You don't think I'm not asking myself that!" I shouted. "I shoulda been looking for him a long time ago. All I was gonna do today, I was just gonna talk to Kenny nice and easy, find out if anyone had been asking questions about that night, but when I found out he was missing, I had—I mean, what the hell was I s'posed to do, Donniker? If I went to the Navy Building, how much time was that gonna take?"

"Okay, okay, take it easy—here, take another drink." He poured a belt, I knocked it back.

Filbert watched me as I took a deep, slow breath.

"Is he dead?" he asked quietly.

"No, God no—your phone, where's your phone?" I jumped out of the chair, spilling my drink all over my jumper and the carpet.

"Hey, hey!"

"Sorry, sorry, but we gotta call the hospital to see if he's gonna pull through! Where's your phone?"

"Hold your horses." Donniker walked to an end table and lifted a black Bakelite from behind a stack of newspapers.

I raced over, took the set, dialed zero, told the operator to ring Providence Hospital. It was the closest emergency room to the Harbor Patrol Station; Kenny had to be there.

Donniker's expression—pursed lips, tilted head, intense gaze—demanded an explanation, answers to the questions he hadn't yet asked. How had I known where the Russians would take the boy—hell, how did I even know they were Russian? Where were they now? How had I gotten the boy to a hospital, how did I end up dressed in a police mechanic's jumper?

"So what this is," I began, dipping my chin at my outfit, "I carried the boy to the M.P.D. Harbor Patrol, it's only a few blocks from—"

"What about the Russians?" Donniker interrupted.

"They ran out the back, I had to bust the window to get—" I broke off as the Providence switchboard came on the line. "Hello, yes, my son, his name is Kenny Newhurst, he's missing, I'm his father, Lyle, and I'm calling all the city hospitals, his mother and I are worried he might have been in an accident, please help us, can you check to see if he's been admitted to the emergency room today?"

The switchboard operator was familiar with frantic calls. She calmly told me to repeat my name and my son's and to describe him. After I finished, she told me to wait. With the headpiece clutched to my ear, I started to tell Donniker what had happened at the Harbor Patrol but again had to stop.

"This is Doctor Tennant, with whom am I speaking?" a weary but authoritative male voice said.

"Lyle, Lyle Newhurst—I'm trying to find my son Kenny, he's been missing—"

"What's your address, please?"

"134 Randolph Place, Northwest."

"Could you describe your son?"

I rushed through a description of Kenny: average height, husky build, acne.

"Okay, Mister Newhurst, I can't tell you much over the phone, but I can confirm your son is here at Providence and he's been hurt. How soon can you get here?"

"Oh my God, what happened—is he, will he be all right? What happened?"

"He's suffered a serious injury but we've stabilized his condition. It's crucial you get here as soon as possible, do you understand, Mister Newhurst?"

"Yes, yes, we'll be there right away!" I hung up. The real Lyle Newhurst would have stayed on the line, pressing the doctor for more answers, but I had another call to make.

Georgette answered on the first ring. "Kenny?!"

"Missus Newhurst, this is William Brady. Kenny's at Providence Hospital. He's been hurt, but the doctors have stabilized his condition. You and your husband need to get there as soon as possible, Providence Hospital." I hung up, cringing at her cry of despair I'd just cut off.

Donniker silently took the phone from my hands and returned it to the table.

"Voigt, what the hell is going on?"

I didn't respond. *He's gonna be all right, he's gonna recover!* For the first moment since I'd learned Kenny was missing, I felt like I had the situation under control, that this mess, this unholy snafu could be untangled, that everything would—

—"d'hell is going on!" Donniker yelled.

I snapped out of my reverie and looked at him.

"What's going on is, they're coming after us, the Russians who shot the kid. That's why they snatched the kid and knocked him around, to find out what he knows. Which means they got descriptions of you and me, and they know we're O.N.I." I didn't tell Donniker I'd let the Russians interrogate me the night before—he didn't need to know, and I didn't want to complicate our next steps.

"Jesus H. Christ. What does Paslett wanna do?"

"Don't know, haven't talked to him yet."

He stared at me in disbelief.

"Donniker, it's not gonna take those Reds long to figure out your name and where you live. Me either."

"Call Paslett now." He pointed at the telephone.

"And tell him what, to send a coupla provost guards over from the Yard?"

"Better make it three."

I picked up the receiver, held it out. "Say I get ahold'a Paslett this minute, say he calls the duty officer. He's gotta type up orders, they gotta get signed, they gotta get delivered to the Yard, they gotta get signed there, on and on. Gonna be two hours at least before those guards arrive."

"I can stay safe for two hours, Voigt."

"I don't know we got two hours."

"M'not leaving my home," shaking his head, taking a long swig of his whiskey.

"Just til Monday, Donniker. Monday bright and early, we'll meet at the Navy Building and see what Paslett wants to do."

"Fine, let's go there now."

"We can't." Leaving it at that.

He studied me silently, clutching his glass. Finally he said, "They knew it was you, trying to get in to save the boy."

"Yeah." Shovel-face and his partner hadn't seen me, but my beat cop act couldn't have fooled them, not for a moment. While I was saving Kenny's life and escaping the police, Shovel-face undoubtedly had made some calls. He'd told staff at the Soviet embassy to find out who Donniker was. He'd told his superiors that he was on his way to my flat to get me—the fact that I was a lieutenant in the U.S. Navy wasn't going to protect me. Meanwhile he'd have N.K.V.D. agents watch the Navy Building—if Donniker and I tried to sneak in, they'd nail us before we got close to any of the doors. The building, one of the awful tempos put up during the last world war, straddled the Mall, offering observers great sight lines on all entrances. They'd sweep us up before we even got close.

"Goddammit, Voigt, what have you gotten us into?" He finished off his whiskey and glared at me.

"Nothing I can't get us out of, if you get gone til Monday."

"What's gonna be different about Monday?"

"We come in with the morning shift, both of us—blend in with the stream. Russians won't risk that kinda commotion, hitting a big group like that."

"You sure about that?"

"No. But it's better odds than we got right now."

"Jesus H. Christ, I'm too old for this horseshit, you know that, Voigt?" He proceeded to drub me but good, a profanity-laced review of my failings as a field agent. I didn't argue, didn't interrupt—how could I possibly disagree, after what I had allowed to happen to Kenny Newhurst? He finished with a question: "Where are you gonna go?"

"I got a place in mind." I didn't elaborate, he didn't press. Better if we didn't know where each of us went—life insurance for each other.

"Just til Monday, huh?"

"Right. Get yourself into the building first thing in the morning, we'll see what Paslett wants to do." I couldn't promise anything more. "How soon can you clear out?"

"Twenty minutes tops."

I checked my watch: 7:27. "The Russians gotta be at my flat by now, watching to see if I show. It's gonna take their embassy a little while longer to come up with your name, so you'll be long gone by the time they get here."

He pointed a finger at me. "If they mess up anything, you're paying!"

"They're not gonna toss your place, Donniker." Though I wasn't so sure. The Russians might well take both our places apart. But I couldn't think about that until I figured out how I was going to keep clear of the Russians for the rest of the weekend. "I'll see you safe and sound Monday, okay?" I added.

"Yeah, sure," he grumbled, looking around the parlor, as if he was considering packing up the whole mess and taking it with him.

"Listen, Donniker, you think maybe I can borrow a change of clothes?"

He looked me up and down. He was shorter than me, and thinner. "They ain't gonna fit."

"I'll make it work."

"You ever gonna tell me how you ended up in that getup?"

"Sure, over a bottle of that kinda whiskey, my treat," gesturing at the liquor he'd served us.

He snorted derisively. "You wouldn't even know where to look for it."

"Then I'll spring for martinis."

He ignored me and went upstairs. I opened up the toolbox and took out the sodden mess that had been the contents of my pockets: wallet (holding six dollars, my O.N.I. identification card, a District of Columbia Public Library card, a coupon for ten percent off my next purchase of books at Lowdermilk & Co.); the keys to my basement flat on Swann Street; dimes, nickels, and pennies totaling sixty-three cents; a plastic comb; and a penknife. Usually I carried a fat money clip, but I'd forgotten to grab it that afternoon after changing clothes. But I was a seasoned naval intelligence officer—if I couldn't stretch $6.63 for thirty-six hours, then I didn't deserve my commission. At least cigarettes only cost eighteen cents a packet—I'd be able to keep smoking. I'd ditch my wet clothes and the toolbox after I left.

Donniker returned with brown trousers, blue dress shirt, shorts, socks, and a pair of battered wingtips.

"What size shoes you wear?"

"Twelve."

"These are ten and a halfs."

"Better than these boots."

He grunted, dropped the clothes on the couch. He poured himself a healthy drink while I changed. The pants were tight and too short, the shirtsleeves weren't long enough, but it was a better outfit than the jumper.

"You want anything else, Voigt, maybe a cup'a cocoa and a peanut butter and jelly sandwich?" he said sarcastically as I sat and pried my feet into the shoes. By tying the laces loosely, I could just fit into the wingtips.

I looked up. "Would a glass'a milk and tuna salad be too much trouble?"

Neither of us laughed. I stood and picked up the toolbox.

"Listen, Donniker," I began, but he held up a hand.

"Save it, Voigt. We both know you owe me, but we'll settle up when this is over."

I nodded. "All right." I turned to leave. "Stay safe, you old goat," I said without looking over my shoulder. Thought I heard a chuckle, wasn't sure.

"You too, Voigt."

CHAPTER 8

I GOT A PLACE IN MIND. SO I'D TOLD DONNIKER. TOO BAD IT WASN'T TRUE. All my usual haunts and hangouts were *verboten*, for sure. Calling on friends or girlfriends endangered their lives. Not that I had any close friends or gals anyway. Bunk in a flophouse? Nix—once the Russians figured out I wasn't coming home, they'd think of the same moves. They'd tour the Seventh Street fleabags, tossing dollar bills to greedy front deskmen until they found me. Stay up until Monday morning, fueled by coffee and bennies? Maybe. For now, I needed to get to a part of the District I didn't frequent, some place that wasn't part of my routine for the O.N.I. or my personal life in any way, shape, or form. Downtown, the public library, the Mall—all off-limits. Union Station was a one-way suicide ticket. There was a Negro neighborhood east of where I lived, but a wandering white man would stick out. A realization tightened my stomach as I walked away from Donniker's house: from my time undercover, I knew the N.K.V.D. had a stable of stooges throughout the District, dues-paying members of the

Communist Party of the U.S.A. as well as parlor pinks and fellow travelers. Look at how easily the Russians had put Mara and her pretend boyfriend into the field. If all these Reds and wannabes went on the look-see, my odds of staying free would get a lot longer.

So what were my best options? I could buy some provisions and camp out in the Rock Creek and Potomac Parkway. Another possibility: take a bus or streetcar to Alexandria, Virginia, or Silver Spring, Maryland, suburbs I'd never been to. Finally, I could flit from one gutbucket tavern to another, nursing dime beers.

One by one, I eliminated these ideas. Camping out was loony. Hikers, bird-watchers, and lovers wandered the parkway's trails at all hours. Sure, I might be able to get through the night undetected, but what about Sunday morning and afternoon, when the recreation area was busiest? As for leaving town, the Russians would tell their stooges to watch the intercity stops. Killing time in taverns was the worst move of the three. It would siphon off my cash, dull my senses, and make me easy to track. So what was I going to do?

Become an invisible man. Be as unnoticeable as wallpaper, a John Doe blending into every scene. Anyone looking for Lt. (j.g.) Ellis Voigt, U.S.N., would eye this fellow head to foot and rule him out because he didn't look like a naval intelligence officer on the run. Say I was a working stiff, 4-F'd because of a medical problem, humping it as a van driver or a warehouseman, bunking in a by-the-week flat with a Murphy bed. This joe—call him Andy, Andy Weldon—was unmarried, young, looking for a good time on a Saturday night, looking for a gal. Where would he go?

The Starlight Ballroom. A former theater on New York Avenue, the Starlight attracted G-girls fed up with chaperoned U.S.O. affairs, where the teetotaler punch and strict curfew were too much like a school prom. And where G-girls looking for fun went, so did guys like Andy Weldon. The owners of the Starlight had converted the theater as cheaply as possible. They'd ripped out the seating, leveled the floor, raised the stage for the band; but that was about it.

I walked north on Third, turned west on M Street. Detoured briefly into an alley to dump the M.P.D. toolbox stuffed with my wet clothes and the jumper. A pleasant evening, day's heat fading, the sun's glare softening, sky azure and traced with wispy clouds. At a newsman's shack I bought a packet of Luckies. Before I went to the Starlight, I had to do something about my appearance. In my brown trousers and blue button-down shirt, I looked like a billing clerk for a dairy. Mister Dullsville, a dud. Andy Weldon was no dandy, but it was Saturday night, he was looking for action, he needed *something* to spruce him up, something flashy to divert attention from the ill-fitting clothes. A bow tie would do, I decided, a real corker, all polka dots and bright colors. I wouldn't be caught dead in a bow tie, but this was Weldon's night, not mine.

I went into a Garrison's variety store and beelined to men's clothing. Picked up a pair of black socks (thirty-five cents), my eyes on a rack of ties nearby. The bow ties were up high. I took two down and feigned interest. One had red and white stripes, the other was maroon with yellow dots. I deliberately fumbled the ties, they fell, I bent to pick them up. Palmed the maroon tie as I stood, pocketed it, returned the striped tie. No one saw me, the clerks were busy preparing to close. I asked the gal at the men's accessories counter about the difference between Royal Crown Hair Dressing and Brilliantine. She let me have a sample and held a mirror as I combed the Royal Crown into my hair. I flashed her a smile and paid for the socks. Outside the store I put the socks into my back pocket and put on the pilfered tie as I finished the walk to the Starlight.

A tick past nine when I arrived. My wallet was still wet, and the doorman scowled as I handed over a damp dollar bill for the cover. I meandered to the bar. A dime's worth of Gunther was fifty cents, it was flat and tepid, but I was going to love that beer like a newborn, cradle and nurse it for hours. Good thing Weldon was a cheapskate—I didn't have to worry about tipping. The band had just set up, the musicians warming up with a listless rendition of "Begin the Beguine." If that was their idea of originality, Andy and I were in for a long night. I skirted the dance floor, scanned the pairs and trios of girls milling around, trying not to look like a man on the make. Good luck, how can a lone joe clutching a warm beer at a cut-rate dancehall not look like he's on the make?

To hell with it, I thought. Strolled up to two gals standing halfway between the bar and the stage.

"Hiya, ladies." Putting my old Chicago—*SheKAWgo*—accent into it.

"All right," one answered frostily. A willowy brunette, straight hair coming to curls above her shoulder. Thin lips, delicate nose, hazel eyes. Flared navy blue slacks, ruffled off-white blouse, crimson silk scarf knotted just right. Pretty, but also pretty unhappy, a bad sign for Andy.

Her companion smiled at me hesitantly. She wasn't a looker. Soft figure, wide waist, round face. Frizzy black hair that refused to submit to pins. Her outfit clashed—floral print dress and black pumps—but when I smiled back, she brightened.

"I'm Andy," I announced.

"I'm Jean," she said. When her friend stayed quiet, dog-eyeing me, Jean added, "This is Vera."

"Hiya Jean, hiya Vera, how ya girls doing tonight?"

"We're okay," Jean said. Vera gritted a smile for a half second, then turned her gaze toward the stage.

"Just okay?" I asked with a lopsided smile, looking straight at Jean. "Okay's for Monday, dis is Saturday night. Lemme hear ya say yer doing great!"

"Oookay, I'm doing great," Jean giggled.

"Hey, that's funny!" I said.

Vera couldn't make up her mind whether to roll her eyes or exhale her annoyance. So she did both. *Walk away?* Vera wasn't looking for action, wasn't happy about being out, a real sourpuss. I decided to see how it went with Jean on the dance floor.

Pretty good, it turned out. She and Vera had arrived an hour before me. Five guys had asked Vera to dance, none had asked Jean. Vera had turned them all down, but that hadn't made Jean feel any better, I could tell. So I told her she was a good dancer and left it at that—if I went on, she'd know what old Andy Weldon was after. Hell, she probably knew already, but he had to play his cards just right if Ellis was going to have a safe place to sleep that night.

"Hey, let's go see how Vera's doing," I said after two numbers on the dance floor. We'd left her at a small table. If she didn't change her mind and accept an offer to dance, she'd get fed up and want to leave, dragging Jean with her. Andy had to find a way to keep Vera around, at least for a bit.

"How come yer friend's so blue?" I asked Jean as we strolled back.

"She hasn't gotten a letter from her fiancé in an awful long time. She's worried 'bout him."

I nodded. Vera was cold-shouldering a punk in a zoot suit. Rejection didn't faze him, he glided off toward a gaggle of girls. I pulled out the empty chair for Jean and grabbed a third from a nearby table, squeezed in.

"Where's he serving?" I asked Vera.

"What?" Surprised.

"Your hubby-to-be, he's in uniform, right?"

"How do you know that?" Vera glared at Jean.

"All's she said was, yer waiting on a letter from yer fiancé, I figgered dat must mean he's in the service. Gotta be rough, being apart like dat."

Good move, Andy. She stayed wary, Vera, but at least I got her talking. Typical war bride story. High school sweethearts, draft order arrived the summer after graduation, he proposed right after Basic, was assigned to the Ninth Army, had been wounded at the Battle of the Bulge, full recovery, now somewhere in the Ruhr. Jean had obviously heard all this many times, so she went to the bar for drinks. God bless her, she shook her head when I made like I was going to pull a roll from my pocket to pay for the round.

" . . . just not like him to not write," Vera was saying when Jean returned, awkwardly holding a glass of Gunther and two gin rickeys.

"Probably, da end a'da war's got the army's mail service all messed up, dat's all," I said.

"You think so?" Vera asked hopefully.

"Oh, you bet."

Andy's dogged geniality did the trick. Vera loosened up, accepted a couple of offers to dance, looked like she was actually enjoying herself. Andy stayed the course with Jean, didn't get fresh, didn't push it, kept his right hand just above her hip during the slow numbers. When Vera said she was tired and wanted to leave, he played the gallant. *Lemme walk you gals home* . . . Jean, God bless her again, took Vera aside and whispered in her ear. Vera eyed me over before she whispered back; I just kept smiling like a happy idiot. Whatever Jean said, Vera agreed to.

Jean hustled over. "I'm just gonna see Vera out, then maybe we can have another dance?"

"Dat'd be great," I said. "Jes great."

CHAPTER 9

S O FAR, SO GOOD, I THOUGHT, HOLDING JEAN CLOSE DURING AN AWFUL cover of "Solitude," the horns bleating like ailing sheep. Only problem: how to keep the night going on the four bucks and change I had left. Thankfully, Jean wasn't much of a drinker—she still hadn't finished her rickey—but she probably expected Andy to take her out for a bite after they left the Starlight. My cash would just cover a midnight snack, but I sure didn't want to start Sunday morning broke. Maybe I could rifle through Jean's purse when I ducked out at dawn? A bum move, for sure, but I couldn't see another angle. Couldn't cadge on the street, that'd hoist a red flag for the N.K.V.D. Couldn't hit up a buddy for a loan, couldn't risk dragging anybody I knew into this mess. Maybe I could get Jean to spring, feed her a line about not getting paid that day, promise to make it up when we went out next. I liked that play, felt like Andy's way of telling a girl he wanted to see her again.

The number was finally coming to an end, and I was about to suggest we skedaddle when a vision of Kenny Newhurst lashed to the wooden chair in the factory overtook me. Just like lightning on a pitch-black summer night, everything lit up brilliantly. His lolling head, his whimpering, Shovel-face yelling. I must have clenched Jean awful hard because she pulled away and gave me a queer look.

"You okay?" she asked.

I mustered up a smile. "Oh yeah, jes had one'a dem shivers down my back, gave me a start is all."

"Somebody walked over your grave." Smiling back.

Jean had no idea how right she was. Another flash: Georgette's instant alarm when I told her Kenny hadn't shown up for work at the Automat. *There's no need to panic, Missus Newhurst.* Had I really uttered those words? Why had I gone to the Newhurst's home, why hadn't I gone straight to the factory? Why had I waited so long to check in on Kenny in the first place? I could tell myself all the live-long day that I'd followed procedure, that I'd done what any trained investigator would have done, but I'd lied to the boy's mother while he was being beaten. Told myself everything was going to be fine—hadn't the doctor said they'd stabilized him?—but that didn't console me, not a bit. *Flash*—Donniker's surprise that I'd gone to the factory alone. *Flash*—wasting time on the rooftop when I should have gone straight in. I was a coward, a simpering punk, the lowest, sorriest, worthless—

"Hey, cat got your tongue, Andy?"

"Huh?"

"I asked if you were having a good time."

"Oh, you bet. Hey, Jean, are ya hungry, wanna grab sometin' to eat?"

"That sounds nice, sure."

We collected her shawl from the coat check girl on the way out. Cool night, clear skies, light breeze. I took a deep breath. Patrons coming and going from the Starlight crowded the sidewalk, hacks rolled down New York Avenue looking for fares.

"Got a favorite place around here?" I asked Jean.

"Uh-uh. Wherever you wanna go's fine by me, Andy."

I steered us northeast on New York, an angled thoroughfare. Instinct: get off the street, pronto. We walked two blocks, passing closed shops and businesses. I took out my cigarettes, extended the packet to Jean, she shook her head. I lit up, inhaled, smiled through the release of gray smoke.

"So, ya been in Washington long, Jean?"

Short answer: no. Jean's answer, not-so-short. She was off to the races, telling me about how after a year and a half, she still got lost, still couldn't get used to the "hustle and bustle," the buses that ran all night, the laundrymen who kept waiting lists, having a roommate. I smoked, nodded, said "uh-huh" a lot, and tried to keep the scenes from the factory at bay. Maybe if I kept her talking and got some food, I'd feel better. Hungry, frazzled, exhausted, beat-down—maybe that's why I couldn't think straight.

A chop suey joint was open. I steered Jean toward its blinking neon sign. Inside, high-backed booths, a clot of rickety-looking tables, and a counter with red-topped stools. By the door, two large fish tanks and potted ferns and plants with wide, drooping fronds. Jean bent to peer into one of the aquariums, watching a gold-scaled carp glide through the murky water. A young Chinese man approached. "Yes, yes, you like," he said, gesturing at a booth. Except for a lone man hunkered over a bowl of soup at the counter, Jean and I were the only patrons. I nodded, we sat. I decided against sliding in next to Jean, didn't want to spook her. The Chinese handed us menus, left, returned almost immediately with two glasses of water. Set them down, smiled, looked expectantly at us.

"I've never had Chinese food!" Jean announced.

"Me neither," I lied. "How's about I jes order us a few things, we'll see how we like 'em?"

"Sure, Andy."

I ordered the sweet and sour soup, egg rolls, and Kung Pao chicken to split. If we didn't get drinks, the bill would come to about $2.50, so I'd still have a couple of bucks.

After the waiter left, Jean said, "Hey Andy, can I ask you a question?"

My stomach tightened. Was something off, did my behavior not jibe? "You bet, shoot," I answered, forcing a smile.

"How come you're not in the service?"

I checked a sigh of relief—I'd been ready for this question all night. "I got hit by a trolley when I was a kid, damn near killed me. I was in a coma for a week, see, and when I came to, I found out I got a steel plate in my head."

"Oh, Andy, that's terrible!"

"Hey, I didn't die, didn't keep me from learning to dance, did it?"

Jean giggled. "No, it sure didn't." Then the dopey smile disappeared. "Gosh, I'm sorry for asking—I mean, it's not like I was thinking you were a slacker, you know, I was just—"

"Hey, kiddo, don't sweat it, I'm used to it. People see an able-bodied joe, dare gonna wonder, right? Not like ya can see the steel plate."

"Does it hurt, having that in your head?"

I barely heard her question. *Flash*—the crack of the pistol, the shot that wounded Kenny. My mouth went dry. "It causes headaches sometimes, real bad ones."

"Migraines?"

"Yeah, dem. Doctors say dare's nuttin' dey can do about it. Jes gotta pop aspirin and wait for it to go away." I took out my cigarettes, lit up, inhaled greedily. *Flash*—Kenny's shirt spotted with blood.

"Are you getting one now, Andy? You don't look so good."

"Naw, naw, I'm fine." I came up with a smile.

Thankfully, the soup arrived, we dipped in. Jean started talking about how much she missed her sister, who still lived with their folks in Schenectady. She asked about my family, but I deflected the question, acted like it was a sore subject. Back at the Starlight, I'd planned to give her a line about a rough childhood to ensnare her sympathy. Tell her I'd been passed from relative to relative as a boy, but that kind of story requires concentration; I was too distracted.

I kept Jean talking through the meal. I paid the bill and asked, "Can I walk ya home, Jean, do ya live around here?"

She nodded, smiling shyly. "Just a few blocks away. Me and Vera, we walked to the Starlight."

Outside, I took her hand after lighting a cigarette and taking a long, deep drag—felt like my hands were about to start trembling. Jean's chubby palm, hot and slick with sweat, gave me the heebie-jeebies, but I held on. She let it drop that her roommate was out of town, she had their flat to herself. Should have put a spring in my step, but all I could think about was Georgette Newhurst at the hospital, sobbing at the sight of her hurt son. My stomach convulsed, bile surged up my throat—I almost vomited on the sidewalk.

"How come ya don't have a boyfriend, Jean?" Saying something, anything, no matter how awkward, to keep myself cemented in the here and now, turning onto M Street, heading toward the flat of this sweet, dull, polite girl from Schenectady, playing the part of the dull, dim-witted Andy Weldon, flat-broke deliveryman with a steel plate in his head and a god-awful bow tie around his neck. Refuge for a night, and sleep—blissful, thoughtless, timeless sleep, hours and hours of it—that's what Voigt needed, so he could start another day on the lam with the strength and awareness he must have to stay alive until Monday.

"Maybe I oughta ask you that question myself," Jean said coyly.

"How come I don't have a boyfriend, ya mean?" Forcing a grin.

She liked the joke, it loosened her up. I kept up the patter, the dopey jive a joe like Andy Weldon thought was smooth.

Back at her first-floor flat—galley kitchen, parlor, and two twin beds jammed into a narrow, windowless room—Jean offered to make tea, shyly explaining that her absent roommate was a teetotaler who didn't allow booze in the place. I said sure, tea'd be great, and put on a record while she was in the kitchen. Art Kassel and His Kassels-In-The-Air Orchestra, delivering scratchy, middle-of-the-road standards. A far cry from the bebop, the Kansas City sound, some called it, that I'd discovered earlier that year at the Lotus Club, where Dexter Pierce and his boys really ripped it up during their last sets. But this was Andy Weldon's night, not mine.

The tea was awful, weak, with leaves floating in it, but I didn't take more than a sip. Asked Jean to dance as Gloria Hart crooned her way through "I'll Be Around," held her close, and leaned in for a kiss. Not much of a move, but tonight I was a stray, damn lucky to have a bowl of cream and a warm corner to sleep in. Reminding myself of that raw fact helped me shut my eyes to Jean's bulbous eyes and the scent of tea and sweet and sour sauce on her lips.

Trying to distract myself didn't help. Andy got through the roll in the hay, afterward he cooed lovey-dovey things to Jean til she fell asleep, but slumber eluded him. Me, that is. Andy Weldon was bushed, for sure, but Ellis Voigt couldn't drive Georgette Newhurst from his consciousness. For all her relief that her son was alive, a terrible question had to be haunting her: *Who did this to my son, who did this?*

CHAPTER 10

I CREPT OUT OF JEAN'S FLAT AT DAWN, WASHING UP QUIETLY AND CHANGING my socks with the pair I'd bought at the dime store. Tossed the garish bow tie and dirty socks into her trash, looked guiltily at her purse on the kitchen table. But I didn't go through it, didn't take her money. Sunday was going to be rough on just two dollars, but at least my sleepless night had given me an idea on how to cadge some moolah.

I was hungry, but the knot in my stomach was stronger. Forced myself to concentrate. I'd gone plenty of nights without sleep in the past, but adrenaline and willpower weren't enough to keep me sharp. Before I scored some scratch, I needed a pick-me-up, something that could carry me another twenty-four hours. I hopped a bus that would get me close to the Eastern Market. The diners nearby attracted musicians finally calling it quits after all-nighters. A lot of jazzbos hadn't slept a wink on a Saturday night since they were kids, but not all stayed awake by habit alone. Sure, I could get what I needed from a Peoples Drug Store, but rumor was, musicians usually had something you couldn't get at the counter.

I walked into Carol's De-Lite, a Formica and chrome palace as sleek as a '38 Packard. Quick eyescan, took in the counter stools, appraised the booths. All full. Booth 1: three Marines in rumpled uniforms, slurping coffee. Booth 2: a morose-looking couple silently eating eggs. Booth 3, in the corner: four joes—three Negroes, one white—in suits, ties loosened, laughing. I beelined for the stool closest to Booth 3, swiveled so I could eavesdrop. Thought I recognized the white guy—he looked like Dexter Pierce's clarinetist, but I wasn't sure. Ordered coffee and biscuits and gravy, downed a glass of ice water in one long draught. Though I'd not drunk much alcohol the night before, my head throbbed, as if the lie I'd told Jean about the steel plate in my head was true. Lighting up, I slid a discarded section of the *Times-Herald* my way and read the listing of that morning's church services as I strained to overhear the musicians . . .

". . . shee-*it*, man, you know that ain't true," one of the Negroes, a stocky man, was saying, in a faint drawl marking him as a native of Baltimore.

"Oh no? Lemme tell you sometin', friend, you don't know nuttin!" Another Negro.

"Was you there? C'mon now, don't be shy . . ."

The clink and rattle of my arriving coffee cup and silverware interrupted their patter. Nothing yet to flag them as Dexter Pierce's boys. Couldn't risk a look from my stool, they'd notice me staring. Sipped my coffee, attacked the gray, steaming mound of biscuits and bits of sausage with my fork, tried not to eat too fast.

" . . . started out with Muggsy Spainer, then came east," the white fellow was saying.

They had a desultory argument about Beiderbecke. None had ever heard him—they were too young—so they debated by proxy, citing trumpeters or trombonists they'd played with who had once gigged with the pianist from the Sioux City Six or the clarinetist from the Rhythm Jugglers, on and on, their breakfast finished, their last cigarettes almost stubbed, my platter just about cleaned. As the biscuits and gravy settled in a lump in my stomach, I could feel the weariness bear down, weighting my eyelids. I nodded at the counterman for another cup of joe, my third.

Then gold.

" . . . naw, we'll be playin' cornball least 'nother year, D.C. ain't ready for it."

I perked up: "it" was bebop, the sound Dexter Pierce saved for his final sets, after the squares had jitterbugged themselves out and toddled home. When the white fellow casually mentioned he'd asked out the coat check girl, a half-Asian, half-white beauty with glossy black hair that fell to her waist, I had my opening—she worked at the Lotus, a place I knew well.

"Great gig last night," I ventured, turning on my stool.

No response, just blank looks.

"How'd you like our 'Crazy Rhythm'?" the clarinetist asked.

"You never played it," I guessed. All the times I'd been to the Lotus, I'd never heard it.

One of the Negroes, a slender man with almond eyes and a mustache, laughed. "Dex hates that number."

I hid my relief behind a sip of coffee.

"You play?" This from the heavyset Negro, who was flipping his Zippo lid open and shut. *Whoosh—clink, whoosh—clink.*

"Nope, just a fan. For what's it worth, you guys are the best in D.C."

Not worth much, my lame compliment. The clarinetist said thanks, the thin Negro yawned.

"Awright gents, ready?" asked the third Negro, who'd been observing me the whole time. He looked alert and restless, like a man who had had a full night's sleep and a pot of coffee. Only there wasn't a cup in front of him.

He's my man, I thought. As the musicians stood, I fixed him with a level gaze and said, "You fellas know where I could find something a cut above a bennie?"

My bluntness bothered the clarinetist, who dropped his gaze to the dollar bills they'd dropped on the tab. The two Negroes who'd spoken to me exchanged quick looks. For an agonizing moment, the fourth man wordlessly returned my stare. Finally he asked, "Rough night?"

I nodded, and left it at that. Anyone could see how haggard I was.

"Just one?"

Another nod.

A smile broke his cool, aloof expression. "Well, for a fan, I guess we can help out." He slipped his hand into his trousers pocket, came out with a slim silver pillbox. With a practiced gesture, he flipped the lid, swept up a red capsule, and extended his hand, palming me as I stood.

"Thanks a million."

"Sure, see you at the Lotus." He pocketed his pillbox, they strode to the front, took their hats down from the pegboard, and left. I drained the last of my coffee and downed the red pill with a long drink of water. The counterman, a lugubrious fellow with a face as creased as last week's paper, suddenly smiled—he'd witnessed the exchange.

"Morning, sunshine," he croaked, laughing with a wheeze.

I left him a fifty-cent tip on my $1.25 tab. That left me just two-bits, but running into Dex Pierce's boys and scoring an amphetamine was an awful good omen, and I wanted to keep my lucky streak alive.

NEXT STOP, THE FIRST CONGREGATIONAL CHURCH AT TENTH AND G, service at 8:30. A lovely morning, pale blue sky dotted with stray clouds, light breeze, temperature in the low seventies. I passed a bakery, its door open, the scent of warm bread and rolls wafting out. A news agent perched in his shack nodded as I passed, a young mother pushing a stroller smiled; I smiled back. I loved Sunday mornings in Washington, loved to walk the streets aimlessly, studying homes and buildings. There was a height limit in the city, something to do with protecting the sight lines of the Washington Monument, so unlike my hometown of Chicago, where architectural wonder was found way up high, the gold flake of the Carbon and Carbide Building, say, or the top stories stacked like wedding cakes downtown. Here in D.C. the beauty was right there in front of you. The redstone arch of a mansion, the copper trim of a mansard roof, a frieze set along a roofline. My first year, I must have logged a hundred miles of Sunday morning strolls, finding tiny manicured parks and overgrown cemeteries. On Sixteenth Street I'd stopped to read some of the names of the city's fallen from the Great War, a maple tree planted and a copper medallion set in a stone for each of the dead. Wandered along the banks of the canal in Georgetown, gazed through embassy gates, passed through the alley slums that honeycomb the city.

A torrent of memories overtook me, random images rushing by like flotsam in a flood. The way a girl I slept with years ago had unhooked her brassiere. The stray cat I'd briefly adopted and named Franklin D. The crooked smile of a fellow naval officer, now dead. The pill was kicking in, for sure. I didn't much use Benzedrine, didn't like the jagged come-down that left your nerve ends flickering and crackling like a cut electrical wire, but I didn't have much choice. And sweet Jesus, this was no ordinary bennie! I felt like a boxer at the first bell, a coiled spring, a bull thundering into the arena. Every sense was heightened. My eyes burned, I had X-ray vision, I could see through walls. How I was going to sit still through several church services that morning, I had no idea, but I did know this: nothing, and no one, not the Russians, not the F.B.I., were going to get in my way. Superman could sleep in, D.C. was all mine that morning.

The First Congregational Church was a fortress of God, stone and brick piled into towers, arches, and entablatures. The entrance, at the top of steep steps, had three keystone-shaped portals (Father, Son, and Holy Ghost?). The greeter, an elegant matron in a peach chiffon dress and pearls, gave me an eyeover as jaundiced as a beat cop's. *Rumpled clothes, no tie, unshaven, trouble?* As her eyebrow arched, I smiled brightly and said I hoped she could excuse my appearance, that I was from out of town, that my work for the War Department had kept me up all night, and that the "First" came highly recommended. Bingo—she gave me a warm welcome.

I appraised the pews before I let the usher seat me. I'd timed my arrival just before the service's start so I could maneuver myself into a sparsely seated pew in the rear. My appearance helped; the usher sat me in the second-to-last bench. As the organ prelude's last chord resonated and a deacon began the call to worship, I had just five pew mates: on my right, two parents and their young son; on my left, an elderly couple. The boy kept staring at me until his mother rebuked him with a hoarse whisper.

I hadn't set foot in a church in years. My folks were lukewarm Lutherans, a cut or two above the Easter-Christmas crowd. I vaguely remembered hymns, Bible readings, a sermon. Hoped the Congregationalists were no different, especially when it came to using a basket to collect the offering. As the good people of the First followed their Sunday routine, I mumbled my way through the Lord's Prayer, joined in the responses, belted out hymns. Seemed like we were up and down twenty times, never seated for more than five minutes before the next round of singing. With that red-hot bennie coursing through my blood, I was thankful for any movement. Was all I could do to keep from drumming my fingers on the well-worn bench or jimmying my leg. The kid sensed my energy and stole looks whenever he thought his mother wouldn't notice.

Until the sermon, the minister, a flabby young man with a florid face and thinning hair, hadn't struck me as much of a preacher. He spoke softly, almost disinterestedly. Turned out he was saving himself for the main event. Is God Still Angry? was the theme of his sermon. His voice picking up tempo and volume, he recounted, with story after story, the absolute wretchedness of mankind. Babies abandoned in dark cold alleys, husbands who beat their wives to death, con artists who bilked the old out of their last dime. What the Japs did to our boys at Bataan, the camps the Germans killed the Jews in. We the people joined together to defeat this evil in Europe, victory is at hand in the Pacific, neighbors love one another here at home; and yet. And yet. *God is still angry.* His left hand outstretched, the minister left his lectern and swept toward us, leaning over the first step of the apse like a tree straining to stay rooted in a windstorm. Sin abounds, temptations flourish, we dance on the borders of Hell. "Having done good in the world, we believe we are inherently good!" he shouted. "That we have no need of God, that we can free ourselves from the fear that is actually love, His love, which keeps at bay the demon's lions, the greedy hungry lions that see their prey."

The congregation was enrapt, even the little boy in my pew, when the vision of Kenny Newhurst tied to the chair blinded my consciousness. His tear-streaked face contorted with pain, now facing me, his lips miraculously murmuring the minister's last words: *God is still angry, waiting, waiting endlessly for you to act righteously.*

"S'the bennie, jes the bennie," I told myself, not realizing I'd whispered the words. The elderly couple in my pew looked over, annoyed. I bit down on my lip, I pressed my hands under my legs, I clenched my eyes shut. Had to pull myself together, had to calm down—the offering was next. That basket was my salvation, but only if I could steady my hands and steel my nerves. *Please God, please help me now, I swear I'll make things right.*

The sermon ended, we prayed, the deacon said a few words about sharing. The choir sang as the ushers came down the aisles. I took an envelope from the rack on the pew in front of me and sealed up my last quarter.

The father on my right put in a dollar, his son took the basket and scooted toward me. He was doing just fine, both hands gripping the basket's edges, but as he let go, I gave the basket a good jostle on the bottom with my left hand, almost upending it. "Peter, be careful!" his mother exclaimed. Everyone was staring at the mortified little boy, here was my split-second chance. I pressed my offering into the basket and palmed several bills, crumpling them into a wad. I passed the basket to the old woman with my left hand, leaving my right hand visible, the fingers slanted downward, to keep the bills out of sight. As the elderly couple and the ushers watched the father berate his son, I slipped the bills into my pocket.

I wanted to beat a hasty exit after the service ended, but Peter's father, a serious-looking fellow with wire rim glasses, said, "Pardon me, sir, my son has something to tell you."

I forced a smile at him and the boy, on whose shoulders his hands rested. Peter, wearing a blue suit just like his father's, looked up at me with red-rimmed eyes. "I'm sorry for being clumsy, sir," he said, his voice quavering.

I blinked away Kenny Newhurst's face and said, "It's okay, it was just an accident, you didn't do anything wrong." I wished the family well and strode away, telling myself, *ordering* myself, to stay composed, to squint away the tears, the pitiful, desperate tears about to trace, at long last, the shame of my sins, my wretchedness.

Bright sunshine blinded me on the church steps. I blinked it away, and the welling tears. At the diner, I'd picked two more church services to attend, but now I resolved to make amends. I'd go to Providence Hospital and tell all to the Newhursts, beg for their forgiveness. What that might do to the investigation, well, I'd just have to let the chips fall where they would.

But I didn't get a chance. Because as I started down the stone steps to Tenth Street, I noticed a man across the street drop the newspaper he was reading into a trash basket and start down the sidewalk in the same direction I was going.

CHAPTER 11

SO MUCH FOR MY ZIGGING AND ZAGGING. THE RUSSIANS HAD FOUND ME. The N.K.V.D. liked to bird-dog, so the shadow was driving me toward the guys with guns. Getting caught here was bad news, it meant they'd had plenty of time to spread a dragnet around the church. I was walking north, but a team had to be positioned south, didn't matter if I switched directions. Could have been worse, I reminded myself—they could have tracked me to Jean's apartment while I was still there. If I ducked back into the church, the Russians would simply tighten the net and wait me out. A block away, at the corner of H Street, I saw a cop in a prowl car, writing a report, his window down.

If not for the pill I'd popped, I probably wouldn't have done what I did. But the idea seized me like an electrical shock, set me tingling, lit up my face. Picking up my pace, I veered toward the prowl car, sneaking looks over my shoulder at my shadow, who pretended not to notice. I let him close the gap until the cop was within earshot, still engrossed in his report.

"Stop it!" I shouted, wheeling around and pointing my finger at my shadow. "Turn off your transmitter!"

He stopped dead, unable to hide his surprise. The cop perked up.

I rushed toward my shadow, a youngish man of average build and soft features: chubby cheeks, snub nose, full lips. "Turn it off, goddamn you, turn it off!" I shouted, shaking my fist.

He took a backward step, involuntarily looked around. The N.K.V.D.'s men had to be close, had to be observing, but they stayed out of sight.

"Are—are you talking to me?" he asked.

"You know I am, you know I am! I told you to stop!" I twitched and jerked my head, like a swimmer trying to eject water from his ear.

"Say, what is this?" the cop said loudly. He'd left his car and was striding toward us, his billy clenched in his right hand. Passersby had stopped to watch, chattering excitedly.

"Make him stop!" I challenged the cop.

"Easy, easy." He raised the club, cupped it in his left hand, glared at me.

I mumbled under my breath, then buttoned up. Couldn't overdo it, couldn't be a ham.

The cop turned his glare on the shadow. "What'd you do to him?"

"Nothing! Officer, I've never seen this man before! I was just walking down the street. All'a sudden, he turns around and runs at me screaming."

"Uh-huh." The cop glanced at me. I was twitching a little but stayed quiet. He sheathed the club and asked the shadow, "Where you going, pal?"

"On my way to the grocer's, my wife gave me a list." He pulled a scrap of paper from his pocket and extended it.

Nice touch, that—always have a good cover story if a tail goes wrong. The cop, a bald man with a wide chin, scanned the list and handed it back.

"How 'bout you, pal, where you going, why're you yelling?"

I drew myself up and leaned slowly toward the cop, making sure not to get too close. "He's following me to make sure the broadcasts are still coming through."

The shadow piped up. "Officer, I got no idea what he's talking—"

"Shuddup, lemme handle this."

The shadow shut up, the cop eyed me up and down. "Broadcasts, huh? Who is it this time? The F.B.I., the O.S.S., Hitler?"

I shook my head. "S'the Russians. They've got a transmitter in Moscow, see, and—"

"Awright, that's enough. Lemme see some I.D., pal."

"I.D.? I don't carry that, they want to take it from me!"

"Yeah, well, I bet they know who you are at Saint Elizabeths, don't they?"

"Saint who?" I gave him a blank look.

The cop sighed. "Awright, you get your shopping done," he said to the shadow. To me he said, "Let's go for a little ride, pal."

"What about the transmitter, the broadcasts—aren't you gonna make them stop?"

"Don't worry, you can't hear anything inside the car, it's got a lead-lined roof."

"For real?"

"You bet." He jerked his head toward his prowl car and waited for me to get going, following closely behind.

The shadow waited for us to get a few steps ahead, then continued north on Tenth, rubbing his chin, looking worried. The Russians would blame him for what happened, but I wasn't out of the woods yet. The shadow would tell them the cop was taking me in, the Russians would follow. For a moment I wondered if I should let the police take me to St. Elizabeths for a chitchat with a shrink—at least I'd be safe from the N.K.V.D. in the nuthouse. But I couldn't risk being identified as the man who'd run away from the Harbor Patrol Station.

"Where're we going, Officer?" I asked as we approached the car.

"Don't worry 'bout that, pal—all you gotta know is, where we're going, you're not gonna hear any broadcasts, okay?"

I nodded eagerly. "Yessir."

He opened the rear driver side door. "Get in there and keep quiet, understand? No squirming, no talking, no nothing—got it?"

"Yessir!" I scrambled in. The cop got in and gave me a long look through the wire screen between the seats before starting the engine.

To get to the closest precinct, I figured the cop would make a right at New York Avenue, which would take us around Mt. Vernon Square, the site of the public library. If I jumped out there, I could bolt to the library's entrance and run for the stacks before the cop got inside. While he rushed back and forth, wondering where I'd gone, I'd exit through the library's sorting area, in the rear.

The cop didn't speak, just kept glancing in his rearview mirror to make sure I was behaving. And I was, keeping still and avoiding eye contact. As he slowed the car to round the Square, I slid to the door, opened it, and jumped out.

"Hey!" the cop shouted—"Ufff!" I grunted. I estimated our speed at only fifteen miles an hour, but that felt plenty fast when my feet hit the pavement. I stumbled and reeled, my arms spinning like a windmill. Luckily I reached the curb before I fell, so my head only hit the grassy strip between the curb and sidewalk. I scrambled to my feet and ran up the steps to the library's entrance. But the cop was quick, a lot faster than I'd expected—he was already out of the car and racing toward me as I grabbed the door handle. So much for my head start.

I tore across the marble lobby floor as startled patrons gaped.

"Outta the way, goddammit!" the cop yelled. He sounded awful close.

I led him toward the circulation desk. A librarian stared in amazement. I didn't look over my shoulder, didn't want to know if he'd drawn his weapon. He wouldn't shoot me in the library with so many people around—I hoped—but what if he cornered me? I veered toward the periodicals, but those cases couldn't conceal me, they were slanted to display magazines and you could see through the gaps between the shelves. Had to keep out of corners, open spaces too—not so easy in a library, I realized.

The reference section, next to the periodicals, had higher shelves. I dropped to my knees, dipped my head, crawled as fast as possible. If I reached the far wall, I could run down a narrow aisle, screened by the reference bookcases, to the sorting area. Now I was out of sight, but I discovered that it's awful hard to crawl quickly, even with the aid of an amphetamine.

I heard the cop shout at patrons to keep back, so he wasn't far. I reached the end of the shelf, turned the corner—and looked straight at a little girl, her eyes wide. She was about ten feet away. I pressed a forefinger to my lips, then beckoned her to come close. She did, warily, as I stood carefully and pressed my back against a reference bookcase.

"There he is!" someone called out excitedly.

"Where?" the cop demanded.

"No, it's just a kid," another voice boomed.

I stayed put and whispered to the girl, "We're playing hide and seek, can you keep a secret?"

She nodded solemnly. Looked about eight, long black hair carefully braided, wearing a polka dot dress with buckled straps. I smiled and pointed for her to go up the aisle between the shelves. She darted away. *For chrissake, don't shoot—*

"He's here, he's here!" the girl shouted.

A buzz rose from the gawkers—"There he goes!"—as I raced toward the library's sorting room and burst through the swinging doors. I seized a cart laden with books, pushed it in front of the entrance, and ran to an exit. I'd just opened the door to the street when I heard a tremendous clatter—the cop upending the cart and tumbling into an avalanche of books. Still running, I went west to Massachusetts Avenue, then slowed to a normal gait, blending in with a crowd waiting for a bus. We were boarded and underway by the time I spotted the cop, limping slightly, coming that way.

I DIDN'T STAY ON THE BUS LONG, DISEMBARKING AT DUPONT CIRCLE TO transfer to a southbound Connecticut Avenue bus. With almost twenty-four hours to go, I'd already had two close shaves. Should have been scared, should have been thinking about digging a deep, deep burrow and hunkering down—but no, all I could think about was how the Russians had found me. Where had I gone wrong? How many Reds, pinkos, and fellow travelers did the N.K.V.D. have on a string? I'd had plenty of brushes with the Russians before, but I'd never imagined they could whistle out so many spotters on a moment's notice. I got off the bus and started walking south on Seventeenth Street. Thought: *Go to the Bureau, ask for Slater, tell him you're ready to talk.* I'd ladle up malarkey, for sure, just enough truth to keep him hungry, stretch it out through the night, then leave in the morning—when Hoover's boys think they got something hot, they'll stay on as long as it takes. But that would be beyond stupid, I realized. I'd surrender control to a hostile agency itching to even a score with me.

I turned off Seventeenth onto H Street. Had to keep moving, had to circulate the streets this way, that way, never staying on the same street or avenue for more than three blocks. Still a beautiful day, the sky an impressionist painting, sun glinting on the Washington Monument, tulips dabbing the street sides yellow, red, orange.

Gotta be a place in this city where the Reds aren't, so think, Ellis, think! Took me four miles, at least ninety-nine corners and turns, and a lot of random pauses to check shop window reflections for a tail, but finally I came up with that place—and I beelined for it.

CHAPTER 12

W HAT PASSED FOR A HOBO JUNGLE IN D.C. LAY NORTH OF UNION STATION, where the Baltimore & Ohio tracks diverged. Warehouses, repair shops, and vacant lots occupied the flat land between the tracks. Before the war, there was a sprawling junkyard here, but years of scrap drives had stripped it of all usable metal, leaving only the rusted hulks of Olds, Studebakers, and Buicks too far gone to salvage. Vags had colonized the wrecks, using the car bodies as shelters. They'd Hoovered them but good, adding on shanties cobbled together from boards and tar paper. The settlement was much smaller than the homeless settlements that had sprung up across the country during the Depression, but the capital's squat had a permanent look to it, as if these men were here to stay. Maybe they were, too—Dougie MacArthur wasn't around to burn them out like he had the Bonus Army.

Which made my entrance tricky. A man couldn't just stroll into a hobo jungle, couldn't just pass around a bottle of sneaky pete and expect a warm welcome. For whatever reasons, these men had dodged a uniform or steady work at a time when sixteen million men were in the service and the nation had a *negative* unemployment rate. That put these bums in an awful elite club, one harder to join than the Cosmos Club. They hated outsiders, they could spot a foreigner a mile away. No way I could pass muster, not in my clothes. I could rub grease on my cuffs and roll my trousers in dirt, but a one-eyed bindlestiff would see fresh paint. Some of these joes had Coolidge-vintage grime, they'd been in the life since I was a squirt. My haircut was barbershop, my shoes clean. If I was going to check in, I had to peddle a damned fine tale.

Still flying on the jazzbo's pill, I reprised my cover identity, Ted Barston, from the case that had landed me in this vat of hot water. Changed the dates, left out the dope habit, and spun a yarn about "Ted" jumping the brig in Norfolk. The vags loved it—they'd all had run-ins with the Man. I clinched my entrance with my account of how I'd skimmed the church offering. A spindly old-timer named Juke accompanied me to the nearest liquor store, at the end of Third Street, and I blew the Congregationalists' cash on rotgut for all. We spent the rest of the day and much of the night drinking and telling stories of the life (mostly I sipped and listened). As the last vag awake staggered off to his '28 Packard for shut-eye, I rubbed my raw, red eyes and slipped away in the dewy air to make my break past the N.K.V.D. into the Navy Building.

WHAT I DID WAS, I FELL IN WITH A GAGGLE OF STENOS, TYPISTS, AND clerks who arrived on the same bus every morning; they boarded together in a house off Rhode Island Avenue. We called them the Andrews Sisters—some wag had overheard one girl trilling a song line once when they were leaving the Navy Building. One of them, Brenda, had been sweet on me and we'd gone on a date or two, but she liked movies and magazines, I liked books; she went for Kenton and Christy, I went for bebop.

"No baby, nobody but you . . ." I crooned, stepping out of the crowd waiting for the bus she'd just left.

Brenda wheeled around. Her favorite, that Gene Roland number.

"Good God, is that you, Ellis?"

"Mi'lady." I took a theatrical bow. The Sisters stared.

"D'hell happened to you?" Brenda asked.

"Would you believe I spent the night in a hobo jungle?"

"Yeah!" she and a Sister exclaimed in unison.

"I think he's drunk," another whispered.

"Nope. Sober as a judge, just had to sip now and then to keep up my cover."

"Cover, right." Brenda rolled her eyes. My work on the countersubversion desk had never impressed her. *Just a big game for boys*, she'd remarked on our first date.

"Listen, will you gals do me a favor and walk me in?"

"For real?"

"We're not gonna get shot, are we?" someone giggled. Nervously.

"Oh no, I'm just doing this to win a bet."

"Gawd," Brenda said, but she held out an arm, and I hooked her elbow. She wore a jade-green dress with a braided belt and a rounded collar. A soft burgundy felt hat draped her forehead, dangling to her plucked eyebrows—always a dish, Brenda. On my other arm, a Sister I didn't know by name, a gal with a toothy smile. We crossed Constitution Avenue and walked to the main entrance as I forced myself not to look anywhere but straight ahead. With the Sisters around me, I'd make it—I hoped.

We got in without trouble, I thanked the Sisters, but I wasn't safe, not yet. Figured the N.K.V.D. or its minions were watching, maybe they had orders to nab me if they could, maybe they just wanted to know I was in the building. Maybe they had someone inside, a Red or a ringer, didn't matter—if he knew his work, he could do his job quietly, quickly, bloodlessly. I'd have to hit the head sometime, a garrote would only take a minute or two, an ice pick even less time. *Easy, Ellis, easy.* Told myself it was the drug finally wearing off, leaving me frazzled, fried, twitchy. Wide awake, sure—but paranoid as hell, a step away from becoming the loon I'd played to shake my shadow the day before.

Donniker. Had the old man beat me to the Navy Building? I sure hoped so—if he was still on the lam, I had a lot of explaining to do and a hell of a lot more worrying to do. I'd already failed to protect Kenny Newhurst from being hurt; what if Donniker became a victim too?

To my immense relief, Donniker was in his ground-floor workshop, sorting through a box of electrical clips as if nothing unusual had happened.

"Jesus Christ, you look like shit," he greeted me.

"Gee, thanks. When did you get in?"

"Same as always, ten after seven."

I didn't ask why ten after seven was his usual arrival time. He sure didn't look like he'd had a stressful night. Freshly shaved, hair combed, clean clothes, shop apron cinched tight around his skinny waist.

"Any troubles?" I asked.

"Nope. Stayed with a pal I know through ham radio."

"What'd you tell him?"

"Besides that little green men were chasing me? D'hell's it matter what I told him?"

"Sorry, it's just that—well, my weekend wasn't so quiet."

"They found you?"

"Almost. I shook 'em, but I had to spend the night in the hobo jungle."

"Huh. That would account for your ripe smell."

I managed a grin. "Maybe you can loan me your cologne?"

He snorted an appreciative laugh, but his gaze was wary and unsettling. Had I overreacted? Were the Russians not interested in Donniker? Maybe their interrogation of Kenny had given them all they needed to know: I had lied, and they needed to pick me up pronto.

"We better go see Commander Paslett now," I said. "He's gotta know what's happening."

"Which is what we shoulda done Saturday night," Donniker complained. "Taking off like a coupla fugitives—what kinda nonsense is that? They're not after me, and I'm starting to wonder if they're really all that hot to talk to you."

I glared at him, remembering Kenny's pale face, his gasping breath, his wound.

"They shot a kid, Donniker! For no reason! They beat him to find out about you and me, and we're supposed to just sit around and hope they don't come after us?!"

"All right, simmer down." He dropped the clip he was holding and took off his apron.

COMMANDER PASLETT HAD A SECOND-FLOOR OFFICE OVERLOOKING THE Reflecting Pool on the Mall. If not for the other tempos on the other side of the pool, it was a postcard view. Not that Paslett spent much time window gazing. He was blunt, he was driven, even obsessive, especially when it came to commies. A lot of brass played politics, they collected and traded favors like rare stamps; they wheedled, connived, and wormed their way up. Not Paslett. He'd earned his desk, he delivered, he had the O.N.I. director's full faith and credit; and I was lucky to serve under him. And boy, did I need a dose of that good fortune today.

I knocked, we entered at his command. Paslett was at the filing cabinet holding his meticulously curated domestic intelligence files. He was as proud of those files as Mellon had been of his art collection. He turned to look at us.

"Hello, Donniker."

"Commander."

Paslett scowled at me. "Why aren't you in uniform?"

"Because the Russians are taking it to the cleaners for me, sir."

"What the hell does that mean?"

"Saturday after duty, sir, I picked up an N.K.V.D. shadow."

A look of alarm. He strode to his desk and sat, motioned for us to sit down.

"Just curious?" he asked. Foreign intelligence tails weren't unusual, sometimes the Russians liked to let us know they were around, hoping we'd waste time trying to lose shadows. Feints, diversions.

"Nosir. What it feels like, they wanna talk to me awful bad. And maybe Donniker too."

Paslett bit his lower lip and lit up a Chesterfield. Grateful he'd taken out his cigarettes, I fired up too, hoping the commander didn't notice the tremble in my hands.

"About Himmel," he said. A statement, not a question. Henry Himmel, the missing Russian agent everyone wanted.

"Yessir, that's gotta be it."

"How do they know you saw Himmel?"

I took a deep breath, exhaled smoke. "There was a kid in the kitchen, sir, at the Automat, when we"—I ticked my head at Donniker—"set up the listening rig. The Russians found the kid."

"How do you know that?"

"After duty Saturday, sir, I went to the Automat to talk to the kid."

"Why?"

I phrased my reply carefully. "With my spec coming to an end, sir, I've been thinking a lot about what happened at the Automat. Who Himmel met with, why he disappeared, if he's gonna turn—"

"Just tell me what happened, Voigt."

"Yessir. So the boy, Kenny's his name, Kenny Newhurst, he didn't show up for his shift that day. So I called the Horn and Hardart office and got his address and went to see his mother."

"You didn't call her first?" He frowned. Donniker, too, was looking at me funny.

"I was hoping the kid was there, sir. Maybe he was goldbricking, maybe he just forgot he had to work."

"What'd his mother say?"

"That he left for work when he was supposed to."

The commander leaned forward to ash his cigarette, smoke drifting my way. "Who'd you tell her you were?"

"William Brady of Horn and Hardart. Gave her a line about how there was theft at the F Street Automat, that her son had reported it and I was supposed to interview him before his shift that day."

"Christ almighty, Voigt! You're about to finish a two-month spec, you want a two-year one? How'bout I bust you to ensign and put you on a water tender west of the Solomons?"

I kept quiet and took it. Donniker did his best to study a corner of the ceiling as the commander dressed me down, ticking off all the mistakes I'd made in just one afternoon: improvising a cover, dragging a civilian—Kenny's mother—into an intelligence case, starting an investigation without orders. When he paused to stub his Chesterfield, I said quietly:

"They shot the kid, sir."

"What?"

I described what had happened at the empty factory and how I'd broken in to save Kenny. Didn't sugarcoat my failure, didn't offer excuses. Telling the story, reliving the horror of staunching the boy's wound and carrying him to the Harbor Patrol, made my mouth go dry, beyond dry—suddenly I was as parched as a dying man in a desert.

Paslett brooded for a moment after I'd finished, poking a pencil eraser against his desk like a steam driver. Thunk, thunk.

"Is the boy all right?" he finally asked.

"Yessir, I called the hospital and pretended to be his father. The doctor said they'd stabilized his condition."

His glare was withering. "If you knew he was in danger, why didn't you tell me back in May? We could've figured out a way to warn his family, get him a different job or something, get him outta the Automat!"

"Sir, I don't know, I just don't know, it all happened so fast the night I was there with Donniker, we were so busy listening to what Himmel and his spy were saying and then I had to rush outta there to try and catch up with Himmel and I told Kenny not to tell anyone we'd been there and I thought, well, I guess I thought that was enough, I never guessed the Russians would come around looking for kitchen staff, I mean, how did they know we were there, but, but . . ."

Paslett stood and walked to his window to give me a moment. Another officer might have angrily ordered me to get a hold of myself or even shaken me—not for the first time, I was grateful he wasn't like most C.O.'s.

"How'd you know where the Russians were taking the boy?" he asked after a long minute, his back still turned.

I took a deep breath, steadied my voice. "When I was undercover at the clipping service, sir, I had to make a delivery to that factory. Seemed fishy, getting a delivery at an empty building. Figured if the Russians were using it as a drop, they might also use it other times." I told myself that it wasn't too much of a lie, told myself I'd tell Paslett about my meeting with the N.K.V.D. agents at a better time.

"And what you heard was, they were asking the boy about Donniker?"

"Yessir."

"Which means they'd already grilled the boy about you."

"M'sure they did, sir."

He looked at Donniker. "Did they come after you next?"

"Nope. But Voigt, he showed up at my house after he saw what they did to the kid and told me I needed to clear out til this morning. So I did."

"Were you tailed? Did anyone unknown to you stop you to ask you questions, anything at all, like for directions or what time it was?"

Donniker shook his head impatiently. "No, nothing like that."

"Where did you stay?"

"With a pal, he does ham radio, known him for years."

"How about this morning? Did you see—"

"Listen, nobody but nobody came after me," Donniker interrupted. "I haven't forgotten my training, you know."

If anyone else had cut off the commander like that, he'd have regretted it. But Donniker had been in uniform, years ago, before retiring and taking his civilian post as our radio and gadgets whiz. I didn't know the first thing about his record, but judging from the commander's respectful nod, Donniker had served admirably.

"Did you go back to your house before you came in this morning?"

"Nope."

"We'll need to check to see if it's been tossed."

Donniker turned to glare at me. "Don't forget what I told you, Voigt. If those Reds busted up my house, you're going to pay for the damage down to the last penny."

"You might need to stay in a safe house a few nights, Donniker, til we're sure the Russians aren't after you too."

"Oh, for chrissake! Goddammit, Voigt, what have you gotten me into?"

Paslett gave me a hard look. He had this face, you see it on a lot of career Navy men, looks carved from flint, a sculptor's rendering of a man who gives orders like the rest of us take breaths. Gray eyes boring down, pincer eyebrows, vise lips prying apart to ask:

"S'a damn good question, Lieutenant: What the hell have you gotten us into?"

CHAPTER 13

P ASLETT TOLD DONNIKER HE COULD RETURN TO HIS WORKSHOP. THE
parting look I got from the old man told me I'd have to buy him a
lot of scotch before he forgave me for disrupting his life. But I hadn't
overreacted, I knew that in my bones, not after what I'd seen Shovel-face
and his partner do to Kenny Newhurst.

The commander walked over to his cabinet. He ran his forefinger along
the top, as if an omen might come off like wet varnish.

"What did you do after leaving Donniker's house?" he asked.

I told him, omitting nothing. After I finished, he returned to his desk
chair and tilted back, the spring creaking.

Finally he spoke. "The Russians think you killed Himmel."

"Yessir." And left it at that.

"He's still missing, you know."

I nodded slowly, as if that was news to me, waiting for him to continue.

"While you were on the nutter line, I had Daley try to find him." Daley—Lieutenant (j.g.) Terrance Daley—had worked with me on the Himmel case, but only I had gone undercover.

"Nothing?"

"Nothing," he repeated.

"What about the front, sir, the clipping service?"

"The Bureau shut it down. At some point, the Russians sent in a team to clear everything out."

"The Bureau didn't have it locked up?"

"A'course. But they had cops watching the place at night. Russians doped a flatfoot's coffee—he always took his break at the same diner—and went in while he snored away in his prowl car."

"Has the Bureau given anything up?"

He gave me a cynical look. *What d'you think?*

"Daley was able to put this together," he said. He riffled through a stack of folders on his desk and slid one over. I took out a packet of stapled documents with the subject line IDENTITY OF HENRY HIMMEL (FOREIGN NATIONAL, RUSSIAN). Daley had worn out some shoe leather. Visits to the Immigration and Naturalization Service, the State Department, the Office of Strategic Services; he'd even gone to the municipal government building to pull the business license for the clipping service.

Himmel (I learned) had emigrated to the States from Pavlograd, a city somewhere in Ukraine. Russian passport, German ancestry. *Volkdeutsch*— a good cover. He wouldn't even have to speak German well; some of those German families had been in Ukraine or Russia for generations. Terrance had obtained a photostat of Himmel's Certificate of Residency, dated August 14, 1934: *Personal description of holder as of date of entry: Age 37 years; sex* Male; *color* White; *complexion* Dark; *color of eyes* Brown; *color of hair* Brown; *height* 5 feet 7 inches; *weight* 140 pounds; *visible distinctive marks* none. Himmel had looked impassively into the camera for his photograph. Cool eyes, tight lips. That same inscrutable expression he'd had the last time I saw him, on the night of the Automat meeting, only now on the younger man in the photograph, no gray in his hair. Not too many Russians, whatever their ethnicity, could have obtained legal entry to the States in the early '30s; the immigration restrictions passed a decade earlier had kept the Russian quota low. I wondered if the N.K.V.D. had greased the wheels for Himmel; the Russians were sure to have a friend or two at Immigration.

Upon arrival, Himmel had settled in New York, where he'd worked at the vaguely named German-American Information Service. Too vague—the outfit screamed front. Probably an offshoot of the Bund, the Nazis' premier organization of American-dwelling Hitler lovers and Master Race hopefuls. "Didn't the Bureau raid them in '38, '39?" Terrance had scribbled in the margin. *Good catch, partner,* I thought. Hoover's boys had swept up the leadership of the German-American Information Service from its New York office right after the Germans pounded into Poland. But Himmel hadn't been there, otherwise the immigration authorities would have deported him. Which meant Himmel had moved on; he'd cut ties before the raid. An easy guess as to why he'd been mixed up with a Nazi fan club in the first place: the Russians wanted to know everything they could about American fascists and their ties to the Nazis.

There the trail went cold, until Himmel surfaced in D.C. with sufficient capital to open his clipping service. Terrance had appended a list of subscribers to the service and he'd come up with short biographies of all the employees. The report closed with *In re: espionage activities of H & H, see report Lt. (j.g.) Voigt, File B-7 5730A.* This was the official designation for Paslett's Do Not File records, the documents he didn't want indexed. Any intelligence agency, the Bureau included, could make an official request for our records, using the Central Files index, so everything we wanted to keep under wraps carried the designation 5730A.

"No wonder the Russians want to find Himmel, sir—eleven years in the States, he knows a thing or two," I said as I handed the report back.

"I was beginning to think the N.K.V.D. had done him in, but with them coming hard after you and Donniker, that doesn't add up."

"Nosir." I lit up.

"But that might be his fear right now," Paslett continued.

"That the N.K.V.D. wants to kill him?"

A nod. "S'happening to a lot of 'em, especially the ones getting long in the tooth, like Himmel."

I thought for a moment. "So he makes the meet at the Automat, he gets the package from their spy, then he takes a powder. Because he knows he'll be killed as soon as he turns over the package. Which means he's holding it as insurance."

"Makes sense, doesn't it? Except—?" Wanting me to finish the sentence.

"But what guarantee does he have they won't kill him once he turns over the package?"

"Right. Himmel's not stupid, he knows they'll break any promise they make."

"Sell it to the highest bidder, then?"

"And who would that be, Voigt?"

"Well, us, sir."

Trace of a smile. "But that puts Himmel back where he started, doesn't it?"

"He can't trust us to keep our promises either."

"Bingo."

"So what d'you think happened, sir?"

"Someone killed Himmel for the package. And the Russians think it was you."

"Sir!?"

"So we gotta find out who it was for real."

"Who killed Himmel, you mean."

The commander shot me an impatient look—who else could he mean?

"D'you think it could have been the spy, sir?"

"But why deliver the package at all if he was just going to kill Himmel?"

"To bring him out, sir. The contact hands over the goods, doubles back on Himmel, kills him and takes back the delivery."

"Awful risky. Why stick his neck out like that?"

"Maybe he wants out, sir. If he kills Himmel and disappears, he could be trying to convince the Russians someone took them both out."

Paslett shook his head. "Too complicated." He sighed, drummed his fingers along his desk. "After you gave me your report about that night, I called Groves and told him one'a my men had spotted someone from his project."

I tried to hide my surprise—and excitement. "Groves" as in Major General Leslie Groves, an old pal of Paslett's now heading up the hush-hush weapons project in New Mexico. The man whom Himmel had received the package from had come from New Mexico. We knew Himmel's clipping service had been the conduit between Russian spies down in the desert and the N.K.V.D., but we didn't as yet know what the weapons project was or how much the Russians had gotten on it. Identifying the man I'd seen with Himmel at the Automat was the first step to answering these questions.

"What'd he say, sir?"

"He asked for your report, which I sent."

"You think he's identified the man I saw, sir?"

"If he has, he hasn't told me. And I'm not holding my breath he will."

"Serious breach like that and he wants to handle it himself?"

"Maybe he already has."

"Say he has, sir. That doesn't bring back what Himmel has. Our man from New Mexico, he could lie or bluff about what he handed over."

Paslett exhaled frustration. "I know that, Groves knows that. But whatever leak he has, he wants to plug it himself. He's already got O.S.S. telling him he needs their help on security."

"What's their angle?"

"They've warned him there's people in his project—civilians—who are cozy with the Russians."

"You think O.S.S. is on to the same man we are, sir?"

"Could be, but I doubt it. They're just trying to keep Truman from axing them by starting new operations with anyone who will say yes. You should see the crap they send me."

If Groves was saying no to the O.S.S., he likely would rebuff us as well. So how to convince the general to say yes? I thought of a news article I'd read years ago about a Swiss mountain climber whose rope broke during a storm. He fell into a crevasse and broke his leg. Unable to climb out, and knowing his fellow climbers couldn't find him in the swirling snow, he realized his only hope of survival was to burrow deeper into the snow, to claw, scrape, and worm his way through the pitch-black, icy depth in hopes of finding another way out. His every instinct resisted going headfirst into that hole, yet somehow he forced himself to blindly traverse the darkness, to go deeper until the crevasse turned and led him out.

I fixed the commander with a steady gaze. "Sir, I need to let the N.K.V.D. pick me up."

"That a joke?"

"For real, sir. We can't let it look obvious, they gotta think they're nabbing me, but once they have me, we can mislead them."

"How?"

"By letting them think we know where Himmel is. What I'll do is, I'll let 'em think I can't hack it anymore, that I've cracked and wanna give up Himmel on my own to get 'em off my back. Or I could play greedy, offer to sell his whereabouts."

"Why would we want to do this?" he said, frowning.

"We both gotta find Himmel, sir, the Russians and us. If I can find out what they know while feeding them misinformation, we can scoop up Himmel and his package before they know we were stringing them along."

He shook his head. "I don't like it. What this sounds like is, you wanna barnstorm back into action after your spec. The Russians are gonna be looking for a plant, they'll work you over something fierce to see if you're faking it. Even if you pull that off, we still gotta give them something on Himmel—and we got diddley-squat on what happened to him."

"What if we shift the blame onto our man from New Mexico, sir?"

He said nothing but gestured for me to continue.

"I convince the Reds that Himmel's contact killed him, killed Himmel, and took the package back, that he arranged the meeting at the Automat to bring Himmel out—just like we were guessing a little bit ago. I pitch that story, sir, I sell it but good. If the Russians think Himmel's dead, they're gonna need to find a way to reach their man in New Mexico. If you can convince General Groves to bring me down, I can sell myself to the Russians as their contact."

Paslett looked doubtful. "If you go to New Mexico and identify the Red spy for Groves to arrest, the Russians are gonna know you pulled a fast one."

"Not if I bring back misinformation, sir. I'll convince the Russians I made contact with the spy and forced him to give me the package he was supposed to deliver to Himmel before I identified him for Groves. We'll give the Reds fool's gold. By the time they figure out they've been had, it'll be too late for them to do anything about it, because their spy will be locked up tight. But you've gotta get General Groves to let me come to New Mexico."

Paslett bit his lower lip, thinking hard, but I caught the gleam in his eyes. Before he could answer, though, there was a bracing rap on his door.

"Who is it?" he called out.

"Agent Slater, F.B.I."

CHAPTER 14

I HAD TO GIVE IT TO HOOVER, HIS BOYS HAD AN IMPECCABLY BAD SENSE of timing. Paslett said to me, "Let's see what he wants, then I'll tell you if I'm gonna let you cozy up to the Russians." Translation: *Not a word about this to the G-man.*

"Yessir," I said.

"Come in," Paslett shouted as I looked over my shoulder.

If you spotted Special Agent Clayton Slater on the street, you wouldn't give him a second glance. Middle-aged, slight build, average height, light brown hair, not close to handsome but far from ugly, too, sporting the kind of face that floats unnoticed through a crowd. His nose wasn't bulbous, broad, hooked, or long; it was just a nose. His lips weren't thin or full; they were just there. Search for words to describe him, and *average* would top that short list. Slater was standard issue G-man, the Model A of bureaucrats, available in two suit colors, gray or blue. That day he wore blue with an ivory shirt and a maroon patterned tie.

"Lieutenant Voigt's here, what a surprise," Slater said after he entered. He stayed directly behind me as I turned around to face Paslett again.

"Yeah, and we're busy, so you'll need to make an appointment," Paslett said smoothly. "I can see you after, oh, I don't know, Labor Day. Maybe."

I watched Slater's reflection in the window. His expression didn't change.

"You'll wanna hear this, Commander, believe you me," Slater said.

Paslett lit a Chesterfield, took a long drag. "I doubt that."

"You know, Commander, I'm here as a courtesy to O.N.I., but I'm happy to tell the director you wouldn't even give me five minutes of your time."

A courtesy. That actually meant the Bureau needed something from Paslett, and John Edgar had sent Slater to get it without saying pretty please.

"Tell him I gave you two minutes." Paslett made a show of looking at his watch. "Starting right now."

"Uh-uh, not with him here." I watched Slater's reflection dip his chin at me.

Slater wanted to tell Paslett all about Philip Greene, no doubt about it. To save his skin, Greene was trying to convince the Bureau that I'd framed him, that I *was* the real killer of Lieutenant Logan Skerrill, the turncoat officer whose death I'd investigated while undercover at the clipping service. Having failed to bait me on Saturday at the diner with Greene's accusation, Slater was casting a line at Paslett. Getting the commander to doubt my loyalty, my honesty—that's what the Bureau was after.

"All right." The commander leveled his gaze at me. "Lieutenant Voigt, you're dismissed."

"Yessir," I answered, snapping off a salute. *Why's he caving?* I started to worry.

Then Paslett said, "Send Lieutenant Daley in, Voigt."

"Yessir," I repeated, ignoring Slater as I passed him. I wouldn't be present to hear what Slater had to say, but my partner would be, and he'd tell me everything after Slater left.

"MISS ME?"

Terrance Daley peered at me through a haze of cigarette smoke. "No." Downturned lips, piercing gray-green eyes. On another man, you'd call it a scowl—from him, that look meant *good to see you, pal.* I'd seen Daley scowl for real—he could rattle Medusa with that look.

"Thanks for keeping my desk clear," I said. During my lengthy exile on the nutter line, my partner had stacked, tossed, dropped, shoved, or flung folders, envelopes, memos, newspapers, grease-blotted hamburger wraps, carbon paper, pamphlets, magazines, and badly folded maps onto my desk, which faced his own in our cubbyhole of an office. Atop one pile, a misshapen clay ashtray with a mountain of butts rested at a precarious angle—a few stubs had already tumbled, like doomed mountain climbers, down the sloping mess. I reached for the ashtray—"Don't touch that!" Terrance shouted.

"Why not?"

"M'trying to get a'hundred butts into it."

"What the hell for?"

"Marcia made it in school. Said it could hold a'hundred cigarettes, easy."

I studied the rough-hewn piece, a thumbprint visible in the glazed clay. "She's got talent," I said.

"Thanks. Have fun this weekend?"

"Fun, that's one word for it. Listen, the commander needs you pronto."

"What's up?" He stood, stubbed his smoke on the edge of my desk, and carefully set the butt atop the mountain. Miraculously, it stayed.

"Our buddy from the Bureau is back. Paslett wants you there."

"Slater." He practically spit the name out. "He's getting to be a real pain in the ass."

"Getting to be?"

"Called for me three times last week. Funny how I couldn't ever find the time to ring him back." He grinned, spreading his palms over the mess on my desk.

"Yeah, funny. Listen carefully, will you? He's got it in for me."

"Don't worry, partner, I'll get it all." He patted my shoulder, checked to see he had his cigarettes, and left.

I sat down in his chair and lit up. Give myself up to the N.K.V.D.—had I picked up a death wish during my weekend on the run? Paslett was right, the Russians would smell a plant, they wouldn't just take my word. It was one thing to say, to *think* I could take whatever they dished out, but another thing to take it for real. No man knows what he'll say to stop the pain, unless he's endured a bout of torture already. And I'd never been put to the test.

But what choice did we have? Keep me deskbound, bunking here? We needed to identify the spy from New Mexico, and we couldn't do that with me in protective custody. I was the only one who'd heard his voice, and I'd seen him. Slim, young, dark-haired, cool, confident. I could quote every word he'd uttered to Himmel that night at the Automat. Whatever was being built down in the desert in New Mexico, we had to keep the Russians from finding out about it. The Germans were *kaput*, the Japs just about; but the Russians were our next enemy—and anyone who believed that Stalin and Company wanted to get along with the United States after the war was a fool.

Paslett had to convince Groves to let us find his spy; I had to convince Shovel-face I was all the way on the Red side of the board. If the Russians eased off, if I could collar the spy, drop him right into Groves's lap, then it wouldn't matter what had happened to Himmel. We wouldn't have to worry about him. Would take a bit of work, but I could bring Paslett around on that subject. Not without that spy, though—I absolutely, positively had to have that S.O.B. tied down and singing loud and long.

I yelped—my cigarette had burned to my fingers. I threw the butt to the floor, ground it out; the telephone rang.

"Voigt here."

"Come on down," my partner said.

Slater was gone, Daley was sitting in the chair I'd used. After Paslett put me at ease, I pulled a chair from the corner and sat next to my partner.

"Hey bruiser, how's it hangin'?" Terrance said, grinning.

"Slater thinks you're a killer," Paslett chuckled. Banter was good, joking was welcome—they were having none of Philip Greene's accusation.

"You tell him I rob banks too?" I asked.

"Funny. But Slater's making some real noise," the commander said.

I said, "The Bureau's gotta cover up their part, sir—they're just trying to get outta the spotlight."

Lieutenant (j.g.) Logan Skerrill, the man Slater believed I'd killed, had served with us in O.N.I. A real whiz kid, he'd turned out to be a Benedict

Arnold, a Red who'd been working for the Russians. Only that hadn't been exciting enough for him, so, like some barrel-chested comic book hero, he'd fashioned himself into a double agent. Presented himself to the Bureau, fessed up to being a spy—and promptly volunteered to be a mole to make things right. How he knew the Bureau would say yes instead of arresting him, we could only guess, but he'd pulled it off. Until he got killed in an alley, that is. Daley and I had investigated the murder—that's when I'd gone undercover to work for Himmel, who'd run Skerrill on the Russians' string. When Himmel found out what his golden goose was doing, he ordered the hit. Despite the proof that Philip Greene was the gunman—hell, I'd found the .38 that had killed Skerrill at Greene's flat—Slater wanted to believe Greene's claim that *I'd* killed Skerrill and planted the gun. Putting the blame on me cooled the heat on the Bureau, which hadn't bothered to tell anyone it was secretly running a compromised naval intelligence officer as its mole.

"Where were you that night, Voigt?" Paslett said suddenly, staring straight at me. Meaning the night Skerrill was killed.

"With my gal, sir."

"Can you prove it?"

"We could ask her, sir."

"The same broad who got you your spec?"

"Yessir." Trying to keep a blank look on my face. That "broad," Lavinia Burling—Liv, always Liv to me—hadn't gotten me my spec. I'd earned it by contacting her while I was undercover, a reckless, stupid stunt that pulled Liv smack into the middle of my investigation. Slater had hauled her in, he'd interrogated her, even though she'd known nothing. She'd left Washington as soon as the Bureau cut her loose.

"Know where she is?"

"Nossir."

Paslett looked at Daley. "How soon could you track her down?"

My partner shifted uneasily in his chair. "Sir, m'sure we could find her pronto, but is that a good idea?"

The commander gestured at him to continue.

"If we alibi Voigt, we're just playing into the Bureau's hand, sir. It tells 'em we think they're right that Voigt is dirty. Whatever alibi we tell 'em, they're gonna hammer it to pieces. They don't just wanna take down Voigt, sir—goddamned Bureau wants to take us all down. Truman hates Hoover—everybody knows it—but if the Bureau can smear O.N.I., O.S.S., and everyone else, then ol' Harry's got no choice but to keep Hoover on."

Paslett was listening intently, I liked that; then he started nodding, I liked that even more.

"Besides," my partner finished with a smile, "Voigt's no killer, else he woulda shot me this morning for what I did to his desk."

I plastered on a grin. My partner had seen right through the Bureau's play, and he'd brought Paslett around. Slater must have laid it on thick, knowing that Paslett was obsessed with Reds, and the ploy had almost worked. But Daley was dead-on right. Coming up with my alibi would only tell the Bureau, and the entire intelligence establishment, that O.N.I. was running scared, that we didn't know if we had another spy in our ranks or not.

"All right, forget finding that broad. I'm gonna see if the admiral"—Rear Admiral Leo Thebaud, O.N.I.'s director—"can stir up a shit storm for the Bureau as our way of thanking Agent Slater for his visit. Besides," he went on, now looking just at Daley, "there's something else I need you to do."

"What's that, sir?"

"Find a safe place for Filbert Donniker to stay the next few nights. Voigt will explain why."

CHAPTER 15

WHILE COMMANDER PASLETT TALKED TO ADMIRAL THEBAUD, DALEY and I returned to our office. I told him about my weekend, starting with what had happened to Kenny and why Donniker had had to go on the lam.

"Why the hell didn't you call me?" he asked when I finished.

For an answer, I pointed to the ashtray his daughter had made for him. He nodded his understanding. He had a son, too, and anyone could easily find out where his kids went to school, could easily come after them.

"These goddamned Russians think they own this city! Why can't we just round 'em up and send 'em to Siberia?"

I didn't reply because he already knew the reason why: the Japs. As long as they were still fighting, we needed the Russians in the war. The deportation of a boatload of Reds, as much as they deserved it, wasn't going to happen. Besides, Shovel-face and his partner were sure to carry diplomatic passports labeling them "Second Assistant to the Directorate of Foreign Trade Missions" or some such nonsense.

"All right, our orders are to find Donniker a safe place, let's do it."

"Um, about that—you're the one who's gonna find him a place."

He shot me his trademark scowl, and as many times as I'd seen it, I still had to suppress a flinch.

"See, the thing is, just before Slater showed up, the commander and I were discussing—well, he might have another job for me, is all."

"Another job. Undercover, again."

"I don't know, he didn't say."

My answer was weak, I was holding back, Daley knew it. We worked well together, had for years, but the murder of Logan Skerrill and my assignment to infiltrate the communist spy ring had strained our partnership but good. I owed him a better explanation than I'd given—hell, I owed him a lot more than that—but until I knew what Paslett wanted to do, I had to hold back.

"Listen, what's going on here, it's not—"

"Better go see the commander," the scowl said.

Felt just like a fight with a girlfriend, but I knew better than to try to placate him. He was steamed, he had every right to be, and nothing I could say could cool him down. Better to tuck my tail and scoot, so I did.

Paslett was bent over one of his file drawers when I entered at his command. He told me to sit.

"Daley working on that safe house for Donniker?" he asked, still poring over his folders, his voice muffled.

"Yessir."

"Good, good," he answered.

I longed to light up but held off, pressing my hands against the top of my thighs and forcing them to stay there. I felt rank, was a mess, could smell my own stink. Hadn't showered or shaved in two days, hadn't washed in more than twenty-four hours.

"All right, okay," Paslett muttered to himself, sliding the file drawer shut with a thud. He returned to his desk, empty-handed, and lit a Chesterfield.

I eagerly tapped the cigarette from my packet and lit up.

"Spoke to the director," he said.

"Yessir." And waited.

"Ever read Westbrook Pegler?"

"Occasionally, sir." Pegler was an op-ed writer for the *Times-Herald*.

"He's gonna leak it the Bureau's coddling a commie killer."

I took a drag, thought about that. Pegler must have had a falling-out with the Bureau. Hoover favored his type, liked to ladle them scoops as they held out their paws and begged. But Pegler must now owe the O.N.I., because Admiral Thebaud wouldn't let Paslett go to the press without a guarantee that the commie's victim, a naval intelligence officer, wouldn't be identified as a Russian spy. The Bureau would push back hard, but it wouldn't leak that detail about the victim either, because then Pegler would reveal that the Bureau had been running him as a double agent. For very different reasons, the O.N.I. and the Bureau wanted to keep Lieutenant Logan Skerrill's treason a secret. Still, using a journalist to poke Hoover in the eye seemed awful risky to me. Intelligence agencies treated newspapermen like pets, either stray cats to throw rocks at or lap dogs to nuzzle; but animals, no matter how tame, are unpredictable, and they can bite. I just had to trust that Thebaud and Paslett could trust Pegler. As long as the ink-slinger delivered, the Bureau was off my back, if only briefly.

"That's great, sir," I said.

"About what you proposed, before our pal Slater showed up. You sure you wanna try it?"

Got no choice, do I? "Yessir, I do."

"All right, here's what we're gonna do. First I want you to write up a Form 47"—an affidavit—"saying you know all the risks." Translation: *I had to sign an advance death warrant, should things go wrong.*

"Yessir, I understand."

"Good. Then I want a brief with your objectives and methods." Meaning the cover story I'd feed to Shovel-face, how I'd stay in contact, everything right down to how many aspirin I'd need if the Russians decided to test my tale with a little pain.

"Yessir, you'll have it this afternoon."

"Get to it, I'll call Groves."

"Sir, a question."

"Go ahead."

"Can I tell Daley what I'm doing?"

He thought for a moment. "No," he said firmly. "Around here, only you and me are gonna know about this."

WHICH MADE FOR A TENSE DAY, AFTER I STOPPED OFF AT THE SUNDRIES counter in the lobby to buy cigarettes. Daley looked up at me but said nothing as I sat down with a blank Form 47 at the typewriter we shared. He had the telephone cradled to his ear, smoke untwining from a cigarette, making calls to find Donniker an out-of-way room—O.N.I. had arrangements with a number of trusted (and well-paid) hoteliers and landlords to provide quick-notice accommodations, no questions asked. I tuned out—typing a statement about the possibility of my death, at age twenty-five, took an awful lot of focus. How should it begin? *The following is a testament that I, the undersigned, understand . . . When, in the course of human events, it becomes necessary for one man to . . . To Whom It May Concern . . .* I decided to skip the preamble and get right to it. Put it all down, not worry about grammar; straight, no chaser. That I was going undercover, that my "treason" was a front to earn the trust of N.K.V.D. agents, that my tasks were to identify the scientist I'd seen meeting with Henry Himmel and to convince the Russians that this scientist, their spy, had killed Himmel. And that I "fully and willingly appreciate any and all risks to myself as a consequence of this operation." I typed slowly, carefully. The motion of the Underwood's keys, snapping forward to strike the paper with a metallic thud, suddenly struck me as violent. My pop was a printer, back in Chicago, and from him I'd picked up some of the trade's surprisingly rough lingo. Margins were slugs, a line that went too far was a bleed; shop tools included scorchers, shavers, and chase trucks. Jesus, why was I thinking about that stuff now? I rolled the Form 47 out of the typewriter, signed it without proofing, and turned to a much harder job: my brief for Paslett. He was a stickler for detailed, precise briefs, especially when it came to "Opers," Navy shorthand for operations.

To avoid further questioning from Paslett, I didn't mention the confab I'd had with Shovel-face and his partner the night before they found and took Kenny Newhurst. The commander would demand to know how they'd contacted me, why I'd gone, and why *for fuck's sake* (a phrase he used sparingly and ostentatiously, like Christmas crystal) I hadn't told him about the meeting. If all went well, no one would ever have to know about that meeting.

I worked through the morning and into the afternoon on my brief. Daley was in and out of our office frequently, our exchanges limited to the workaday: where a file was, or a certain form. He was waiting for me to tell him what Paslett was having me do. But telling him I couldn't tell him would only anger him more. The scowl was bad enough, but the *smolder* was worse, much worse.

PASLETT ORDERED ME TO REWRITE THE BRIEF THREE TIMES, WHICH KEPT us both late, close to 10:00 P.M. Every change he wanted, each addition, was true-blue, and I wasn't bent at all about the extra work. It was my neck being stretched out, and Paslett had a jeweler's eye for planning. Despite the hazards I was facing, my excitement grew as I retyped the final version, Daley long gone, a gooseneck lamp shining like a spotlight on the Underwood. Because the commander wouldn't stay all night to rework the "Opers" unless he had talked to Groves—I hoped.

But Groves hadn't as yet returned his call.

"What do you think that means, sir?"

Paslett shrugged. "He's a busy man. Could just mean he hasn't had the time. Like I told you before, he's busy trying to keep O.S.S. out of his hair."

"Sir, what if you were to tell him what I'm doing, pretending to be a Russian spy?" As much as I wanted to go to New Mexico, I was hoping—praying—that Paslett said no to this idea.

"No, no, that's a bad idea. Just you and me—we've gotta be the only two who know what you're doing." Translation: *If there's a leak, you die.*

"Then what are we gonna do, sir?"

"We start the operation, you go under tonight. You do your part, I'll do mine—I'll get Groves to say yes."

I didn't answer, just took a deep breath, let it out. Then: "Absolutely, sir."

"Good. Dismissed, Voigt, and good luck."

CHAPTER 16

NO ONE TAILED ME, I TRAILED NO SHADOW ON MY BUS RIDE HOME.
Jesus H., did I want a drink, I needed bourbon like Crusoe needed
fire, but until I got myself cleaned up, I wasn't fit to bend elbows with
fellow humans, not even in a Seventh Street gutbucket slogging nickel
beers. Thanks to the coins in my desk drawer, I was able to buy a shortie
of bottom-shelf rye from a liquor store near my basement flat. *How soon
til they pick me up?*

My hand trembled as I dug in my pocket for the door key. If I were
the Russians, I'd have two men waiting inside my flat, tipped off that
I'd left the Navy Building and was taking the bus. Or would it be a blow
from behind as I came down the steps? A car rolling up, a fast snatch? My
imagination ran wild, my pulse raced, my breath quickened. Street empty,
locust trees casting shadows, whisk of my shoes on the pavement; I could
even hear the rye gurgling in my back pocket.

What I got was nothing I'd imagined. Not even close. What I got was Mara on my steps as I approached, key in hand. Mara, the Southern belle and fellow traveler who'd been dispatched by the Reds to let me take her home the night of my interrogation at the deserted factory.

"Hello there," she chirped. "Ah was just leaving a note on your door because you haven't called, you naughty boy." Giving me a flirtatious smile.

"I've been busy," I managed. *What the hell is she doing here?*

"Ah figured so." Still smiling, but giving me an eye sweep her thick lashes couldn't hide. Her jaw clenched slightly as she noticed my grimy, wrinkled clothes and greasy hair.

I met her smile and took a quick step closer. "Would you believe I've been working undercover in a junkyard?"

"Why yes, yes Ah would." She made a show of waving her hand in front of her nose and laughed ever so briefly. *Ah ha, ha.* A true finishing school touch, that laugh, as perfectly timed as a Bob Hope crack. I wondered if the headmistress had required her charges to practice in front of a mirror. *A lady never giggles, or chuckles, and she never, ever guffaws . . .*

"Hence my disheveledness," I said.

"Ah didn't know that was a word."

"'Hence' or 'disheveledness'?"

"Ah ha, ha." Smile fading.

"Well, Mara, you've caught me in a less than presentable state, but won't you come in and have a drink while I freshen up?"

"Why, that would be lovely, Ellis!"

Now I got it, I saw why she was there. My solitary return had thrown the Russians. Everything I'd done to evade them over the weekend, and now I was riding the bus home alone? Shovel-face and Company smelled fish, they didn't like it, they suspected a trap. So they'd rustled up Mara on short notice, and ten to one, she was carrying a Mickey Finn. The Russians were waiting, she'd spike my drink, they'd wait for me to pass out and then move in. Smiling, I slipped past Mara and opened the door.

She followed me in. I wasn't much of a housekeeper, but the place was presentable. Motioned for her to sit in the lone upholstered chair while I switched on the tabletop Motorola. Artie Shaw came on, "Many Dreams Ago," Helen Forrest singing.

"I'll build us those drinks, then get cleaned up."

"Ah'll mix the drinks if you like," Mara said brightly.

I bet you'd like. "Now, what kind of host would I be if I let you do that?" Big, big smile.

"Well, if you're sure, Ellis."

"Oh, but I am, I am."

She forced a laugh as I kept grinning.

"Something to read?" I asked.

"Why, if it's no trouble."

"No trouble." A few copies of *Collier's* and *Esquire* were on the table by the radio. I grabbed two and brought them over. "Back in a jif."

I went into my tiny bathroom, then the kitchen, where I took down two highball glasses, added ice cubes, and poured two fingers of bourbon in each. Fortunately, I had sweet vermouth, to soften the cheap booze. I broke three sleeping capsules I'd taken from the bathroom and dumped the contents into the first drink. Stirred vigorously with a spoon, then brought the glasses into the front room. Mara was sitting upright in the chair, legs primly crossed at the knees, single pleat gray skirt just above her shins. Drab-green short-sleeve shirt, short string of pearls and matching earrings, black pumps with a decorative buckle fashioned as a bow tie.

She set down the *Collier's* and smiled as she accepted the drink with the dissolved sleeping pills.

"I'm outta gin, hope you like rye," I said.

"It's my father's favorite drink."

I set my drink down on a cork coaster on the end table next to my chair. "Won't be long, promise," I told her. Went down the hall to the bedroom, made sure she could hear drawers opening and shutting as I collected a change of clothes. Showered, shaved, and dressed as quickly as possible. How long would it take for the sleeping pills to work? Fifteen minutes, twenty?

I returned to the front room, feeling like a new man, rubbing my clean-shaven cheeks and relishing the scent of Murray and Lanman's Florida Water. Bad sign: Mara had barely touched her drink. Good sign (in a fashion): my glass was perfectly centered on its coaster, which meant she had handled it, as I'd left it close to the coaster's back edge. She'd spiked the drink, now she just had to get me to drink it.

"May Ah offer a toast?" she asked.

"A'course."

"To new beginnings." Smiling pertly as she extended her glass.

I reached to clink glasses, we both sipped. I let the cold liquor touch my lips and run back into the glass.

"Now may I propose a toast?"

"Surely."

"To many happy returns."

We clinked glasses, another lip press for me. If I pulled this off, maybe I'd write a book: *Party Tricks That Might Save Your Life Someday*. To keep Mara from noticing that my drink wasn't going down, I set my glass behind the stack of books on the end table. Wasn't hard to rattle the ice cubes every time I took a "drink" and I kept my hand wrapped around the glass. To speed her along, I spun a tale about the rye we were drinking, how a buddy of mine in the Navy was from Kentucky, how his pop and brothers were master moonshiners, how they had a generations-old recipe, how lucky we were to be drinking it.

"Why yes, it's quite, well, unusual," Mara said gamely.

"Can you taste that hint of cardamom, just as you finish swallowing?" I asked, raising my glass and feigning a big gulp.

"Why no, Ah can't say Ah do . . ."

"Try it again—you'll taste it on the back of your tongue."

"Why yes, there it is . . ." Slurring her words slightly.

I checked my watch: twelve minutes since I'd sat down. Now she yawned mightily, set her glass down suddenly, frowning. For an instant, her eyelids fluttered.

"Ellis, do you think—could Ah have a glass of water, please?"

"Right away."

When I returned, she was dead asleep, slumped in the chair, hands resting on her thighs. I drank the water for her and took the glasses, including my spiked drink, to the kitchen. Dumped out my glass, rinsed it, poured in the rest of the rye from the bottle. Left Mara in the chair, her breathing deep and rhythmic, and unlocked the front door. Sat back down, raised my glass. "Here's mud in your eye," I said to Mara. Took a long, long drink to start my wait, Tommy Dorsey on the radio, working magic with his trombone.

I was almost done with the rye and Mara was snoring when the door clicked. Lucky me—Shovel-face and his partner entered. No caution, no apprehension, no weapons drawn, came in just like cats at dawn, rolling their shoulders, stepping lightly. They looked around quickly, taking in the scene in a snap.

"She did not notice you switch drinks?" Shovel-face asked, alert but not alarmed.

"I didn't switch drinks," I said, and left it at that.

He shrugged, not caring what I'd done. He barked something in Russian at his sidekick, who reached over the chair and grabbed Mara under her arms. He roughly pulled her down the hall and into the bedroom, where I heard her weight thump on my mattress. Shovel-face sat down in the upholstered chair. In short order his partner returned with a chair from the kitchen. Clearly this wasn't their first visit to my flat.

Shovel-face said, "Clever of you, Lieutenant." Ticking his head toward the bedroom.

Anger swelled within me. The man who had shot Kenny Newhurst was sitting across from me, and I couldn't do a damn thing. Instead of avenging the boy's injury, I was playing a game with Russian spies. I could call it an "operation," I could call it "duty," I could call it "the national interest," but no label could banish my frustration at not being able to punish these two N.K.V.D. agents until we knew what they were after.

When I didn't respond, Shovel-face shrugged. "You have been avoiding contact, Lieutenant. Why?"

"I figured you'd drop by eventually."

"You were at the Navy Building all day."

"Well, yeah, it's where I work, after all."

"What did you do?" Not one for sarcasm, Shovel-face.

"Caught up on my filing."

"With Filbert Donniker?"

"We didn't work together today if that's what you're asking."

His expression tightened. He didn't like me jumping ahead, I'd have to watch myself.

"You told him to run."

"A'course I did. When I found out the boy from the Automat was missing, I knew we were next." Paslett had decided bluffing the Russians was a bum move, they'd know we were working an angle. So he'd told me to admit we knew something had happened to Kenny Newhurst without letting them know I'd seen what had happened.

"What boy?" He was trying to slip me up.

"There was a boy in the kitchen the night Donniker and I listened to Himmel. Saturday afternoon, I went to talk to him. He hadn't shown up for his shift at the Automat. So I went to see his mother, she didn't know where he was. Turns out he's in the hospital with a gunshot wound."

"How did you know where to find him?" Shovel-face asked. He wasn't fazed at all to learn Kenny was alive.

"A child goes missing, first thing you do is call the hospitals. Don't you do that in Russia?"

He ignored the crack and spoke quickly in Russian to his partner, who nodded, his eyes on me during the exchange. *They know I was there, know it was me pounding on the door, know I saved the boy's life. Why don't they care?*

"Where is Donniker?"

Did they know he had arrived safely at the Navy Building that morning? I decided to play dumb. "I don't know."

"You're lying."

"No."

"The Navy is protecting him."

"I don't know where he is."

He made a dismissive noise, a sort of *pffft*. "Why would you tell him he is in danger?"

"You want to know where he is, don't you?"

"Lieutenant Voigt, how can you be so certain we have gone after this boy from the Automat? Of what value is he? Or this Donniker?"

He was toying with me, and with a sickening feeling I understood why he wasn't pressing me to admit I'd come to the factory looking for Kenny.

He knew if I really wanted to see him punished for shooting Kenny, I wouldn't be here—I'd be working with the police to have them arrested.

I gulped the last of the rye and banged the glass down. "Look, god-dammit, why don't you just come out and ask me already!" Practically hearing Paslett's voice from that afternoon, when we'd gone through the paces. *Get steamed, Voigt! Spit in their eye, let 'em have it.*

Shovel-face said calmly, "We know you didn't tell us about your equipment. Your headset, the receiver—what is that word you have? Gadget, yes, gadget." He pronounced the *dg* as a *j*.

The answer I'd expected, because they'd extracted it from Kenny just before they shot him. But I managed to keep up my act.

"You better not be surprised! No way in hell I was gonna tell you about the rig and how we listened. I had to give Paslett something, didn't I? Doesn't change anything I told you about Himmel and his contact, and everything I already told you is how it happened. I met Himmel outside the Automat at seven-thirty, we walked to the Hancock statue, he asked me about the F.B.I., he left walking south around eight, I don't know what happened to him."

"What did the man at the Automat give Himmel?"

"I don't know."

"No?"

"If he picked up something, he musta put in his jacket pocket—I never saw anything."

"But you heard everything."

"They didn't talk about a pickup."

"You recorded this conversation?"

"No. Donniker's rig only had a microphone. It picked up their conversation and sent it by a radio signal to the kitchen—I listened through a headset."

"Donniker also heard everything?"

"No—he couldn't, he wasn't close enough."

Shovel-face didn't like that answer. He leaned close and stared straight into my eyes. His dark eyes glinted, I could see the stubble on his chin.

"How could he not hear if he was close enough to use a microphone?"

"That's how it works, it can pick up sound the human ear can't."

"I don't believe you."

"I don't give a rat's ass what you think," I said defiantly. "Donniker didn't hear anything, we didn't record what they said."

Shovel-face shot his partner a look. He stood, came around behind me. Paslett and I'd planned for this, he'd convinced me I had to let the Russians believe they were putting the squeeze on me, that no matter what, I couldn't put the proposition to them, not even if they put a gun to my head. Because they knew I'd spent all afternoon with my C.O., they suspected we'd cooked something up, they were trying to draw it out by scaring the bejesus out of me.

Which they sure as hell were. "Get the hell outta here," I blurted. No courage, I was trying to keep my lips from trembling. "And take your little Red pixie—"

Then everything went black.

CHAPTER 17

I CAME TO IN A WINDOWLESS, SMALL, DARK ROOM. COLD WATER WAS thrown onto my face, a lamp was shining on my eyes. *Good morning, sunshine*, I thought absurdly. Hadn't a stranger recently said that to me? Or had I heard it in a movie? Had to focus, going loopy wasn't going to help. Blinked the water away, shook my head, flexed my arms and legs. They'd lashed me to a wooden chair, hands behind my back, ankles to the chair's front legs.

"There will be no preamble, Lieutenant—we're all professionals here, and I see no point in wasting time explaining what will happen if I don't get complete, truthful answers." The voice: reedy but precise, unmistakably American, a mid-Atlantic accent. The man speaking: a shadowy, slight figure, seated in a chair about six feet away. With the room's only light on my face, I couldn't see his features or even what he was wearing.

"Agreed," I said tersely. Who was he? Where were Shovel-face and his partner? I sensed others' presence, the whisk of a shoe sole on tiles, a muted cough. How many, I couldn't tell. Two, three? Cigarette smoke lingered in the air, but no one was smoking now—they weren't going to let me see their faces. What did that mean, that they wanted to stay hidden? I shook off the question. No distractions, only unassailable concentration. Funny, when I'd earned a coveted O.N.I. berth, I'd daydreamed myself into stardom, the Melvin Purvis of the Navy. Be careful what you wish for, natch—now I was starring in my own show, on the stage with the spotlight trained on me. *Break a leg, Ellis . . .*

"Why did you decline to tell my colleagues about your surveillance of Henry Himmel and his contact at the Automat?"

"I was holding that back as insurance." *True.*

"Explain."

"I didn't like being called to an empty factory at night. But I also wanted a reason to be called back." *True.*

"Understood. But withholding information hasn't made your position any more secure, has it?"

"Thought you said we'd skip the unnecessary explanations."

He laughed, but that didn't put me at ease. Sadists like feisty prey, makes them feel even more powerful.

"You said your equipment didn't record the conversation at the Automat."

"It didn't." *True.*

"Did you hear the entire conversation?"

"No. I missed the first few minutes while we got set up." *True.*

"Tell me what you did hear."

Decision time. So far, telling the truth was easy, the answers couldn't hurt me. I wasn't so sure about my next response. Still, I opted for the truth. Most of it.

"Himmel's contact is a scientist working on a weapons project in New Mexico. He came to Washington to see Himmel in person. Himmel was upset, he had wanted to use a courier, he didn't want him to come in person, but the scientist dismissed his concerns, said he was sure he wasn't followed. Then he said he wanted Himmel to memorize something."

"What was it?"

"He said, 'To diffuse the Uranium-235, use uranium hexafluoride and a metal filter with submicroscopic perforations. Do not use a mass spectrometer.'"

Without missing a beat, my interrogator repeated, word-for-word, what I'd just said. "Correct?" he asked.

"Yes."

"Then what?"

Now I held back. That night at the Automat, Himmel had demanded to know how the scientist had made his discovery, and the man had taunted him. *What, a Ph.D. in physics from Yale at age twenty-two isn't sufficient bond?* The Russians and their American friend must never know I had this vital piece of identifying information. So I said, "He told Himmel that, quote, our visitor from afar, unquote, had helped them figure out what he'd just said about the uranium." *True.*

"Did he or Himmel use this so-called visitor's name?"

"No." *True.*

"Do you know who he is?"

"Yes. Gerhard Trechten. A physics professor, a Nazi, went on the lam, we picked him up in the Canary Islands and brought him to the States, to New Mexico." Which my interrogator already knew. Because Logan Sker-rill, the officer whose death I'd investigated, had been part of that mission to fetch Trechten, and he'd told all this to his Red handlers.

"What else?"

"The scientist said something like, your physicists will know what to do with this, as long as you remember what I just told you."

"With what—did he give Himmel something?"

"I don't know. Remember, I couldn't see them. If he did hand some-thing over—"

He interrupted. "Your technician, Filbert Donniker, he was close to their table, to position the microphone, correct?"

"Yes."

"What did he see?"

"I don't know, he didn't tell me if there was an exchange."

A long pause. "You heard an apparent reference to a delivery, and yet you didn't ask him what he saw afterward." His tone was low and ominous.

"No, we didn't have a chance to speak, I had to get Donniker outta there and on his way so I could try to follow Himmel." *True!* But I had a sinking feeling the truth was no longer helping me.

"That's difficult to believe, Lieutenant."

"It's what happened. I didn't ask Donniker what he saw."

He spoke, but not to me. Rapid Russian, to a figure behind me. I checked the urge to speak—pleading would only make me sound like I was hiding something. Which I sure as hell was. I'd followed Himmel, and how I was going to keep that secret, I had no idea. Especially after the first electrical shock hit me.

They gave it to me on the nape of my neck. Went down my spine, through my innards, through my legs, to my toes, and right through the floor to the earth's core. I'd heard, somewhere along the line, that electricity delivers pain like you've never felt before. *True.* No blow, no cut, no burn could match the fire that coursed through my nerves, that turned my muscles to jelly and my brain into a buzzing bee-hive, that rattled the fillings in my teeth, that blurred my vision. The second shock lasted an eon, I was living in geological time. If you can call what I felt *living.*

Somewhere beyond the Milky Way, the voice of God said "Stop," and the monster left my neck, leaving me quivering, moaning, crying, and soaked in my own piss.

"Again, Lieutenant. What did Filbert Donniker see?"

The vampire swept down and shook me like a rag doll. When the command to stop came, sometime after the passage of the Ice Age, I heard a chortle, from a familiar voice: Shovel-face was wielding the prod.

"Answer promptly, Lieutenant. You're flat broke, promptness is the only way you can buy reprieve."

Flash: *Just tell 'em Donniker saw an envelope, you need time, gotta figure out how to really lie.* A voice I'd never heard before, that of a broken little boy, whispered through my lips—bleeding, because I'd gnashed them—"Okay, okay, he saw the scientist pass over an envelope."

"Good. Now, you might not believe me, but I find this type of coercion distasteful. So your continued compliance will make the situation better for all of us."

I took that to mean that more shocks would cause me to shit myself, chew off my tongue—or worse. And that he didn't like messes.

My interrogator continued. "I have several problems with your account of what happened next, Lieutenant. Specifically, what you told my colleagues about your little stroll with Himmel."

Why's he calling these goons 'colleagues'? I managed to wonder. Was he a professor? Highly educated, for sure. "Want me to go over it again?" I croaked.

"No. Just answer my questions."

I nodded. At least, my head lolled on the throbbing stump that had replaced my neck.

"First, why would Himmel want to talk to you about the F.B.I.?"

"Because they'd questioned me, he wanted to know what—"

"Stop. You had ample time to tell Himmel about your interview by the F.B.I. after it occurred. You were undercover, working as his courier—"

"You stop!" My outburst surprised everyone, including me. "All the time I was at the clipping service, I was posing as Ted Barston, a discharged commie shipfitter second class who'd just got outta the brig. I kept that cover always, even when Himmel and I were alone. You know that's good tradecraft, you know Himmel would follow it too." *True.*

I braced for a punishing shock—I could hear Shovel-face shuffle closer, no doubt he was drooling in anticipation—but it never came. Instead:

"I see your point. All right, tell me what you and Himmel talked about."

"I told him the Bureau knew he was running spies outta the clipping service. Told him they knew I was his courier."

"What else?"

"That's all." At least, that's all I'd told the Russians during my interrogation at the factory.

"I don't believe you."

"Okay, I also told him the Bureau didn't know I was O.N.I."

"What else?"

"Nothing." I tried to brace myself, but my muscles had turned to flabby flesh, my bones had dissolved, the rope that bound me to the chair had taken the place of my spine. I heard Shovel-face approach. In spite of myself I cried out.

This shock knocked me out. No reprieve, though—the pain brought me back awfully quick.

"I'll ask just once more, Lieutenant: What else did Himmel say?"

"Nothing. Why would he tell me anything?"

"What happened to him, where is he?"

What had I told Paslett? *I convince the Reds that Himmel's contact killed him, killed Himmel, and took the package back.* Had I really said that, had I really believed I could sell this story to the Russians? Sure—because in Paslett's office I wasn't being electrocuted. No way I could pull off that lie now. They'd keep shocking me, demanding evidence. *Had we found a body, how had Himmel been killed?* And they'd want to know why I hadn't mentioned this during my first interrogation, back at the factory. I had to improvise:

"He took a powder, he's scared, he's hiding."

"Why do you think he's on the run?"

"Because he likes life in our bountiful nation. He likes Pepsi, peanut butter, and scotch whiskey. Hell, he just plain likes life."

The Professor laughed derisively. *Not good enough . . .*

"Look, we know what's happening to the Reds who get long in the tooth. Himmel showed all the signs of a man who wants to keep his teeth."

Our knowledge that the N.K.V.D. was on a tear, knocking off the most veteran Russian operatives in D.C. and up and down the Eastern seaboard, was a closely guarded secret, and I hoped by sharing it I was proving my trustworthiness.

But that revelation didn't work either. The Professor said, "Maybe those who aren't so long in the tooth, either, what do you think, Lieutenant?" His voice—calm, precise, level—hadn't changed, but there was an ominous undertone in the question.

"You've already rattled me good, in case you didn't notice." Begging myself not to beg, not to plead for a second chance. Somewhere out beyond the moon, I could see the logic behind that decision—if I begged for my life by telling them I had orders for New Mexico, they'd know it was a setup—but right then and there, every remaining nerve in my body was twitching for me to beg. But I didn't, I said:

"Go ahead and get it over with, why don't you? Fuck you all, just do me straight, you owe me that, goddammit." I'd managed to say what I had to say, but I couldn't hold back the tears, which streamed down my face. Shovel-face lurched up behind me. Was he gripping the same gun he'd shot Kenny Newhurst with? Poetic justice, wasn't it, if it was the same gun . . .

"Hold it," the Professor intoned.

CHAPTER 18

W HAT ARE YOU HIDING?" THE PROFESSOR ASKED.

"Does it look like I got anything left to hide, you bastard?" Teeth gritted, breathing shallow, bowels loose, whole body trembling. Would I hear the report, would that be the last sound I ever heard? Or just my pulse pounding in my temple?

"Perhaps you do, Lieutenant, you've proven quite resourceful so far."

Was this my opening, my way out of the crevasse? Or must I burrow deeper into the dark? The only thing I knew for sure was this: I couldn't take another electrical shock, couldn't endure even seconds more of that pain.

I said, "Maybe I just don't want to tell you how short-sighted you're being."

"Oh, I think we can handle a little criticism now and then."

"Good, then handle this: Himmel's gone, and if he wants to save his skin, he's already destroyed whatever he got at the Automat. If you want the recipe featuring Uranium-235 molecules, you need another visit from your friend in New Mexico."

"A child could tell us that, Lieutenant."

"Could a child get you close to your friend, on that protected base in New Mexico?" Trying to say it calmly, trying not to think about how my life was riding on the Professor's answer.

Long pause. Somehow, I willed myself to stop trembling.

"You're being sent to New Mexico," he finally said. A question, not a statement.

"If I leave here in one piece."

"Tell me your orders exactly as you received them, every detail, right now," he demanded.

He was good, damn good—if I was lying, I'd stumble, I'd hem or haw, um or er, as I struggled to craft my story. But Paslett and I had anticipated this moment, he'd drilled me, we'd gone over my orders again and again, so I could do the same with the Russians. So I told them, recited my orders in the rote drone of a schoolboy giving his lesson, the Professor listening intently, not interrupting once. Behind me, I could hear Shovel-face's husky breathing.

When I finished, the Professor asked, "Why hasn't General Groves isolated him for questioning?" *Him* being the scientist who had met with Himmel. The Russians and the Professor knew his name—we didn't.

"Groves doesn't know who he is yet."

"Come now, Lieutenant, that's fantastical. How many scientists on that project had leave on those days? We know even civilians need permission to step foot off that base, how could he *not* be identified yet? Perhaps you need a reminder of why you shouldn't lie—"

"No, no more shocks, call off your Russian wolfhound *now*. If you want the whole truth, and nothing but the truth, I need to think clearly."

"Fine," he said breezily. "But don't waste time convincing me."

"We don't know Himmel's contact is a scientist. I've been calling him a scientist because of all the gobbledygook he said to Himmel, but for all we know, he's just a messenger who flunked freshman chemistry. There's what, at least a thousand men on that base, and like you said, every one of them needs a hall pass to leave. Coulda been as many as fifty, sixty, who had permission to leave that week. That's a lotta folks to check out, and that's why General Groves wants me down there pronto, to help him make the I.D. quicker." I offered a silent prayer that Paslett was, right at this moment, convincing Groves to bring me down. Because if those orders fell through—

"Why doesn't Groves do it himself, with his men?"

"He will, I'll be there to verify. Nobody wants to make a mistake on this one."

"What's Groves going to do after you make the identification?"

I didn't fall for the trap. "That's a decision way above my rank. After I do my work, they'll hustle me outta there without telling me anything."

"If so, then what's the value of us letting you go to New Mexico, Lieutenant? After all, we already know who this man is."

"I'm the only one who can get another copy of the diagram he gave to Himmel."

"We have other options."

But none better than relying on me, I wanted to say—otherwise, Shovelface would already have fired that shot into the back of my head. What the Professor didn't know is that I'd heard his man from New Mexico tell Himmel that he was out, he was done, he wasn't going to lift his little finger to help the Russians any longer. He was running scared, laying low, hunkered down on the base in New Mexico where the N.K.V.D. couldn't touch him. Without the missing Himmel, without a way to reach their man, the Russians didn't have the dope on whatever weapon we were building down in the desert. They wanted it in the worst way, and the only way to get what they wanted ran through me.

I said, "Here's how we should do this. You give me your contact's name, I go to New Mexico and go through the motions of identifying him, to make it look good for Groves. Right away, I'll tell your man I'm a courier, sent to get another copy of the blueprint out."

"Can you?" the Professor asked.

"I won't be searched upon leaving. My kit, sure, maybe a pat-down, but a full body search? Uh-uh."

"I'm curious, Lieutenant. Why would you do this?"

"Maybe I like Pepsi, peanut butter, and scotch whiskey too. Maybe I just want outta this mess."

"Or maybe not, but that is irrelevant. Although I have a certain grudging admiration for the audacity of your proposal, you're not in a position to negotiate. Here are my terms. You will not get our man's name. You will go to New Mexico, you will identify him on your own, and you will get a copy of what he gave to Himmel. Waste no time. We'll be continuing our search for the absent Himmel—if we find him, and get what he was supposed to deliver to us, then you're no longer of any use to us. Same for our friend in New Mexico. Do you understand?"

I nodded grimly.

The Professor spoke in rapid-fire Russian, I heard Shovel-face lurch forward, I tried to steel myself—didn't matter. The prod came down, and the screams of a terrified, almost broken man filled the still-dark room. *Shut up, shut up,* I tried to tell him, but he didn't stop until I passed out.

I WOKE UP IN A WEED-CHOKED FIELD. THE RUSTLE OF CREATURES—RATS, squirrels?—brought me around. Groaning, I struggled to my knees, head hanging low, taking long, slow breaths. Aches veneered the throbbing pain in my entire body, my neck burned. When I touched the spot where Shovel-face had electrocuted me, I cried out. Whimpered, really—my voice was too hoarse for a cry. Add wrinkles, silver my hair, and I'd have looked like I felt: an old man with a terminal condition. An optimist would have told me I was lucky to be alive, but at the moment, I wished, if only fleetingly, that I was dead. The thought of dragging myself out of that field and making my way home appeared impossible, an act of strength beyond even Hercules's powers. If only it was winter, I thought, I could close my eyes, shut out the pain, and let the cold take me away.

But pity turned to anger, weakness to determination. Neither duty nor courage drove me out of that field, just revenge. *Must kill Shovel-face.* I muttered the phrase, and that goal rallied my weary, broken body. I repeated the words, they became an incantation, they energized me and brought me to my feet; they steadied me. *Must kill Shovel-face.* Afraid to break the spell, I kept muttering as I tottered out of the field, milkweed grazing my trousers. Checked my watch: five past two in the morning.

"Where am I?" I beseeched the first passerby, a slight young man in coveralls, his cap pulled low. He shot me a suspicious look and quickened his pace to go around me. "Please, I've just been mugged," I said, "they hit me on the head, I need to get home."

"Oh." He stopped, still wary, keeping his distance. "Are you—do you need a doctor?"

"No, I just need to get home."

He eyed me over. Given my appearance, my story wasn't hard to believe. "That's Virginia Avenue and Seventh," he said, turning to point behind him.

Which meant I was in Southeast D.C. Pennsylvania Avenue was just a few blocks north, I could catch a bus and transfer at Sixteenth Street, on the north side of Lafayette Square. "Thanks," I said.

"Sure." He let me pass, then called out, "Good luck."

I waved an acknowledgment but didn't answer. I was already whispering, "Kill Shovel-face, kill Shovel-face," ignoring my parched tongue and cracked lips.

The bus rides seemed interminable, the pain worsened. At least that kept me from falling asleep. I let myself into my flat and shut the door with a loud, reassuring *ker-thunk*. I had aspirin in the bathroom, I'd chase the pills with the rest of my whiskey and go to bed. At least that was the plan until I heard a voice call out from my bedroom: "Who's there?"

Mara! Nothing like a long bout of torture to make you forget about the fellow traveler who'd tried to Mickey you earlier in the evening. Without answering, I walked down the hall and flicked on the bedroom light. Mara turned her head, blinking. Hair mussed, hand pressed to the side of her head. Clothes rumpled, shoes still on. What time had I doped her? Half-past ten, maybe a little later, I guessed.

"Sleep well, Mara?" I asked, standing in the doorway.

"You drugged me!" she said indignantly.

"What's good for the goose, right?"

"Where are they?"

"Your Russian pals? We had a nice talk, shared some yuks, promised to do it again soon." I stepped into the room. "Rise and shine, now it's our turn to chat."

"Oh no, Ah'm leaving." She swung her legs over the bed and stood, smoothing out her shirt and skirt.

"Not yet." I strode close, clapped my hands on her shoulders, and sat her down on the edge of the bed. I pulled over the chair from the corner. "How do they contact you?"

"Let me go," she said defiantly. Her makeup was almost perfect: lipstick glossy, mascara barely smudged, eyelashes still curled.

"Soon as you answer my questions. How do they contact you?"

She looked away but didn't answer, her fingers gripping the bedcover.

"It doesn't matter now," I said. "You won't be hearing from them anymore."

"You don't know that."

"You're done, Mara, they're not gonna use you after what happened."

She shook her head, to my disbelief—didn't she know how lucky she was to be out?

"Look, I've known who you were from the moment we met," I said.

"How?"

Because I'd been interrogated for an hour by N.K.V.D. agents before you came on the scene! But I couldn't tell her that.

Instead I said, "Your pretend boyfriend, he gave it away."

"Dale did?"

"He kept glancing my way when you two were staging your row," I lied. "Dead giveaway."

"For real?" Sounding doubtful, like she wanted to be convinced.

I nodded vigorously. "Three times I counted."

"Ah knew it! Ah told him to follow my lead, Ah coached him, we went over it again and—"

"Listen, forget about Dale—tell me how they contact you."

"Ah'm not going to tell you that."

She still believed they'd use her, I could see it in her eyes, she was busy thinking, already working out how she'd tell them it wasn't her fault, that "Dale" had given them away, that she was still A-One. Arguing with her wouldn't change her mind, sure as hell wouldn't help me. Was she a true believer, a bred-in-the-bones Red all dewy-eyed for a Marxist utopia? Or was she a baller, in it for the excitement and the rush? I decided to try a different play.

"Then I guess there's no point talking to you anymore," I said slowly, standing up and gesturing at the door. "Good luck."

She stood but didn't leave. "Why do you want to know how they contact me?"

"Doesn't matter now. Sorry about doping you, but . . ." I gave a little shrug.

"What aren't you telling me?"

"I don't think you wanna know."

"Tell me."

"Your Russian pals offered your head on a platter. Told me if you were still here when I got back, I should run you in on an espionage charge for trying to turn me."

"You're lying." Glaring at me.

"You wanna find out if I'm on the level, get in touch with them and see what happens."

She sank down on the bed. "Ah've no reason to trust you."

I sat back down. "Not yet." I leaned close, looked her straight in the eye. "Mara, do you know why the N.K.V.D. is after me?"

She shook her head.

"Would you like to know?"

Now a nod. And a gleam in her eyes.

"Then I need you to contact them and then tell me what happens."

"They wouldn't like that."

"They don't need to know, do they?" I placed my hand on her thigh and squeezed.

"How will Ah contact you without them knowing?"

I slipped from my chair to the bed. "That's easy enough to figure out," I whispered in her ear, my hand still on her thigh. She turned her head, pressed her lips to mine, closed her eyes. My exhaustion and pain vanished as a surge of excitement, of desire, energized me. What drove Mara's desire, I couldn't say, but of this I was certain: her cries of pleasure weren't part of her cover this time.

CHAPTER 19

STRINGING MARA WAS ONE BIG HEAP OF STUPID, FOR SURE, AWFUL RISKY. Maybe the Russians had fried too many brain cells, maybe the shock had messed with my instinctive wariness. I couldn't trust Mara, but if she ran straight to the Russians to tell them I'd tried to turn her, which is what I was counting on, that helped me. Despite having convinced the Reds I was working for them, I feared it still looked like a setup. What if the Professor, after a good night's sleep, started thinking harder about my sudden eagerness to help after spending days on the lam? He might conclude I wasn't worth the risk—bad for me, very bad. As much as I knew about how they operated, they'd not hesitate to kill me. Sure, they'd cover their tracks by making it look like an accident, but that wouldn't do me much good. If the Professor believed I was operating as a double agent by trying to turn Mara, perversely he would be reassured; his suspicions about me would ease. Thinking he knew what I was *really* up to would make him think he could better control me, through Mara. She was my life insurance, carrying a double indemnity against commie distrust. Just before I fell asleep, I decided I wouldn't tell Paslett about this arrangement. He wouldn't like it, not at all, but it was my neck on the block, not his.

The jangling alarm bell finally woke me up at nine. I'd set it for seven but hadn't heard it for two hours, I was that beat. My entire body ached, every move hurt. Wished I had a bathtub, but a long, hot shower had to do. Shaved, made instant coffee, heated up a can of tomato soup, the only chow in the cupboard. Put on my uniform, stepped out into a day so pristine it almost choked me up. Azure sky, temperature in the high seventies, light breeze. The azalea in the tiny front yard of my flat smelled fresh, bountiful, good. Last night, a brush with death, then unexpected sex, now a beautiful summer day—the last twelve hours had whipsawed me but good. "Jesus, I want to live," I murmured, then berated myself. Going namby-pamby wasn't going to help. I needed to get to the Navy Building pronto, had to find out if Paslett had persuaded Groves to let me post to New Mexico. I'd told the commander I'd be in by eight, I was now almost two hours late.

Shook off my worries, hailed a hack. Went straight to Paslett's office, found him smoking, brooding. He put me at ease and spoke before I could ask about Groves.

"Expecting his call any second."

"Yessir."

"Why're you late?"

"Russians didn't waste any time, sir. Picked me up at my flat right after I got home." I tipped off my cap, turned my head so he could see my neck. He whistled.

"Jesus, what'd they do to you?"

"Electric shocks. Two Russians, one American. Russians were waiting for me when I got home last night, sir."

"Know where they took you?"

"Nosir. Knocked me out in my flat, I came to lashed to a chair."

"Tell me about them."

"Russians I didn't get a good look at, sir, and they didn't talk much. Stayed behind me. They kept a light in my face so I couldn't see the American, but I could hear him just fine. Educated, lots of silver dollar vocabulary, accent I wanna say is Ohio, maybe Michigan. Arrogant, cocky, real sure of himself. First impression, a professor a'some sort."

Paslett snorted derisively. "Those goddamned eggheads, they're all Reds or pinkos. Did he ask about Himmel?"

"Yessir. Like you said, they think I killed him. Kept juicing me to get me to admit it."

"What'd you say?" Paslett might never have been tortured, but he sure as hell knew what men did to stop the pain.

"Told them we knew the N.K.V.D. is busy knocking off veteran operatives and officers up and down the East Coast. Told them Himmel musta known he was next soon as he turned over the diagram from New Mexico, so he went on the lam."

"They bought that?"

"Yessir. But that's not what finally made them happy."

"You sold them New Mexico?"

"Yessir. Wasn't easy—the American, this professor-type, he wanted to know why Groves hasn't identified the spy yet. Didn't think it was too hard to figure out how many scientists coulda had leave the week of the meeting with Himmel."

"What'd you say to that?"

"Told him Groves doesn't know for sure he's a scientist. Coulda been anyone who got the diagram and smuggled it out. I guessed fifty, sixty people coulda had leave and said that's why Groves wants me down there, to speed up the identification."

"Good thinking—couldn't'a been easy, either, coming up with that line while they were—"

"When you said you're waiting for him to call, sir," I interrupted, "does that mean he's thinking about it or he's just briefing his men first?"

"I don't know, Lieutenant, I just don't know. I gave it my all, believe me. He said he'd call by noon. This wrangling with the O.S.S.—he didn't say anything about it, but it's driving him nuts, I can tell."

Checked my watch: a few ticks past ten. What if Groves said no to me coming to New Mexico. What then? Move into the Navy Building, become a virtual prisoner? Get orders for the Aleutians or Iceland, try to dodge the Russians for the rest of my life?

"Sir, if Groves says no, what am I gonna tell the Russians when they pick me up next?"

"Been thinking about that. What we might be able to do is—"

A firm knock on the door.

"Goddammit, we're busy in here!" Paslett shouted.

"Sir, I'm sorry, but there's a detective sergeant from the Metropolitan Police here, says it's urgent."

My heart pounded, my mouth went dry. The commander gave me a long look.

"All right, let him in."

A warrant officer opened the door, I turned to look as the sergeant entered. Short, with a ruddy face faintly traced by acne scars, reddish hair bristling out beneath his hat brim. His expression—tight lips, cop stare—didn't change as he looked directly at me. A familiar face. Detective Sergeant Durkin and I had met in April, a few months or a lifetime ago, depending on how I measured it. Durkin had been assigned the murder of Lieutenant Logan Skerrill, had been investigating all of twenty minutes when Paslett sent Daley and me in to take the case away. Durkin had pouted, he'd glowered, he'd tried to beat us to the coroner's office for the autopsy, but we'd boxed him out. Then without asking, I'd roped him in on the interrogation of our suspect because I needed a local cop present. But Detective Sergeant Durkin wasn't here to get an apology.

From the hallway, the warrant officer closed the door and Paslett simply asked, "Yes?"

"Gotta take him in," Durkin said, pointing at me.

"Why?"

"We got a boy in the hospital, he's been shot. His mother tells us a fella showed up on her doorstep on Saturday asking lotsa questions about her son. Said he was from Horn and Hardart, the boy's employer. Said his name was William Brady. Thing is, there is no William Brady at Horn and Hardart."

Durkin stepped forward and dropped a folded sheet of paper onto the desk. Paslett unfolded it as the sergeant said, "Boy's mother sat down with an artist to describe this Mister Brady. Some kinda resemblance, isn't it?"

Paslett didn't have to answer: it was a drawing of me.

CHAPTER 20

W E ALL STARED AT THE DRAWING, AS IF WE EXPECTED IT TO TALK. Then Paslett broke the silence. "Lieutenant, you better go with him." Durkin gave us a baleful look. I stood up. My legs turned to jelly, my mouth went dry—I gripped the back of the chair to steady myself. Last night, I'd suffered interminable pain at the hands of the Reds, but at that moment, if I had a choice between another bout of electrical shocks or being interrogated about what had happened to Kenny Newhurst, I would have taken the prod without hesitation. That sketch was like a ghost, appearing to haunt me. *You did this, you alone.* I could tell myself that what had happened to Kenny had happened because of my case, that once I'd realized the danger he was in, I'd acted without hesitating, that I'd *saved* him, but I knew, deep down, such a rationalization was utterly unconvincing, weak salve for a deformed conscience. If I was just doing my job, why had I lied to Georgette? Why hadn't I identified myself to her as well as to the police at the Harbor Station? Why so many lies? Were my instincts to protect my cover that engrained, or was it high time I asked myself if there were other reasons to keep lying?

"Detective, give us a moment, will you?" Paslett said.

For a moment, Durkin didn't speak. Then he nodded, picked up the sketch, and left.

Paslett said, "Tell them everything."

"Yessir. Including about the Russians?"

"Everything. What happened to the boy, it's been weighing on me all night. We're in a war, we all know that, and boys Kenny's age are still dying in the Pacific. But he's not in uniform, he still lives at home with his folks, he's a schoolkid. He was just in the wrong place at the wrong time. You and Donniker, you did what you had to do at the Automat, we had to know what Himmel and his spy were up to, but we should have looked ahead, we should have anticipated what the Russians would do once Himmel went missing. And we went looking for the boy too late."

We meant *me*. No one knew better than I did the danger my actions had posed to Kenny Newhurst.

"Yessir," I repeated numbly.

"The goddamn Reds can't just shoot a kid in our back yard and expect to get away with it! Burns me up just thinking about what they did. But it shows how desperate they are to find out what we've got cooking down in New Mexico."

"That's for sure, sir," I said lamely.

"There's another side to this, too, Voigt. We want the M.P.D. to chase down the two Russians who shot the boy, we want them to feel heat."

"But they've got to have diplomatic cover, sir, we can't even arrest them let alone—"

"I know, I know, but if Durkin is able to pick them up, then we'll let the press know what happened. That story'll splash across page one, the Soviet consulate will have to recall those two pronto. And that'll slow down their operation here in a big way."

A brilliant ploy, I had to admit, but my awe for the commander's genius also disgusted me. If I stayed in this game—if I survived this game—was this the future that awaited me, having the monomaniacal mind-set of a Commander Paslett, puppeteering everyone and everything in the name of the case? Or was my path even lonelier, more despicable? I didn't want Shovel-face and his partner expelled from the U.S., I wanted real revenge, I wanted to kill Shovel-face for what he had done to Kenny. And if I managed to get away with that, could I ever return to the straight and narrow, or would I stay rogue?

DURKIN'S UNMARKED PLYMOUTH WAS PARKED ON SEVENTEENTH STREET.

"How's the boy doing?" I asked.

He didn't answer, I didn't ask again. Neither of us spoke a word during the drive, his contempt as thick as the smoke from the cigarettes we smoked. The station house was cramped and cluttered, astir with that mix of idleness and excitement peculiar to police stations and emergency rooms. Citizens slumped in rickety chairs, a desk sergeant yelling into his telephone, two beat cops jawboning about a Golden Gloves card, a crying woman trailing behind a plainclothes pulling a disheveled, cuffed man in a dirty T-shirt. I followed Durkin to an interrogation room. Without speaking, Durkin motioned me to take the hot seat, slapped his notebook down. It was in a monogrammed leather case, worn and scuffed along the edges. He sat and took out a pencil and licked the tip, flipped the notebook open.

"How do you know Kenny Newhurst, Voigt?"

"From the Automat where he works," I answered.

"When were you first there, what were you doing?"

"Night of May Ninth, we were following a mark, we wanted to listen in, we had to set up the rig in the kitchen."

"We?"

"Filbert Donniker, civilian, our gadgets guy. Old fella, he sat close to our mark, had a hidden mike. I was in the kitchen listening on a headset."

"What time was this?"

"About seven."

"How long were you there?"

"Forty minutes, give or take. We hustled outta there when the mark left. Donniker went back to the Navy Building, I tried to follow the mark."

"Tried?"

"I lost him."

"Did you go back to the Automat?"

"No."

"You say anything to Kenny before you left?"

"Told him it was military business, secret stuff, and he shouldn't say anything to anybody about us being there."

"That's it?"

I nodded. "We had to get outta there, I had to get after the mark, there was no time to coach him. Kenny, I mean."

"Did you follow up with him?"

"Not until Saturday."

Durkin shot me a cold look. So much time had passed since that night at the Automat—why had I waited so long?

"Nothing was happening with the case, and the mark we'd been listening to just disappeared," I explained. "I guess I thought it was better not to visit the kid, we didn't want him to get excited, didn't want him to start talking about that night to his friends or other Automat workers."

"This mark—he's Russian?"

"Yes. Name's Himmel, he's the owner of the clipping service I went undercover at."

"And you didn't ever think your case put Kenny in harm's way."

"Not until this last weekend."

"What happened over the weekend?"

Here I had to be careful. *Tell them everything,* Paslett had ordered me. But I hadn't even told him about my interrogation by Shovel-face and his partner on the night before they shot Kenny.

"Himmel's been missing since that night, and the Reds are awful anxious to find him. Saturday, it occurred to me I oughta go see Kenny, ask if anybody had come to see him."

"It occurred to you," Durkin repeated acidly. "Two months go by, you do nothing, then it occurs to you. Something happened, what?"

Flash thought: *Durkin and Paslett aren't going to compare notes, Durkin's too good'a cop to snow, gotta give him something.* So, "Two Russians came to see me the night before, asking about Himmel."

"You visit regular with the Russians, do you?"

"That case I was working, it's still open. My job is to string the Reds along, just like I did at the clipping service. I don't have to tell you, you gotta keep—"

He cut me off. "So these Russians, whatever they say, it gets you worrying about Kenny."

"Right. I go to the Automat the next day, he hasn't shown up for his shift, so I go to see his folks next."

"This is when you tell Georgette Newhurst you're William Brady of Horn and Hardart. Why lie?"

"Instinct. Training. Stupid, I know, I didn't think about how it would—"

"What'd you do after you peddled your story to the mother?" Durkin was having none of my excuses. Who could blame him?

"I went looking for Kenny."

"Alone?"

I nodded.

"Why didn't you get your partner?"

"No time."

"Not even to call? Have him catch up with you?"

"All I was thinking about was finding Kenny."

"S'a big city, Voigt—where'd you know to look?"

"Figured if the Reds had picked him up, they'd probably take him to the same place I met them at."

He lit a cigarette before responding, snapping open a well-worn brass Zippo.

"The empty factory." A statement, not a question.

"Right. But when I got there, what I saw, what was happening . . ." I trailed off, unable to continue. I lit a cigarette, hoping that would help, but I almost choked on the first inhale. I set the Lucky on the ashtray with a trembling hand.

"What happened, Voigt?" Durkin's tone had hardened.

I told him. My voice was steady but sounded remote, different, as if I was listening to a stranger recite words I was thinking. *Got on the roof, saw what was happening . . . banged on the door, shouting I was a cop . . . Open up! Open up! . . . heard the shot, broke a window to get in . . . had to stop Kenny's bleeding* . . . The stranger tried to finish my statement, but the words were crushed in a convulsing sob, a total breakdown, a man who had never cried in front of another man now bending forward, head clasped in his hands, tears streaking his cheeks.

Durkin reached across the table, knocked my chin up with his knuckles, and backhanded me, hard. Out of his chair now, he grabbed me by the collar and yanked me across the table, eyes blazing. His cigarette fell to the table, smoldering, smoke drifting into our faces.

"You don't cry, understand? You don't have that right, you miserable sonofabitch. You're crying because you got the kid shot? What do you think his mother cries for, Voigt? Where do her sobs come from?"

The table edge pressed against my ribs, my breathing was constricted, but I didn't jerk free, didn't protest.

"Is he all right?" I finally managed to ask, looking straight into Durkin's pale gray eyes.

Again no answer. He shoved me away and picked up his cigarette, stubbed it, lit a new one, and flipped to a clean page in his notepad.

"What happened after you gave the boy first aid?"

I picked up my Lucky from the ashtray, drew deeply, composed myself, and recounted how I'd carried Kenny to the Harbor Patrol, how I'd shanghaied the portly workman, my good Samaritan, into helping me. Durkin wanted to know how I'd escaped, I told all.

"You pissed all over those Harbor boys, Voigt—they're itching to have a long moment alone with you."

Nothing to say to that, so I asked if they'd let the good Samaritan go without too much trouble.

Durkin shook his head. "Jesus, some nerve! After the pickle you put that poor joe in, d'hell d'you care what happened to him?"

Nothing I could say to that, either—claiming I'd had to protect my case was no defense.

"Back to the Russians, I wanna know everything about them, no holding back."

I dutifully described Shovel-face and his partner down to every detail, even mimicking their accents.

"No names?"

"Wouldn't matter even if we had some, they use so many aliases. What you're gonna need to do is, you're gonna need to start with the State Department, the Consular Service, you wanna get a hold of a'joe named Hendrick Thorsen—"

"What I need to do?" Durkin interjected.

"You wanna find these bastards, don't you?"

"And you don't?!"

"A'course. But I might—I gotta leave town."

"Might? Or gotta?"

"For the case," I said.

A reply so weak Durkin didn't even bother to swat; it shriveled and died on the table like a moth in a flame.

"Look Durkin, these Reds didn't shoot the boy for the hell of it. What we're trying to do here, what we're trying to prevent, it's awful goddamned big. There's a lotta lives at stake."

He snorted derisively. "There always is, for you cloak-and-dagger types. 'Lives at stake.' Funny how it's never any of you who lose their lives."

That wasn't true, but I wasn't going to argue with him. Jesus, I was exhausted, yet I felt like I'd never sleep again, doomed to permanent wakefulness, every moment of the rest of my life haunted by my sins, my misdeeds, my failure to be a decent human being. All my service so far, *the* case had always washed away the wrongs I'd done in its name—but not this time, not anymore.

"Look, Durkin, I want these two to dance from the end of a rope for what they did."

"D.C. doesn't hang in capital cases."

"You know what I mean."

"Do I? Maybe I'm just a flatfoot, a thick-headed city cop, but if you want these two Russians brought up on murder charges, why're you walking away?"

"I'm not walking away, I told you, after you get the files from—"

"That's bullshit!" Durkin exploded. "You're gonna look at some photos, then we're gonna pick these two Russians up, huh, that's all you gotta do? Another bum's rush, Voigt, just like last time."

He had me there. Durkin had been assigned to investigate the murder of Lt. Logan Skerrill, the case that had led us to Himmel and his nest of spies, but we had wrenched it away from M.P.D. and locked them out—until we needed their help.

"Commander Paslett told me he wants the Russians arrested, okay? That means O.N.I. is gonna give you whatever you need to find them. Just because I'm not with you doesn't mean you're on your own."

"Funny how I don't believe that."

I wasn't going to argue, I couldn't, weariness was overtaking me.

"Would you tell me how the boy's doing already?" I said, practically pleading.

Durkin stood, walked to the door, rapped twice.

"Why don't you ask his mother, Voigt?"

CHAPTER 21

AFTER AN AGONIZING MOMENT, THE DOOR OPENED. STARING AT ME WITH horrified recognition was Georgette Newhurst.

"That's him!" she shouted. "That's William Brady!"

Durkin shook his head slowly. "No, Missus Newhurst, this is Lieutenant j.g. Ellis Voigt of the Office of Naval Intelligence."

She was a wreck of the woman I'd met just days earlier, her pretty face now puffy, smudges of lost sleep beneath her eyes, hair unkempt. Durkin gestured for her to enter. A man next to her gently took her arm and guided her to the table. Kenny's father, Lyle. Late thirties, stocky build, receding brown hair cut close to leave a sharp widow's peak. An angular face: sharp nose, pointed chin, thin lips. Kenny had his father's eyes, round and expressive. Lyle glanced at Durkin, then me, his look hardening.

What had I done to this family? The fear that had transfixed me the night before surged back. When Shovel-face had loomed behind me, gripping the electrical prod, I'd told myself the impending pain was my penance, my punishment, for what I'd let happen to Kenny. Not even close, I now realized.

Durkin pulled two chairs from the wall to the table, lined them up next to his. He motioned for the Newhursts to sit, then took the chair on my right.

"I don't understand," Georgette said quietly, "he came to the house, he said he was from Horn and Hardart, he said his name was William Brady."

"Missus Newhurst, I lied to you," I said.

"What?"

"I had to follow a man. For a case I'm working on, for the Navy, for our—" I bit off the word *country*. "This man, he's a foreign national, and he went to the Automat for a meeting with another man. They're spies, both of them, and I needed to watch them from the kitchen. Kenny was there that night. I asked for his help."

"You dragged our son into a spy case." This from Lyle, every word pounded, like nails driven into wood.

My head swarmed with *Wait, no!* but I shut out the excuses. Instead: "Yes."

My reply shattered what remained of the Newhursts' composure. Georgette cried out and she gripped herself tightly, knuckles white on her clenched biceps, as if she was trying to compress herself, make herself disappear. Lyle jumped to his feet, his chair skittering away like a startled animal. He flung himself over the table, tipping my chair over, gripping my collar.

"Did you get my son shot?" he shouted. He pounded my head against the floor, but I didn't fight back, didn't try to push him off. Only the first blow hurt—the second, the third, felt remote and dull. My vision dimmed, my thoughts fogged. *Darkness, yes,* I thought numbly.

But I didn't black out. Durkin wrenched Lyle away. I thought I heard a chair picked up, thought I heard the muffled sobs of Georgette. Now the pain crashed in. My head felt swollen to twice its normal size, the sore spots from my electrocution blazed anew. Groaning, I struggled to my feet, gripping the table edge to keep from collapsing. My eyes watered, blurring Durkin, the Newhursts, the grimy room. My breathing was shallow, forced, rapid.

"I, I didn't think any of this would happen, please, believe me," I managed to say, voice hoarse and cracked.

"Tell them what happened," Durkin said coldly. "Just like you told me." He'd moved his chair to the other side of the table, next to the Newhursts.

"This case, what's happening is, we're trying to prevent the theft of a military secret. A really important one." Jesus H., I sounded like a two-bit character in a lousy radio serial. I clenched my eyes shut and rubbed my temples, trying in vain to ease the pain so I could concentrate.

"Who hurt my son?" Lyle demanded. He was seated but still breathing hard from the thrashing he'd given me.

"The Russians," Durkin said firmly. "Voigt's playing patty-cakes with the Russians."

Any other situation, I would have immediately denied what Durkin had just said and reported him for compromising an investigation. But this wasn't any other situation. *Tell them everything*, Paslett had ordered me. He meant the police, but I couldn't hide behind the skirts of investigatory secrecy anymore. Whatever happened, I had to come clean with the Newhursts.

The Newhursts looked confused. I could almost hear their thoughts. *Aren't the Russians our allies?*

"Detective Sergeant Durkin is right. The man I was following is Russian, he was meeting with one of his spies. I needed to hear what they were saying, we had equipment to do that, we had to set it up in the Automat kitchen. Kenny was there that night."

"Why didn't you get him out of there?" Georgette's voice was barely more than a whisper, but it lashed like a whip.

"Only my partner and I knew Kenny was there, the Russian and his spy never saw him."

"You said Kenny helped you," Lyle challenged me.

"I just meant he let us set up our equipment. He never left the kitchen—there was no way the men out front knew he was there."

"Kenny never told us any of this." Georgette again, softly.

"I—I asked him not to tell anyone we'd been there."

From Georgette, an anguished cry; from Lyle, a furious roar.

"Charge him!" he shouted at Durkin, pounding the table with both fists. "He's an accessory to attempted murder, he's negligent, what he did's the same as pulling the trigger!" He pointed at me. "If Kenny had told us what had happened, we would have made him quit, you understand? He listened to you, he *trusted* you, he kept your dirty secret, and look what happened! He almost got killed."

I didn't protest, didn't defend myself.

"We've drafted charges, Mister Newhurst," Durkin said ominously, looking my way. His way of telling me the M.P.D. and the U.S. attorney could come after me. For impersonating William Brady, for lying to the police, for fleeing the Harbor Patrol Station. The charges wouldn't stick—the Navy would kill them—but Durkin wanted leverage to force me to help him find the Russians.

Lyle appeared ready to lunge at me again, but a quiet question from his wife turned his head.

"Why didn't you protect him?"

"That's why I went to the Automat, Missus Newhurst, that's why I came to your house and said I was from Horn and Hardart, because I was trying to protect your son, I was trying to find him—"

"Before that," she cut in. "Before these, these Russians came looking for him."

Too late, too late. I'd realized the danger to her son much too late. I had no reply for her, I had no good reason, I had absolutely nothing to say. I could tell her and her husband about how I'd found their son, how I'd tried to stop the Russians, how I'd broken into the factory and carried him to safety. But none of my desperate, last-minute deeds could excuse my weeks of inaction, when I had all the time in the world to protect Kenny.

"I have no answer for you, Missus Newhurst. I failed to see the danger when it mattered the most. When I realized what the Russians were doing, I did everything I could to stop them. I went straight from your house to where I believed they'd taken your son, and—"

"Why did they kidnap him?" Lyle interrupted. "He's just a boy, what could he possibly know?"

"The Russian who met with the spy is now missing. The Reds need to find him in the worst way. They found Kenny because they wanted to know what happened at the Automat that night."

"They didn't have to hurt him," Georgette said, her voice trembling.

Her anguish shamed me into silence for a moment. Lyle glared with hatred at me, Durkin's face was set in stone.

"No," I said. "I didn't believe they would go to such extremes. But I should have known."

For a moment, no one spoke, my words hanging in the air. My head throbbed, I was thirsty, I wanted to crawl under the table and hide like a child.

"They tell us two men brought Kenny to the police station," Lyle broke the silence. "Were you one of them?"

"Yes."

"Who was the other man?"

"A passerby. I asked him to help me, he did."

"You don't know him, not even his name?"

I shook my head.

Durkin said, "We have his name, Mister Newhurst, I can tell you it after this."

Lyle nodded, his eyes still on me. "They tell us you ran away from the police after you brought Kenny in—why?"

"Because the man who came with me to the Automat was also in danger. I knew if the Russians had come after your son that he was next. I had to get to him before the Russians got there."

"Did you?" This from Georgette, quietly.

"Yes."

Lyle slapped the table in disgust. "You take care of your own, don't you, but the rest of us, people just living their lives—we don't matter to you at all, do we?"

"I have no excuse for what I failed to do, Mister Newhurst. None."

Another long silence. Then:

"How, how is Kenny doing?" I asked.

"Goddamn you, you got no right to ask that!" Lyle shouted.

"He'll be all right, he'll be all right," Georgette said softly, more to herself than to me.

"I'm sorry for what I've done," I said. "For what I didn't do."

Lyle lurched to his feet and stormed to the door, shooting me a look of unrestrained, feral anger as he yanked the door open and left. But his hatred didn't rattle me as much as the sight of Georgette as she stood slowly to follow her husband, her eyes on me. Abhorrence, despair, grief, disbelief—I saw all on her tear-streaked face. *How can such a man exist?* she appeared to be thinking.

DURKIN LEFT WITH THE NEWHURSTS, I LIT A LUCKY WITH SHAKY fingers and thought about what I'd say when he returned. No need— Agent Clayton Slater of the F.B.I. came in instead. I wasn't surprised. Durkin knew we'd tangled with the Bureau when I was undercover. When he had recognized me from the sketch, he must have asked Slater to come in.

"You're looking a lot less cocky than the last time I saw you, Lieutenant," Slater said, taking one of the chairs across from me.

Nothing to say to that.

"Your rough patch is only getting started, Voigt."

Four days ago, I would have thrown his comments right back in his smug face. But I had no fight left, not after facing the Newhursts. I deep-dragged my smoke.

"I don't think you and Commander Paslett know what you're getting into. What you're already neck-deep into, I should say."

"What do you want, Slater?"

"How's an accessory to kidnapping charge grab you, Voigt? I talked to the boy, know what he remembers after the Russians snatched him? They were working him over, asking him a lotta questions, hurting him, then there's a gunshot, the pain's unbearable, then all'a sudden he sees your face. Now, how are we gonna know you weren't there the whole time unless we have an investigation and a trial?"

His way of telling me the Bureau wasn't letting go of what Philip Greene kept saying: that I'd framed him for the murder of my fellow officer Logan Skerrill. Slater wanted me off the street, wanted me behind bars. Even if he couldn't keep me there, I'd be out of his way. But if the Bureau was going to charge me, Slater wouldn't have come to taunt me. Like the N.K.V.D., the Bureau picked up defendants quietly and expertly, dark-suited agents swarming the target and hustling him into a black sedan. My best play, keep mum, wait him out.

"Hoping the silent treatment keeps me chatty, huh, Voigt? Let me oblige: you talk to Rosario Moreno lately?"

I took one last drag on my Lucky, crushed the butt hard. Slater dropping that name was bad, bad news. In high school, in Chicago, I'd dated Moreno's daughter, not knowing for a time he was a union organizer and member of the Communist Party of the United States of America. If the Bureau had his name, that meant the Chicago field office was doing an honors history thesis on my young life, paging through yearbooks, talking to old classmates, scrutinizing the Bureau's card file on radicals. It also meant Hoover's boys had a magnifying glass on my eight years in the Navy. *Seek and ye shall find.* Bureau 101. If they didn't find what they were looking for, whatever they uncovered would do with a little touching up.

So I did what an innocent man would do: I stood and walked out. All I could do was hustle back to the Navy Building and find out what Groves had said. *If he says no, if he says no* . . . that thought turned and whirled, like metal on a lathe, waiting for me to shape it. But I couldn't concentrate, not with visions of the Newhursts' grief and Agent Slater's parting shot—*Enjoy your last breaths of fresh air, Voigt*—ringing in my head.

PART 2

Confessions

Los Alamos, New Mexico
July 13–16, 1945

12 July 1945

MEMORANDUM TO: Chief of Staff.

The plan to handle the alleged security problem at Site Y is now underway. The adding of O.N.I. is necessary due to fact one of its officers is able to identify suspect. Colonel Latham assures me this action will be conducted separately from the other steps being taken. Providing there are no unforeseen problems, the breach will be sealed prior to the Trinity test in four days. Dr. Oppenheimer assures me there will be no delays. He is fully confident of Trinity outcome and I have no reason to question his expectation.

L. R. Groves,
Major General, USA.

CHAPTER 22

THE DREAM JOLTED ME OUT OF UNEASY SLUMBER. A LITTLE BOY CRYING, "No, Mommy, no." She was nudging him, marching him across the concrete floor of an empty factory. "Be a good boy," she was pleading. I was watching helplessly from the corner, paralyzed, my arms and legs dead weight, my voice gone.

Awake—disoriented, blinking, wiping slobber from my chin. Didn't need Freud to interpret that one. Bright light, back aching, right arm numb from sleeping on it. The carriage rolled smoothly, movement barely noticeable. I looked out the window at flat, furrowed fields, the damp black earth shot through with tall rows of corn. Indiana, Illinois? I'd drifted off shortly after the Cincinnati stop. Across the aisle, a few seats up, a young mother was spooning medicine to her toddler. The boy was sick, had a cough, was fussy. "No, Mommy, no!" He squirmed, he kicked; but she got the spoon in, he swallowed—*ack, ack*—and started wailing. An elderly man leaned into the aisle to glare at the mother. When he saw me dog-eyeing him, he frowned but turned around.

I was aboard the B & O's National Limited, bound for St. Louis, where I would switch trains for Santa Fe. Commander Paslett had wanted to put me on an Army transport plane, but General Groves had said no, that kind of arrival would start chatter, draw attention. Better I come in like the junior officer I was, even if it cost us two days. I didn't mind, not a bit; I needed the time to think, brood, decide. Groves *had* said yes, had signed orders to post me to Los Alamos to find his spy, but trouble still followed me.

Trouble like Clayton Slater and the F.B.I. The Bureau hadn't been able to keep me from going to New Mexico, but it wasn't going to stop trying to get me pulled from the case. Working Chicago, digging into my past, field agents would snuff and paw relentlessly, interviewing old friends and teachers, my family. No matter how benign the stories told, the memories shared, Slater would find a pattern. I could anticipate the language. *As a teenager, Voigt already displayed a disposition to defy authority . . . there have been received numerous reports that Voigt associated with radical and foreign-born elements as a youth in Chicago, including known communist Rosario Moreno . . .* Add to this the Bureau's version of the last case I'd worked, and I'd come out looking awful hinky. Slater would make sure Groves's boys got his report before I even arrived in New Mexico, so I had to watch for Bureau land mines with every step I took.

More trouble: the O.S.S., which kept turning up like a bad penny. Paslett had told me more than once that the agency was trying to shoehorn into Groves's operation in New Mexico. What if the general also said yes to the O.S.S.? My operation was dicey enough without also trying to work with O.S.S. officers eager to prove themselves and keep the agency alive.

Finally, the N.K.V.D. I'd come within a cat's whisker of being killed the night they tortured me. If I messed up my assignment in New Mexico, the Russians would put a bullet in my head without pausing to ask what had gone wrong. My double-game with Mara wouldn't save me, Paslett couldn't protect me; I couldn't run, I couldn't hide. The Russians never forgave and they never forgot. Just ask Trotsky.

ALL THIS MESS, THIS TANGLED, STICKY WEB—KENNY NEWHURST, SHOT; Hoover's bloodhounds racing to tree me; the N.K.V.D. and Mara—was my making. *You made your bed, now lie in it:* So my mother had chided my brother Eddie and me when we got into trouble as kids. Never quite understood the adage—wasn't making your bed a good thing? *Time to pay the piper:* Pop's preferred saying, just as obscure. Much clearer, the plain phrase of my high school gymnasium teacher: *Own up, own up!* Who snaggled the jump ropes, who left the baseball bat at the plate? *Own up, boys, own up!*

Time for me to own up, to tell the truth, to be honest *with* myself.

And the truth was, I did kill the N.K.V.D.'s agent Henry Himmel.

I shot him at close range on the grounds of the Jefferson Memorial, which was closed for renovations, on the night of May 9, after confronting him outside the Automat and persuading him to go to a quiet place to talk. I borrowed a rowboat from a camper at East Potomac Park and used stones from the construction site to weight the body. Dumped him into the Potomac, returned the boat, and went home, as if I'd been out for a quick fishing trip. Only what I'd caught was a schematic, a plan, for the weapon being built in New Mexico. The man whom Himmel had met at the Automat was, in fact, a scientist who traveled to Washington from New Mexico. Along with the plan, he'd had Himmel memorize the following: *To diffuse the Uranium-235, use uranium hexafluoride and a metal filter with submicroscopic perforations. Do not use a mass spectrometer.* But these instructions, whatever they meant, were useless without the blueprint the scientist had also shared with Himmel. By killing Himmel and taking the plan, I'd prevented the Russians from getting the dope on our secret weapon. That plan, a schematic, was now folded into a tiny square and hidden in the works of a mantel clock I'd bought at a junk shop. I'd hocked the clock at a pawnbroker's on G Street. The stub, hidden in my flat, was now my most valuable possession, truly priceless, because there wasn't enough money in the world to pay for what that sheet of drawing paper could buy me.

Redemption. Absolution. Salvation. The unhocking of my conscience. Most of all, a future. Because I hadn't killed Himmel in the name of national security—I'd killed him to save myself. The Bureau's bloodhounds weren't barking up the wrong trail in Chicago. I'd known Rosario Moreno, I'd known he was a Red, I'd dated his daughter Delphine. More than dated—we'd been in love, the stupid, head-over-heels-to-hell-with-the-rest-of-the-world love that only the young are blessed with. Or cursed. I'd watched Delphine die on Memorial Day 1937, when the Chicago police fired on unarmed strikers in a field outside Republic Steel. Rosario had organized the march, Delphine and I had posted flyers all over town, we'd gone. A cop shot Delphine in the back, she died in the dirt, wide-eyed and bewildered, spitting blood, trying to speak, clutching my hand. The cop who murdered her was never identified; no one was called to justice for her or the ten men the police also killed. I was seventeen, I wanted revenge. Headstrong and hot-blooded, roiled with unspeakable grief and anger, I wanted so much more than to strike back at the cops—I wanted to destroy the men who pulled their strings. The men who owned Republic Steel, the men who owned and traded its stock, all the men who owned the corporations that enslaved the proletariat, all the men who started wars to make even more money . . .

No need to spout the commie manifesto, I knew it by heart, and it didn't matter a bit now if I'd ever believed in it. At my pleading, Rosario had put me in touch with the no-name Reds who ran the Party's secret apparatus. I passed their tests, they ordered me to enlist; I did, happily. By the time I realized nothing I did for the Party or the Soviet Union would ever change anything or even avenge Delphine's death, it was too late to drop out. The N.K.V.D. had me by the shorts.

Which is why Himmel ordered me to kill Logan Skerrill, the naval intelligence officer who had also been a Red spy. And I'd never known it! The Russians were that good, they raised and ran us as lone wolves, nurtured and trained apart from the pack. Skerrill had signed his death warrant by going to the Bureau for a turn as a double agent, and Himmel had selected me as his gunman because he wanted me to investigate the very murder I'd commit. Had to give it to Himmel—he was the best in the business I'd ever encountered. Brass balls, steel nerves. He'd arranged for me to shoot Skerrill on Navy property so that O.N.I. would take the case; and he knew, because of all I'd told him about Paslett, that the commander would order me to go undercover to infiltrate the news clipping service Himmel ran as a front for his espionage. Himmel knew I'd be desperate to frame someone for Skerrill's murder. Sure enough, I planted the gun I'd used at the flat of Philip Greene, Himmel's office manager and a loyal commie, so I could "find" it. By going to the Bureau, Skerrill had compromised Himmel's spy ring, so the Russian didn't care if one of his underlings took the fall. Meanwhile Himmel used me to feed false discoveries. I didn't know we were being played until I eavesdropped on Himmel at the Automat. That was his game all along: kill Skerrill, throw O.N.I. and the Bureau off the scent, and take delivery of the package from the scientist from New Mexico.

The fast-fading bell of a crossing signal brought me back to the here and now. As in, what was I going to do, here and now. *Arrive in New Mexico, identify the scientist spying for the Reds.* I'd told no one—not Paslett, not Shovel-face—that I'd gotten a long, good look at this scientist from the window in the Automat kitchen door on the night of May 9. Young, thin. Thick, arched brows that gave him an intense appearance. Dark eyes, black hair parted to the side. Delicate features: high cheekbones rising from a narrow chin, thin wrists, slender fingers. His appearance and his voice—surprisingly deep—were burned in my memory. All I had to do was see him once—bingo! Groves would lock him down, put him in total isolation for ceaseless interrogation. I'd return to Washington, get the schematic out of the pawnshop. Modify it, bitch it up. Change the measurements, alter the scale, erase a few lines, anything—then turn it over to Shovel-face, telling him I'd obtained it from the scientist before I told Groves who he was. Once the Russians had the schematic, they wouldn't care any longer what had happened to Himmel; but by sabotaging the blueprint, I'd keep the Reds from building their own weapon. At the same time, catching the scientist would give me bona fides, the kind that not even Special Agent Clayton Slater and the Bureau could wreck. Sure, they had Philip Greene in custody, he'd convinced them I'd pulled a frammi; but it was still my word against his. Not even J. Edgar could discredit a naval intelligence officer who'd nabbed a Red spy in a top-secret weapons program. And if I had to answer additional questions about my youthful associations with Rosario Moreno, I'd say, sure, I knew he was a Red, that's why I'd stopped seeing his daughter.

If everything went according to plan, I'd be fine. I'd have the Russians and the Bureau off my back. If everything went according to plan, I'd look like a hero. I wouldn't be a hero, of course, but being a fraud sure beat being a traitor. Or being dead. *If everything went according to plan.* What had Von Moltke, the Prussian general who drafted Germany's war plans in 1914, once said? *Planning is everything, but at the moment of execution, plans are worthless.* Anybody who doubted that advice needed to remind himself how that particular war had turned out for the Germans.

CHAPTER 23

THE TRAIN WAS RIGHT ON TIME, WE ARRIVED AT SANTA FE A TICK SHY of four the following afternoon. I'd spent a fitful night in my sleeper, the pint of rye I drank after dinner no help in chasing away the anxieties filling my skull. Spent the morning and afternoon gazing out the window at the craggy desert landscape, unable to concentrate on the book I'd brought along. *The Narrative of Arthur Gordon Pym of Nantucket*, by Edgar Allan Poe. What the hell had I been thinking, packing Poe? I knew the answer: Liv had recommended it, in one of the last conversations we had before she left town. Liv . . . Liv . . . full name Lavinia Burling but I'd only known her as Liv, ignorant of her family name, just as she had only known me as El. Not truly my "gal," we'd never "gone steady," but our infrequent dates in the spring had been a sorely needed refuge from the wreck I'd made of my life, my work.

So I finished the journey thinking about Liv. Remembering her, us together. How she absently played with a lock of black hair when she talked, how her bracelets slid up and down her slender forearms when she was gesturing. Her quirky greeting. *How will you be?* Never *How have you been?* or even a simple *Hiya*: always *How will you be?* Her winsome smile, her love of the moment, the way the past appeared not to exist for her. I never learned anything about her family; she never once told a story about being a girl or about her life before she turned up in Washington to work as a typist for a war agency. *Live free, and the rest will follow.* Her slogan, her mantra. We never set dates in advance, I never knew when I'd see her next. Might come home to find a cryptic note slipped under my door—if I deciphered it correctly (somehow I always did), I'd find her that night. Were we "steadies"? Did we have a future together? I learned not to care about those questions, learned to embrace living free.

As Liv was doing now. I tried to stay within my memories, tried not to wonder where she was—how could I know for certain? If she had chased her dream, she was in San Francisco, waiting out the war, primed to leave for the South Pacific as soon as the Japs called it quits. But maybe she'd changed her mind, maybe en route to California her fancy had taken another flight. Maybe she'd met someone else. Try as I did, I couldn't shake that thought. It wasn't jealousy but envy. A jealous man wants his lover all for himself, but the envious man wishes he could be like her. *Live free, and the rest would follow.* If only I could, if only I could.

THE SERGEANT SPOTTED ME RIGHT AWAY, BEFORE I'D FINISHED SCANNING the platform. "Lieutenant Voigt, sir, over here!" Waving like a kid, practically on his tiptoes. He was short, the top of his cap barely reaching my shoulder. Round face with indistinct features, a bit pudgy, Army greens rumpled. "I'm your driver, sir."

I snapped off a salute, he lowered his arm and reached for my kit. I gladly handed it over, rubbed my shoulder.

"Any other bags, sir?" Slight drawl, not quite Southern. Southern Illinois, maybe Missouri. Nametag read McALLISTER.

Shook my head. One duffel, that was it. Call it superstition, but I was hoping the less I brought, the shorter my stay.

"All right then, this way, sir."

I followed him across the busy platform and down a short set of stairs to a Chrysler jeep that looked new, the late afternoon sun glinting on the drab olive body. To keep my duffel from dragging, McAllister had to cinch up the strap, but he didn't let the burden slow him down. He hefted the bag into the jeep and hopped into the driver's seat. Pressed the ignition, slipped on dark glasses, looked over at me.

"Did you bring sunshades, sir?"

"Sure didn't."

"Here, take these, sir." He reached under the seat and came up with glasses identical to his. "The glare is something awful." He gestured vaguely at the horizon. Flat mountains dotted with short, dark green conifers, scattered expanses of reddish soil devoid of foliage. I slipped on the glasses and was immediately grateful for the tint—I hadn't realized how much I'd been squinting.

"Nice trip, sir?"

"Nice enough. Been a while since I spent that much time aboard a train."

"It can get boring, I bet."

"Been stationed here long, Sergeant? At Los Alamos?"

"Sorry sir, I can't tell you that."

"For real?"

"Yessir."

"Pretty tight security, huh?"

"Airtight, sir. General Groves's orders."

"So I can't even ask where you're from?"

He took his eyes off the road to grin at me. "You can ask, sir, you can even order me, but I won't answer."

"All right. How about this: How far to the base?"

"Nope, can't even tell you that, sir."

"But I can just get that from a road sign!"

"Not anymore, sir—they took down all the signs."

"Jesus H., what can you tell me?"

Another quick grin. "Just that before you get your billet and orders, sir, you'll go through inspection and get briefed on security."

He didn't say another word. I'd never been to the Southwest before and marveled at the scenery like a tourist without a care in the world. Flawless blue sky, rolling mountains with swathes of trees, craggy bluffs. I watched a hawk take flight from a conifer, wheeling away. I'd expected blazing heat, but the temperature was tolerable, no more than eighty degrees, I guessed. Not much traffic, just an occasional delivery truck and passenger sedan. After about fifty minutes, we arrived at a nondescript post outside a barbed wire fence. I'd been through my share of gate checks while in uniform—all were perfunctory, the guards bored, going through the motions. Not at the Los Alamos Project Main Gate. Two Army MPs approached the jeep, one to talk to McAllister, the other with his carbine at port arms, his eyes trained on us. If McAllister was a regular driver, then he'd probably presented his credentials any number of times to this corporal, but the soldier acted as if he'd never seen the sergeant before. Nor did he acknowledge the sergeant's rank. McAllister held out a laminated badge—I was startled to see it had a photograph. Nobody in D.C. carried an identification card with a photograph.

"Destination?" the corporal asked. He was tall, wide-jawed, broad-shouldered, trim-waisted. Born to be a right tackle, a doorman, or an MP. Maybe all three, eventually.

"H."

"Stops?"

"None."

"Him?" The corporal eyed me over.

"Intake."

"Okay." To me: "Step out and come to the post. Bring your kit."

I'd never been stopped by the police while driving, but I imagined this was just what a pull-over was like—if the cop thought you were Pretty Boy Floyd. I clambered out, shouldered my duffel, followed the corporal. Gravel crunched under the boots of his partner as he turned to watch me, his weapon still at arms. I followed Notre Dame's future star recruit into a small wood-framed structure. The interior was striking for all the things it lacked. Cheesecake calendar, base map, wall clock, clipboards dangling from nails, overflowing ashtrays, hot plate on a cluttered counter—the standard fixtures of sentry posts everywhere were nowhere to be found here. This sentry post was as barren as a surgery, and almost as clean, featuring only a broad wooden table in the center, no chairs, and a small wooden desk in the corner.

"Your orders," the corporal said.

I handed the sheaf over, he read them carefully, every page, the onion skin rustling in his hands.

"Okay." He returned the packet. "You armed?"

"No."

He studied me. Then his eyes drifted to my duffel.

"My sidearm's in there, sure," I said.

"Loaded?"

"A'course not."

"Okay. Empty your duffel on the table."

"Empty it?"

"Take everything out for inspection."

I wasn't a stickler for rank, but taking orders from a corporal was a new, and unpleasant, experience. But I did what I was told and didn't speak as he went through my clothes, shaving kit, shoes—every item in the duffel. He even riffled the pages of my book and shook it by the spine to see if anything came out. He removed my Colt M1911 from its holster and expertly checked the magazine. Reholstered the pistol and set it to the side, along with the unopened cardboard box of ammunition I'd packed.

"You'll get these back when you leave."

"That's an authorized weapon, Corporal."

"Not here it isn't, Lieutenant."

"All right."

"You can put your kit back together."

As I repacked, he filled out a custody form for my weapon and ammunition. I signed it, took my carbon; he chin-nodded toward the jeep.

At any other post, McAllister and the other MP would be jawboning, smoking, telling jokes. But the sergeant sat ramrod straight in the jeep, the MP was still at attention. I tossed my duffel into the back, got in; McAllister fired up the jeep. Only then did the MPs open the gate topped by barbed wire, and we entered the post.

"They enjoy that?" I asked.

"If they did, they'd be reassigned," McAllister said. "Them ignoring rank, sir—they've got orders to do that. From the top."

I nodded, getting it now. "Security matters more than anything else, so everyone gets treated the same."

"That's right, sir. You see them when they're not at the gate, they'll 'sir' you."

"Destination H" turned out to be the administration headquarters, an irregularly shaped wooden structure in the center of the base. At first glance, Los Alamos looked like any other army base. Unadorned rectangular wooden structures; winding interior roadways; dusty parked cars; sheds, garages, and outbuildings strewn about like autumn leaves. But two features were unique: massive brick chimneys, at least six, attached to several buildings; and watchtowers with armed guards. The prior year, the Washington papers had run stories about camps the Nazis had built in occupied Poland. According to an escaped prisoner, the Nazis were gassing Jews in those camps and burning their bodies in massive crematoria. I was pretty sure the Los Alamos chimneys had a very different purpose, but the similarity, however invalid, was still unsettling.

McAllister stopped the jeep in front of Building H's main entrance, left the engine running. "I'll take your kit to your billet, sir, while you get briefed."

"Where'm I bunking?"

"They'll show you when you're done, sir. Good luck."

"Thanks, Sergeant. Maybe I'll see you around."

"Maybe you will, Lieutenant."

Another sergeant was waiting for me. He made McAllister look like a real gabber. Just read my nameplate, saluted, and said, "This way, sir." The sounds of a bureaucracy at work carried from the offices lining the long corridor. Clattering typewriters, *thump-thump* of a mimeograph, indistinct telephone conversations. The sergeant opened a door with POST SECURITY stenciled on its opaque window and shut it behind me without entering. For the first time since disembarking from the train, I was alone. Two small windows, an unmarked door, an upholstered couch with matching chairs, a low-slung table with dog-eared magazines and an ashtray, a faded war bond poster, the one with the grim-faced Bataan prisoner: *Remember Me?*

Before I could sit down, the interior door opened. An army officer stuck his head out. "We're ready, Lieutenant Voigt."

Ready for what? I wondered. Involuntarily, I shuddered—the electric shock treatment the Russians had given me was still a fresh memory. But I dutifully entered a windowless, brightly lit room lined with metal file cabinets and wooden card catalogs like those found in libraries. In the center was a long table with chairs. The officer who had spoken to me was lanky, with a long, thin face. He wasn't wearing his cap, and his wispy, light brown hair was combed over a bald spot. Looked to be about thirty. The colonel already seated at the table was much older, at least sixty, with a creased, tanned face. His piercing blue eyes expertly appraised me. His crew cut was fully white. My guess, a sheriff or a cop whose service during the First World War had fetched him this commission. I saluted; he put me at ease and gestured at the chair directly across from me.

"Welcome to Site Y, Lieutenant Voigt. As in the twenty-fifth letter of the alphabet, not the adverb." He sure didn't sound like a sheriff or a cop—so much for my hunches.

"I'm Colonel Latham," he continued, "this is my adjutant Lieutenant Dahlen. I'm in charge of security for Site Y. As you already know, we do things differently here. The gate inspection, for instance."

"Yessir."

"The purpose of Site Y, what's being done here, I ask you to put that out of your head. I make this request knowing full well that it is all but an invitation for you to spend every spare moment letting your imagination run wild. You will want to conjecture, surmise; above all, guess, and guess some more. This is a human tendency, even a necessity. Are you familiar with the Buddhist faith, Lieutenant?"

"Nossir."

"The Buddhists believe that man is born to suffer. The cause of this suffering is craving. Our longing for material as well as intangible things, like love, can never be sated. Therefore we suffer. How do you think a Buddhist would advise we cease our suffering?"

"By not craving things, sir."

He offered me the smile of a pleased teacher, but it was fleeting. "Very good, you catch on fast. But now I'm afraid I must raise an unpleasant matter."

Nothing to say to that, so I waited.

"It is your contention, Lieutenant, that I have a security problem, a very serious one, a spy. I believe, however, you are incorrect, though Lieutenant Dahlen phrased my response much more bluntly, didn't you?" He glanced at Dahlen, who looked uncomfortable but still spoke up.

"Yessir, what I said was, 'This Voigt's full'a horseshit.'"

CHAPTER 24

OULDN'T BLAME DAHLEN AND LATHAM FOR BEING INCREDULOUS. They were in charge of security for Site Y, and to have a lieutenant j.g. from the Navy expose the lapse added insult to injury. Even worse, if Commander Paslett was correct, the O.S.S. had already told them they had a breach. Had someone from the O.S.S. already finagled a meeting with Latham to break the bad news? But I wasn't about to ask pesky questions or argue with Latham. To leave Site Y unscathed, my secrets and sins undetected, I needed their cooperation every step of the way. I responded diplomatically.

"It's an extraordinary charge, I know."

"Of course we've read the report your commander sent, but I'd like you to review the evidence for us yourself," Latham said.

"Yessir." I took out my cigarettes, drawing a pained look from the colonel.

"About those, Lieutenant—I'm allergic to tobacco."

"Sorry, sir." I slipped the Luckies back into my pocket. As concisely as possibly, I told them about my undercover assignment at the clipping service, told them how Himmel had fed me fake finds to throw O.N.I. off the scent. I described Himmel's Automat meeting with the spy from New Mexico, holding fast to the lie I'd told everyone—Paslett, the F.B.I., the Russians—so far: Himmel had received an envelope that night and slipped away before I could follow him. But I did repeat verbatim what I'd overheard the spy tell Himmel: *To diffuse the Uranium-235, use uranium hexafluoride and a metal filter with submicroscopic perforations. Do not use a mass spectrometer.* I'd said this gobbledygook so many times it had become an incantation in a language I didn't understand, like a prayer in Latin.

If the instruction about uranium meant anything to the two officers, they didn't let on. Dahlen scribbled notes, his head down, as Latham listened quietly, asking no questions, tilting back in his chair, eyes cast upward, fingers steepled and pressed lightly to his lips. After I finished, the colonel remained silent for a long moment, the scratch of his adjutant's pen the only sound in the room. Then:

"Why did you follow this Himmel to the Automat?"

An excellent question, one I had to answer carefully. "Himmel fired me that day, sir. It struck me he had hired me, as Ted Barston, just as suddenly as he let me go. Seemed too cut and dry, so I followed him from his residence to the Automat. I was beginning to suspect that he knew I was not who I claimed to be." *Understatement of the year,* I thought.

"You were able to arrange the surveillance astoundingly fast." A question, not a statement. The colonel still had his gaze on the ceiling.

"Our civilian technician is quite good, sir. I went straight from Himmel's hotel to the Navy Building to get him and his rig."

Now Latham straightened up, looked at me. "How were you able to go to the Navy Building if you were following Himmel to the Automat?"

"Sorry, sir. I didn't mention that I bribed the doorman at the hotel to find out where the taxi was taking Himmel—the doorman had overheard him give his destination." All true, but it sounded weak, sounded complicated, and I didn't want Latham scrutinizing every detail of my account.

He looked mild-mannered but he was good, he was sharp—perilous for me to risk his suspicion.

"Never leave anything out, Lieutenant—if a detail, fact, or observation is irrelevant, I'll make that call, you shouldn't."

"Understood, sir."

"Given your success in trailing Himmel to the Automat, why weren't you able to follow him after his meeting?"

Is he on to me? I wondered uncomfortably. Had Agent Slater contacted Latham, told him the Bureau was digging up the bones of my past, told him the Bureau thought I was bent? I eased that worry to the side and reminded myself that Latham was behaving normally, as any security chief would when confronted with a major lapse in his operation. He simply didn't want to believe he'd missed a spy.

"I lost too much time packing up my technician."

"Your technician couldn't do that himself?"

"I shoulda let him, sir. I made a big mistake not hustling outta there."

Latham looked sideways at Dahlen, his way of saying *Be sure to write down "big mistake."* "So Himmel escapes, with an envelope, contents unknown, as well as the statement his contact had him memorize."

"Yessir."

"And it's your contention that the man Himmel met came from Site Y, that he's a scientist of some sort. What's your proof?"

Your proof. Shading his words, casting a shadow of doubt. Subtle, but troubling.

"Himmel's contact said he came, quote, from the desert, unquote, sir."

"And you're just assuming that meant he came from Site Y." He said *assuming* as if the word was coated in acid.

"Can we afford to assume he didn't, Colonel?" I dared.

His bright blue eyes flashed, but he didn't rebuke me. Instead, tersely, "Describe him, the man from, quote, the desert, unquote."

"I never saw him, sir." A bald-faced lie, that, but I had to keep that man's image, now burned into my memory, completely to myself. Offer up a description, and Latham could easily find him without me. I needed that man brought before me, had to look him in the face and declare *He's the one* while Latham watched. If I wasn't the star, the spy-hunter who bagged his prey with witnesses, I wouldn't leave Site Y with the luster necessary to blot out the shadow cast by the F.B.I.'s suspicions of me.

"So how are we to find him, Lieutenant?"

"I know his voice, sir. If I hear him talk, even a little, I'll recognize him immediately."

"What you want then is a lineup, a listening session as it were, of all the men stationed at Site Y who were off the base on the date of the Automat meeting."

"Yessir, I believe that's the best approach."

He said nothing, just drummed his fingers on his desk. Deliberating, not liking it, but not saying no, not yet. Then he asked, "Why would the Soviets set up a front in D.C. for a contact they may or may not have here?"

"Safest transmission to Mother Russia, sir. Diplomatic pouch or a coded transmission."

"Why not someplace closer, like San Francisco?"

"Do they have operatives they can trust in Frisco, sir? Veterans who know their tradecraft, who don't make mistakes. Himmel is one of their best on the East Coast."

Latham glanced at Dahlen, who stopped writing.

"Let's review your scenario," the colonel said. "This spring, working undercover at a Washington clipping service, you discover a communist spy ring, but its owner, who uses the name Henry Himmel, knows exactly who you are. He then feeds you false information about the front's espionage in order to mislead O.N.I. and the F.B.I. This ruse frees Himmel to meet with an alleged Site Y employee, who traveled to Washington to deliver sensitive data, both orally and in writing. Because you didn't witness the meeting, never even saw the alleged Site Y employee, there's no way to confirm that something on paper actually exchanged hands. And to date, the only evidence to suspect a Site Y employee is because the man you overhead—but never saw—claimed to come from, quote, the desert, unquote. Is this an accurate summary, Lieutenant?"

I wondered if Latham was an attorney in civilian life. His summary was one hundred percent correct, yet every emphasis, every nuance, added doubt. I had no choice but to agree with him.

"Now, about this Himmel," he went on. "You believe he took flight because he believed the Russians planned to kill him after he turned over the received data. What's your evidence for this theory?"

"The N.K.V.D. has been eliminating veteran operatives since the early spring. These men have been in the States a long time—in Himmel's case, more than ten years—and the Russians get awful suspicious of anyone who spends too much time away from watchful eyes. Do you know what the Russians are doing to their P.O.W.'s, sir, the ones who managed to survive the war in German camps?"

He shook his head.

"Sentencing them to hard labor in Siberia. All because Stalin believes they became German spies in order to survive. What's happening to their operatives here, it's part of the same pattern."

"A pattern is not proof."

"Nosir, it's just a theory."

"As I see it, Lieutenant, the disappearance of this Himmel is peculiar and, as yet, insufficiently analyzed. But that's not my concern. What is my concern, my obligation, relates to the alleged presence of a Site Y employee in Washington in May."

"Of course, sir. No one would be happier than me to find out that Himmel didn't meet with someone from this base. Like you said, one quick reference to the desert doesn't prove we're dealing with a breach here. But if we're not, then the sooner we rule Site Y out of the equation, the faster we can figure out who Himmel's contact was. So maybe, as Lieutenant Dahlen suggested, I'm fulla horseshit"—I cracked a friendly smile—"but let's find out."

I wasn't wrong, of course; the plan I'd taken from Himmel after I killed him was a schematic of a new type of weapon, and all signs pointed to Site Y as the place where that weapon was being built. But I had to placate Latham, had to coax him into believing I wasn't a threat; above all, I had to act like an intelligence officer who was telling the whole truth, and nothing but the truth, every minute of every hour.

For a long moment, no reply. Then Latham said, "We'll let you know when we're ready for you." He nodded at his adjutant, who handed me a badge. Orange, my name printed in ink, no photograph. "Until then, your security clearance only gives you access to your quarters and the officers' mess and club."

"Understood, sir." I wanted to ask if he and Dahlen would begin compiling a list of all male Site Y employees who were off the base in early May but knew better than to press. The colonel dismissed me, and Dahlen led me to the anteroom.

A YOUNG W.A.C. WAS WAITING, A SLENDER GIRL WITH REDDISH-BROWN hair piled beneath her garrison cap. She took me to my billet, driving slowly. The roads were unpaved, and it must have not rained in some time, because the soil was rock-hard and bumpy. We passed young women in civilian clothes: denim pants, checked shirts, headscarves. Many trailed toddlers or cradled babies. What kind of base was this? But I knew better than to ask, remembering what both McAllister and Latham had told me about asking questions. I kept quiet, drawing hard on the Lucky I'd been desperate to smoke during the briefing.

Officers' quarters were in a two-story wooden building with a wide veranda. I signed the usual forms, accepted the carbons, collected my allowance of towels, bedding, soap. Listened patiently to the private from the Army's quartermaster as he told me about the mess and the club. Dinner was still being served, I was hungry, but I decided to stay in my room. If I went to the mess, the steward would seat me with other officers, we'd chat. I had to worry about Latham setting a trap, assigning an overly friendly fellow to try to get me to talk about why I was there. One wrong word, and Latham would pounce, would tell Groves I was no good, couldn't be trusted, should be sent packing. So, no dinner while I worked out my next move and figured out how to handle Latham. If he continued to stonewall me, I'd be boxed in, all but confined to quarters.

Didn't take me long to unpack. Spartan furnishings: single mattress on metal springs, three-drawer dresser, a wooden chair, nightstand, rickety clothes rack with three wire hangers. The room was about ten by twelve feet, with a sash window overlooking a cluster of prefabricated, two-story buildings with tarpaper roofs. They looked a lot like the tempos that clogged the National Mall in D.C. On the horizon, squat trees with twisted trunks dotted the mesa. Junipers? Pinions?

I changed into khakis and a T-shirt, hung up my uniform and clothes, made my bed. Drawing on another cigarette, I suffered a terrible coughing jag, my lungs constricting. Stubbed the smoke and sat down on the bed, gasping—*what the hell?* Then I remembered the sign at the Santa Fe station: *Altitude 7,199 feet.* Awful thin air this high up, I'd better go easy on the Luckies until I adjusted.

Stretching out on the bed, I laced my fingers behind my head and stared at the ceiling. I could understand Latham's hostility. All this security, so many precautions; and yet a leak. If General Groves wasn't worried about a breach, he wouldn't have signed off on my posting—that meant Latham had to give in. Once he did and he set up a lineup, I wouldn't have much difficulty singling out the man who'd come to Washington. I'd listen carefully but also make sure I got a look at every suspect so I could make a one hundred percent correct identification. Latham and Groves would toss him in solitary and sweat him but good. I'd have an easy trip back to D.C. I'd doctor up the schematic I'd taken from Himmel and hand it over to the Russians, claiming I'd managed to get it from their spy before he was locked up. Then I could figure out a way to do right by Lyle and Georgette Newhurst for what had happened to their son.

Suddenly my hopefulness vanished. I was building castles in the air, scheming and dreaming, mistily envisioning a future where every one of my problems, every misdeed, vanished like morning fog, and I got off scot-free. Who the hell did I think I was? Did I really think I could pull all this off?

CHAPTER 25

H OW HAD IT COME TO THIS, HOW HAD I JAMMED MYSELF UP SO BADLY?
I was no commie, no Red. That kind of commitment requires idealism,
faith, beliefs—no such principles had tempted me down Benedict
Arnold Boulevard. My motive had been revenge, born of blinding anger
and wrenching anguish. I could say that Delphine Moreno's father gulled
me, tricked me, back in Chicago, that he was a nefarious Red who'd captured a naive kid for his cult. But that wouldn't be true. At discussions at the
Moreno dinner table, he'd gently questioned the assertions I'd made with
the cocky certitude of youth. Me: *The owners built the business, why shouldn't
they keep all the profit?* Rosario: *But did they build the factory, do they assemble
the autos, Ellis?* Never correcting, never haranguing, always listening, always
asking. I didn't become a communist under Rosario's tutelage, I became a
better citizen, a well-informed one, capable of understanding how a crip-
pling depression could last eight years with no signs of quitting.

Besides, I wasn't in the Moreno home to see Rosario—I was there for
Delphine. Five feet tall, at seventeen she already had the striking figure of

a grown woman. Whip-smart, a voracious reader, confident and unafraid. Almond eyes, black hair, the dusky complexion of her maternal Sicilian family. But Delphine was indifferent to her beauty, proud only of the flowing hair she wore in a braid. Young girls were supposed to be quiet and deferential, opinionless, to say things like "What do you think?" and "My parents want me to . . ." Delphine brandished opinions like other girls wore bracelets and charms. She knew more about Shakespeare than our English teacher, she was a Dos Passos fiend. Her writings—stories, poems, observations, essays, aphorisms—filled notebooks. I'd watched her spurn advances from so many classmates that I was almost dumbfounded the day she struck up a conversation with me after English class. She asked if I agreed with our teacher's description of *Macbeth*—no, of course not, I said immediately, sensing that was the right answer for Delphine even if I had no idea what I was going to say about *Macbeth*. What I said, she must have liked, because she kept asking me questions, kept telling me what she thought; and from that day, we were inseparable.

Until the cops opened fire on the strikers in that field outside Republic Steel. We heard the gunfire, panicked strikers raced past us. I tugged Delphine's hand so we, too, could run, but she wanted to find Rosario. So we pressed against the stampede, and I was so intent on keeping us from being trampled that I didn't know what had happened until Delphine dropped to the dirt, gasping her last breaths with her eyes wide open, unable to speak as I cried and shouted, begging God to keep her alive. My first and final prayer, denied.

"A stray bullet," wrote one newspaper. "Warning shots gone awry," reported another. As if the execution of Delphine and so many men was an unfortunate accident, unavoidable, no one's fault. I knew who was to blame. The cops were just the hired guns, stooges for the bosses, Pinkertons on the public payroll. I wanted to hurt, really hurt, the men who sat in the boardrooms, who racked diamonds on their wives' hands while chiseling workers' wages and cheating on their taxes. Everything Rosario had been teaching me now made sense; the logic of Marx, Engels, and Lenin shone as brilliantly as the light that blinded Paul on the road to Damascus.

But I didn't want to learn more, didn't want to preach or proselytize. Instead, I would bore deep into "the system," my vague term for the economy and the government, and weaken both by helping the communists. I wouldn't be one of them, just a one-man Abraham Lincoln Brigade—ours would be an alliance forged from overlapping but distinct goals. For the communists, revolution; for me, revenge. What I imagined happening was never clear in my mind. I suppose I envisioned pickets of armed workers turning on the police and mowing down the bosses. I suppose I wished for chaos and cleansing fire, flames from sea to shining sea, a corrupt nation burned to the ground to be rebuilt like the Soviet Union. I don't think I ever thought much about what, exactly, would or should happen. I merely trusted that whatever I did would satisfy my bloodlust and palliate the pain of losing Delphine. Naiveté, grief, fury—I was ripe for exploitation by the Party. Hell, I was seventeen, and I unassailably believed I could bend the world to my will.

I begged the grieving Rosario to put me in touch with the unseen functionaries who recruited spies, organized cells, and couriered for the Party. He didn't want to do it, but I was persistent, and he was too consumed by his own guilt and grief to put me off more than a couple of times. I took tests, endured hours of interrogation, and when I'd proven myself, they told me to enlist in the Navy. When they told me to find a way to get an officer's commission, I did. When they told me to finagle an assignment to the O.N.I., I did. And when they told me to kill Logan Skerrill for going to the F.B.I., I did, and then manipulated the investigation to frame the communist Philip Greene for the murder I'd committed. Killing Henry Himmel was hastily planned, not quite spur of the moment but far from methodical. But eliminating him had cracked open my cell door, offered me an escape route from the clutches of the Party. And, if all went well, his death yielded the possibility of atoning for my treason. I'd long ago stopped believing that what I was doing for the Party, for the Soviets, would bring me solace for losing Delphine. Yet how to get out? The N.K.V.D. ruthlessly killed anyone even suspected of wavering—to break openly would sign my death warrant and do nothing to repair the damage I'd done to my nation. But if I could identify the Site Y spy, if I gave the Soviets an unusable schematic of the weapon being built here—then, and only then, would I be redeemed.

I fell asleep; a nightmare woke me up. I was locked in a prison cell, convicted of espionage, sentenced to death. They'd told me I'd be hanged at dawn, and a prison guard was pounding on the cell door, shouting for me to wake up, shouting they had a lot of hangings that day, they had to start and I was first on the list.

It was more than a nightmare, though—someone was actually pounding on my door in the morning. Six-fifty-five, to be precise. I rolled out of bed, blinking—the overhead light was still on. My mouth was parched, my empty stomach growled.

"Who's there?" I croaked.

The door swung open, an MP strode in, a corporal. "General Groves wants to see you, sir," he announced, saluting listlessly.

"Okay," putting him at ease. I shuffled toward the clothes rack, rubbing my eyes.

He didn't leave as I dressed, but I didn't protest—figuring out why General Groves had to see me immediately took all my attention.

THE MP LED ME TO A DUSTY JEEP AS I SMOKED MYSELF AWAKE. DESPITE the early hour, the base's roads bustled with jeeps and cars. He drove badly, braking hard and jerking the steering wheel as we passed other vehicles. Finally we lurched to a stop in front of a nondescript, two-story wooden building with small windows and a tarpaper roof. Army architecture: cheap, functional, bland.

I didn't say anything as I stepped out of the jeep, and the MP immediately drove off. Lieutenant Dahlen was waiting for me inside the door.

"What's with the rousting?" I asked.

He shrugged. "General Groves wanted to see you first thing this morning."

More to it than that. But I kept that thought to myself. Groves was waiting for us in a spacious, neat office. Rowed file cabinets, wall map of New Mexico, hulking safe, metal desk with just a Bakelite telephone, a manila folder, and a calendar. Colonel Latham was seated on the left side of the desk; the man behind it was Groves. Bristle of a mustache, beady eyes, wavy hair with a streak of gray brushed back from a broad forehead. His brown uniform, slightly rumpled, didn't sport any fruit salad—not a single medal or campaign strip, just the ribbon with stars on his epaulets.

Latham put Dahlen and me at ease, and we sat in two wooden chairs placed in front of the desk.

"I have to know if an envelope exchanged hands, Lieutenant," Groves greeted me, leaning over his desk. Not quite a glare, his fix on me, but awful close.

"Sir?"

"Wake up, Voigt! In Washington in May at the Automat, this Himmel you followed—how do you know the man he met passed him an envelope? You told the colonel"—here a tick of his head toward Latham, who nodded slowly—"you never saw any part of the meeting. So how do you know papers, a package, anything, got handed over?"

"I—I could hear the rustling on the table, sir, I could hear an envelope sliding over." I hid my cringe. Jesus H., this was the weakest part of my story. I had the envelope, I knew what was in it, but how could I convince anyone it existed if I wasn't supposed to have seen it?

They pounced like circling wolves, Dahlen, Latham, Groves: "It coulda been a newspaper."—"Your hearing's that keen?"—"Maybe he was wiping his hands with a napkin!"

Things were going bad fast, I had to recover.

"Donniker saw the envelope, General," looking straight at him.

"Who's Donniker?"

"Filbert Donniker, sir, O.N.I.'s gadget man, a civilian, I'd brought him along, I needed him, he set up the listening gear."

"Where was he?"

"Seated two tables away from Himmel and his contact. For the rig to work, Donniker had to have a microphone near them. It was made to look like a pen. He saw the envelope change hands."

"Why isn't that in the report, it's not, is it, I don't remember seeing it," Groves blustered as Latham shook his head vigorously, murmuring, "S'not in the report, nosir, not in the report."

"General, if I may?" I interjected.

He nodded grudgingly.

"I don't know what's being built down here, sir, and I don't wanna know, but I do know this, just like I wrote in my report: The man who came to the Automat flat-out said he was done, he was out, he wasn't going to meet with the Russians anymore. That's why he arranged the meeting, that's why he took the risk of coming all the way from Site Y to D.C. He had to convince the Russians he meant it, and he had to give them something big, something tremendous, otherwise they wouldn't accept him breaking free."

All this, true. The spy had told Himmel, "Now memorize this: this is my last delivery, my last contact," and I'd cited this verbatim in my report.

Latham protested, "We don't know for certain that a Site Y employee was the man Voigt heard—"

Groves waved his hand impatiently at Latham, who zipped it.

"Then who has that envelope?" Groves's tone was ominous—I had a lot of story left to sell.

"Henry Himmel, sir."

"Where is Himmel, where is that goddamned envelope?!" He slapped his desk, the metal rang, the telephone receiver twitched in its cradle.

"Three possibilities, sir. Number one, Himmel's hiding, dug in deep, where even the N.K.V.D. can't find him. Biding his time, waiting to cash in that envelope as his life insurance. Number two, someone killed him and took the envelope. Number three, he went back to the Russians, gave them the envelope, and they've done whatever they've wanted to do to him."

Groves exhaled loudly. "Goddammit, every possibility is bad news, the worst headache I've gotten since I opened this base—and believe me, Lieutenant, I've had some One-A migraines here."

I believed him. "Sir, can I tell you what I think is most likely?"

He flicked his wrist impatiently.

"I don't believe the Russians have him, sir. The way they came at me, it's no dodge, they're not trying to mislead us into thinking they don't have the envelope. I worked undercover for Himmel, I got to know him—he got real spooked at the end, just before the meeting at the Automat. He's been in the States since the thirties, he's awful clever, he's had plenty of time to work out his disappearing act. So he doesn't want the envelope to come to light, it really is his life insurance. Gotta figure he's stashed it with someone he trusts. That way, if the Russians catch him, he can leverage an exchange—the Russians let him go in exchange for the envelope."

Groves was nodding, I liked that, I needed him not to worry about Himmel, needed him to see the problem my way.

"But if we don't figure out who met Himmel in Washington, then the envelope isn't our biggest headache," I went on. "Because the spy here at Site Y can get another copy to the Russians if he can get off this base. Or even mail it."

"Not by mail, not a chance," Latham piped up. "We handle every piece of mail leaving and arriving."

"All right, not by mail," I said. "Which means as soon as we set up a lineup so I can identify the man who came to Washington, the Reds will be locked out. You can put the spy in solitary til he tells all. No need for another agency to be involved," I added, alluding to the O.S.S., "because we'll be able to handle everything here, quickly and quietly." Laying out my plan so baldly was risky, might sound suspicious, but this was my only chance to erase Groves's doubts and prevent him from relying on the O.S.S. to find his spy. And if I had Groves's ear, Latham might fall in line.

Or not.

"We still don't know that the man Voigt overheard in Washington came from Site Y," Latham said to Groves, who murmured, "I know, I know."

Neither man commented on my suggestion. Dahlen, who still hadn't said a word, scribbled away, recording the conversation in shorthand.

What was I missing, what wasn't I seeing? The man at the Automat had said he'd come from the desert—admittedly, that was vague, even trifling, but how many secret weapons programs in this war could be located in an American desert?

Dahlen stopped scribbling, Groves and Latham continued to brood. In the worrisome silence, my stomach tensed up as I perceived the reason why Latham still doubted Site Y had produced a spy.

Because Site Y wasn't the only base for this project.

Whatever weapon the military was building with Uranium-235 was so enormous, so complex, that even a base of this size and functions couldn't do all the work.

There were other sites, maybe two, maybe ten; I had no way of knowing. Maybe each one was designated by a letter of the alphabet, which would mean I was on the twenty-fifth such base.

And maybe all the sites were in American deserts for security reasons.

Jesus H., did I need a cigarette, but no one was smoking out of consideration for Latham's allergy. If the spy I'd seen and heard in Washington *hadn't* come from Site Y, if he was located at a base I didn't even know existed, I was in big, big—

"You'd better do the lineup to make sure," Groves broke the silence, addressing Latham. "After the other briefing."

"Yessir."

Groves checked his watch and stood, motioning us to stay put. "I've got a meeting off base, so Colonel Latham will take it from here, Voigt."

"Yessir."

With that the general left. I was so relieved Groves had approved the lineup that I didn't think much about the reference to "the other briefing."

But I should have.

CHAPTER 26

L
ATHAM REMAINED SEATED BEHIND GROVES'S DESK. HE NODDED AT
Dahlen, who finally spoke.

"We need you to report to our office in Santa Fe."

"Aren't we here already?" I asked, confused.

"No, this office is in the city itself. All civilian personnel go there first for briefings before coming up to Site Y. Dorothy McKibbin is in charge, she's been here since Day One. We want you to tell her about the voice of the man you overheard in Washington. This'll help with the lineup."

"All right. How do I get there?"

"You'll take a jeep from the motor pool," Latham answered. "Dahlen will walk you over there after you get a security badge. You'll report back here at fourteen-hundred—we'll be ready to do the lineup by then."

Dahlen stood, and I followed him out of the building. Still cool, but the sun had risen. Clods of dirt crunched and broke under our shoes. To the west was the compound of buildings I had glimpsed while the corporal was bringing me to Groves. A tall barbed wire fence surrounded these structures. A protected base within a protected base—was this the brains of the operation? Dahlen gave no sign that he was interested in chatting, so I lit a cigarette and tried to make sense of the just-ended briefing. A lot had happened, much of it troubling. General Groves had approved the lineup to identify the Automat spy, but . . .

What if the spy was working at a different secret base? I'd assumed Site Y, here in the remote New Mexico desert, was the only location for the weapons project, but now I wasn't sure. He has to be here, I told myself—otherwise, why had the Russians released me the night they tortured and interrogated me? Because they knew their man was in New Mexico, and they believed I was going to help them get their missing data. But . . .

The Russians didn't trust me, and neither did Groves and Latham. Sending me solo into Santa Fe was a ruse. If Dorothy McKibbin could be helpful, Latham would send for her so she could be present at the lineup. He didn't need her help to draw up a list of the civilians who were off the base in early May—as the head of security, he already had those records. He and Groves were sending me into Santa Fe to see if I would meet with anyone. They were having me watched and followed, every move, every minute, while I was in Santa Fe. Paslett's endorsement hadn't sufficed; Groves and Latham wanted to see for themselves if I was squeaky-clean.

I hid my dismay with another cigarette as Dahlen and I continued our silent hike to another nondescript wooden building, where a private from the Signal Corps took my photograph for my security badge. He snapped two pictures and we waited while he finished the badge. At the motor pool, Dahlen gave my orders to a sergeant and handed me an inexpertly drawn map with a circle around an address, 109 East Palace. He told me I'd find Dorothy McKibbin there and reminded me to return by 1400.

The drive to Santa Fe forced me to think about subjects other than my predicament. Such as when the jeep's brakes had last been checked. Or if it was possible to leap out of the driver's seat if a wheel went over the side of the guardrail-less, narrow, rutted cow trail mistakenly called a road on my map. At first the descent wasn't too steep, but in second gear the engine started to whine, hard; I killed it trying to find third. Had to ride the brake to keep from rolling while I fired the ignition and started over.

A gentle curve, the unpaved dirt road lined by junipers, soon turned mean, then downright wicked. On my right was a craggy embankment tufted with scraggly weeds; on my left, a breathtaking vista of a steep hill, dropping to a ridge, dropping to a cliff, dropping to a thicket at least one hundred feet below. Not that I could afford more than a panicked, second-long glance, but that look was more than enough to take my breath away. I managed to find third gear, the jeep picked up speed, I started pumping the brake. Wrestled the stick back into second, told the protesting engine to shut up, and just managed to come to a stop for the hardest left turn I'd ever made, a switchback so sharp I was certain it defied the laws of geometry. The steering wheel fought my frantic pulls, the engine conked out yet again.

Finally, I got smart and shifted into neutral without touching the ignition. Growing up in Chicago, its terrain as flat as a table, my experience with inclines was limited to sledding on a hill at the lakefront. I'd sled this jeep to Santa Fe or die trying. CAUTION: TURN AHEAD! a wooden sign exclaimed as the jeep picked up speed on a straightaway. Spinning the steering wheel, I realized that the "ridge" I'd seen from above was actually the road, which meant I was now on the edge of the cliff. Drops of sweat blurred my vision, my legs and arms ached, I desperately wanted a cigarette; but I didn't dare take my white knuckles off the wheel.

I reached Santa Fe as wet as a fever victim. Rattled, I walked by 109 East Palace twice before I noticed it. Were Latham's men already watching me? Did the Russians know about this place? I pushed these questions aside, trying to gather my wits before I went in. The entrance was an iron gate opening into a shaded courtyard with a brick path. No sign, just the address numbers above the doorway. The building looked like a residence, a tourist's colorwash postcard of a historic New Mexico home. Thick adobe walls, sienna roof tiles, small square windows, French doors. The courtyard featured pale lavender flowers in clay pots and rows of gray-blue grass. I knocked hard on a heavy plank door. The clatter of typewriters and cigarette smoke drifted through an open window.

"S'open," a male voice shouted.

The door creaked on its hinges and I entered a low-ceilinged, raftered room packed with mismatched wooden desks arranged into T shapes to make the most of limited space. A stout man, his black hair mussed, didn't look up from his Underwood, his fingers dancing over the keyboard, ash dangling perilously from a jutting cigarette.

"Straight ahead, friend," he said through immobile lips.

I thanked him and picked my way through the crowded room. A brightly colored tapestry hung from a knurled rod set between the windows. The wooden sills and panes were painted canary yellow. In the corner, a fireplace with glazed tiles was piled high with boxes of office supplies: stationery, typewriter ribbons, envelopes. I ducked beneath a wooden beam to enter a small room with just one desk, behind which sat a middle-aged woman with frizzy brown hair cut short. She wore a collarless blouse and a wooden bead necklace. She had a pleasant, soft face—people probably told her she reminded them of their favorite grammar school teacher.

Looking up from a sheaf of typed papers, she asked, "Are you Lieutenant Voigt?"

"Yes ma'am."

"Have a seat." She took in my still-shiny brow and the sweat-darkened patches on my uniform. "Drove yourself down, did you?"

"Wouldn't call it driving, ma'am, but I'm here." I eased into the wooden chair in front of her desk.

"Call me Dorothy, and tell me about the man you saw in Washington."

I had to answer carefully. At the Automat, Himmel had questioned the authenticity of the information he was receiving. *What, a Ph.D. in physics from Yale at twenty-two isn't sufficient bond?* the man had challenged Himmel. I'd told no one this detail. If I had, there was no reason to send me to Santa Fe—Groves and Latham could easily identify the spy without me. And, of course, I couldn't admit I'd seen him and knew what he looked like. So I only described the sound of his voice.

She scribbled notes. Then, rapid-fire questions.

"Did he speak with an accent, foreign or regional?"

"No."

"Did he sound educated?"

"Yes."

"Did he say where he came from?"

"He mentioned the 'desert,' nothing more."

"Did he say how long he'd been traveling?"

"No."

"Did he mention any names?"

"No."

"Did he use any technical vocabulary?"

I hesitated—Latham hadn't told me how much I could share, or not share, with McKibbin.

"S'all right, Lieutenant, this briefing has Colonel Latham's full approval." She smiled tersely and waited.

Was Latham setting me up? Did he want me to tell her about the Uranium-235 just so he could tell Groves I was blabbing classified information? But if I didn't answer, I'd look like I was hiding something.

"Yes, he did," I responded. "Just before he handed over an envelope, he said, 'To diffuse the Uranium-235, use uranium hexafluoride and a metal filter with submicroscopic perforations. Do not use a mass spectrometer.'"

If that meant anything to McKibbin, she didn't let on, just wrote it down, in shorthand.

"Anything else you can tell me, Lieutenant?"

"Yes: This man is self-assured and confident, so much so that it wouldn't surprise me if those who work with him find him cocky, even arrogant."

She noted that, too. Then looked up and asked, "When are you supposed to report back to Site Y?"

"Fourteen-hundred."

She looked surprised. "It's not even eleven. You've got some unexpected leave, don't you, Lieutenant?"

I pretended to happily agree and asked where I might get something to eat. She recommended Joe King's Blue Ribbon Bar, just a few blocks away. I thanked her and walked out, well aware that Latham's men were following me, marking my every move. No way to pick out my shadow. Was he the elderly man sitting on a wooden chair under the awning of a grocery store, newspaper folded to the crossword, or was she the young woman carrying a shopping bag across the street? An innocent man wouldn't look over his shoulder or scrutinize passersby, so I kept my gaze forward and my gait leisurely. Santa Fe seemed like a pleasant town, its streets lined with one- and two-story stucco and brick buildings, but I was too anxious to enjoy the view.

Despite the early hour, the Blue Ribbon had customers. Several workmen in dusty overalls leaned against the bar, beer glasses and sandwiches in front of them. At a table, three young women dressed like stenos were chatting. The barmaid was listening to one of the workmen tell a joke as she rolled a cigarette. She looked to be on the right side of forty, slender, her hair tucked beneath a colorful bandana. She wore a baggy chamois shirt and dungarees as well as that fixed look of patience all good barkeeps put on for the joke they've heard a thousand times before.

I sat on a stool at the end of the bar and took in the place. My uniform caught nothing more than a quick glance; no doubt the regulars were used to seeing servicemen since Site Y opened. Standard-issue watering hole: high-backed booths, wooden tables and chairs, jukebox and a telephone booth, tin beer signs, hand-lettered placards touting daily drink specials and the sandwiches. The back bar featured rows of whiskey and tequila bottles and taped-up postcards. I lit up, inhaled with relief. The barmaid came over, her hand-rolled already half smoked.

"What'll you have, hon?"

"A ham and cheese sandwich and a root beer."

She nodded, walked over to a reach-in cooler, and took out a wax-paper-wrapped sandwich and a bottle.

"Wanna egg, they're right there," ticking her head at a large jar to my right.

"Thanks," I said, dropping a dollar bill. I unwrapped the sandwich and took a big bite.

The cash register *da-dinged*, she brought my change. The workmen were entertaining each other; the young women were still talking happily; and the bartender didn't say anything more to me. No one was looking at me, and I was sure no one would strike up a conversation or buy me a drink, as often happened to a man in uniform rubbing elbows with civilians in a tavern. The locals might spend endless hours guessing at what went on up in the mountains, but by now they knew better than to ask questions of newcomers. But were any of the patrons plants, there to watch me for Latham? Dorothy McKibbin had to know I was being watched, so she likely had called Latham as soon as I left 109 East Palace to tell him I was going to the Blue Ribbon. The three young women, the workmen—they all looked as if they'd been in the Blue Ribbon for a while, but I couldn't be certain. A good shadow always fits in, looks natural, never draws attention.

Rules that don't apply to someone trying to find you. A woman wearing sunglasses and a wide-brimmed sun hat slid onto the stool next to me.

"Mind if I join you?" Mara asked, smiling.

CHAPTER 27

*J*ESUS H. CHRIST! WHAT WAS MARA DOING HERE—HOW IN THE HELL did she know I had come to New Mexico? My mind raced as I tried to keep my composure. The N.K.V.D. must have sent her to keep an eye on me. Shovel-face had gulled me into thinking they were dumping Mara after she failed to dope me. I'd come up with a half-cocked scheme to keep Mara on a string, not realizing the Russians had another mission for her. But what? Flash: Mara as honey bee. She'd told Shovel-face we'd slept together again, or he'd guessed it. *Does he love you?* he'd challenged her. *A'course*, selling it. The Russians had peculiar views of love and sex in the States; they believed we Americans were hopeless romantics, gripped by passions straight out of Pushkin, flinging ourselves into torrid, doomed affairs. Figure Shovel-face wanted Mara to vamp me but good here in New Mexico, get me in the sack, dope me right this time, and I'd come to lashed to a chair for another live wire dance to verify I was being a good boy, doing their bidding and only theirs. Even if I could dodge that, how was I going to explain to Latham who Mara was? I had no choice now but to acknowledge her—giving her the cold shoulder would look awful suspicious. Could I manipulate our encounter in some way to shield myself? It was my only angle, and I had to hope—pray—Mara was sharp enough to follow my lead.

"Why sure," I answered her question about joining me at the bar. "I'm Ellis," I added, quietly and quickly. *We're strangers, we never met, please please please play along—*

"I'm Elizabeth," Mara promptly replied. The Southern accent was gone, replaced with a barely noticeable mid-Atlantic inflection.

The barmaid came over, gave Mara a swift eyesweep. Was she Latham's plant, or was she simply sizing up a new customer?

"Something to drink, hon?" she asked.

"I'll have a root beer too."

"Care for a sandwich?"

"No, thank you."

"Are you, uh, are you local?" I asked.

"Oh no, I've just come here to Santa Fe for a few days before I return home."

"Vacationing, then."

"Well, I suppose you could call my visit here a vacation, but I've been helping my sister—that's why I'm here in Santa Fe."

"Oh?"

"Elizabeth" proceeded to tell me all about her older sister. She had tuberculosis, needed a sanitarium, needed dry, hot air. So, Santa Fe. A good but obvious cover—I sure hoped the Russians had set it up for real. There had better be a "sister" in that sanitarium, and her story—every detail, every fact—had to match Mara's. The Russians wouldn't send Mara here blind, they had to know Santa Fe was crawling with Army intelligence, their eyes peeled for outsiders who called themselves tourists but who asked questions about that place up in the mountains. Could Mara brace her front after Latham's boys hauled her in?

"Where is home?" I asked.

"Ohio. Zanesville."

"When do you head home?"

She shrugged. "I'm in no hurry. Everyone in Santa Fe told me it's just so pretty over here, and they're right. Don't you think so?"

"Pretty as a picture." Which also described Mara. She wore a calico cotton dress, the hem hitched just above her knees, a sheen on her bare thigh. No careless gesture, that; the etiquette matron at the finishing school would have drilled her charges on the necessity of always keeping a skirt pulled over a young lady's knees. Muted, rose-colored lipstick and turquoise-tinted eyeliner accented Mara's patrician beauty, the smooth planes of her cheekbones, her inquisitive blue eyes and thick lashes. She noticed me looking at the engraved silver band glinting on her left wrist.

"I picked this up from a delightful little Indian woman here, she says her husband makes them." She held out her hand, I took it, my thumb lightly touching her palm as I gently turned her wrist to admire the piece.

"S'lovely," I said, slowly releasing her hand, lingering as she almost imperceptibly squeezed my thumb.

"Thank you." She dropped her hand to her knee. "I may be a visitor, but I already know not to ask what you're doing here." Was that a twitch of a smile on her lips? The woman had nerve, had to give her that.

"Like they say, you can ask, just don't expect an answer."

"But can I ask where you're from?"

"A'course." So I repeated the biography I'd shared with her the night we met. Chicago, Navy, war, Washington. Jesus, did those four words frame the canvas of my life? But the drab picture brush-stroked over my secrets. *Spy. Traitor. Communist sympathizer. Soviet agent.* Mara's hidden portrait, too. How much of the truth about me did she know? She knew I was O.N.I., for real; she knew I was clandestinely working for the N.K.V.D. But did she believe I was feigning my allegiance to the Russians as part of my undercover work for Navy intelligence, or did she believe I was feigning my allegiance to America because I was a Soviet plant? Shovel-face wouldn't have given her much, just her instructions. *Is he following orders, is he getting what we want?* The Russians wouldn't tell her I was supposed to be collecting plans for the weapon being built at the secret base, but Mara was a bright penny, she must have guessed that. What could I tell her that would convince the Reds I was being a good boy without saying anything incriminating my shadows might overhear? How the hell was I going to explain this encounter to Latham? I could try to convince him she was part of my operation in Washington, that I was running a double game on her. Problem was, he'd immediately verify that with Paslett, and I'd never told the commander about Mara. Latham wouldn't just cancel the lineup, he'd arrest me. There was only one way out, I decided.

"Must be lonely, traveling by yourself," I said. Translation: *Are there any Russians here in Santa Fe?*

"It can be, but I'm meeting interesting people. And before I go home, I'm going to see my sister once more." *I'm here alone, to see you—I'll report to them after I leave Santa Fe.*

So I only had to deal with Mara at the moment—and Latham's shadows.

"What are your plans for the afternoon?" I asked.

"Thought I'd look for some souvenirs to take home."

"Would you be so kind as to let me tag along? There's a special lady I'd like to buy a bracelet like yours for." I reached and gently turned the silver bracelet around her wrist, letting my forefinger trace across her veins.

"Your gal?" Eyebrows arched, hint of a smile.

"My mother. For the moment, I'm single."

She laughed. "Such a thoughtful boy. It would be my pleasure if you joined me, Ellis."

"Wonderful."

I left the change on the bar to cover Mara's root beer and a tip. The barmaid gave us a knowing look as we said so long. She knew a pickup when she saw one—was she buying this one? Or had it looked forced, would she be calling Latham the moment Mara and I left the bar? Take it easy, I told myself. I had no reason to suspect the barmaid. I knew I had shadows, but the less I worried about them, the more natural I'd look.

We strolled, we chatted. Mara donned a white hat with a wide, curving brim that shaded her face. I tilted my officer's cap against the sun's glare. Hot, but bearable—a sticky July day in Chicago was worse. A cloudless sky so blue, so beautiful, no photographer or painter could capture it. Santa Fe didn't look like a Western town, but what did I know? Movies and comic books had filled my head with clichés. No cowboys here, no cows, no brawl spilling out of a saloon's swinging doors. Instead, two-story adobe buildings with recessed verandas. Shops, mostly. Hardware, groceries, clothing, hats. Under the shade of awnings and porches, men sitting on benches, chatting, pausing to watch us stroll by. Passersby, too, women with children, an elderly couple walking slowly, elbows linked. Some said hello, we hello'd back. With the sun almost directly overhead, Mara and I barely cast a silhouette. *Where are my shadows?* I couldn't stop wondering. Every hat-brimmed face was suspect, even though we were likely being watched from behind. I stole close looks at everyone we passed, to see if their gaze wandered over our shoulders to someone else, but Latham's tails knew to stay well behind us. The city was small enough, I realized, that we could also be watched from the window of the hotel on the block.

I distracted myself by telling Mara about my mother, who worked at a jeweler's in Chicago. How she'd started making her own jewelry, bracelets and earrings. Mara listened attentively, kept me talking by asking questions. Stringing me along, keeping me chatty, no doubt hoping for a slip, an admission, something she could tell the Russians after she returned from Santa Fe. But for once, the truth couldn't hurt me—my folks and brother Eddie knew nothing about my treason, my spying. They were proud of Lieutenant (j.g.) Ellis Voigt, U.S.N., as their letters made clear, telling me how everyone in the neighborhood was always asking how I was doing. Of all the terrible, and deserved, troubles that would fall like bricks on me if I was exposed as a spy, the crushing of my family's love and respect for me was the most dreaded. Maybe that's why I was fighting so hard to free myself from the Russians' grip without confessing—to protect my family. Or maybe that was yet another lie I told myself to justify what I was doing. At the moment, no matter; the mission was the mission, and to succeed I couldn't make a single mistake in how I handled Mara.

She found the shop, we cooed over the wares as the Indian woman nodded wordlessly.

"I'm sure your mother will love it," Mara said of the bracelet I picked out.

She would. The piece featured a silver filigree so delicate it looked like spun thread. "S'lovely, for sure," I said.

"Are you in any particular hurry?" Mara asked after we left the shop.

I made a show of checking my watch. "Got some time yet."

She smiled. "Then you've got time to walk me back to my hotel, yes?"

Yes. I saw her to her room, I accepted her offer to come in. She didn't ask me to sit. Instead, she walked over, her eyes locked on mine, and gracefully pivoted, turning her back to me and taking my hands to place them on the hem of her dress, on her thighs damp with sweat from our walk in the sun.

"Help me out of this?"

Yes, yes. I gently pulled the dress, my fingers tracing the line of her panties and her stomach. She shivered, pressed against my groin; I pressed back. Then whispered in her ear.

"Assume the room's bugged, everything's gotta sound natural."

"Mmmmhmmm," lustily, bringing my hands up to her breasts. Neither of us spoke as we undressed each other, still standing, embracing after every stitch of clothing and our shoes lay haphazardly on the floor. Mara's kiss was long and deep, sticky-sweet with the root beer she'd drunk—that kiss, more than the slow traverse of her right hand round my hip, my thigh, inching closer to my desire—made my legs shaky.

She led me to the bed, parted her legs. Joined together, I leaned to press my lips to her ear, feeling her nipples high on my chest.

"Every word covered," I murmured, and she offered a slow, audible exhale of pleasure. I responded in kind, we eased into our rhythm. The spread fell to the floor, a bed board *tick-ticked*. So easy to go on, to stop whispering, to let every utterance, gasp, moan come naturally. *Focus, focus!* I ordered myself.

"They're arranging a lineup," I said, my mouth locked on her ear. Our lovemaking continued. A minute, or two, or more, passed.

Suddenly Mara raised her head, nipped my earlobe, tugged me to her lips. "When?"

After a moment, "Soon."

"Not too soon!" Translation: *You've got to get the schematic before you identify him, you've got to make contact before the lineup.*

"No, no, not yet!" *Understood, I'll have the schematic before he's locked up tight.*

"So good, so good . . ." *This'll make the Russians happy.*

"Yes, yes, yes . . ."

Mara clenched me, her nails pressed into my biceps, and her urgent cry brought forth our climaxes.

We separated. I rolled onto my back. Stared at the stucco ceiling, not speaking, listening to our breathing, our exhales slowing. Finally, I said the words I'd carefully put together in my head:

"A fine way to spend the afternoon, Elizabeth."

"Yes, very much so," Mara said.

"I hope you won't consider me rude, but I've got—"

"To get going, I know."

I got out of the bed, lit a cigarette, passed it to Mara. Lit another for myself, started dressing.

"I'm glad neither of us are saying it," Mara said after a deep drag on the Lucky.

"That I'll call?"

A wicked smile. "Or we should do it again soon?"

"Exactly."

"Why spoil a fine moment with clichés?" I forced a grin, playing along, but my gaze gave away my anxiety. *Don't overdo it.*

She sensed the tension and nodded, just once. Neither of us spoke again until I'd finished dressing and lacing up my shoes, the bed creaking as I sat and then rose. Mara shifted to lean on the pillows against the headboard. Didn't pull the sheet over her, her shapely legs crossed insouciantly at the ankles, the light overhead catching the sheen on her skin.

"Will you do me a favor, Ellis?"

"A'course."

"Tell the bellboy to bring up ice and lemonade."

"Sure. Anything else?"

"Leave me your cigarettes, please? I'm fresh out."

I started to hand her the packet, but she shook her head. Pointing to the pad of hotel stationery on the desk, she made a scribbling motion.

For a split second, confusion, then I caught her drift. She needed to bring proof to the Russians that she'd seen me. I wrote *Kilroy was here* on the pad, tore off the sheet, folded it into a square, and tucked it into the packet. The Russians had plenty of samples of my handwriting, and using the hotel stationery proved I'd been here.

Mara nodded approvingly as I brought the packet over to her.

"I hope you have a nice last visit with your sister," I said.

"Thanks." She stubbed her cigarette. "So long, Ellis."

"So long, Elizabeth." And with that I left, not looking back, squaring my shoulders and coming out of the room, the cock of the walk, not quite strutting but trying to look awful pleased with myself in case Latham's shadows were watching. In the lobby, I told the bellboy to take up the ice and lemonade. Bought a coke for myself, drank it greedily on the walk to the jeep.

I hoped the drive back up wouldn't be as tough as the drive down, because I had plenty to think about. That bit with the cigarettes and note: Mara had been awful smooth. And the way she'd played along from the get-go at the bar—fine tradecraft, too. Maybe I'd underestimated her. Just because I'd switched the Mickey Finn into her drink the night she'd come to my apartment didn't make her an amateur. Flash thought: What if she and the Russians had planned her screwup with the drugging of my drink all along? Maybe she'd wanted me to catch on, maybe the Russians wanted me to sell her short. She'd fronted "Elizabeth" effortlessly, like a stage actor, without hesitation, delivering all her lines effortlessly, never sounding stilted.

Which was good, real good. I couldn't trust Mara as far as I could throw her, but now my fate was in her hands. Latham's boys would be sweeping her up any minute, hauling her in for interrogation. Her story had to hold up, she had to keep the note I'd written hidden deep in the Lucky packet I'd given her, and she had to sell but good the nooner we'd just had.

And so did I. Thank God I didn't know who was going to be in my audience when I returned to Site Y—if I had known, I might have just let the jeep miss one of those hairpin turns on the road back.

CHAPTER 28

ARRIVED AT LATHAM'S OFFICE PROMPTLY AT 1400. THE COLONEL AND Dahlen weren't there. A typist asked my name, her face tightened for a second when she heard it. Told me they were expecting me in Room 1410A, right down the hall. I knocked, thinking about the typist's expression. I knew Latham was going to confront me about my encounter, but did he also have something unexpected waiting for me?

Did he ever. Special Agent Clayton Slater of the F.B.I. was seated next to the colonel at a long wooden table. Dahlen was there, also a steno, a young woman with glasses and brown hair. Four unfriendly faces staring at me, Slater's hatred glittering in his eyes.

"Sit," Latham practically hissed.

No mistaking where, just one metal folding chair on the other side of the table. Flash thought: Groves had said he had a meeting off base. Who with—Slater? Had Slater come from D.C. on a plane that Groves had gone to meet? All the time I'd been in Santa Fe, Slater must have been briefing Groves and Latham, laying out his case against me, all the suspicions, the innuendo. Considering how much Latham already didn't trust me, Slater must have sounded awful persuasive. What if the Bureau had turned up something on me in Chicago? Lying my way out of this trap was going to be like picking my way across a minefield. Worse—death wouldn't be instant on a wrong step.

The door behind me opened and shut. I stole a glance at the reflection in the steno's glasses: two MPs, burly, helmeted, armed. They stood at parade rest, eyes forward.

"Your friend's already in custody—"

"Agent Slater's told us quite a story—"

"Don't waste our time with lies, Voigt—"

Quite a barrage, that—one, two, three. In rapid fire, Dahlen, Latham, Slater. The steno's fingers danced over her machine. *Click-click, click-click-click-click.*

Get cocky? Play dumb? Blow my stack? Cook up a cover? Instinct said no, all three were pros; and I was sure Slater had told them about my modus operandi when I'd been undercover in D.C. and first tangled with the Bureau. All feints they'd parry, cutting me at every thrust, too. My best move, ignore the third-degree staging and act like I was on the same side of the table.

"So who is she?" I asked matter-of-factly.

Dahlen and Latham had already reloaded, itching to fire—my question threw them. Why wasn't I protesting, throwing a fit? But Slater didn't blink, fixed me with the patented G-man stare, lips pressed as straight as a ruler, brow furrowed, eyes bearing down.

"Who's her contact, how does she find them?"

I ignored Slater and looked straight at Dahlen. "The round heel, who is she and why didn't you bring her in earlier?"

"The better question is why did she find you, Lieutenant Voigt?" Latham asked.

Slater's expression tightened. The colonel might think he was in control, but even acknowledging my question gave me an opening.

"Now look here," I said quickly, before Slater could jump in. "I went for lunch after my briefing with McKibbin, stumbled into an easy nooner, took it. If that's against the rules, how come you didn't tell me that before you pushed me into a jeep and sent me down the trail?"

The steno blushed but didn't miss a word. I hoped I wasn't laying the cad act on too thick.

"You don't actually expect us to believe you don't know her?" Latham was getting hot under the collar.

Slater shot him a look. Colonel or not, he was fouling up the interrogation.

"She's telling all, Voigt, so drop the act," Slater said. "You're not leaving this—"

I cut him off to address Latham. "Colonel, I know the drill—if you meet a girl, and one thing leads to another, s'long as you don't tell her what you do, it's A-okay. And I sure as hell didn't give this gal my life story. So why are we sitting here talking about that when we should be doing the lineup?"

"Forget the lineup, Voigt."—"That's not why we're here." Latham and Slater, talking at the same time. Showed they'd expected me to change the subject. My tight spot had just gotten tighter.

"Delphine Moreno," Slater said.

Delphine Moreno. How long since I'd heard her full name? Since her death, countless hours of memories and what-ifs, but names aren't needed in that realm. Besides, I'd always called her Delphi. *My oracle,* we'd joked. Just kids, we'd borrowed from the Greeks, like so many doomed do, not understanding tragedy. No one does until it hits.

I said nothing, waited.

"Her father, Rosario, was a field organizer for the Communist Party in Chicago."

I didn't respond. The day Delphine died was beautiful, sunny, warm. A strike for steelworkers' rights *could be* dangerous, we'd sensed that, we'd known the police would be protecting Republic Steel's property, but we were seventeen years old, and no one that age ever dies. It was a strike, a protest, peaceful and right—how could anything bad happen? We didn't even hear the first shots. Strikers running, rushing past us—the stampede had frightened us, but we'd stayed on our feet.

"You knew who Rosario was, you knew what he did," Slater continued in a monotone. "We have affidavits."

My God, what have they. Delphine's last words, uttered when we saw a fallen striker. A question unfinished, a sentence incomplete, a life snuffed out. The bullet spun her around, dropped her in a blink. She didn't die instantly, but the ground and the grass knew she was theirs, the thump of her body sickening, an unnatural embrace, a horror in my ears all the surrounding noise couldn't silence.

"'God only knows how many hours he spent with the Morenos' . . . 'He and that girl were two peas in a pod, let me tell you' . . . 'They put up handbills for the protest, sure, all over the neighborhood and by school.'" Dahlen, reading from the affidavits the F.B.I. agent had just mentioned.

What did my former classmates know about Delphine and me? They'd been a blur to us, faceless figures shuffling around us, mumbling—first love, real love, does that, it banishes those around you to the background. They'd not understood us then, what could they possibly remember now to tell a persistent Bureau questioner?

"How bad does it look that you never mentioned Rosario Moreno when you put in for O.N.I. service?" A statement, not a question, from Latham.

"For once, Commander Paslett's paying attention," Slater chimed in. "Going over all your cases, looking for irregularities."

"'Voigt was really broken up when his girl got killed' . . . 'Walked around like a zombie for weeks.'" Dahlen again, reading the affidavits like a script.

Do you think I could be a playwright? Delphine's question the week before she was murdered. A lovely spring day, we were at the lakefront, lying in the grass, looking at the blue sky, eating candy. *A'course. S'that what you wanna do?* A smile. *To start.* Of all her remembered words, those two still sting, still carry the hurt of loss, injustice, emptiness. *To start.* Who'd stolen that start, all the brimming promise of a seventeen-year-old girl with her life ahead of her? Stooge cops doing the bosses' bidding.

"That's when it happened," Slater said. "Moreno had been feeding you the commie line for months, you'd been lapping it up—he was the heroic father of your puppy love. Three of you could hardly wait to mix it up with the cops at Republic Steel, that was your first taste of agitation and revolution. And when that recklessness, that stupidity got the girl killed, you and Rosario didn't blame yourselves—Reds never take responsibility for the troubles they cause. He recruited you, got you into the secret side of the Party, all before you even joined the Navy."

Slater was wrong—Rosario hadn't recruited me. The mission of revenge was all mine. Grief had consumed Rosario, he wasn't even leaving home. Grief had overtaken me, too, but glimpsed through the blackness, I saw a path. *Tell no one you were there . . . ask Rosario to back you up . . . find a way in . . . it's the only way to hurt them for killing Delphine . . .*

"Your silence is pretty damning, Voigt," Latham said.

So was their posturing. If Paslett really was combing over my files, Slater and Latham would have waited to confront me until they had hard evidence, not the half-baked memories of people who knew me when I was a kid. And if Mara really was telling all, I'd be in a cell, the charges ringing in my ears. Her story was holding up, they hadn't broken her. The surprise appearance of Slater, the opening salvo of blunt questions, the looming MPs—a bluff. A full-tilt Bureau squeeze, classic John Edgar, don't let up until they squeal.

"Want me to talk, how's this: Slater's little show here stinks," I answered the colonel.

"Bluster can't save you," Slater shot back.

I ignored him, still talking to Latham. "How many times did he tell you the Bureau should take over this case?"

"Now listen here," Slater interrupted, but I continued.

"With all due respect, sir, has it occurred to you that Slater's here, waving laughable affidavits and painting me Red, just so the Bureau can get its foot in the door? Did he also arrive with a draft memorandum of understanding already signed by John Edgar to assign a permanent Bureau liaison team to Site Y to help you with security?"

Bull's-eye. Latham was nodding, Slater glowering. Dahlen looked dumbstruck. *How'd he know?*

"If I'm a goddamned Red, why aren't you arresting me?" I almost held up my wrists, but I was afraid they'd shake, so I kept my hands tight on my legs.

"Colonel, remember what I said, Voigt's a slippery one, you can't trust a word he says—"

"—Colonel, if I was a Red agent, why would I be here identifying the Russians' number one spy?"

"—this is exactly what I mean, Colonel! This is how Voigt operates, Jesus Christ himself would fall for his 'I'm-as-pure-as-the-white-driven-snow' act—"

"—Colonel, if I'm a Red agent, would I say this to you now: Don't let me near the spy after we do the lineup, don't let me say a single word to him? Would I?"

That clinched it for Latham. Slater started to sputter, but the colonel held up his hand. Looked at me, looked at Slater. Then ordered Dahlen: "Call McKibbin, see if the girl's story checks out."

"Goddammit, Colonel, I told you the Reds will have her covered! We've got to keep pounding away at her til she cracks!"

Bad move, cursing a senior Army intelligence officer. Latham glared at Slater, who finally had the good sense to shut up. Dahlen stood, exited.

The next three minutes were agonizing. At least when the Russians had been torturing me, I'd blacked out briefly. No choice here but to sit still, try to control my breathing and clamp down on the growing quiver in my hands and legs. Slater busied himself scribbling in a notepad, no doubt recording my mendacity and Latham's incompetence. The colonel simply closed his eyes, but he wasn't sleeping—his chin was tilted up. Concentrating, thinking? I remembered his reference to Buddhism when we met—didn't Buddhists meditate? Looked like a good idea, but I no more knew how to meditate than I knew how to fly an aircraft. So I kept my eyes on the scuffed tabletop and kept my thoughts firmly in the past, remembering the thrill, the exhilaration of our first kiss, Delphine and me, how we were seated on the sofa in her parents' parlor, not working on our homework, how our hips were touching and her bare arm brushed up against mine and my heart was pounding and I swallowed hard as she murmured something about the play we were reading and her tongue nervously touched her upper lips and her lashes fluttered as I dared to lean my head closer and—

The door swung open. I jolted out of my reverie, Slater stopped writing, Latham opened his eyes. We all looked at Dahlen.

"She's clean."

"No! No! Colonel, you've gotta let me question her, I know how these Reds operate, I know how they set up their covers, I know what they overlook. Take me down there, now!"

First a curse, now an order—Slater was digging his hole deeper.

"The woman's committed no crime," Latham said evenly. "What do you propose we do? Jail her without a charge?"

"Charge her with prostitution, anything! Just please keep her detained til I can question her."

"This is the United States of America, Agent Slater. We don't fabricate charges." He looked at me. "We'll do the lineup right now—Dahlen's got the names of all male civilians and military personnel who had leave the first week of May." To Slater he said, "You can observe the identification, but that's it, understand?"

Slater said yessir but he was looking straight at me. The hatred in his eyes had turned to cold, hard resolution. He was absolutely, positively convinced I was a fraud, a liar, a traitor, a Red. And I knew he wouldn't stop until he had evidence.

I'd wiggled my way out of this jam, but I was, for real, a fraud, a liar, a traitor, a Red. So how long did I have before Agent Slater proved it?

CHAPTER 29

WE DID THE INTERVIEWS IN A CRAMPED, WINDOWLESS OFFICE IN THE Administration building. Metal table, wooden chairs, blank walls. Latham, Slater, Dahlen, and the steno with brown hair sat facing the lone chair reserved for the suspect. Latham ordered me to lean against the wall behind the suspect. He didn't want me watching the suspects' faces, just listening.

Fine by me. Despite my run-in with Mara and the arrival of Slater, my plan was working. As soon as I recognized the spy's voice, Latham would immediately arrest him. I'd be ordered out of the room, of course, to appease Slater—didn't matter. I wanted nothing to do with the spy, I truly wanted Latham to keep me away from him. Mara and the Russians would never know I hadn't spoken with him, and where the spy would be going, he'd never be able to tell them we'd never talked. Latham would send me straight back to Washington, where I'd doctor the schematic the spy had originally delivered. Give it to the Russians, get them off my back—then I'd figure out what to do about Slater and the Bureau. And the Russians, too, when they finally realized the schematic was hooey. For now, my goal was not to drown—I'd find my way out of the water later.

Six men on the list: Klaus Fuchs, Fred Dawes, Richard Feynman, Gary Ackerly, Paul Scheppel, and Mason Adams Brode. Latham didn't tell me anything about the men except their names and that he and Dahlen were certain they were the only Site Y personnel who could have traveled to Washington in May. Again, fine by me. I knew my man's voice, I knew what he looked like, even if I'd only peered at him through the window of the kitchen door at the Automat. I also knew—because he had boasted about it during the conversation I overhead—he had earned a Ph.D. in physics from Yale at age twenty-two. That fact I hadn't shared with anyone. Not that I expected Latham to ask these men where they'd gone to school, but a guy who gets a doctorate one year after becoming old enough to vote sure wouldn't talk like a mechanic.

The first man, Klaus Fuchs, looked to be in his early thirties. Serious, almost forlorn expression on an otherwise blank face, notable only for big round eyeglasses and hair rippling back from a receding hairline. Trying hard not to look nervous. The man I'd seen hadn't worn glasses and wasn't losing his hair. Still, I wanted to hear him speak. It's easy to alter an appearance using spectacles and a wig, much harder to disguise a voice.

"Doctor Fuchs, we called you here because we're investigating a possible breach of security in the Theoretical Physics Division," Latham announced. "We've just a few questions for you, then you can get back to work."

So Fuchs had a Ph.D.—that caught my attention. He nodded energetically at Latham's statement but didn't speak.

The colonel slid a stapled sheaf of papers across the table. "This is your signature here," pointing.

"Yes."

"Indicating the removal of the papers identified on the log from Safe TP Four on July seventh at twenty-two-thirty-five."

"Yes . . ."

Dammit, Latham, get him to say something besides yes!

"Why is there no time of return of the papers on this log?"

Fuchs peered at the log, looked up, scanned the faces watching him, cleared his throat.

"Well, I, er, I am not sure, certainly I returned the papers, but I must have simply forgotten to update the log, that is all, I did not—are the papers missing?"

"No, Doctor Fuchs, the papers are secure. But you didn't indicate when you locked the papers back in the safe. A failure to maintain timely and accurate logs for classified materials greatly undermines our security measures—"

"Is it other papers that are missing? You said there is a breach. Because if there are, other missing materials I mean, I do not know anything about it."

I tuned out Latham's response. Fuchs was rattled, speaking rapidly, but I'd listened long enough: He was not the man I'd seen and heard in Washington. Fuchs spoke with a German accent, and it wasn't faked. My parents were immigrants from Germany; I'd grown up hearing English being spoken with almost the exact same inflection.

". . . you may return to work, Doctor Fuchs," Latham finished.

"Yes, thank you—I am terribly sorry about my neglect of the log, it will not happen again, Colonel, I promise you that." Fuchs pushed his chair back and stood, eyeing me over as he hustled out of the room.

As soon as the door shut, Latham looked straight at me. "Well?"

I shook my head. "He's not the spy. Fuchs is German, right—the accent? The man I heard at the Automat speaks one hundred percent American English."

"All right," he said. He started to tell Dahlen to bring in the next man, but Slater piped up.

"Hold on, Colonel, if you will. I think we should give this Fuchs another look."

"We?"

"I mean your office, Colonel, of course. But just a quick glance at the file raises all sorts of red flags about Fuchs's background. He was born and raised in Germany, at a time when the Communist Party there was quite active, and—"

"Doctor Fuchs is now a British citizen. Last I checked, we're still on the same side as the British."

Slater ignored the crack. "Be that as it may, Colonel, I think it prudent to continue questioning him."

"Fuchs went through a thorough security screening before he set foot on Site Y. And we just heard Voigt say he's not the man who came to Washington."

Everyone—Latham, Slater, Dahlen, the steno—looked at me.

"He's not the spy," I repeated.

"What if he's wrong?" Slater said, addressing Latham. Translation: *What if he's lying?*

The colonel's expression of impatience suggested this wasn't the first time Slater had raised the possibility. I had to admit, the F.B.I. agent had a point. If I was a Red spy, I might very well lie to protect the spy. But when I identified the spy, I'd throw that theory out the window.

"Agent Slater, let's get through the list as quickly as possible, as we agreed. If we need to bring Fuchs back in, we know where to find him."

Slater was unhappy, but he nodded. The second man on the list, Fred Dawes, was short and fat, his neck rippling over his collar like a melting pudding. He worked in metallurgy, so Latham asked him about the stock of aluminum bars. Sounded like a pretense—unlike during the questioning of Fuchs, Latham didn't produce a log or an inventory, so his queries were broad. *Have you ever had a problem with missing bars? How do you keep track of your stock?*

Problem was, Dawes wasn't much of a talker. At all. *Dunno. Couldn't say.* Nodded his head for yes, shook his head for no; I watched the fat rolls jiggle. Exasperated, Latham finally asked him to tell us, in his own words, how the aluminum was inventoried and stored.

"Now look, Colonel, dis here's a royal waste'a time, awright, dat alOOh-muNUM is locked down tighter dan virgins in a CAHNvent, you wanna know about how it gets inventoried, don't waste yer time talking ta me, I gotta get back to work, I got a man already out sick, I got a lathe down . . ."

Dis, dat, dan: Dawes was a Midwesterner like me, a city boy, not quite Chicago, but close, Rockford or Milwaukee. Wherever he was from, he sure hadn't learned to talk like that at Yale. Latham dismissed him as soon as I shook my head.

"Definitely not our man," I said once Dawes was out of the room.

Not even Slater disputed my appraisal. We waited in awkward silence as Dahlen fetched the next man. Latham appeared to meditate, Slater scribbled notes. I ached to light a cigarette, but we were all still abstaining because of the colonel's tobacco allergy. My legs were starting to tire from standing, though I knew better than to ask if I could sit. Latham didn't care for Slater, wasn't going to let him shoehorn his way into Site Y; but that didn't mean I'd become the colonel's pet. Making me stand away from the table was a not-so-subtle reminder I was still the outsider, here to do one task and then get gone. *Fine by me*, I thought. My mantra for the evening, that phrase. I wondered if Latham's men had released Mara yet. She was made of tougher stuff than I'd first thought—keeping her cover tight during a lengthy interrogation was mighty impressive. I hoped she knew she'd be followed all the way from Santa Fe. If she met with the Russians, as she was supposed to, then the jig was up, for sure. Felt my pulse quicken, my mouth go dry. Told myself not to panic, not to spin what-ifs. Mara had just fooled Army intelligence; she wasn't about to make an amateur mistake.

The arrival of the third man interrupted my worrisome thoughts. Richard Feynman came in smiling, confident, scanning the room like a Borscht Belt comedian sizing up his audience. He barely glanced at me as he took the lone chair facing his tribunal. He was thin and rakishly handsome, with arched eyebrows and dark eyes. His baggy brown trousers and white shirt badly needed pressing.

"Time for *Professor Quiz* again?" Feynman said, still smiling.

Latham smiled faintly at this crack about the radio show. "We've received more reports of tampered safes."

Both Slater and I perked up. *Tampered safes?* Was this for real or a ruse, like the story of the missing aluminum bars?

"Well, I'm not your man," Feynman answered, "no sir, I learned my lesson, you schooled me rightly, I keep my fingers off the dial, the safe dial that is. The radio dial I don't dare touch. *Take It or Leave It* is even better than *Professor Quiz*, don't you think, Colonel?"

This Feynman was awful close to being insolent, but Latham didn't dress him down. *Why not?* I wondered. The colonel had rebuked Fuchs for failing to sign a log, but Feynman wasn't even getting chided for safe tampering (alleged). He must be awful important to the project, I decided, or else he'd seen right through Latham's pretense and was having fun with the colonel.

No matter—Feynman wasn't the spy. The pitch of his voice was higher than the man I'd heard, and Feynman had a habit of stretching out one-syllable words. *Keeeep, saafe.* Latham told him he could go. He left—after making an exaggerated bow. Slater's face reddened with anger. What tales he'd tell Hoover!

"Well?" Latham asked.

"Not him, sir."

"I see," he answered cryptically, looking at me long and hard. I didn't like his expression—at all.

"Colonel, what's this about tampered safes?" Slater piped up.

"Don't get excited, it's not what it sounds like. We had a small problem with Feynman playing jokes. He's so good with numbers he can crack the codes and open safes. He was leaving jokes on scraps of paper inside the safes he opened. Obviously, we put an end to *that*."

"What?!" Now the color drained from Slater's face. "Good Lord, do you have any idea . . ." I tuned out the familiar Bureau bluster and Latham's indignant response, Dahlen watching the back-and-forth like a tennis match.

Why the cold look from Latham? And that reply? *I see.* Three men had come and gone—I'd denied each was the spy. Was the colonel coming around to Slater, was he starting to suspect that I wasn't going to identify the spy in order to protect him? I wasn't going to do that, of course—but what if I couldn't recognize the spy's voice or his appearance? What if he had disguised himself when he came to Washington and now looked different? What the hell would I do then?

CHAPTER 30

TOLD MYSELF NOT TO PANIC, I HAD THREE MORE MEN TO OBSERVE, ONE of them *had* to be the spy. But now I couldn't stave off the what-ifs, they swept in like locusts. What if the man I'd seen in Washington had just been a courier, pretending to be a hotshot scientist from Site Y? What if Latham had overlooked my man, what if he had found a way to get out of Site Y without leave? What if the spy was posted at a different secret site? If the spy wasn't here, for whatever reason, Slater would sink his teeth in and shake me like a rag doll. I couldn't claim Latham had made a mistake, all my credibility rode on this identification. More than credibility—my life. Because if I didn't put the spy into the clink here, at Site Y, the Russians would be able to ask him if I'd made contact, as I was supposed to do, and when he said, *What are you talking about?* I'd be a walking dead man.

Plan's solid, stay steady, I told myself. A new mantra, those words. Plan's solid, stay steady. Still, I wished I could smoke—a Lucky would have gone a long way toward smoothing my nerves.

The fourth man, Gary Ackerly, was small and slight, with an angular face and a bristle brush of a mustache. *Could he be the spy?* I wondered. The man I'd seen in Washington had been thin and also had a sharp chin. No mustache, but he could have easily grown it since his return.

Latham gave him the same line he'd used with Fuchs: there had been some security breaches, this time in the Experimental Physics Division. Another scientist—we were getting warmer.

"What kind of breaches?" Ackerly calmly answered. Confident, like Feynman, but not cocky. Voice soft but clear, no accent.

"Classified materials improperly logged. Safes left open."

"Colonel, I'm keenly aware, as are all my colleagues in the division, that any and all observations relating to said problems must be immediately reported to your office. Therefore, I propose that we dispense with pretense and you ask me whatever it is you really want to."

If Ackerly was expecting a retort or a lecture on the importance of security measures, he didn't get it. Latham calmly asked, "Doctor Ackerly, have you ever failed to correctly log classified materials and return them to their assigned safe and properly secure the lock?"

He had a Ph.D. too! Appearance, work, education—Ackerly shared three traits with the spy. And his tone of voice and the words he used strikingly resembled the man I'd heard in D.C. Arrogant, confident, officious. The professorial phrasing. *Any and all . . . said problems . . . therefore.*

"No, Colonel, to my knowledge I have never failed to properly handle classified materials."

Was he the man? I badly wanted to say yes, but something didn't feel right. I needed to hear more. Catching Latham's eye, I circled a forefinger in the air. *Keep him talking.*

"Very well, thank you," Latham said to Ackerly. "Next question: Have you been out to Trinity recently?"

A smirk. "Like a competent trial attorney, you already know the answer to that question, Colonel."

"Let's pretend I'm not a competent trial attorney."

"It so happens I was at Trinity a week ago Tuesday," the scientist said.

"For how long?"

"Just a day, thankfully, the conditions are beyond wretched. I cannot fathom how we're expected to work in that heat and dust."

Something wasn't quite right, he had an enunciation that didn't jibe with the spy's. Ackerly didn't draw out his words, as Feynman did, but he did hit second syllables like some people smack staplers. *Wret-CHED* . . . *fath-UHM*. The man at the Automat had the same verbal tic, hadn't he? I couldn't be certain, too much time had passed. If only I could ask where he'd gone to college, if only I could find out if he was a Yale man. Told myself to concentrate. Ackerly continued to complain about the terrible conditions at this place called Trinity, some site in the desert. Finally I thought to close my eyes and imagined myself back in D.C., the headset over my ears, the spy's voice right there, then and now . . . *in a coupla months, maybe less, the whole world's gonna find out what a big, big bang of a success we've pulled off* . . . as Ackerly droned on in the background . . . "time and again we have lodged our complaints with Robert and he has promised to get the general to do something, but nothing has changed, not a thing!"

I opened my eyes, looked at Latham, and shook my head. Contractions: the man I'd heard used them, Ackerly didn't. *We* have *lodged* . . . *he* has *promised*. For all the apparent similarities, Ackerly wasn't the spy.

Latham dismissed Ackerly, who barely looked at me on his way out. If I was important, surely I would've been seated at the table. Would *have* been seated.

The three men facing me had noticed my hesitation; they'd seen me close my eyes to concentrate. Latham said, "Bringing any of these men back in will raise their suspicions, Voigt." Translation: *This is your only shot to get it right.*

"I understand, sir. I just needed to listen a little longer, that's all. Ackerly has a similar way of talking to the man I heard in Washington. But it's not him. The man I heard uses contractions, Ackerly doesn't, plus the inflection is a little off."

Slater shook his head in disgust. "Colonel, we're not rehearsing characters for a play here. Voigt's obviously incapable of identifying the spy." Another way of accusing me of being a liar.

"We're down to just two men," Latham replied. "If Voigt leaves us empty-handed, we'll consider doing things your way."

The colonel didn't so much as glance at me, but that statement was a definite shot across my bow. Speaking as if I wasn't in the room, giving Slater encouragement—Latham was letting me know that if I didn't come through, I was finished at Site Y. And Slater's "way" might well include detaining me on suspicion of being a Red agent. I was utterly alone—Paslett couldn't protect me, not here.

My blood pressure shot up when the fifth man, Paul Scheppel, came in. He was stout, short—and completely bald. His shaved head caught the overhead light as he sat. I tried to hide my dismay, had to appear to concentrate. *No one knows you saw the spy, so listen hard.* Scheppel worked in the Chemistry Division, he was asked about a laboratory accident. Looked surprised, said he'd already been asked about that; Latham told him they needed to go over it again. Scheppel shrugged, said okay, talked. East Coast accent, Boston or Rhode Island—what did it matter? Five men had come in—I hadn't recognized one.

Slater couldn't contain his triumph when I shook my head after Scheppel left.

"At this point, Colonel, I have to wonder why we're even bothering to bring these men in. Voigt is playing a game, trying to stall us to keep us from digging further into what he's been up to."

Latham regarded him coolly, like a teacher who's had it with a bright but obnoxious pupil.

"Perhaps. There is also the possibility that the man Voigt heard didn't come from here."

Slater's look of surprise was no consolation to me. Like me, the F.B.I. agent assumed Site Y was *the* sole location of this weapons project. But if the sixth man wasn't the spy, no way in hell was Latham or General Groves authorizing me to travel to another secret site. Latham would hustle me off the base, Slater on my heels. I'd report back to Paslett, but why would he back me after I'd failed so miserably? And the Bureau wasn't even my greatest threat—the Russians were.

"Anyway, let's finish this," Latham told Slater. To me he said, "Depending on how this last examination turns out, you may be confined to quarters, Voigt. This is a standard security measure here for personnel without an assigned duty, and it would just be temporary until I receive instructions."

"I understand, sir," I answered the colonel. That line about standard procedure was complete bullshit, we all knew it, even the steno, who suddenly lowered her head when I noticed her looking at me; but what could I do? Lose my temper, put on an act, storm about?

The final man was brought in: Mason Adams Brode. He eyed me over as he entered; I kept my gaze disinterested. He was well dressed. Brown sport coat, white shirt, striped tie, tan trousers. Freshly shined wingtips. Thick eyebrows accentuated an intense gaze and dark eyes. A smoothly planed face, not quite handsome, but striking. Average height, slight build, a shade too thin. I watched as he sat and placed his hands on the table, his cuffs sliding up. Long, slender fingers; delicate wrists.

The spy had arrived! His first words confirmed my visual identification:

"Colonel, your timing couldn't be worse." The pitch of his voice, his enunciation, the accentless American English—Mason Adams Brode was the man I'd seen and heard in Washington. The man who'd turned over a schematic of the weapon being built at Site Y, the man who'd said, *To diffuse the Uranium-235, use uranium hexafluoride and a metal filter with submicroscopic perforations, do not use a mass spectrometer,* was now seated not six feet away.

"We won't be long, Doctor Brode. We just need to ask some questions about security measures in your division."

"Ah, the familiar song-and-dance routine, and me without my top hat and cane." He must have smiled at the steno, because she looked down at her machine. *Click-click, click-click-click.*

"Have you ever failed to secure classified materials in their assigned safe?"

"Maybe you should ask Feynman that question, he's the one with the light fingers." I couldn't tell if he was smirking, but he didn't need to—his sarcastic tone told us he knew Feynman had been called in, too.

"Just answer the question, Doctor."

"No, never."

"Have you witnessed the mishandling of classified materials during your work in the Tech Area?"

"No, never." Brode drummed his fingers—tap-tap, tap—as he spoke. Playing games.

Latham kept his cool. "Have you found classified materials where they shouldn't be?"

"Colonel, you have to know that's a difficult question to answer, quite leading. How should I, a lowly physicist, know where *all* classified materials should be at *all* times? We have quite the galaxy of classified stars and planets, as it were, here, don't we?"

The more I listened, the more familiar he sounded. Not just his voice, but the breezy arrogance. Where Feynman had been playful and Ackerly imperious, Brode was flat-out sassy.

He blithely answered Latham's last few questions and accepted his dismissal with "Toodle-loo." Gave me another eyeover as he exited, but I wasn't worried—no way he'd seen me at the Automat, because I'd viewed him through the kitchen door window.

"What did he mean that your timing couldn't be worse?" Slater asked.

Latham ignored him, looked straight at me.

I nodded firmly. "No doubt about it, he's the spy—he's the man I heard in Washington."

Slater started to protest, but Latham waved his hand angrily to cut him off.

"You're sure, Voigt, absolutely sure?"

"Yessir. The voices are the same, the way he talks, even his manner, his, uh, way of being overbearing, a know-it-all—that's the man I heard in Washington. Colonel, believe me, once you arrest him and put the heat on, your interrogation will prove I'm right."

I took a deep breath. Jesus H., that had been close! Why couldn't Brode have been the first man on the list, or even the fourth? Having him come in sixth had sweated me but good. Yet my mantra had held. *Plan's solid, stay steady.* In mere minutes, Brode would be swept up by MPs and locked down in isolation. In a day or so, I'd be on my way back to D.C.—maybe I could even talk my way onto a transport plane to Washington. I'd doctor up the schematic I had hidden and turn it over to the Russians. *Plan's solid, stay steady.* Or so I was thinking until Latham responded:

"That's the problem, Voigt—we can't arrest Brode, not now."

"Maybe not ever," Dahlen added ruefully.

I was so stunned I didn't even notice this was the first time Dahlen had spoken since we started the lineup.

CHAPTER 31

Y OU CAN'T ARREST HIM?!"—"YOU'RE LETTING HIM WALK AWAY?!" Simultaneous outbursts from me and Slater. We glared at one another, but he got the jump on me.

"Colonel, setting aside the question of whether or not Voigt's telling the truth about Brode, why can't you arrest him? Any of these men can be locked up, there's nothing legally preventing a precautionary detention."

"You don't think I know that, Agent Slater?" Latham shot back, finally losing his temper. "This has nothing to do with the law!"

"Do you know who Mason Adams Brode is?" Dahlen asked quietly.

Slater asked, "He's not related to the senator, is he?"

Latham and Dahlen nodded; I groaned; Slater, for once, had nothing to say. Senator Harrison Wright Brode was a Washington giant, an American legend, a character not even William Dean Howells or Mark Twain could have conjured up. Now in his seventies, Brode claimed his parents had been killed by marauding Sioux in the Dakota Territory when he was an infant. He claimed the Indians took him, reared him as their own until he ran away at age thirteen. Hell, maybe it was true—he spoke the Sioux language. Brode claimed he found work following railroad track gangs, toting buckets of water and beer for the Chinese and Irish laborers. The bejeweled cane the old man was never without now was needed, he claimed, because of the damage done to his young spine from bearing a yoke day after day. The cane itself was famous—carved from a rare wood that could only be found in Paraguay, it featured a snake's head with rubies for eyes.

Hence the name everyone knew Brode by but dared not say to his face. *Snake Eyes.* No future in being a human ox, the boy decided; he ditched the railroad for Colorado's boomtowns. He had a head for numbers, nerves of steel—a gift, he liked to say, from the stoic and brave Sioux—and quick, nimble hands. First cards, then dice; and only dice after his first big roll. He amassed a fortune before he was eighteen. He grew tall and had broad shoulders, and, it was said, his eyes were as blue as the Western sky. After Colorado, he settled in Wyoming. No long-term future in gambling, either, the young man realized. He'd seen too many card sharks, rollers, and casino operators meet violent, premature deaths. (And, it was said, he'd delivered that fate to more than one rival.) The real action was in the sanctioned rackets, law enforcement and politics. So, Sheriff Brode. Then, Mayor Brode. Then, Water Commissioner Brode (apparently a powerful position in a state like Wyoming). While still in his thirties, he became Senator Brode. Scourge of the Monopolies, Champion of the Working Man, Friend of the Red Man—he could have worn the appellations he collected during his decades on Capitol Hill like service ribbons on a uniform—but that one nickname told you all you needed to know. *Snake Eyes.*

A man of iron will who chewed grudges like terriers break rats, Brode's allegiances were mercurial, shifting. Teddy Roosevelt had believed he had Brode's support for a certain conservation bill until something transpired between the two men. An argument, an affront, a forgotten favor, no one knew for sure. But Brode suddenly killed the bill. T.R. raged, he fumed, he stormed; he unleashed his power and allies like a winter blizzard against Brode, who refused to yield. Taft, Wilson, Harding, Coolidge, Hoover—one president after another had taken on Brode and failed, on issues ranging from tariffs to torts, Versailles to farmers. Only the other

Roosevelt had figured out how to deal with Brode: Don't stand in his way. With his swept-back silver hair and weathered, creased face, the still-sparkling blue eyes, Brode was the very embodiment of a senator, a Cicero of the Prairie.

He had married late in life, in his fifties. Janice Adams was a descendant of *those* Adamses, a striking beauty with raven hair and an elegant manner. Her marriage to Brode had stunned the Social Register, which considered the union scandalous (she was just twenty-eight), though no one had the guts to say that in print, mindful of Brode's peerless talent for visiting ruin upon his enemies. Only one child, the man we'd just seen, Mason Adams Brode. No wonder he was so self-assured and confident—being that senator's son was akin to being the favored offspring of Zeus.

"If the questioning is done *in camera*, the senator won't even know what's happening," Slater suggested.

"The senator regularly corresponds with his son," Dahlen said. "Letters every three, four days." Translation: *Mason was the apple of his father's eye, and he couldn't be held incommunicado without attracting the senator's attention—and wrath.*

"Don't forget, the senator is chairman of the appropriations subcommittee of the Senate Interior Department Committee," I added. During my stint undercover in Washington, I'd learned that the tremendous costs of the Site Y project were concealed as Interior Department expenditures.

"I know that," Slater snapped. "So what? A coupla days is all we need to interrogate Mason Brode, and as soon as we have his confession, not even his father will be able to protect him or interfere with what's happening here."

"And if he doesn't confess?" I asked Slater. "Do you wanna be at Hoover's side when the senator demands to know why his son was arrested as a suspected Red spy?"

His clenched jaw was all the reply we needed. Rumor was, J. Edgar Hoover—the man who had incriminating files on all of Washington's rich and powerful, including presidents—was himself compromised by certain information and evidence held by none other than the senator. Who also chaired the appropriations subcommittee of the Senate Justice Department Committee, as well as the naval appropriations subcommittee.

"What the senator can or can't do to us is irrelevant," Latham piped up. We all looked at him; he sighed. "Miss Imes, you can go, thank you," he said to the steno.

She nodded, gathered up her machine, and left.

"We can't arrest Brode right now because he's indispensable to Trinity," Latham explained.

Trinity. Latham had asked Ackerly if he had been to Trinity recently. The scientist had said yes, he'd complained about the conditions, the heat and dust. Trinity must be a branch of Site Y, I guessed, within driving distance but even more remote, without even the simple amenities of Site Y. With all the resources here, why was another base even needed? Again, I recalled what the spy had said in Washington: *In a coupla months, maybe less, the whole world's gonna find out what a big, big bang of a success we've pulled off.* Remembering how Brode had uttered that line had allowed me to eliminate Ackerly as the spy—and now it answered my question. The weapon being built was too dangerous to handle here. They needed a test site, a proving ground, far enough from Site Y to keep the main base safe in case something went wrong. *Big, big bang . . .*

"Colonel, before you go on, I think it would be prudent to dismiss Voigt," Slater said.

Latham gave me a long look as he considered the suggestion. I checked the urge to protest—that wouldn't help me. I'd managed to convince the colonel the Bureau had ulterior motives for sending Slater to Site Y, that Hoover wanted a permanent detail of his boys on the base. As an intelligence officer, Latham knew that the affidavits Slater had brought concerning my long-ago relationship with Delphine and her father were circumstantial. If the Bureau had hard evidence of me being a Red spy, they'd have used it already. And thanks to Mara holding fast to her cover identity, I'd managed to brush off my encounter with her in Santa Fe. But now that I'd served my purpose—identification of the spy who'd come to Washington—Latham didn't need me. Letting me know why Mason Adams Brode was so important to the Site Y project wouldn't help Latham figure out what to do. And what if Slater and the Bureau were right, what if I was compromised? The smart move, the only move for Latham, was to get me out of the way, send me packing. It's what I would have done if I were the colonel.

As if he were reading my thoughts, Latham nodded. "Lieutenant Dahlen, take Lieutenant Voigt back to his quarters." To me he said, "Voigt, I appreciate you making the identification. I'll let General Groves know how helpful you were, and I'm sure he'll let your commander know that as well. We'll make arrangements for your return to Washington as soon as possible, but until then, I'm instructing you to remain in your quarters or the officers' mess until you leave. Is that understood?"

"Yessir. I'm glad to have been of service." I kept my gaze trained on him, but Slater's smirk was still visible.

What had just happened? Somehow, I'd deflected the Bureau's charges and dodged detention for meeting with Mara; I'd kept secret my shame, my treason, my betrayal; I'd identified the Russians' top spy. But the other half of my meticulous plan had just crumbled before my eyes. All I needed was for Mason Adams Brode to be locked up, with no contact with the outside world—that's all! Even Slater wanted him locked up tight. Only then could I complete my deception of the Russians and, at long last, redeem myself.

Why was Mason Adams Brode indispensable? What, exactly, was Trinity? Would Latham ever arrest Brode? My mind whirred with questions, but the one that stood out was the hardest one of all to answer: How would I convince Latham to not send me back to Washington?

CHAPTER 32

DUTIFULLY FOLLOWED DAHLEN OUT OF THE INTERROGATION ROOM, lighting up a long-awaited Lucky. Neither of us spoke as we trudged down a hard, baked road. Ahead of us, a small pond. To our left was a high wire fence topped by angled barbed wire encircling a compound of two-story wooden buildings painted olive drab. A dozen or so dusty cars were parked haphazardly on a gravel lot alongside the road. The Technical Area, I guessed—the heart of Site Y, the workplace of our spy Mason Adams Brode. We turned in the opposite direction, passing a cluster of small wooden dwellings with porches. Some had laundry hanging from lines; others had been screened in. The tree-dotted mountains on the horizon looked like the background in a nineteenth-century landscape, the colors soft.

Dahlen clearly wasn't going to speak. *Should I?* I wondered. But I was caught in the suspect's enduring dilemma. Silence *and* protest alike hint at guilt. My only play, I decided, was to make one simple statement, and leave it at that. So we continued in silence until we reached the officers' quarters.

"Here we are," Dahlen said awkwardly.

"Quarters and mess only, got it—I won't stray," I reassured him.

"It's not like you're under arrest, it's just, well, it'll be easier for all'a us if—"

"I don't cause trouble, I know."

He looked relieved.

"Dahlen."

"Yeah?"

"Don't forget, the chessboard has more than one pawn."

"Right," he said uneasily. After a pause, "Well, then, you can expect more information about your departure tomorrow. Wait, sorry, not tomorrow, the day after, probably."

I didn't ask what was happening the next day, and with that he left.

I WAS RAVENOUS BUT I NEEDED TO THINK BEFORE I ATE. THINK, AND plan. Took a long shower, put on comfortable civvies: dungarees, T-shirt. Stretched out on the bed, closed my eyes, breathed deeply, and tried to focus. But my eyelids drooped, and I couldn't stay awake. I slept a couple of hours, yet even refreshed my mind wandered, memories rolling over me like summer storm clouds. All the treasonous acts I'd committed since I gave myself over to the Reds.

The tiny camera they gave me, my courier "Geoffrey" showing me how to use it, his lesson terse, his demonstration swift. *Point, press, advance; repeat . . . keep the lens parallel to the documents.* He was an American, Geoffrey, red-haired and freckled, a burly build. Looked like a longshoreman, not a spy, but disguise was our stock-in-trade, right? Masks, covers, deceptions.

A humid, sweltering Washington night, July 1943, my face slick with sweat, one drop, then two plunking and blotting the onionskin papers I was photographing furtively. They looked like oversized asterisks, the stains, and for a panicky moment I envisioned a rebuke from my courier, now a middle-aged man named Henry. *They want to know the meaning of these marks . . .* There I was, in Paslett's office, photographing a memorandum of understanding between O.N.I. and the O.S.S. regarding an intelligence source in Istanbul—and I was imagining the N.K.V.D. grumbling about the sweat of my brow?

February 1944: a dead drop in McPherson Square, an impression of a key I'd made in clay, per my instructions. A low gray sky, a stiff breeze, my ears red, lips chapped. Thinking how reckless the drop was—nobody was lingering outside on this winter day. The urge to look around to see if I was being watched was maddening, like an itch you can't reach. Here the memory fades. Like a photograph I could see myself on that bench, blowing on my hands to warm them up; but after the drop, where did I go? Probably to a diner for coffee, maybe even a tavern for a whiskey.

All this, the incomplete docket of my crimes, my autobiographical bill of attainder. Not so neatly presented, of course; memory is not a finicky file clerk. Instead, a montage, a drift of images and details as crisp and colorful as autumn leaves falling in no particular order. And leaves yet to drop.

When did I realize nothing I was doing would ever alter the conditions, the circumstances, the powers, the *system* that had caused Delphine's murder? Funny how I could recall with clarity these crimes against country but I couldn't envision the moment and place I "woke up." Maybe it was an accretion of uncomfortable questions, a creeping awareness. *How does giving the Soviets the January 17, 1944, report of the O.N.I. liaison in Lisbon punish the owners of Republic Steel? Why am I giving a foreign power a coastal survey of the Faroe Islands?* A moribund conscience stirred, getting restive, resisting suppression.

Focus, dammit, focus! Had to push the memories back into the box and deal with the present. What was being built here at Site Y, what was this weapon, what was the *big, big bang* Brode had spoken of? Several times I'd studied the diagram he had brought to Washington, which I'd so carefully hidden. Brode had told Himmel to give it to Soviet physicists, that they'd know what it meant. I was no physicist, no scientist; I'd passed high school chemistry, that was it. How could I possibly guess what the diagram showed?

External signs—the money, the resources, the secrecy, the determination of the Russians to get this diagram—pointed to some kind of super weapon. Our version of the V-2 rockets the Germans had desperately launched late in the European war? The V-2s were remarkable—unmanned, directed bombs—but for all the terror and destruction they'd caused, the rockets were but a tactical diversion. They hadn't slowed, let alone stopped, an Allied victory; they'd not saved the Nazis. I sensed the Site Y project was much bigger than the V-2. From one bomb, one building to one bomb, *one city.* Destroyed, leveled, pulverized—and buried in the rubble and ashes, the bones of fifty thousand people, maybe even more. The stuff of comic books and science fiction, I realized, a phenomenon that beggared the imagination and defied the laws of nature.

But what if? What if that *big, big bang* could burst from just one bomb? What would that take? I did possess part of that answer: Uranium-235. Brode had referred to this element in the conversation I'd overheard in Washington. He'd also explained a process involving uranium hexafluoride. Here, at Site Y, they were diffusing uranium hexafluoride—the reason why, he hadn't said. But he was proud of what he was helping to build: *in a coupla months, maybe less, the whole world's gonna find out what a big, big bang of a success we've pulled off.* That was on May 9; it was now July 15. Just over two months since his prediction. They had to be close.

I closed my eyes, took a long drag of my umpteenth cigarette. Tried to picture the periodic table that my chemistry teacher had drilled into us. Uranium was at the bottom, in the 90s, down there with mythological-sounding elements like neptunium, plutonium, thorium. All part of the same series—was it lanthanide? Actinide? But what could be done with those elements, how could they be weaponized? Bombs require energy, which must be kept stable until detonation. *Atoms,* I muttered, dredging that word from the muck where so much of my high school learning had settled. Was it possible to obtain energy for a weapon from atoms, the tiniest bits of matter in the universe? That made no natural sense, though— in a Newtonian world, you couldn't create energy from next to nothing.

Flash: What if the atoms weren't the source, what if they were the carrier? Wherever the energy came from, what if the atoms delivered it, spread it? Atoms are everywhere—if Mason Adams Brode, Gary Ackerly, Klaus Fuchs, and all the other eggheads had hit upon a way to use atoms to carry TNT or some other explosive, where would that end? One bomb, one city—Jesus H. Christ. But with something so new, so unworldly, how would they know if it could work?

I jumped up from the bed, ash falling everywhere. *Not tomorrow, the day after, probably,* Dahlen had said about my departure. I couldn't leave *tomorrow* because they were testing the weapon tomorrow. I had to see Latham immediately, I had to convince him to let me remain on Site Y.

I PUT MY UNIFORM BACK ON AND RUSHED FROM THE BUILDING. DIDN'T GET far—a lanky MP jumped to his feet from a wooden chair on the porch of the officers' quarters. I wasn't surprised. If I were Latham, I would have posted a guard to keep an eye on me. Question was, how detailed were the MP's orders?

"Ready for dinner, Lieutenant Voigt?" he asked.

"After a quick detour, Corporal," I said. HUGHLEY, his nameplate read.

"Um, no detours, sir."

"Lieutenant Dahlen forgot to collect this," I said, holding up the security badge I'd been issued.

"Well, I can give it to him for you." He didn't look more than nineteen, acne still dotting his cheeks. His helmet was askew, casting a shadow across his sharp chin.

"But who'll mind me, then?" I asked with a disarming smile.

He frowned and took the badge, studied it, as if he expected the man in the photograph to give him an answer. I'd never had an I.D. card with my photograph on it. Hadn't smiled for the camera, my expression a bit stern. Head slightly tilted, close-cropped brown hair riffled from being awakened abruptly. Was the twenty-five-year-old man in that picture handsome, or just an average-looking joe? Who was I to say? It was my face, I'd seen it in a mirror almost every day of my adult life, the image no longer had meaning or uniqueness; its features were neither attractive nor unpleasant. Just a man's face concealing secrets tamped down deep.

"I'll just give it to him later," Hughley said brightly.

"How are you gonna explain to him how you got it?"

"Can't I just tell him you gave it to me?"

I shook my head solemnly. "Better if I give it to him directly, Corporal. Let's just pop over to his office together, then I'll go to the mess."

"I don't know about that, sir, my orders are to, well, I'm supposed to just make sure—"

"You got your orders from Lieutenant Dahlen, right?" I took a guess.

"Yes."

"Nice enough fella?"

His nod was uneasy—an officer asking an enlisted man about another officer usually wasn't a promising conversation from the subordinate's point of view.

"Well, we don't want him to get in trouble with Colonel Latham, do we? What if the Colonel asks for the badge before you get a chance to give it to Lieutenant Dahlen? If we go over there now, that won't happen."

He looked unhappy but agreed. "Well, all right, I guess."

WE WALKED IN SILENCE. WHAT WAS THERE TO SAY? *THINK THEY'RE building a bomb here, Corporal?* Or, *Pleasant evening, huh?* Which it was, the evening air cool, the sky a purplish and dark blue, stars bright and proliferate—no ambient light here to dull their pinpoint brilliance. Early in the war, while the blackout was still in force in Washington, it was also possible to glimpse the galaxy beyond the undiluted sky. My work for the Russians sometimes caused insomnia, and on those sleepless nights, I'd slip outside to gaze at the stars. One night, I saw Mars, a red-washed orb burning a hole in the dark sky. I'd held the ember of my cigarette, struck at how the glow resembled the mottled surface of the planet. *Is Mars pleased with what he sees down here?* I remembered thinking.

"Well, I'll just be back in a jif, sir," Hughley told me when we'd reached the administration building.

"I'll wait right here, Corporal." I made a show of lighting a cigarette and leaned against a wooden post supporting the porch roof.

He nodded approvingly and hurried into the entrance. I gave him a beat, flicked my smoke into the air, and beelined to Latham's office. If he wasn't there, I'd have just enough time to scurry back to the entrance before Hughley returned to escort me to the officers' mess, where I'd figure out another way to find the colonel. But if my hunch was right, if the test was tomorrow, Latham would be burning the midnight oil.

His door was shut, but I heard the murmur of voices. I knocked, waited.

"Who is it?" Latham called.

I checked my sigh of relief—finding the colonel was only the first challenge.

"Lieutenant Voigt, sir—it's urgent that we speak."

No reply. He spoke rapidly but quietly to the other person, and I couldn't make out any words. *Open up, goddammit!* I thought nervously. Dahlen's office was close; Hughley might see me any minute. My head jerked at the sound of a door opening down the corridor. Just as I decided to barge in, Latham opened his door.

"Why aren't you in quarters?" he asked with a scowl.

My answer really had to zing, it had to fly high and take the colonel soaring—if it flopped, I was finished. So:

"Brode's got a contact on the base, sir, and he's gonna use him tonight to send more materials to the Russians."

"What? Who's his contact?"

"Me."

CHAPTER 33

AS LATHAM GAPED, I DARTED INTO HIS OFFICE.

"Sir, I can explain everything."

"I'll bet," the other man said. I couldn't tell if he was being ironic. He was on the gaunt side of thin, a belt cinching his baggy trousers, his shirt collar slack at the neck. Drawn cheeks, long nose, deep shadows under his eyes. His thinning, dark hair was cut short but somehow was still mussed, tufts that wouldn't stay combed. He looked like a man recovering from a long illness, pneumonia or tuberculosis, but his eyes were bright and lively, studying me. Sprawled in a wooden chair, his bony knees and elbows jutted in all directions. He reached to stub a cigarette in an ashtray perched precariously on the edge of Latham's desk and immediately took another from a packet of Chesterfields. So much for the colonel's allergy to tobacco.

Latham pushed the door shut, glaring at me.

"Sit," pointing at a chair in the corner. I obeyed, feeling like a miscreant schoolboy sent to the principal's office. If only my troubles were so trifling.

"I don't know if you need to hear this, Oppie," Latham said to his visitor.

He laughed. "Know how long that list is, all the things I don't need to hear but do? I take it our interloper is the visitor the Navy's been kind enough to send us?"

Latham nodded. "Maybe you want to get a little sleep before we head to the site?"

"Sleep remains an impossible dream, Jim, you know that. Besides, Kitty's all but banished me from the house until this is finished. Apparently I'm no longer convivial company."

Jim? Whoever this "Oppie" was, he knew Latham pretty well to speak to him with such familiarity, not to mention to smoke in the colonel's presence.

"Anyway, I'd better just get all the bad news about our *enfant terrible* at once," he added.

I took that to be a reference to Brode. If Latham had already told him about Brode being a Russian spy, then Oppie had to be important to the project. *Another scientist?* I wondered.

Latham sighed. "And I thought being department chair was a burden."

Oppie shot me a sly smile. "Did you know the intrepid Colonel Latham is professor of Eastern religions and cultures at the University of California?"

I shook my head, feeling light-headed. The moment was becoming surreal. Was I actually in my quarters, fitfully dreaming of a mysterious encounter between Latham and a skinny stranger named Oppie? Had a talking cat strolled in, I don't think I would have blinked.

"All right, Voigt, let's hear it." Latham returned to his chair, wrinkling his nose at the smoke drifting over his desk. He caught me looking longingly at the cigarette dangling from Oppie's long fingers and shook his head fiercely. "No, you can't smoke too, Lieutenant!"

"Yessir." I waited for him to introduce Oppie, but he gave no indication he wanted me to know who exactly his visitor was.

So I took a deep breath, pretended it was a long drag on a cigarette, and began.

"The N.K.V.D. believes I'm working for them, sir. In Washington, Commander Paslett and I worked up an operation. I contacted two known

Soviet agents and convinced them I would come here and get another copy of what Brode delivered in May."

Latham held up his hand to pause me and glanced at Oppie, who nodded. Which meant the colonel had already briefed him about Brode's trip to Washington and the diagram that everyone believed was missing along with Henry Himmel.

"And the N.K.V.D. didn't smell a plant?" Latham asked.

I pulled down my collar and displayed the still-healing burn on my neck.

"This is my souvenir from them seeing if I was lying."

"Electric shocks?" Oppie asked.

I nodded slightly. Just thinking about the experience set my hands trembling, my heart pounding; I gripped my thighs to hide the tremor.

"And you didn't crack?" This from Latham.

"Nossir."

He looked doubtful.

"Colonel, believe me, I'm not trying to sound like some kinda hero. I passed out, I wept like a baby, I pissed myself. I even begged them to shoot me to get it over with, the pain was so bad. But never once did I admit I was a plant.

"The other thing is, I've been working the Reds long enough that I've built up some credibility with them—they've been eyeing me as a possible turncoat for a while."

"Does Slater know any of this?"

"Hell no, sir—we wouldn't let the Bureau within ten miles of this operation."

"What about any other agencies?"

I assumed he meant the O.S.S. I shook my head.

"So is that why Slater's convinced you're a Red, because of your flirtations with the N.K.V.D.?"

An innocent-sounding question, and a trap.

"Nosir," I answered without hesitation. "Slater and the Bureau are after me for the reasons he gave—they really do think I became a commie as a kid." That was without a doubt, the rashest, most reckless thing I'd ever said: I'd just told an Army intelligence officer how I'd become a traitor! Is a confession for real if no one hears it as such?

Oppie honored my hazard with a laugh. "You aren't the only one, friend."

Latham shot him a look, then said to me, "Why didn't you or Paslett tell General Groves and me about your undercover assignment?"

"We didn't want that detail traveling across even a secure line, sir."

"What about after you arrived?"

"These things get out, sir, they always do."

Latham closed his eyes, tilted his head back, and briefly rubbed his temples as if he had a crushing headache. I expected a tongue-lashing. Instead:

"Brode, Voigt, Trinity . . . Brode, Voigt, Trinity," he murmured. Then he fell silent, but his eyes remained shut.

This was even stranger than a talking cat.

"Is he—is that meditation?" I whispered to Oppie, who looked amused.

"Jim, are you meditating?"

"You know I'm not," Latham said to the ceiling.

Oppie took a long drag on his cigarette. "When someone meditates, he doesn't speak. He's just thinking through the problems your revelation has caused."

"Not anymore," Latham sighed, straightening his head and opening his eyes. He looked at me, he looked at Oppie. Then back at me. "You"—now pointing—"show up claiming one of my top physicists is a Russian spy. Your evidence? You overheard a man with a similar voice brief a Soviet agent at a meeting in Washington in May. According to you, the spy also passed an envelope to that Soviet agent, who is now missing, along with the envelope. Also according to you, you're now posing as a Soviet spy in order to trick Brode into replacing the missing materials."

"Sir, check with Commander Paslett—"

"Don't interrupt me, Lieutenant."

"Sorry."

"Then I have a special agent from the F.B.I. show up claiming that you are in fact a Soviet spy. According to him, you were recruited by a communist immigrant, the father of your high school sweetheart who was shot by the police at a violent strike years before the war. So far, so good?"

"Well, no, sir, I wouldn't say anything Slater's said is good, it's all—"

"I'm not asking you to dispute the facts, Voigt, just to acknowledge if my summary of the situation, *as I see it*, is accurate."

"Understood, sir. Yes, so far, so good."

"And then, while you're in Santa Fe, you have an assignation with an attractive woman who Slater claims is your liaison to the Soviets and who you claim is just a tourist you met in a bar. Is that correct?"

"Assignation?" I asked.

"Sexual encounter," Oppie piped up.

"Well, uh, yes, all correct."

"Now, it is impossible for both you and Slater to be telling the truth. Either you are for real a Soviet spy, or you aren't; and either the woman you met in Santa Fe is your liaison to the Soviets, or she isn't."

"Two tautologies, Jim, nicely done," Oppie said with a smile.

I had no idea what he was talking about, and Latham ignored the comment.

I said, "I can make it very easy for you to determine who's telling the truth, sir."

"I'm listening."

"If I'm a Soviet spy, as Slater claims, would I ask you to have your scientists doctor the plan I get from Brode and pass on bum information to the Reds?"

"Indeed you might, in order to save your own skin and prevent your exposure as a Red spy. Your continued, undetected placement in naval intelligence might be worth more to the Soviets than obtaining an accurate replacement of the missing material from Brode."

Jesus H., he was good—he was seeing the problem from every side, like all good intelligence men do. Fortunately, knowing so much about how the Russians worked gave me an edge.

"Colonel, without knowing exactly what is being built here at Site Y, I can say without hesitation that whatever it might be, it is worth *much* more to the Russians than any single agent they might or might not have in our military. Now, I am *not* one of their agents, but if I were, they would not hesitate to kill me if I failed to return from New Mexico with what they want."

"He's got you there, Jim."

"Oppie, please!"

"Oh c'mon, having been on the receiving end of these chitchats, it's fun to watch one."

"Watch, yes; comment on, no."

Oppie shrugged ambivalently. His interruption was helpful—any distraction of Latham allowed me to press my case.

"Colonel, consider why Henry Himmel, the Russian who Brode met in Washington, is missing. We know the N.K.V.D. didn't kill him, otherwise they wouldn't need to replace the envelope. Our best explanation for why Himmel's missing is that he's in hiding, sir. He's been in the States an awful long time, we know—he knows—the Reds have a nasty reputation for getting rid of their people who've been in a foreign country for a while. He's worried his bosses will have him killed after he serves his purpose, so he's laying low until he can figure out a way to surface and give the N.K.V.D. the envelope without losing his head after the exchange."

Latham asked, "Any evidence Himmel has fled?"

"No hard evidence. Just precedent." I resisted the urge to keep talking. Latham might be quirky, an egghead, but he wouldn't be head of Army intelligence at Site Y if he didn't know what he was doing. He received the same reports O.N.I. did, and according to a recent memo from the O.S.S., the Russians had "liquidated a substantial share of their U.S. assets since late 1944." Not a phrase you easily forgot, not when "assets" meant "people" and "liquidated" meant "killed." After all, I was one of those assets—reading that report had brought sleepless nights.

A long, difficult silence. Then Latham said, "If you're correct, then Himmel can't afford to wait much longer to reestablish contact."

"Nosir."

"You're proposing we allow Brode to pass on the data to you, then skew it before you give it to the Russians."

"Yessir."

"Say we set this up. How will Brode know you're a Soviet spy? What if he suspects the truth, that you're an American posing as a spy? If he balks, we get nothing."

I felt as if I was trapped in an amusement park fun house, staring at trick mirrors. I was a Soviet spy, posing as an American intelligence officer, desperately trying to break free of my treason and become an honest man by posing as a Soviet spy to fool another spy. All my identities reflected back on me, warped and distorted; and yet I needed to see everything with clarity and precision. The colonel's instincts were excellent—Brode might smell a trap and play dumb.

"That's why you're gonna have Agent Slater arrest Gary Ackerly, sir."

"Explain."

"Every man we questioned today knows he's a suspect. Soon as they hear someone else has been identified as a spy, they relax."

"An old trick, that. Brode's too smart to fall for it."

"Not when I tell him I set Ackerly up so that I could approach Brode."

"Again, he'll see it as part of the ruse."

"Not after he hears what the N.K.V.D. ordered me to do if he doesn't cooperate."

"And what's that?"

"Kill him."

I'd hoped this line would land like a knockout punch in the tenth round—it did. Latham flinched, Oppie whispered *Jesus*.

"For real?" Latham asked quietly.

"Absolutely. In Washington, I heard Brode tell Himmel that he was out, that he was done spying for them. The Reds aren't happy about that, not at all, and they told me to kill Brode if he doesn't cough up another copy. Brode thinks the Russians can't touch him as long as he's at Site Y. If I show up, identify myself as a Red spy, and tell him the Russians want me to kill him if he doesn't produce a copy, he'll be too rattled to think it's all part of a sting." That wasn't true—I hadn't been ordered to kill Brode—but it sounded plausible, given the way the Russians worked.

Latham thought for a moment. "Even if this works, what happens if Himmel comes forward and gives the Soviets the original data? Or they take it from Himmel if they find him. Then they'll know what you gave them is baloney."

"That's the beauty of this plan, sir. As long as we get our documents in the Reds' hands before Himmel, they'll believe we gave them the real McCoy. They'll think Himmel's materials are false—they'll suspect him of trying to dupe them. He's already untrustworthy because he fled. No matter what, they're going to kill him and tell their scientists that what *I* gave them is legitimate. Instead of being able to copy what's being done here at Site Y, the Russians will be headed in the wrong direction."

The colonel didn't answer. As he had done previously, he closed his eyes, tilted his head back, and murmured, this time too softly for Oppie or me to hear. I waited in dread, not daring to look at Oppie. Instead I stared at my hands pressed tight against my thighs.

Finally, "What do you think, Oppie?"

"If he can get Brode to play along, we could modify the . . . nim . . . item to appear real. As you know, there's a . . . nim . . . process we attempted that was quite time-consuming and ultimately failed, so we could—"

"Voigt doesn't need to know about that," Latham interrupted crisply. Given Oppie's struggle to find the right words—where others said *er* or *um*, he said *nim*—the subject was clearly sensitive.

"Right, sorry."

To me Latham said, "All right, we'll do it."

"One other thing, sir. To look convincing to Brode, I need to be armed."

He nodded. "I'll order your sidearm returned to you."

Oppie crushed his umpteenth cigarette of the evening. "You're in for a memorable night, my friend."

Memorable didn't even begin to describe it.

CHAPTER 34

HORTLY BEFORE MIDNIGHT, I LEFT SITE Y IN A TRUCK WITH SIX MPs. *Get some rest*, the colonel had advised when I'd left his office. Fat chance, I'd thought, and yet, as soon as I'd stretched out on my bunk, I'd fallen asleep again, waking only when my alarm rang. I should have been a jangle of nerves, keyed-up and dread-weighted—was I too exhausted physically to appreciate my predicament? Or was I beyond the point of caring, had I resigned myself to failure, to exposure, to ruin, to prison, to the gas chamber? My plan—no, my machinations—seemed so fantastical, so absurd and implausible, that perhaps my body was giving up on my mind and seeking out a last few hours of comfort and timelessness through sleep. During Guadalcanal, the *Washington Post* had published a story about Marines trudging into battle, submissive and dead-eyed. I still remembered the description that had gotten the correspondent recalled and the desk editor fired: "The men appear resigned to death, their only hope that the end is swift and they feel but fleeting pain." Had I fallen into such hopelessness?

Jouncing in the rear of the 4x4 with the MPs, I shook off my selfish self-pity. I wasn't a nineteen-year-old Marine facing Japs in battle—I was a twenty-five-year-old officer who had made the choice to betray his country. The Marine accepts his orders, even if they guarantee his death, because he must; but I was chasing a golden opportunity. If I succeeded, I would negate my treason. I would, on my own, keep the Russians from learning the secret of Site Y. Brode would be arrested, we'd dupe the Reds with a fake. Wasn't that enough to absolve me? That I regretted my decision to help the Reds, that I'd repented my sin (if only to myself) wasn't enough; I must also right the wrongs.

Our destination was the Alamogordo Bombing Range, but the MPs called it Trinity. They didn't tell me why, I didn't ask. My presence had been explained simply as "additional security"; they didn't ask why a naval officer was riding with them. Indeed, they ignored me during the bumpy ride. The flare of a Zippo or a match lit our faces as we chain-smoked, the only illumination in the dark truck. A light rain tinked the canvas canopy. The MPs weren't happy about their orders. Apparently they'd just spent a week at Trinity and had only just returned to Site Y. Trinity was hot, really hot—"fucking blazing," one man muttered. In the middle of the night, with rain falling, it was hard for me to imagine the heat the men were complaining about. "Les jes hope we're outta thare before that sun's too high," an MP drawled. Which told me that whatever was about to happen would happen at dawn. Even before dawn? Why else leave at midnight?

The truck rattled to a stop at a compound of buildings on flat hard clay traced with countless tire tracks. Metal roofs painted gray, tar-papered walls, casement windows—Army construction, just like at Site Y. Two wooden windmills stood like sentries, the blades turning briskly.

"Jesus Christ, it's gonna storm," an MP grumbled as he studied the sky. The cloud cover did look low and dense, and the wind was stronger than it had been at Site Y.

Latham had told me to report to the McDonald House. The MP with the drawl pointed the way. He and his comrades headed to a barracks, their helmets glistening from the rain. No utility lines to be seen, but the compound was well lighted. On eaves, rows of bulbs served as miniature streetlights, illuminating the paths between the buildings. There were no curtains on the windows, and every room was lit, a hive of activity, men in military uniform and civvies crossing back and forth.

The McDonald House was a home, a ranchstead with a wide veranda. No doubt the McDonalds had been paid off and moved out, whether they wanted to leave or not. A stocky MP checked my badge, grunted for me to wait, and went inside. Latham returned with him and motioned me to follow. We walked through an expansive living room with a plank floor and stucco walls. Flimsy plywood partitions had been put up to create workspaces. Men were bent over folding tables, some using slide rules, others adjusting knobs on consoles with meters. Skeins of cables ran along the baseboards of the halls and dangled from sixteen penny nails.

"In here," Latham said.

I followed him into a small room that must have been a bedroom. Now it held three desks and a safe, and the lone window had been boarded up. An upright metal fan stood in a corner but it wasn't on. Despite the hour, the room was stuffy—no surprise, since each desk was occupied. Latham pointed as he made terse introductions: Captain Gerald Foley, Lieutenant Paul Jarowsky, Dwayne Meacham. Foley and Jarowsky were Latham's security liaisons at Trinity; Meacham was one of the assistants to the chief of the Trinity scientific team, Dr. Kenneth Bainbridge.

"They've all been briefed," Latham said. "Captain Foley will catch you up on the situation here." He sat in a chair by the door. There was no other place to sit, so I remained standing.

"Right, okay," Foley said. He scratched his temple and looked at me before continuing. He looked about thirty. Square-jawed, broad nose, wide forehead, reddish-blond hair parted precisely. "Might as well start with your biggest problem, Lieutenant." He tried a grin.

I obliged with a tight smile. He had no idea what my biggest problem was.

"The problem is, Brode's in the arming party. Which means, uh, that he and several other individuals, they, uh, they need to—"

"—they need to complete certain duties in places where you can't be present, Voigt," Latham finished for Foley, who looked relieved. Briefing someone at Trinity who didn't know what was going on was clearly not an everyday occurrence.

"Which limits my time with Brode," I said.

"Exactly." This from Latham.

"But we have a solution," Foley continued. "Dwayne is going to ask Brode to check some figures on the humidity measurements of the H.E.'s at the tower—" He broke off abruptly and looked anxiously at the colonel.

"Just stick to the facts Voigt needs to know to do his job," Latham told his subordinate.

H.E.'s—high explosives. A tower—was it for some kind of new bomb? What other job would an arming party have but to ready a bomb? Distracted, I remembered what Latham had told me when I arrived at Site Y. *The purpose of Site Y, what's being done here, I ask you to put that out of your head.*

Foley's *yessir* to Latham brought me back. "So while Brode's checking these figures, here in the ranch house, you'll slip into the room where he's working."

"That'll look fishy," I said.

"Everything looks fishy at this point," Latham said. "You've never been to Trinity—Brode's been here a hundred times if he's been here once. You only just arrived to Site Y. Brode's a smart one, and around here, that's saying a lot. The best we can do is give you a rock-solid reason to be here in the first place."

Jarowsky cleared his throat. "And we've only had a few hours to come up with that reason." He was a few years younger than Foley. Black hair in a crew cut, pudgy chin. Narrow-set eyes gave him a slightly malicious appearance. "The challenge is, how do we avoid making it look like you're a plant, right? As the colonel said, you just got here, so if you suddenly sidle up to Brode and tell him, 'Hey, guess what, I'm a Red, too!' he's not likely to give you the secret handshake no matter how good you are at pretending to be a commie. Right?"

"Right," I promptly agreed.

"So this is what we came up with: you're here to interrogate Doctor Oppenheimer."

I stared blankly.

"You met Doctor Oppenheimer in my office today," Latham said.

Oppie, of course—short for Oppenheimer. "How will me claiming to be here to question this Oppenheimer convince Brode he's not being set up?"

Foley held up a thick black binder. "Doctor Oppenheimer had some, uh, dubious connections when he was younger. And his wife, Kitty, oh boy, lemme tell—" A glare from Latham cut off that sentence. "Anyway, what you're gonna do, Voigt, is, you're gonna memorize everything in this binder—you gotta know more about Oppenheimer than he knows about himself. Because you're gonna tell Brode you've been sent here to reinvestigate Oppenheimer as well as Ackerly, Fuchs—everyone you helped interrogate today, including Brode."

"I didn't question anyone—I was just a silent observer."

"That's actually good—makes you look more authoritative. Like you're letting the local yokels do their thing before you take charge and do it right. No offense, sir." Foley smiled weakly at the colonel.

"None taken. Just part of the cover story, after all."

"That's right," Foley said. "You're gonna tell Brode that the brass in Washington think something hinky's happening down here, that the Reds have penetrated the project."

"Which sadly is the truth," remarked Meacham, who hadn't said anything yet. We all looked at him. He was middle-aged, his brown hair going gray. Reading glasses perched on the end of his nose, along with his off-white shirt and red striped tie, gave him a teacherly appearance.

"Let's stay focused on what Voigt has to do," Latham said after a moment of uncomfortable silence. Translation: *If Voigt succeeds, the Reds get nothing.*

"Anyway, you'll tell Brode the brass don't trust *us*"—Foley circled his finger at himself, the colonel, and Jarowsky—"to question Oppenheimer because we've known him too long."

"This explains why you just got here and why you're here tonight at Trinity," Latham added.

I nodded. It was a good story, plausible without being complicated, a passable cover. But only if I could learn my lines. I walked over to Foley and took the binder from him.

"How long do I have?" I asked him.

"One hour," Latham answered for him.

"Jesus, that's not much time. Sir."

"Then you better get started, Lieutenant. The ruse we have for Brode only flies if we bring him here before the arming party heads out."

CHAPTER 35

J AROWSKY TOOK ME TO ONE OF THE PLYWOOD WORKSPACES IN THE living room. A folding table was buried beneath precarious stacks of clipboards, rolled charts, and more black binders. One bump, and the whole mess would plummet to the floor.

"Don't touch anything," Jarowsky joked. He checked his watch. "See you at oh-one-twenty."

I sat down in a battered folding metal chair and carefully slid my knees under the table. Fortunately, the previous occupant had managed to squeeze an ashtray onto the table. I lit up, opened the binder, started cramming. Facts like fallen leaves, strewn across a vast lawn, collected pell-mell in the blades of my rushing rake . . .

J. Robert Oppenheimer, born April 22, 1904. *J* for Julius, his father; but he never used that name. Only Robert or Bob. A Dutch scientist nicknamed him Opje, that got Americanized to Oppie. Upper-class German Jewish family, New York, private schools, Harvard. Graduate work overseas in laboratories in Cambridge and Göttingen. At twenty-four, he was already a professor at the University of California at Berkeley and at the California Institute of Technology in Pasadena, some sort of dual appointment. Brilliant physicist, producing important papers one after another. How quantum mechanics explains molecule movements. The mass limits of certain stars' neutron cores. All Greek to me, the science; but the bare biographical details weren't much more useful. Facts you could get from *Who's Who* or a puff profile in a magazine. J. Robert Oppenheimer, present; Oppie, absent.

Rake, rake. Away from the lab and the blackboard, he read French poetry and Dostoevsky. His wealthy father bought him good cars, he drove recklessly, even wrecked a Chrysler racing a train. He socialized with his students, made them omelets in his apartment and treated them to expensive dinners. Money was no worry, his parents supplemented his salary. Adjectives and impressions from field interviews with friends, colleagues, neighbors, and landlords offered glimpses into his personality. *Charming. Intense. A true Renaissance man, quoting poetry in one breath, doing mathematics in the next.* And this: *He's popular and well liked, but even at a crowded party he seems like the loneliest man there.* That comment stuck as I read about an incident from his time at the Cambridge laboratory, where he left an adulterated apple on his tutor's desk. The man wasn't poisoned, but Oppenheimer, just twenty-one, was almost expelled. Was it homesickness? Depression, mental instability? That mix of melodrama and impetuousness that afflicts the young? All the theories and explanations in the binder missed the symbolic significance of the deed, I thought. Was a deeper bite into the fruit of knowledge really what he was meant to do with his life? He kept to the science, yes, but at Berkeley he also learned Sanskrit to read an ancient Hindu text known as the Bhagavad Gita. (That explained the friendship with Latham.) A genius mastering the science of the universe who was also entranced by that same universe's most insoluble mystery: Why are we here? The loneliest man, indeed.

Rake, rake. At age thirty, a sudden interest in politics. Radical politics, including communism. "There had to be a girl," I murmured, an image of Delphine consuming my attention, as brilliant and blinding as a lightning flash. Delphine watching me over the top of her textbook as we studied—attempted to study—in the school library, a secretive smile on her lips. She tilts the book cover (*Chemistry for the Modern Age*) to reveal another book: Edna St. Vincent Millay's translation of *Flowers of Evil*. Brings the book upright, continues reading, her lips now moving silently as she savors every word, every line. Will she pass our chemistry test? She doesn't care, I don't care, I give up trying to learn about alkalis and wonder if later, once we desert the library and find a quiet corner, will Delphine whisper a line from Baudelaire in my ear, her breath hot, her tongue like an electric charge—

"Oppie, Oppie," I muttered, bringing myself back to Trinity. Sure enough, he had tumbled into radicalism via romance, during a long relationship with a woman named Jean Tatlock. Daughter of a Chaucer scholar, she was a full-time medical student and part-time communist, penning indignant articles for the *Western Worker* and marching for the rights of migrant farm workers. She recognized the evils of Hitler and Mussolini long before most Americans did, advocating the Popular Front. Fight fascism, empower the workers, defer the revolution—that cocktail intoxicated Oppenheimer. He attended rallies, arranged for Jewish relatives in Germany to emigrate to the States, and cut checks to the Abraham Lincoln Brigade and to the farm workers ("Oppie for Okies," I couldn't help but joke to myself). He and Jean socialized with a bevy of California communists. He sponsored a German-born longshoreman named Bernard Peters for graduate study of physics and made him a note taker for one of his classes. With fellow Berkeley professor Haakon Chevalier, he discussed Marxism and French literature. When Scottish-born doctor Tom Addis asked him to give money directly to the Party, Oppenheimer happily obliged. His younger brother Frank, to whom he was close, joined the Party—the binder even had Frank's roll number and false name (Frank Folsom). No doubt about it, by the late 1930s the brilliant, popular physicist J. Robert Oppenheimer was a radical.

Oppenheimer loved Jean—more than once, he proposed—but she was given to bouts of depression and sharp mood swings. In 1939, she broke off the engagement. Soon Oppenheimer was seen in the company of a twenty-nine-year-old married woman named Katherine "Kitty" Harrison. Physician Richard Stewart Harrison was her third husband. Her biography read like the notes on a character in a melodrama. Her mother was descended from European royalty—Kitty's uncle was the king of Belgium—yet she grew up in Pittsburgh. Her first husband was apparently a dope fiend and a homosexual; they were divorced after just a few months. Her second husband, Joe Dallet, had spurned his wealthy upbringing to become a long-shoreman and communist organizer. Kitty embraced his politics, living in abject poverty and selling the *Daily Worker* on the streets of Youngstown, Ohio. The deprivations proved too much, and she bolted. They reconciled in Europe when Joe came to fight in the Spanish Civil War, but he was killed in battle. In November 1938, she married Harrison; by the summer of 1940, she was pregnant with Oppenheimer's child. Harrison magnani-mously agreed to divorce Kitty so she could marry Oppenheimer.

I couldn't help but marvel at Oppenheimer's elegant waltz with the Reds, such a vastly different experience from my own. Where Oppenheimer had written checks and attended lectures, I had pilfered classified documents and learned to do dead drops. For him, communists were lovers and friends, fellow party-goers and do-gooders. He welcomed doctors and dock workers alike into his home. For me, communists were always pseudonymous fellow spies and taciturn, distrustful Russian-born operatives for the N.K.V.D. I led a furtive, illegal, dangerous life, one locked far away from my life as Lieutenant (j.g.) Ellis Voigt, U.S.N.; Oppenheimer glided effortlessly and openly between his radical, personal, and professional realms. He was the star guest at a never-ending garden party, while I was the mole burrowed beneath the green grass. Measuring the contrast didn't embitter me—I'd made my choices, I had to live with the consequences—but did people like Oppenheimer ever wonder about the subterranean world the communists had tunneled right beneath their feet?

Another question: had he ever been a dues-paying communist like his younger brother? The damnedest thing was it didn't matter if he was on the Party's roll, not with lovers and associates like Tatlock and the rest: Oppenheimer should never have been cleared for a military project. Hell, my only known connection to communism was Rosario Moreno, Delphine's father, a man I hadn't seen in eight years. Yet Agent Slater wouldn't let go of that slender straw—he was determined to bring me down, and as much as I hated him, I couldn't deny (to myself) that he was right: I'd turned

Red because of what happened to Delphine. If all went well, Slater would never expose me, but Oppenheimer had already been exposed as a major security risk. His presence at Site Y, not to mention his friendship with the head of security, meant that he was indispensable. Without Oppenheimer, there was no Trinity, no test, no secret weapon, whatever it was.

At a quarter after one, I closed the binder and lit yet another Lucky. My ninth of the hour, the butts in the ashtray told me. I was a quick study, but I didn't have a photographic memory. Even if I did, spewing facts about Oppenheimer wouldn't impress Brode. Latham was right, Brode was a smart one in an already crowded field. More important, he was shrewd. Wasn't enough to be a genius to get away with spying for the Reds as long as Brode had, you also had to be clever, a natural reader of people, with a keen nose for sniffing out their ulterior motives. To earn Brode's trust—or at least to avoid his suspicion—I needed to act like I had nothing to prove when it came to Oppenheimer. It helped that my "role" as an outside security investigator was a secondary one. My leading part was to play a Russian spy, and wasn't that an assignment that needed no rehearsal?

Jarowsky fetched me just as I was stubbing out my cigarette.

"Ready?"

I nodded. He took the binder and I followed him back down the hallway.

"Brode will be in here in a few minutes," he told me, pointing at the room next to the one where I'd been briefed. "The door will be closed. Go in without knocking, close the door immediately. You'll have five minutes tops. Slip out, shut the door, come back to our room. Don't say anything til you get a signal—we can't take a chance of Brode hearing you. Doctor Bainbridge will be coming to get Brode just a few minutes after you leave him, so it won't be long."

"Understood."

We went into the briefing room to wait. Latham, Meacham, and Foley were gone. I didn't ask where and Jarowsky didn't tell me.

"What's the first thing you're gonna say to Brode?" he asked.

"'Get to the ballpark much here?'"

"Funny guy. For real, though."

"How's this: 'They think I'm here to interview Oppenheimer.'"

Jarowsky thought that over. "Yeah, that's good. Gives your cover but gets him thinking, too."

"Thanks."

He lit a cigarette, so did I; we smoked in silence. After a moment, he stood and turned on the fan. The papers on the desks undulated with each pass of the fan head.

"Colonel Latham really allergic to tobacco smoke?" I asked.

Jarowsky shrugged. "Can't smoke around him, so yeah, I guess so."

"Reason I ask is, when I met with him at his office at Site Y, Oppenheimer was there and he chain-smoked the whole time."

He smiled. "Well then, lotsa rules get bent for the professor."

Indeed they did. And who was I to question that? I thought about why I'd persuaded Latham to return my weapon, now concealed in a holster beneath my left arm. Even if the Russians wanted me to kill Brode, I couldn't shoot him, not here, not during the test. But what-ifs kept scratching.

What if Brode panicked after giving me the copy I'd been ordered to get? What if he tried to take it back from me, believing that the diagram was his only leverage with the Russians? What if during that struggle, Brode tried to seize my weapon, tried to shoot me?

And what if I shot him first?

Wild what-ifs, for sure—Brode wasn't the panicky type. But if I had the opportunity to shoot Brode unobserved, if I was confident I could convince Latham that a struggle had occurred, should I kill the young physicist? Every word I said to Brode that night to get the diagram would be learned by the F.B.I. during their interminable interrogation of Brode. Getting him locked up was all part of my plan, but I hadn't considered the risks of my contact. To get Brode to talk, Slater and the Bureau would let him know that they didn't trust me; to save his skin, Brode would feed their suspicions. Jesus, he might even lie and tell the Bureau I had admitted to being a longtime Red agent.

But if Brode was dead, he couldn't tell the Bureau anything.

Stop it! I resolved to banish that thought from my mind. That's how murderers got caught, by cooking up self-serving schemes that only appeared plausible to themselves. Killing Brode would make me look far more guilty than anything Brode told the Bureau, true or false. A yarn about a struggle, the gun going off, would unravel immediately. No matter what, I had to let Brode live and trust that a successful operation to trick the Russians was all that I needed to block the Bureau from learning who I really was.

The door swung open, Foley nodded curtly at Jarowsky, and disappeared. Jarowsky looked at me. He held up his wrist, tapped his watch, and raised his right hand, fingers splayed. *Five minutes.* I ticked my chin and stood.

As instructed, I opened the door to the adjacent room and strode in, shutting the door behind me. Brode was leaning over a desk and looked up abruptly. His surprise turned to recognition—he remembered me from the interrogation at Site Y.

"Why are you here?" A challenge, but calmly said. His dark eyebrows were arched, his black hair precisely parted and shiny with Brilliantine.

I was just about to say *They think I'm here to interview Oppenheimer* when the obvious connection finally hit me: What if Brode and Oppenheimer were working together to deliver the secret of Site Y to the Russians?

CHAPTER 36

'M—THEY THINK I'M HERE TO INTERVIEW OPPENHEIMER," I GOT OUT.

"Oh, you're a reporter, not a sailor?" His smugness was no act—he looked every bit as self-assured as he sounded. He deftly flipped shut the binder he'd been examining and folded his arms, his gaze first on my face, then my nameplate.

If Oppenheimer's a spy, he can make sure the Russians get a correct diagram . . . I tried to shake that dreaded thought, tried to focus. Forced myself to step closer and meet his stare. I said, "To diffuse the Uranium-235, use uranium hexafluoride and a metal filter with submicroscopic perforations, do not use a mass spectrometer." The exact words he had said in Washington while I covertly listened. I still had no idea what that statement meant, but I knew it was the key to what was about to happen here at Trinity. And quoting it was a surefire way to get Brode's attention.

His haughty grin remained. "I have no idea what you're talking about."

How can I pull this off if Oppenheimer's dirty? Dismay—the crush of looming defeat—distracted me. I felt sucker-punched, but is it even possible to sucker-punch yourself? I'd been a Soviet spy for eight years. How could I have deluded myself into believing that self-extraction was possible?

"No idea, huh?" I scoffed, buying myself time to regain my concentration. "You can drop the act, Brode—I heard you say those exact words to your Russian contact at the Automat in Washington in May. The old man in work clothes close to your booth? His toolbox was a wireless rig, and I was in the kitchen listening on a headset."

The flickering of his eyes hinted at a mind racing through all possible responses, like a chess master surprised by a bold move from an inferior opponent.

"Whatever you may or may not have observed in Washington is irrelevant," he said. "There are just two salient facts. One, you didn't say anything about this alleged Automat encounter during today's joke of an interrogation. Two, you're here, alone, to make this charge at a most inopportune moment."

Translation: *My earlier silence and now sudden appearance were highly irregular, definitely out of step with protocol.* Brode was savvy enough to wait for me to tell him why I was violating procedure.

As much as I needed to engage Brode, I couldn't avoid more dreaded thoughts. Brode had been able to elude identification as a spy for years, and Oppenheimer had been cleared to direct this project despite his Red-stained past, making them the perfect cell. Both were genius physicists, carrying out work only a handful of other scientists could comprehend. The two could spend—and no doubt had spent—countless hours working together without raising suspicions. Oppenheimer knew he couldn't leave Site Y without being followed and watched constantly, so had Brode served as the courier? Meanwhile Oppenheimer's comfortable relationship with Colonel Latham eased security concerns. If General Groves ever questioned Oppenheimer's loyalty, Latham was there to vouch for him. With Brode as his coconspirator, Oppenheimer could focus on his work, behaving and talking like an innocent man. Was that why the N.K.V.D. had agreed to release me after torturing me, so that I could come to Los Alamos and, without even being aware, receive a coded message from Brode that

Oppenheimer wasn't under suspicion? Maybe the diagram Brode was supposed to give me would include a notation, an equation or a sequence of numbers, that would tell the Russians that Oppenheimer was safe.

"You forgot a third fact," I said, trying again to push those what-ifs out of my mind.

"Did I?"

"Oppenheimer."

"Yes, you said 'they' think you're here to interrogate him. Identify *them*."

"Army intelligence and the F.B.I."

"Why aren't they doing the interrogations—why you?"

I glanced at my watch. Jesus—I'd already wasted two of my five minutes. "I haven't got the time to tell you why. Here's all you need to know: I'm one of you."

"One of what?"

"Don't play dumb, Brode!" My urgency wasn't feigned, and my surging panic at running out of time finally dispelled the worry about Oppenheimer being a spy—I could only deal with that potential snafu if I persuaded Brode to believe me. "Did you hear that Gary Ackerly's been arrested?"

"Of course."

"I arranged that to keep the Bureau busy. While Special Agent Slater's raking Ackerly over the coals, I'm free to meet with you, but we've only got a few minutes. Latham sent me here to trick you into believing I'm a Red spy so that you'll make a copy of the diagram you delivered to your contact in Washington. Your contact disappeared after that meeting, and so did the diagram. What Latham doesn't know—what no one knows—is that I'm with the Russians too, I have been for years. Latham's going to have the replacement diagram you give me doctored, and I'll deliver it to the Russians. Before he does that, I'll make sure I have a true copy to hand over."

There it was, in one dense paragraph, the entirety of everyone's scheming: the N.K.V.D. and their spies; U.S. military intelligence and the F.B.I.; above all, me. So much information, so swiftly delivered, would cow and confuse even a smart man, who would sputter questions. What happened to the original diagram? What happened to my contact? How did you fool

Latham, how did you get orders to come to Site Y? How much does the F.B.I. know? Can I really trust you?

But Brode only had one query:

"What was their penultimate question?"

For a split second, I was lost—he'd given me no context. What was he asking? Then I got it. *They* meant the Party's spy recruiters, who'd screened me, and, of course, him. We all went through the rigorous testing and interrogations alone, but the process was too organized to be ad hoc. What I was asked, he was asked; if I answered correctly, he would know, without any further corroboration, that I, too, was a Red spy. And the penultimate—that is, second-to-last—question had been—

"Are you ready to say good-bye to your family forever," I answered Brode in an even voice.

"Very good, you pass. Now I have a surprise for you, Lieutenant Voigt: I'm going to arrange for you to be part of the arming party."

That was a surprise—a shock, even—but I checked the urge to ask why. I sure as hell wasn't as smart and sly as Brode, but I sensed his reason: he wanted the N.K.V.D. to know just how important he was to the Site Y project. He wanted an eyewitness to his part, either to protect himself from the Russians or because of his vanity. Maybe both.

His motive didn't matter, I reminded myself. Being a part of the arming party, whatever its duties, helped me. Such evidence of Brode's trust would convince Latham and his subordinates that I had succeeded, and that would help keep Slater at bay a little while longer.

As I slipped out the door to return to Latham's office, I couldn't help but remember the last question my communist recruiters had asked me and Brode: Are you ready to die for the Party?

"HE SAID WHAT?" LATHAM EXCLAIMED.

"He wants me to be part of the arming party," I repeated.

"Jesus Christ," Jarowsky swore.

Meacham and Foley looked equally unhappy. After leaving Brode, I had returned to the office. As Jarowsky had instructed me, I had said nothing until we heard Brode leave the room next door and go down the hallway. The silence had seemed interminable, though it had only lasted a few minutes. Seated at their desks, the four men had tried to keep working, their attention directed toward papers and folders spread out before them, but they were just as edgy as I was.

"There's no reason for you to be in the arming party," Meacham said. "Everyone has a specific purpose, all highly specialized tasks, and Voigt isn't—well, he's just not qualified for anything they're doing!"

"Let's not worry about that for the moment," Latham said. "Why does he want you there, Voigt?"

"As an eyewitness, sir. Either out of caution or vanity, probably both, he wants me to tell the Russians everything I saw him do. This will show how vital he is to the project."

"My God, you can't be telling the Russians what you saw!" This from Foley.

"Of course I won't do that. All I'm gonna do is, I'm going to hand over the doctored diagram to my contact in the N.K.V.D. without saying a word."

"Will they let you do that?" Jarowsky asked.

"Sure. Once I tell them the F.B.I. is watching my every move, they won't wanna come near me." Volunteering a reminder that the Bureau didn't trust me was risky, but I needed Latham to agree to put me in the arming party.

"What if they try to contact you later for a face-to-face?" Foley asked.

"After I deliver the doctored diagram, Captain, believe you me, I'm getting outta this operation for good. My job will be done, and I'm coming out from under my cover." Speaking the truth, even if my listeners didn't know the *full* truth, was a relief.

"Colonel, I think it's a good sign Brode wants Voigt by his side—it shows he trusts him," Jarowsky put in. I silently thanked him—having him make this observation rather than me gave it added validity.

"Brode bought your line about being here to question Oppenheimer?" Latham was watching me closely.

I had to answer carefully. After Brode was arrested, his interrogation would go over every detail of our encounter. Given how hard Slater was charging at me, I couldn't risk leaving holes in my story. Better to tell the truth—at least a part of the truth that would help keep my secret buried.

"I started to tell him, then I changed direction."

Latham grunted his dissatisfaction.

"Five minutes wasn't enough time to sell that story, sir. Instead I told him flat-out that no one knows I'm actually a Red spy and that I'm here to get another copy of the diagram he delivered in May."

"Goddammit, Voigt, we went over this—Brode's too smart to believe that! He'll just think you're posing."

"That's why he challenged me straightaway. And what I said satisfied him that I'm really a Red spy."

"What did he ask?" This from Jarowsky.

"He said, 'What was their penultimate question?'"

"D'hell does that mean?" Foley asked.

"He was referring to the second-to-last question the Party asks of its spy recruits as they come to the end of their screening. The question is, Are you ready to say good-bye to your family forever?"

"How do you know this?" Latham asked.

"O.N.I. had a source, a former communist spy, who revealed this to us. It's also something I'm sure the Bureau knows."

Latham nodded slowly. Would he verify this detail about communist spycraft with Slater? Despite the obvious hazards to myself, I hoped he would. Once again, I recalled the story of the mountain climber who had survived a fall into a dark, icy crevasse by wriggling through it backwards. That true-life adventure had inspired me to convince Commander Paslett to let me get picked up by the N.K.V.D. after I'd spent desperate days on the lam from them. Only by tunneling deeper into my secret could I escape it. It was as if I was turning my real identity inside out: by constantly asserting that I was only *pretending* to be a Red spy, I could make the assertion true.

But was I being too clever? O.N.I. did *not* have a former communist spy as a source, unless you counted me. Upon my return to Washington, I would have to fabricate such a document, predate it, and slip it into our central files. And if I didn't make it back to Washington, the fictional report wouldn't matter—because that would mean I'd been exposed.

"All right, let's set it up," Latham announced. He looked at Meacham. "Dwayne, you better tell Doctor Bainbridge he's a got a new member of the arming party."

CHAPTER 37

WE FOUND BAINBRIDGE IN THE LIVING ROOM OF THE RANCH HOUSE. He looked about forty, maybe older, his thin brown hair combed back from a broad forehead. He wore a khaki work shirt and brown trousers. A quiet but intense conversation with another man kept him from noticing me and Meacham, who finally cleared his throat and said, "Ken?"

He looked up from the chart both men had been looking at. "Yes?"

"Lieutenant Voigt"—Meacham ticked his chin at me—"has been added to the arming party."

I braced for bluster, for protest, but Bainbridge's doleful expression didn't change. "Oh?"

"Colonel Latham thinks it would be helpful."

"Of course." Bainbridge looked at me, his thin lips pursed. "Can you drive?"

"Yes."

"Then you'll be our driver."

This distressed Meacham. "This is Lieutenant Voigt's first visit here, he doesn't know the site, maybe he should—"

"Dwayne, there's only one road where we're going—he can hardly get us lost."

Meacham shook his head unhappily but didn't argue. "Is the schedule still the same?"

"Yes," Bainbridge said. "You better—"

"I know, I know," Meacham interrupted. He motioned for me to follow him. We went out the door and into the yard. A light rain still fell. The lights burning in the house and outbuildings only made the night appear even more oppressive. No stars, no lights in the distance, just depthless darkness.

"The car's right here," Meacham said, pointing to a late-model Plymouth coated in wet reddish grit. The windshield was clean only where the wipers reached, which irritated Meacham.

"Goddammit." He yanked a rag from his back pocket and tried to swipe away the grit, to little effect.

"Look, Meacham, why don't you leave that alone, the windshield's fine."

He wheeled around, glaring. "Do you have any idea what's about to happen here? Everything is planned down to the last second, everything must be done exactly right, there's no margin for error. None! Yet here you are, being assigned to drive the arming party to the tower when you have no clue what's going on! You don't even know the way!"

Meacham wasn't so much angry at me as he was overwhelmed by weeks of stressful work and anxiety over what was about to happen. I let him rant, nodding sympathetically. *What is going to happen?* I wasn't supposed to know—Latham had been very clear about that when I arrived at Site Y—but wasn't the cat out of the bag now?

"Let's check the car, Meacham," I said when he finished. "We'll check the fuel and temp, okay?"

"Okay."

We got in and shut the doors. We left the windows up. The engine fired right away, and I turned on the dome light so we could see the gauges. The tank was full, the temperature and electrical gauges were both normal. I shut the engine off.

"See? All good."

"We should check the tires. If you were to get a flat—"

"We'll check the tires. But first I need you to tell me what's going to happen, what I should expect."

Meacham looked stricken. "You're not cleared for that."

"I'm not asking for a full report, I just wanna know where we're going and when. Just give me what I need to know so I'm not wondering what the hell is going on while I'm also trying to accomplish my task with Brode."

"All right." He looked at his watch, sighed deeply. "At oh-four-twenty, the arming party will leave for the zero point, which is two and a half miles north. Lieutenant Jarowsky, Doctor Bainbridge, Doctor Kistiakowsky, and Doctor Brode make up the arming party. Once you reach the zero point, Bainbridge, Kistiakowsky, and Brode have several jobs to do at the tower. We've estimated it will take them fifteen minutes to finish. Jarowsky will have a field telephone in case communication is needed with us. You should remain in the car and leave the engine running.

"Once the arming party is ready to leave, you'll continue up the road to Shelter A, which is thirty thousand feet northwest of the zero point. Colonel Latham will be there—if there's anything else he wants you to do, he'll tell you. Zero time is oh-five-thirty."

My mind raced. Shelter A, our final destination, was more than five miles away from the zero point. I was no Einstein, but this problem only required simple deduction. A weapon—a bomb—was in place at the zero point, most likely at the top of the tower Meacham had mentioned. The arming party—three physicists—would activate the detonation sequence. Either the firing was set to a timer or controlled remotely—either way, we had plenty of time to get from the zero point to Shelter A. Even though it was more than five miles from the point of detonation.

Five miles plus! What kind of bomb was this? Berlin, Dresden, Hamburg—we'd pounded those cities into rubble, but the destruction had required thousands upon thousands of sorties, waves and waves of Flying Fortresses and Lancasters delivering kilotons of ordnance. The bombing of Dresden—carried out on a single night in February—had produced horrors that would make even Dante flinch: Fires so powerful that their oxygen draw swept children and the elderly off their feet and hurled them into the maelstrom; civilians boiled alive in the city's canals; broken bricks still warm to the touch weeks after the bombing. But even this hell, unleashed by untold numbers of bombs, hadn't come close to touching people five miles away from Dresden.

If I was guessing correctly, Trinity was testing a single bomb. I keenly remembered Colonel Latham's admonishment to stifle my curiosity if I wanted to avoid suffering, but the enormity of what Meacham had just told me couldn't be ignored.

"What in God's name is happening here?" I asked in a hushed voice.

Meacham said nothing. After a moment, he reached into the back seat to rummage in a box. He held up a square piece of dark glass in a plain wooden frame.

"At the shelter site, you'll be told to lie flat in trenches with your feet pointed toward the zero point and to hold one of these over your eyes. Not everyone will—some of the scientists will stand and face the zero point— but I'll be in one of those trenches, holding one of these, and I advise you to do exactly the same."

"Jesus Christ."

"Jesus Christ, indeed. Are you religious, Voigt?"

"No."

"Me neither. Even if I were, I sure wouldn't count on Jesus Christ, God, or the Holy Ghost being anywhere around here this morning."

I didn't respond. So far, my complicated scheme to save myself had taken all my energy and attention, but for the moment, dread about Trinity caused my heart to race and my mouth to go dry. What forces of the universe had Oppenheimer and his mad geniuses harnessed and bottled into a single bomb? We were going to be more than five miles away, and yet still lying in trenches with dark glass over our eyes. No wonder the Russians had put so much effort into infiltrating Site Y. Consideration of what the Russians could do with such a bomb was even worse than imagining the bomb test itself.

Meacham snapped me out of my nightmarish thoughts. "Only ten minutes til you leave," he said, tapping his watch. "Let's move that box"—he motioned at the back seat—"to the trunk and check the tires."

THE PLYMOUTH'S ENGINE DRONED AS I STEERED THE CAR DOWN A NARROW asphalt road. The rain had stopped and the eastern sky had begun to lighten, though the sun hadn't yet risen. Jarowsky rode in front with me; the three physicists shared the back seat. The headlights captured the smooth, unmarked pavement and scrub brush.

"Look!" exclaimed Bainbridge, who was seated directly behind me.

The others turned their heads to look out his window as I glanced at the driver's side mirror. I caught a flash of several animals' hind legs, bounding away into the darkness.

"Antelope," Jarowsky said.

"Poor bastards," Bainbridge murmured. None of us asked what he meant.

No one said anything more for the rest of the drive. I stole a look in my rearview mirror. Bainbridge's head was bowed, while Kistiakowsky— a serious-looking man in his fifties—chewed absently on an unlit pipe. Brode, who sat in the middle, stared back at me, his expression steady and sure.

When we reached the tower, Bainbridge directed me to park the car so the headlights shone on the tower's base. He and Kistiakowsky had a brief exchange about whether or not the Plymouth cast enough light.

"Let's just see, shall we, George?" Bainbridge said good-naturedly.

Kistiakowsky shrugged and they exited, the doors clattering shut one after another. Meacham had told me to stay in the car with the engine running, but Jarowsky didn't repeat this instruction, so after a moment I engaged the parking brake and got out, leaving the engine running. Bainbridge was standing close to the tower, a clipboard in his hand.

"North relay four," he said loudly.

Brode was crouched in front of an open metal cabinet affixed to one of the tower's pylons. He clicked a switch.

"Check," Kistiakowsky, who was standing behind Brode, called out.

I walked over to Jarowsky. He was standing just outside of the headlights' beam, so as not to block the light. Smoke twisted from the cigarette in his right hand as he gazed up at the tower. I'd expected a formidable structure, but the tower was spindly. A metal ladder reached to a deck at the top. Wires dropped from the deck, stretching in all directions to sturdy T-poles embedded in the desert soil.

I lit a Lucky. "What's up there?" I asked, figuring I had nothing to lose. The worst Jarowsky could do was say I didn't have clearance.

But he answered, his gaze still directed upward. "The gadget."

"Funny."

"For real. That's what they call it."

"The gadget?"

Now he looked at me, taking a long drag. "If they used its real name, would any one of us know what they meant?"

"Good point."

"Looks like a goddamned diving bell," Jarowsky said.

I was about to ask him more when Bainbridge caught our attention. "Mason's going up," he announced. "Should be back down in five minutes tops, then we're done."

"Okay," Jarowsky responded as we watched Brode deftly, swiftly climb the ladder.

I felt a surge of complex emotions. Curiosity, because I wanted to know what, exactly, the gadget was; dread, because I couldn't know until the detonation what, exactly, the gadget was; apprehension, because unless I left Trinity with Brode's diagram of how the gadget worked, I wouldn't save myself; and grudging admiration at how thoroughly the Russians had penetrated this project. After all, a Russian spy would be the last human alone with the gadget before the zero time. For a moment, I wondered if Brode would sabotage the gadget so that the test fizzled. Wouldn't a bred-in-the-bone Red want the United States to fail while ensuring that the Russians succeeded? Then I remembered how proud, how boastful Brode had been when he had come to Washington in May to deliver the diagram. He wanted the bomb to work to prove how smart he was, and he wanted me to tell the Russians what I'd just seen: Brode was the last scientist to handle the gadget.

After three minutes, Brode calmly descended the ladder. He handed a sheet of paper to Bainbridge, who scanned it.

"Okay, we're all set, let's go," he said.

We got into the car. The tires crunched slowly as I backed up, then steered onto the road.

"Oh-four-fifty-seven," Kistiakowsky announced, looking at his watch.

"Wonderful. Lieutenant Voigt won't have to speed," Brode quipped. Everyone laughed, releasing our pent-up tension.

And I didn't speed as I drove the remaining five miles to Shelter A, though it took conscious effort to keep my foot from pressing down on the accelerator.

SHELTER A CONSISTED OF TWO BUNKERS INSIDE EARTHEN BERMS AND A wooden shed half-buried in the ground. At Bainbridge's instruction, I parked the Plymouth behind one of the bunkers.

"Everybody, roll down your window," Kistiakowsky said, then he and Bainbridge beelined for the larger bunker.

"I'll brief Colonel Latham," Jarowsky told me as he left the car.

Brode remained in the middle of the back seat. His gaze was already locked on the rearview mirror when I looked at it. All around us, MPs, officers, and scientists came and went, busy with their tasks, but none paid any attention to us. Even with the windows down, Brode and I could talk unobserved.

"Did Meacham tell you about the suntan lotion?" Brode asked.

"What?"

"I'll take that as a no. You should rub suntan lotion over your exposed skin, especially your face, before the firing."

"What the hell is about to happen here?"

"'References to 'Hell' and 'Heaven' are proving to be quite popular as we prepare to embrace our destiny. If I were given to hyperbole, I might say that what's about to happen will rip the angels from heaven. But why seek flourish when simplicity will do? Trinity, despite its portentous name, is uniquely American. Think about it, Voigt! Here we are, about to unleash the most powerful force in the universe, and we're preparing for it like a day at the beach. Put on your dark glasses, rub on the lotion, and get comfortable in the sand. There's no ocean, of course, but there will be plenty of sun. The most beautiful sunrise you'll ever see in your life, Voigt, so I advise you to look closely. They'll tell you not to, not even with the glass, but I'll be watching, and you should too, Voigt."

"Lying down in trenches might remind some people of a graveyard, not a beach."

He snorted dismissively. "A senseless precaution is no precaution at all. Trust me, if my baby gets colicky, lying flat won't save you. You'll merely be buried rather than blown away. Why not stand beside me and enjoy the show?"

His *baby*? The man's arrogance was boundless. My already strong dislike of the physicist intensified, but I wasn't here to make a new friend.

"Let's not forget the work we have to do, Brode."

"You and me, the two of us, alone; that work, right? Tell me, Lieutenant, how have you been able to stay hidden so long, even as you rise ever higher?" Translation: *Why hadn't I yet been identified as a Red spy?*

"I could ask the same question of you."

"But you already know the answer, don't you?" *The gadget couldn't have been built without me, so what makes you so vital?*

I let that ride, still watching Brode in the mirror. A grim expression had replaced the cocky smile. "Before we get to our work, what happened to my friend in Washington?" He meant Himmel, his contact, to whom he had delivered the first diagram of the gadget.

"He retired."

"Without clearing out his desk?" *Without delivering the diagram?*

"He's worried he can't enjoy retirement without sufficient life insurance." *He kept the diagram so the Russians wouldn't kill him.* I sure wasn't going to tell Brode that I, in fact, had killed Himmel to protect myself. As long as Brode, like the Russians and the Americans, believed Himmel had gone on the lam, I was safe.

"Paranoia really creates problems, doesn't it? With just a small measure of trust, all of this intrigue, all of the effort to send you on your beach holiday, could have been avoided. I'm going to tell you the same thing I told our retired friend: I'm out, got it? Be sure to let the bosses know."

Before I could answer, a male voice boomed from a speaker on a tripod behind the bunker: "T minus fifteen."

"Just fifteen minutes til showtime," Brode said.

"Then you better get busy," I said, suddenly anxious. If Brode wouldn't or couldn't give me another copy of the diagram, I was in deep trouble.

"Here you go." A tri-folded sheet of paper dropped onto the seat next to me.

I snatched it up and jammed it into my pocket. "When the hell did you do this? I sure hope you haven't been carrying—"

"Easy, boy, easy. I know the rules. Here's a hint. I did it in the last hour." He slid across the seat and got out of the rear driver's side door. The only time Brode could have drafted the diagram was when he was on top of the zero point tower, making the final check of the gadget. He had only been up there a few minutes. Was it possible to draw the plan from memory that quickly? What kind of confidence and brilliance did he have?

He leaned into my window. "What do you say, Voigt, are you ready to hit the beach? Ready for a day of fun in the sun?"

CHAPTER 38

GOT OUT OF THE PLYMOUTH, OPENED THE TRUNK, AND RETRIEVED THE frame of dark glass. Then I went into the closest bunker to find Jarowsky and Latham. The small space was jammed with worktables and consoles of electrical equipment. Four civilians, all men, were monitoring gauges or talking. I left and headed to the other bunker, which was larger. An MP stood at the entrance.

"Where's Colonel Latham?" I asked.

He shrugged. "Not in there, I can tell you that, sir."

Another MP rushed up. "We're supposed to get behind the photo shelter."

I watched them trot off toward the wooden shed. Photo shelter? The structure resembled a gun emplacement, buttressed with sandbags and featuring a long, narrow firing window. Instead of Browning machine guns, this position apparently had Kodaks pointed at the zero point. Brode's beach metaphor took on added meaning. *Don't forget your camera.*

I ducked to enter the bunker. Bainbridge, Kistiakowsky, and Oppenheimer were intently talking with one another. Brode was seated by himself at a small table, looking like he didn't have a care in the world. I tensed up. I couldn't ask if anyone knew where Latham was, not in front of Brode. Not that the three scientists paid attention to me. Brode stared at me but said nothing. *Does he suspect me?* I couldn't help but wonder. Unnerved, I left without saying anything.

"T minus ten," the PA announced. "Ten minutes until detonation, ten minutes, all personnel should assemble at their observation positions."

Where was the announcer located? Was he one of the men I'd seen in the first bunker, or was he located at another shelter, miles away? Was he even real? No experience in my life, nor any novel, not even *Alice's Adventures in Wonderland*, had prepared me for the disorientation I now felt. I was lost in the desert, wandering in and out of gadget-packed grottoes as I gripped a piece of darkened glass, waiting for someone to give me suntan lotion, waiting for someone to tell me which trench was mine to lie down in, waiting for the zero minute, waiting for the detonation.

"Voigt!"

Jarowsky was motioning to me. He was standing with Captain Foley, Colonel Latham, and an MP behind the larger bunker. I gratefully trotted over. Foley finished saying something to the MP, who nodded and started walking to the photo shelter.

"So?" Latham asked.

I looked over my shoulder to make sure Brode wasn't in sight. Then I wordlessly handed the folded diagram to Latham. He slipped it into his jacket pocket without looking at it.

"He bought your story about being a spy, obviously," the colonel said.

"Yessir, he did."

"Did he just do that in the car?" Jarowsky asked.

I shook my head. "He did it at the zero point."

"But how, he was busy the whole time and we were there for only . . ." Jarowsky trailed off as he realized that Brode had sketched the diagram while atop the tower. "Holy shit!" he exclaimed.

"Can it be done that quickly?" Foley asked, incredulous.

Latham scowled. "We better hope so, but we don't have time to check now."

"He's in the bunker right now," I said.

"We know," Jarowsky said.

"If the test goes well, we'll take him into custody right afterward," Latham told me.

"And if it doesn't go well?" I asked.

"We leave him be. Oppie will need him to figure out what went wrong."

"Unless it goes really wrong—then none of us will be around to care," Jarowsky cracked.

No one laughed.

What if the gadget failed? That possibility hadn't occurred to me. A dud would foul me up but good. As long as Brode remained free, my plan was at risk. If I gave the Russians a bum diagram and they were somehow able to make contact with Brode, they'd know I'd tricked them. I pushed that ugly thought out of my head. I had to assume the bomb would work, and I had to get a fast answer to the question of where, exactly, I should be at T minus zero.

"Are we really supposed to lie down in trenches?" I asked.

"The MPs are, but their position is closer than ours. We're going into the bunker," Latham said.

"What about them?" I pointed to a group of several civilians who had also assembled behind the bunker. They were talking animatedly; one was gesturing wildly with his hands. They looked like they were dressed for church: suits, ties, hats.

"More scientists," Foley said. "They built it, they wanna be present at the creation. I get why, but I'm not taking any chances."

"Brode said something about suntan lotion."

Latham looked uncomfortable. "Some of the scientists think—they're advising that putting the lotion on your skin may offer some added protection."

"We're five miles away from the zero point, sir. If the distance isn't enough, why do we need this"—I held up my piece of glass—"and suntan lotion?"

"There's going to be a flash, and we don't know for certain how bright it will be," announced Oppenheimer, who was approaching. "Frankly, I don't think the suntan lotion will do anything, but I definitely advise you not to look in the direction of the zero point. Jim, a moment?"

He and Latham stepped to the side and conferred quietly. A sidelong look from Oppenheimer at me hinted at the topic: Had I obtained the diagram from Brode? Yet again, I wondered if Oppenheimer was trustworthy. If he was a Red; if, somehow, Groves and Latham had failed to uncover his true allegiances—

"T minus five, T minus five," the PA interrupted that troubling thought.

"Well, that's all the reminder I need," Jarowsky said. "Time to stake my claim in the bunker." He started walking to the entrance.

"You coming with us?" Foley asked me.

Joining the other officers in the bunker certainly was the prudent decision. But as Latham and Oppenheimer finished their conversation and Oppenheimer walked over to the other scientists gathered around the bunker, I knew I wasn't going inside—I would stand and watch, just as Brode had tauntingly told me to do.

"No, I'm going to stay out here," I told Foley.

He shook his head. "Remember what they said about not looking in the direction of the tower."

He left. Latham glanced at me as he passed but said nothing. For a moment, I was alone. As I watched Oppenheimer converse with his fellow scientists, I suddenly felt anxious, like a lonely teenager afraid to approach a clique of popular kids. Would they abruptly fall silent as I approached? The absurdity of my fear made me smile—we were minutes away from something extraordinary, and I was worried about an awkward social encounter?

I shambled over. The piece of glass was now grubby with fingerprints. It was still dark, though the predawn sky was starting to lighten. I lit a cigarette, inhaled deeply. One of the scientists was rubbing lotion onto his face, but his companions declined the bottle when he held it out. He shrugged, dropped the lotion into his pocket, and dabbed his face with a handkerchief. Another scientist with distinctive, bushy eyebrows was ripping up a sheet of paper. His explanation to a querying colleague made no sense to me—the only words I recognized were "shock wave." Oppenheimer was standing next to a post, his left hand resting on its top, a cigarette in his right hand.

"Good morning, Lieutenant."

"Morning, Professor."

"I heard you did a bang-up job chauffeuring the arming party." Translation: *You got the diagram from Brode, good work.*

"Well, I've got the easiest job round here."

"Perhaps."

We both took long drags on our smokes. I glanced around. There were seven of us, but Brode wasn't present. *Where is he?* I wondered.

"Professor, a question."

Oppenheimer gave me the slightest of nods. He looked exhausted, his wrinkled shirt loose on his bony shoulders, his face drawn, his eyelids puffy.

"What's this bomb made of?"

"Made of? That's not an easy question to answer, as you might imagine."

"Maybe that's my problem—I can't even imagine what's about to happen. What little I've been told only makes it harder to envision what your gadget will do."

He flicked his cigarette butt into the air, its ember tracing an arc to the ground, and immediately lit another Chesterfield.

"None of us can imagine what's about to happen . . . nim . . . we can only predict what will happen, and those predictions vary. One of my colleagues has even conjectured our action could, nim, ignite the atmosphere."

"If that happens, I guess this won't be of much use." I held up my piece of darkened glass.

Oppenheimer didn't laugh. "No, it wouldn't."

"Brode says your gadget will rip the angels from heaven."

"If there is a heaven, Lieutenant, perhaps."

"And if the angels haven't already decamped for a safer place."

"T minus two, two minutes remaining," the PA announced. He said nothing more, but a moment later, there was a gurgle of static and then, absurdly, we heard a few bars of classical music before the frequency went silent.

Oppenheimer smiled wearily at my confusion. "That happens a lot. The Trinity frequency is close to an Albuquerque station that broadcasts music."

Bainbridge and Kistiakowsky approached, clearly wanting to talk to Oppenheimer. I edged away to give them privacy. My watch read oh-five-hundred-twenty-eight and forty seconds. I looked to see if Brode had joined the gaggle of scientists while I was talking with Oppenheimer, but he hadn't. Where was he? Had he chickened out and gone into the bunker after all?

"Voigt!"

I turned and looked up. Brode was standing atop the bunker, hands on his hips. He'd donned a canvas bush hat, its strings dangling, and wore dark glasses.

"C'mon up, the view's incredible."

I shook my head in amazement. How could he be so sure of what was about to happen when even Oppenheimer himself was waiting with dread and anticipation?

"T minus one, T minus one, countdown to begin at T minus ten seconds," the PA announced. There was a distinct edge to the man's voice.

Two of the scientists knelt and lay on their stomachs, feet pointed toward the zero point and hands laced behind their heads, like soldiers who had just been disarmed and taken prisoner. Oppenheimer, Bainbridge, and Kistiakowsky remained standing, but Oppenheimer clenched the top of the post with his left hand. The coal of his cigarette cast red light onto his tense face. *Should I at least crouch?* I wondered. With both hands I held the dark glass in front of my chest, ready to raise it during the countdown. My mouth was dry. The glass started to tremble—for a split second, I thought the detonation had somehow already begun. Then I saw my hands were shaking. My legs felt weak.

"Ten . . ."

Better crouch . . .

"Nine . . ."

Don't look . . .

"Eight . . ."

Breathe slowly . . .

"Seven . . ."

Not alone . . .

"Six . . ."

Don't panic . . .

"Five . . ."

Head down!
"Four . . ."
Glass up!
"Three . . ."
Please God . . .
"Two . . ."
Let this work . . .
"One . . ."
Please?
"Now!"

CHAPTER 39

THE STARS VANISHED, THE NIGHT VANISHED, AND THE LIGHT OF UNTOLD suns blinded us. I'd never known such brightness, no human ever had. It was as if the universe had become nothing but light—now no galaxies, no planets, no earth, no mountains, no humans, only light. This brilliant, celestial light absorbed all of us. For an instant, we ceased to exist as individuals and we disappeared into the light, transformed into energy, beautiful and boundless, never-ending. I was no longer Ellis Voigt, wretched schemer—I wasn't a human being at all. Neither was Brode, neither was Oppenheimer. To even conceive of ourselves as individuals seemed stupendously wrongheaded, for the bomb transcended all known frames of reference. No ego could shield itself from the bomb's transformative power. The bomb hadn't ripped the angels from heaven, it had made *us* angels.

But only for an instant.

The rumbling blast slammed into us with breathtaking ferocity that shook the earth. The force wrenched us out of the light and hurled us back to earth as our former selves, frail and vulnerable beings. The blast upended me, sent me hurtling backward from my crouch like a mad gymnast somersaulting uncontrollably. The darkened glass I'd been clenching flew off into the air. A berm stopped me and I rose unsteadily, gasping, blinking, besmirched with wet dirt. Had I the lung power, I might well have wailed like a newborn, a primordial cry the only way to respond to my admittance into this terrifying world, for with the blast came heat, as intense as a stoked furnace. I could barely breathe, the hot air scorching my lungs. The bomb had lifted us high only to let us plummet.

Oppenheimer had pinwheeled off the post he'd been clutching and had fallen to his knees. He, too, came to his feet shakily.

The blast had flung Kistiakowsky into a mud puddle. He scrambled to his feet and hugged Oppenheimer.

"We did it, Oppie, we did it!" he shouted.

"And now I am become death, the destroyer of worlds," I heard Oppenheimer say.

The other scientists all stood, unhurt, though one—I recognized him as Richard Feynman, the mathematician we had interrogated the previous day—was blinking furiously and waving his hand in front of his eyes. "I can't see, I can't see," he exclaimed.

No one tried to help or comfort him—we were awestruck by the clouds billowing across the now dark horizon. No sunset had ever colored the sky so vividly. Orange became green, green became red, red became purple. This rainbow of clouds rolled like an avalanche as three gigantic smoke rings ascended from their center. We gaped, and groped for words. "Jesus Christ," a scientist murmured. "What have we done?" asked another. No one responded. "My God, it's beautiful" was answered with "No, it's terrible." Bainbridge approached Oppenheimer. "Well, now we're all sons of bitches," he said. Oppenheimer merely nodded. He hadn't spoken since his comment about becoming death, the destroyer of worlds. A quote of some sort, I guessed, but I'd never heard it before.

The shelter observers gathered around us to watch the clouds.

"Check on the MPs!" Latham shouted at Foley, who rushed toward the photo shelter.

The order jolted me back into the here and now. Where was Brode? I wheeled around to look atop the shelter—he wasn't there. I scanned the crowd—he was nowhere to be seen. A wonderful, terrible thought excited me: Had the blast killed him, swept him off his feet and broken his neck? How perfect would that be if Brode died, a casualty of his own creation and hubris, his day on the beach his last on earth! His death would be a windfall to my plan to trick the Russians and extricate myself from their grasp.

Yes, I was once again a wretched schemer.

BUT BRODE HADN'T BEEN KILLED. THE BLAST HAD KNOCKED HIM OFF THE shelter and thrown him like a rag doll to the ground, but his only injury was, remarkably, a sprained wrist. That didn't prevent Latham from ordering him to be handcuffed as we arrested him.

"Not done playing question and answer, Colonel?" Brode said, showing no sign of distress or even pain.

Latham ignored him. He ordered Jarowsky to sit in the Plymouth with Brode while he briefed me.

"Oppie now has the diagram. He'll work with Doctor Fuchs to alter it. When they're done, we'll make arrangements for your return to Washington, Voigt, so you can deliver it to the Russians."

"Yessir. What about Brode?" I asked.

"Agent Slater and I will conduct the interrogation—it's best if you're not present."

"Understood."

Keeping me out was sound protocol—by obtaining the diagram from Brode, my task had been completed—but I dreaded to think what Brode would tell Slater. The physicist would sense that Slater didn't trust me, and he'd worm his way into the F.B.I. agent's mind, feeding his doubts and suspicions. Brode would see through the elaborate ruse we'd just carried out. *Voigt claimed to be a Red agent, but what if that's really true?* he'd say to Slater. *What if the Russians sent him here to double-cross me and you?* Brode would immediately understand that we'd tricked him into giving me a diagram of the bomb in order to fudge it before we let it get into the Russians' hands, but he could raise pointed questions about my role. *What if Voigt took a photo of the diagram before he handed it over, what if he gives that photo to the Russians? What if the Russians want you to think they've accepted a false diagram so your security services breathe easy?* One of the surest ways to trip up an intelligence agency was to convince its officers that the other side's credulity was actually calculated deception. Worst of all, Slater now knew that I knew the N.K.V.D.'s recruitment challenge: "Are you ready to say good-bye to your family forever?" Believing he now had all the proof necessary to arrest me, Slater wouldn't wait—he'd insist that I be detained immediately. I had to convince Latham to send me back to Washington as soon as possible.

"How long do you think it'll take them to doctor the diagram, sir?"

"I have no idea, Voigt, I'm not a physicist. They can't just change a few lines or equations—it's gotta look like the best way to build such a bomb, otherwise the Russians will know it's a fake straightaway."

I couldn't dispute that fact, so I said nothing more. I could only hope that Fuchs and Oppenheimer were, like Brode, quick draftsmen who would finish their task before Latham and Slater finished theirs.

I rode back to Site Y with the same MPs I'd arrived with—Latham didn't want me in the car with Brode. Again, good protocol, but also another reminder that I had absolutely no control over what Brode would now do or say. The MPs were subdued but still talkative. They shared stories of what they'd experienced. "Jesus, that heat," one said, "it was like a ball of fire going right over me." "I thought for sure I'd gone blind," said another. "Had my eyes closed and the glass covering them but it still felt like I was staring straight at the sun." They spoke of a comrade who had been blown out of his trench. "Bet he wasn't lying down," the MP with the Southern accent said. "Probably stuck his fat head up and that wind jes picked him like a big ole balloon."

I learned from the MPs how the Army was explaining the flash, blast, and clouds to area residents. An official statement already released claimed that a "remotely located ammunition magazine" had accidently exploded, detonating a "large amount" of high explosives. The MPs had a good laugh about that cover. "Ain't nobody gonna believe that horseshit," the Southerner said. He didn't have to explain why: Anyone living near Trinity or Site Y had seen too much secrecy, resources, and personnel for the last three years to believe that it was all for an ammunition magazine.

How would the Army tamp down the inevitable speculation and news reports? Hundreds, if not thousands, had witnessed that flash, had felt the heat and the blast. As capacious as Trinity was, it wasn't big enough to contain the full-blown effects of the gadget. Now I understood Oppenheimer's distinction: We can predict, but not imagine, what will happen. I wondered what went through his mind at the moment of detonation. Did he feel any thrill or excitement, was he ecstatic? I knew nothing of the mechanics of the gadget, other than that it required Uranium-235, but it didn't take a genius to know that the science involved had required marshaling the finest minds in the field, giving them unlimited resources and plenty of time. Even so, success hadn't been guaranteed, so it seemed unlikely that Oppenheimer didn't feel some pride in what he had helped create. And yet his words at the moment of creation: "And now I am become death, the destroyer of worlds."

Destroyer indeed. If Oppenheimer and his team had built one workable gadget, they could build another, and another. How many total? Three, five, ten? Was it possible to detonate them aerially? For that, of course, had to be the primary purpose in building such a weapon: to finish off the Germans and the Japs. The Nazis had surrendered more than two months earlier, but the Japs fought on. In Washington, the subject of the final assault of Japan dominated all conversations. When, and where, would the first amphibious landings take place? How many troops were needed, how many would die if the Japs fought as hard as they had at Iwo Jima and Okinawa? And the biggest question of all: What would just one of these bombs do to Tokyo, or any other Jap city? We had sheltered *five* miles from the zero point and still had been blown off our feet. What were the blast and heat like at the center of the explosion? Even if the destructive radius was only—only!—three miles, one bomb could level most of a major city. In Washington, such a bomb, detonated near the White House, would utterly destroy the Pentagon, the Capitol, Union Station, downtown, and so much more. My own apartment was less than two miles from the White House. If the Germans had built such a weapon and used it, I would have been incinerated, along with tens of thousands of other Washingtonians.

After what the Japs had done in this war so far, I—along with all other Americans—had no reason whatsoever to show them kindness, but I still hoped Hirohito and his generals would come to their senses and surrender soon to spare the untold number of women and children who would die unspeakable deaths when these bombs were used. Or was it better for humanity in the long run for one of these bombs to fall, so that all the world could witness the top-secret horror of Site Y and Trinity and collectively resolve that never again should such a weapon be used?

The truck had just clattered to a stop at Site Y's gate when the significance of something Latham had said finally dawned on me. Dr. Klaus Fuchs, whom we'd questioned yesterday and cleared, was going to doctor the diagram along with Oppenheimer. If Oppenheimer was, in fact, a Red agent, he wouldn't falsify the diagram—he'd guarantee it was accurate!

But that panicky thought quickly vanished. Obviously Oppenheimer couldn't leave the diagram untouched without Fuchs, who was also a physicist, knowing. And Oppenheimer couldn't pressure Fuchs to cooperate without exposing himself. The conclusion was obvious: despite his Red-checkered past, Oppenheimer wasn't a Russian agent. Only Brode was.

And me.

CHAPTER 40

M Y RELIEF AT FIGURING OUT THAT OPPENHEIMER WAS CLEAN DIDN'T last long. Slater was waiting for me as soon as I stepped off the truck. "You and me, we need to talk," he greeted me.

"Sure." The conversation wasn't going to be pleasant, but it would delay his interrogation of Brode, giving Oppenheimer and Fuchs more time to falsify the bomb diagram.

I followed him to the building where we'd questioned the suspects the day before. It was still early, but the streets of Site Y were crowded with people excitedly discussing the Trinity test. The sight of three young mothers talking on the porch of a residence brought a realization: no women had been present at Trinity. General Groves must have prohibited them, in case the test went terribly wrong. *Last act of chivalry in our old world*, I thought.

Slater had appropriated a messy, cramped office in the Administration building. Folders bulged from open file cabinet drawers, a miniature mountain range of papers and books dominated the desktop. The only chair was behind the desk, but Slater didn't sit, choosing to lean against the desk. I closed the door and lit up a cigarette.

"Nifty trick you pulled on Colonel Latham, Lieutenant, convincing him we should arrest Ackerly."

"It worked, didn't it? We got Brode to talk."

"*You* got Brode to talk. I'm awful interested to hear what he has to say about your conversation out there in the desert." Slater was baiting me, hoping I'd get defensive and rush to give him my version of what had been said. Which was exactly what a guilty man would do to bolster the appearance of innocence. I had to behave like a loyal officer who had only pretended to be a Red spy.

So I shrugged. "Not really my concern what he says—I did what I was supposed to do."

"And how did you do that, Voigt? D'you just say to Brode, 'Hey, I'm working for the Russians too, let's work together'?"

I checked the urge for sarcasm. *You're beat, you haven't slept, you're a man with nothing to hide—play that part.*

"Like you said, Slater, Brode's gonna tell you all about it."

"But you don't wanna tell your side? Awful suspicious, wouldn't you say?"

"It'll all be in my report to Paslett and Latham. M'sure the colonel will give you a copy."

"How are we supposed to know if Brode's lying if we don't have your account?"

His trap, sprung. Latham didn't need my side of the story because he believed I had only pretended to be a Red spy in order to deceive Brode. The purpose of the interrogation was to determine how much Brode had compromised the bomb project, not to analyze my methods; and Slater knew that. *What would an innocent man say?*

"You wait for my report, Slater, like everybody else."

He shook his head in disgust. "You think you're gonna come outta this a hero, don't you? Won't make the papers, a'course, but you're banking on being the darling of O.N.I. and the Army for what you did down here. Do you really think that's enough insurance, Voigt? Think that'll protect you when the evidence I have now about who you really are comes out?"

His questions sliced right through me. Jesus, he was good—he'd sussed out my scheme. He believed I was a Red, so he'd asked himself, What would I do in Voigt's shoes to keep my secret? But if he actually had evidence, he already would have arrested me. *So how does an innocent man respond?*

I took a drag and studied the curved, long ash drooping from my cigarette's ember. Without an ashtray, I hadn't been able to tap it.

"Put this out for me, will you?" I said, flicking the Lucky at Slater. He instinctively shirked backward into the desk. The mountain of papers and books began cascading to the floor, almost causing him to lose his balance. His flailing arms only knocked more items off the desk.

I turned and left, calmly shutting the door on his stream of curses.

MY LAST HOURS AT SITE Y FLEW BY. I WENT STRAIGHT TO THE OFFICERS' mess and wolfed down a breakfast of eggs, sausage, and oatmeal. Skipped the coffee, for I wanted nothing more than to sleep the sleep of the dead. Though considering what I'd witnessed that morning, perhaps that wasn't the right turn of phrase. I was worried Latham might find me and dress me down for the stunt I'd pulled with Slater, but either the F.B.I. agent didn't tell him about his embarrassment or Latham simply didn't care. He had a much greater concern. The success of both the Trinity test and our mission to deceive the Russians didn't erase his failure to identify the spy in his domain. Colonel Latham had a lot of explaining to do to General Groves as soon as the hoopla over the bomb died down.

I was asleep mere seconds after pulling my shoes off. A hard knock on the door rousted me around 1300. I padded to the door, disoriented and disheveled, with a tremendous thirst. Unfortunately, the MP waking me up hadn't brought a tall glass of water, only an announcement that he was there to take me to Colonel Latham and that I should bring my kit with me. We had a terse exchange about whether or not I had time to get cleaned up and change my clothes; I prevailed. The hot shower and shave and change of clothes left me feeling like a new man. I packed hurriedly and was at Latham's office by 1340. He was alone and put me at ease, motioning me to sit.

"We haven't got much time—you're on a transport plane bound for D.C. that leaves in half an hour."

"So Oppenheimer and Fuchs finished the diagram alteration, sir?"

He held up his hand. "We'll get to that. I've briefed General Groves, and he has some concerns."

"About what?"

"How you're going to approach the Russians, for one."

Told myself not to get impatient. Groves had every right to be worried, considering the stakes, but I didn't want him taking over the operation.

"Well, sir, you can tell General Groves I'm not gonna approach the Russians—that's not how these things work. I'll wait for them to find me."

Latham frowned. "How long will that take?"

"Not long at all. They're awful eager to have the diagram."

"That brings me to the general's next concern: How will you present the diagram?"

"Like I'm their mailman with that morning's post, sir. No fanfare."

"The general is wondering if it will get a close look in your presence."

"M'sure they'll look at it, sir, but will they have an expert with them? I doubt it. Anyone who can tell them what that diagram means is in Russia. Even if they have someone they can use in the States, they wouldn't risk letting me see his face."

"Okay. Now, about what you'll say to the Russians about what you saw this morning. The general and I talked about it, and we decided it's advantageous for us if you don't hold back."

"We want them to get excited," I said. Latham didn't need to spell out the reason why: We wanted the Russians to spend a lot of time and money building their own bomb the wrong way.

"Exactly. As for you, are you going to stay undercover, Voigt?"

That sounded like his question, not Groves's, but there was no reason not to answer honestly.

"Nosir. I've been under too long already. This business with the F.B.I. offers me the perfect exit—I'll tell the N.K.V.D. there's too much heat on me. They won't take my word for it, of course, but when they check up they'll see I'm telling the truth."

"What are you going to do about Slater? He seems awfully persistent."

I tried to sound unworried. "Slater's just an attack dog for J. Edgar, who's had it in for O.N.I. for years. Smearing a lowly officer like me is just part of their mission to take over some of our operations once the war's finally over. Bureau's doing the same thing to O.S.S."

"About them, O.S.S. Have you heard anything from Commander Paslett about their interest in this case since you arrived here?"

A strange question—Latham had to know I'd had no contact with Paslett since leaving Washington. But I wanted to get out of Site Y without any more complications, so I shook my head.

"All right, the last thing we need to talk about is what happened at Trinity today."

"What's Trinity and what happened there today, sir?" I asked evenly.

"Excellent response, Lieutenant." He took a regular-sized envelope from his desk drawer and slid it across the desk. "Oppie and Doctor Fuchs finished this just before you arrived. No doubt I don't have to tell you not to let this leave your person until the delivery."

"Understood, sir." I considered wishing him luck with his interrogation of Brode, then thought better of it. I stood. He returned my salute and I started to leave.

"Voigt?"

"Yessir?"

"I appreciate what you did here." Translation: *Thank you for nailing Brode.*

I shrugged. "Thanks, sir." I stopped myself from saying *Just doing my job*, for the cliché would have tasted like ash in my mouth. Instead:

"Sir, do you know this quote: 'Now I am become death, the destroyer of worlds'?"

He gave me a strange look. "Where did you hear that?"

"I'm not sure. It was a while ago."

He clearly didn't believe me, but he still answered. "It comes from the Bhagavad Gita, an ancient Sanskrit text. The title translates as 'Song of the Lord.'"

I thanked him and left.

THE FLIGHT TO WASHINGTON WAS BUMPY AND LOUD. THE DRONING engines of the Douglas C-47 inhibited conversation, as did the seating layout: the other six passengers and I had strapped ourselves into metal seats welded parallel to the port and starboard sides of the fuselage. Wooden crates were stacked and belted to the two tracks in the center of the deck. PHOTOGRAPHIC EQUIPMENT—HANDLE WITH CARE was stenciled onto the crates. So were a lot of TOP SECRET warnings. Fitting, I supposed, that as a witness to the Trinity test I was now unofficially escorting the photographs of the detonation and its aftermath to Washington. I couldn't help but wonder what the developed film would show. As much as I had seen, how much of the bomb's beauty and horror had I not seen? I didn't recognize any of the other passengers, but it was a safe guess that some, if not all, were the technicians who had set up and operated the cameras at Trinity.

But I had more important subjects to mull over. Would Paslett agree that I must break cover and end this operation? Yes, I had conceived of it and I had convinced Paslett to authorize it, but he was still my C.O. Its success might well whet his appetite. *What else can we get from them while they trust you?* I could practically hear his eager voice. To save myself, however, I really did have to make a clean break, I had to tell the N.K.V.D.'s American agent, the professor-type who had overseen my interrogation and torture in Washington, that I had no choice but to hibernate because of the F.B.I.'s suspicions of me. I was confident they'd believe me once they checked out my story, as I'd told Latham; but what about Paslett? What if Slater's persistence, and the circumstantial but still troublesome evidence the Bureau had uncovered in Chicago about Delphine and her communist father, started nagging Paslett? He hated the Bureau, sure, but not so much that he'd turn a blind eye to a thick file of documents that cast suspicion on my loyalties and actions. If Slater and the Bureau persuaded Paslett to distrust me, if they convinced him to participate in a full investigation into my past, I was finished. But I had to tell Paslett about Slater's suspicions. There was no way to keep them secret, after Slater had waylaid me in New Mexico, and wouldn't an innocent man immediately tell his C.O. that he'd been falsely accused?

Then there was the problem of what I'd said to Brode to convince him that I, too, was a Red spy. How would I explain to Paslett how I knew the Russians asked every recruit whether or not he was willing to say good-bye forever to his family? As soon as possible, I needed to forge and backdate a document detailing how I'd learned this detail from a previous investigation. It would have to be misfiled, to explain its absence from the main file, but that was a manageable challenge.

Another urgent task was to check on Kenny Newhurst and his recovery from the shooting. My throat went dry just thinking about seeing him and his parents, but I had to know he was all right. I had to ask for his forgiveness, and for the forgiveness of his parents. I wouldn't dare tell them that Kenny's sacrifice and pain had been expended for a greater good—since I couldn't tell them the truth, I couldn't lie, either. If I was still wretched, at least I could try to redeem myself from one of the consequences of my scheming.

Not that I was yet free of my own entanglements. I had to learn what had become of Mara. Her ability to withstand an interrogation after our encounter in Santa Fe still amazed me. Holding fast to her cover was quite a feat, but what had happened to her after her release? For sure, the Bureau would have placed a full tail on her to see where she went after Santa Fe. Did she shake it? Even if she had, the Bureau would check up on the family she supposedly had in Ohio. Had the Russians conjured such a deep cover that fellow travelers, duly rehearsed, would convincingly answer the field agents' questions when they came knocking?

As the flight dragged on, my worries about Mara mounted. I'd never told Paslett about her—what if he learned about her role on the Russian side of the operation? What if the Bureau took a crack at her and this time she broke? No way I could explain away my hiding of my contact with her. Paslett would drop me, Slater would have me; all my machinations would collapse like a tower of toothpicks. I'd planned everything so carefully, and I was so close to succeeding, but Mara could doom me.

Foolish me: I'd thought I could get some sleep on the flight.

PART 3
Redemption?

Washington, D.C.
July 16–17, 1945

CominCh File

FF1/DR

OFFICE OF NAVAL INTELLIGENCE
Sabotage, Espionage, and Countersubversion (B-7)
NAVY DEPARTMENT

SECRET   Washington, 25, D.C.   16 July 1945

From: Commander Burton Paslett
To: Rear Adm. Leo H. Thebaud
Subject: O.N.I. mission, New Mexico

Army Intelligence reports Lt. (j.g.) Ellis Voigt has identified security breach at site as Dr. Mason Adams Brode, son of Senator Harrison Wright Brode. Dr. Brode is currently detained and being questioned at site. F.B.I. involvement unavoidable but manageable (see below). Greater problem for O.N.I. concerns Senator Brode given his assignment Naval appropriations subcommittee. O.S.S. investigation now significant and urgent yet presents opportunity for O.N.I. All signs point to dissolution O.S.S. pending Japanese surrender.

Recommendations
1. O.N.I. should reconsider O.S.S. offer to continue joint mission. O.N.I. will carry on mission after expected O.S.S. dissolution.

2. F.B.I. Director will insist Bureau handle continued interrogation of Dr. Mason Adams Brode. We should expect President to defer to Director but Chief of Naval Operations must argue necessity O.N.I. leading investigation of Senator Brode.
3. Chief of Naval Operations should request letter of support from Major General Leslie Groves detailing O.N.I. vital part in identifying Dr. Brode as Soviet agent.

CHAPTER 41

WE LANDED AT BOLLING FIELD, ALONG THE POTOMAC IN SOUTHWEST Washington, at 1910. During our banked descent, I occasionally glimpsed the nighttime city through the portal window across from me. Cars and trucks moved in fits and starts, the capital's distinctive lattice of diagonal avenues, straight streets, and expansive traffic circles precisely illuminated by streetlamps. (The blackout had ended months earlier.) This yellowish light, added to the penumbra of countless business, government, and apartment building lights, gave the city a theatrical appearance, as if it were nothing more than an impossibly elaborate and miniature set design for a never-ending play. Had I returned from Site Y just one night earlier, I would have marveled at this sight, my first aerial look at Washington. But now the incandescent vista filled me with dread as I imagined the beautiful horrors of Trinity smothering the city. What Lot's wife had seen had turned her into a pillar of salt, and what we of Trinity had witnessed had transformed us into speechless prophets, burdened with top-secret visions of another Apocalypse. *Now I am become death, the destroyer of worlds.*

My O.N.I. partner, Terrance Daley, was waiting for me in the run-down Chrysler we always seemed to get from the motor pool. He was leaning against the driver's door, a cigarette poking from his meaty hand, his hat high on his broad forehead. Was he still angry with me for withholding the details of my undercover assignment? To my relief, he broke into a big grin when I approached, my duffel slung over my shoulder.

"Well, look who got a nice suntan."

"D'hell you're talking about?"

"Take a look." He stepped away from the car and I leaned to peer into the side mirror. Sure enough, my face and neck were red—I'd been so exhausted when I shaved earlier that day that I hadn't even noticed. I should have used the suntan lotion after all.

"Damn! You know that comes from hard toil under the blazing desert sun," I told Terrance. It took a lot of effort to sound carefree.

"Sure it does. Get in."

During the short drive to the Navy Building on the Mall, we avoided the subject of my assignment and the work Terrance had done in my absence, instead chatting about his wife, Marie, and their kids, and how much of a chance the Senators had to win the American League. But as we parked, I couldn't help but ask a pressing question.

"How's Paslett?"

"Dying to see you. An early morning cable from General Groves riled him up but good, and he can barely keep still waiting for you to stroll in. But you wouldn't know anything about what that cable said, would you?"

The edge to his voice told me his resentment hadn't fully faded. I resolved to repair my relationship with my partner as soon as possible. After I saw Paslett, after I made the delivery and broke ties with the N.K.V.D., after I checked to see how Kenny Newhurst was doing, after I determined what had become of Mara. But would *after* become *later*, would *later* become *never*, as was so often the pattern of my behavior? *No, things are different*, I told myself. *From now on, I'm a new man.*

COMMANDER PASLETT WAS INDEED IN AN AGITATED STATE.

"Jesus H. Christ, what did they do down there?"

A question I wasn't supposed to answer. To hell with Latham's order to keep quiet, I decided. If Groves had cabled the commander, then he knew the test was successful; knowing the details wouldn't compromise the secret. And Paslett might be more amenable to releasing me from my undercover work if he fully appreciated what had happened at Trinity.

So I told him. I described the spindly tower that had held the gadget and how I'd driven the arming party to the shelter more than five miles away; told him of the MPs who had lain in trenches with their feet pointed toward the zero point and the pieces of darkened glass we were all issued; described the scientists who had assembled behind the shelter to witness their creation. And I described the creation, the gadget being born: "Sir, it unleashed the light of heaven and the heat of hell, and even five miles from the detonation, the blast knocked us all down and gave me this sunburn." I pointed at my face. Then I told him about the unnaturally colorful clouds that issued forth, enveloping the predawn sky, and the three rings that had ascended.

"Holy motherfucker," Paslett whispered when I'd finished.

The curse startled me. The commander wasn't averse to swearing, but I'd never heard him use that epithet. Yet it was apt. Who could deny that Trinity had spawned one hell of a holy motherfucker?

"Commander, believe you me, the Japs are finished for sure when we start dropping these bombs."

"Do you know how many lives will be saved?" he asked in an awe-filled tone. "If we can get these bombs in theater pronto, there'll be no landings."

I nodded energetically. "Gonna be a lot of happy Marines and G.I.'s."

For a moment, he said nothing, his gaze directed toward his window and the darkened city visible through it, lost in his thoughts. I lit a cigarette and tried to push Trinity out of my head. I needed to focus, needed to get the commander's support for the endgame I'd plotted.

"Sir . . . ?"

"Right, sorry, Voigt. Groves cabled me you succeeded—let's hear it."

I kept my account brisk, concise. Covered the interrogations, the identification of Mason Adams Brode as the spy, and the reason why we couldn't arrest him immediately. Paslett nodded approvingly as I explained how I'd arranged for an innocent scientist to be arrested to lull Brode into a false sense of security. As I detailed my conversation with Brode in the car at Trinity, I pulled out the envelope from my jacket pocket and laid it down on the desk between us.

"Two physicists doctored the diagram Brode drew for me."

"It's all set for you to hand over, then."

"Yessir."

"How did you get him to trust you as a fellow Red?"

"He challenged me with the second-to-last question the N.K.V.D. apparently asks Americans being recruited for espionage."

"Which is?"

"'Are you ready to say good-bye to your family forever?'"

"Lucky you knew that." Translation: *How do you know the question?*

"I'll say. It came up during that case we had a while back involving the Navy Yard provost guard." We'd had a couple cases involving provost guards, which made it easier for me to type up and backdate a document for the file in case the commander checked. I hoped Paslett wouldn't ask for details now; fortunately, he was eager to move the debriefing along.

"Who's handling the interrogation of Brode in New Mexico?"

"Colonel Latham and, believe it or not, our old friend Clayton Slater." He stared at me. "You gotta be kidding me! When did he show up?"

"Right after I got there, sir."

"He had to have G-2's blessing to be there," he said. Army intelligence. "So why did Latham . . ." He trailed off as the answer occurred to him. "Slater claimed you couldn't be trusted and Latham heard him out."

"Bingo. Slater had the Bureau's Chicago field office dig up dirt from when I was a kid. Interviews with classmates, teachers, neighbors. All he got was, a gal I briefly dated when I was in high school, turns out her pop was a commie."

"For the love of Mike, that's what he presented?"

I took a long drag and exhaled the smoke over my shoulder. Time to address the real reason Slater was gunning for me: He believed that I had framed someone else for the murder of Logan Skerrill, whom the Bureau had run as a double agent. At all costs, I had to keep Paslett from learning that Slater's hunch was correct, that I had killed Skerrill under orders from Himmel and had then framed an innocent man and killed Himmel to protect myself.

"Sir, remember how Slater told you and Daley that Philip Greene, the commie who did Skerrill, says I framed him?" At his nod I continued. "Slater flat-out told me the Bureau's digging, and digging deep, to use his phrase, til they find something. That's why he came in waving affidavits from people I haven't seen since I was a kid. He wanted Latham to sideline me and put him in charge of finding the spy."

"Obviously Latham saw right through that B.S."

"Sure, he knows Hoover wants to take security operations away from Army. A'course, he also needed me to make the I.D. of Brode since I know what his voice sounds like. But he did let Slater take part in the lineup."

"Did Slater come to Trinity?"

"Nosir. I convinced Latham that Slater should be the one to arrest the innocent scientist and question him during the test while I made contact with Brode."

"Good move. And once you make the delivery"—he tapped the envelope—"and we write up our full report, the Bureau will come out looking like sore losers."

"Speaking of sore losers, sir, have you had any additional trouble from O.S.S.?"

He gave me a strange look. "Why do you ask?"

"M'sure it's not important, but during my debriefing at Site Y Colonel Latham asked if I'd heard anything from you about O.S.S. while I was there, at Site Y."

"I don't know why he would ask you that. He knew we weren't in contact." His tone was neutral but forced—was there more to the O.S.S. angle than he'd let on?

"Exactly what I was thinking, sir. Which is why I mentioned it—seemed like an awful queer question."

"I'd forget about it if I were you, Voigt."

"Yessir." I picked up the envelope and returned it to my pocket. "Now we wait for the Russians to pick me up."

CHAPTER 42

D IDN'T TAKE LONG FOR THE RUSSIANS TO FETCH ME. SOMEONE MUST
have been watching my flat, for I'd only just changed out of my uniform and poured a tumbler of rye when I heard a hard knock on the
door. I sighed, took a long, long drink, and made sure I had my cigarettes
before I opened the door.

Shovel-face glared at me. Without speaking, he pointed to a dark Ford
sedan parked across the street. He stepped aside to let me go first, then
followed close on my heels, his rasping breath audible. Whatever he'd had
for dinner, it had lots of onions.

The rear driver side door opened from within the car and I got in.
Shovel-face's sidekick sat in the back on the passenger side. He handed
me a black hood.

"Put this on and stay down," he ordered.

The thick cotton fabric stank of another man's sweat. As I sank down
in the seat, propped against the door, I closed my eyes and tried not to

think of what had happened to the hood's previous user. The N.K.V.D. had tortured me while my eyes were wide open, so what had they done to that poor soul? Telling myself the Russians had no reason to hurt me now didn't help. Shovel-face had had no reason to shoot Kenny Newhurst, but he had done it anyway. No matter how good my story was, they might use the electrical prod to make sure I wasn't holding anything back. My heart raced and I sucked in my breath at the memory of the pain, the timeless agony of being shocked. The drive, whatever our destination, wasn't far, four miles at most, but it felt like an interminable journey.

One of the Russians walked me from the car into a building and pushed me down into a chair before yanking the hood off. No surprise, a bright, hot light was trained right onto my face. I almost smiled—the N.K.V.D. couldn't know that no light could ever blind me now, not after Trinity.

"Welcome home, Lieutenant."

I recognized the professorial-sounding American who had interrogated me while Shovel-face had tortured me.

"Can I smoke?" I answered him. Since they hadn't even let me finish my drink before sweeping me up, the least they could do was let me smoke.

"Go ahead."

I took out my Luckies, lit up, and stole a glance upward during my first exhale. I glimpsed a high, arched ceiling supported by steel trusses. The floor was cement, and the vast space smelled of motor oil and grease. A service garage, I guessed. Behind me, I heard a whisk of shoes, a scraping against the cement, and the creak of jointed wood. Shovel-face and his sidekick, sitting down. Knowing the two attack dogs were seated rather than standing comforted me only slightly.

"Do you have our package?"

I said nothing, just pulled the envelope from my jacket pocket and tossed it. It landed with a soft slap in the darkness in front of me. I couldn't see the hand that picked it up.

"Check it out," the Professor told an unseen fourth person, who walked away briskly toward the far wall. I heard a door open and close.

"How's your memory, Lieutenant?"

"When my brains aren't being scrambled, excellent."

He chuckled. "There shouldn't be any need for prompts tonight, as long as we're satisfied with your answers."

"Then let's get to it."

Get to it he did. His questions and instructions were precise, comprehensive, relentless. They ranged from the picayune—*What was the name of your train and what time did it arrive in Santa Fe?*—to the profound—*Describe what you saw and felt when the weapon was detonated.* He asked a lot of questions. How had I made contact, how did I convince "our man" (Brode) I was "a mutual agent," where did we meet, was anyone else present when we talked? He wanted me to estimate the size of Site Y and describe the facilities I'd seen. Who was Colonel Latham, was he a capable officer? Why was an F.B.I. agent present? Who was in charge: names, duties, personalities. He wanted to know everything; having the diagram wasn't enough. For the Russians to even think of building a gadget of their own, they needed to have a sense of the resources, manpower, and logistics required. I wasn't a scientist or an engineer, of course—I could only share what I'd seen as a layperson, as it were—but even the skimpiest of impressions would be helpful to them, and I had no choice but to be truthful, in order to sound convincing when I did have to lie. I assuaged my conscience by reminding myself that Oppenheimer and Fuchs had doped the Russians but good by falsifying Brode's diagram.

And many were my lies and omissions. A real whopper: that I'd convinced Latham and Groves there was no spy present at Site Y. I couldn't reveal that Brode had been arrested, of course, or that we'd questioned a slate of Site Y personnel in order to identify Brode in the first place. I had to fabricate entire conversations and scenes. Brode and I, walking along the perimeter of Site Y one evening; Brode working dutifully on the diagram in his quarters while I waited in the officers' club; Brode confiding in me that he'd lost his nerve, that he was worried Army intelligence was on to him, that it was high time for him to cut ties with the Russians. This last lie was my insurance policy. Eventually, the N.K.V.D. would learn that Brode had been arrested. I wanted the Professor and his Russian handlers to believe Brode himself was responsible for getting caught, wanted them to believe that I'd done all I could to bolster his confidence and give him a pep talk while I was at Site Y. Admittedly, Brode as a nervous Nellie was a stretch, but to my relief the Professor didn't get suspicious.

The interrogation had gone on for hours, according to the pressing ache of my swollen bladder, before the Professor finally asked me about Mara. He did so obliquely.

"Did you ever leave the base before going to the test site?"

"Yes, Colonel Latham sent me to Santa Fe."

"How did you get there?"

"I drove myself in a jeep from the base motor pool."

"And you went by yourself?"

"Yes."

"Why did he send you to Santa Fe?"

"To be briefed by a woman named Dorothy McKibbin."

After I answered a slew of questions about her, he asked, "What did you do after the briefing?"

"I went to get lunch at a place she'd recommended called Joe King's Blue Ribbon Bar."

"Did you meet anyone there?"

Time to push back, I resolved. "You know I did."

"Excuse me?"

"Your favorite fellow traveler Mara sidled up to me at the bar."

He responded quietly but firmly. "The treatment for insolence is the same used for memory gaps, understood?"

"Understood." I'd hoped to rattle him a bit, but he was too good.

"Tell us about your conversation with her and leave nothing out."

I complied but deliberately omitted our visit to the shop where Mara had bought a bracelet. They might shock me for "forgetting," but I had to know if Mara had made it back too.

"Is that everything, Lieutenant?" the Professor asked. He knew I was leaving something out, which meant Mara had returned and told him everything about our encounter. She wasn't in F.B.I. custody, then.

I hid my relief in an exhale of smoke. "Yes, that's all we—wait, I'm sorry, I forgot, we visited a little shop after the bar. She bought a silver bracelet as a souvenir."

"Anything else you might have forgotten?" There was an edge to his voice, but I was ready to push back again.

"No, but I do have some bad news."

"Oh?"

"I'm done, I'm out, I'm finished, for a long while at least." He started to interrupt, but I plowed on. "Agent Slater has a hard-on for me a mile long. He's got the Bureau's Chicago field office digging into my past. Until I figure out a way to trip him up, I can't have any further contact with you or any of your friends."

I flicked my cigarette butt to the floor, watching the ember scatter, and pressed my hands against my thighs to keep them from trembling. The Professor might agree—or not. And *not* could turn out very badly for me. He might insist on keeping the status quo, or he might decide that making the problem—me—go away was the best solution.

"Well, that is a problem, but—"

I cut him off. "The good news is, General Groves, Colonel Latham, and Commander Paslett are awful happy that I proved there was no spy at Site Y. Right now I'm their fair-haired boy, so if I go dormant and take care of the Bureau, then it goes without saying that I'll be highly placed for any future operations you might have."

This was my lifeline, the pitch to keep them from liquidating me.

A long pause. "Yes, I see what you're saying, Lieutenant," the Professor finally said. "Maybe you should hibernate for a while."

I nodded curtly and stood up, my legs aching. When I turned to leave, Shovel-face was looking at me with a curious mix of disinterest and malice, as if I were a buzzing fly he couldn't be troubled to swat. With barely controlled fury, I recalled my mantra from the night he'd tortured me with the electrical prod. *Kill Shovel-face.* I couldn't kill him, not here, not yet—perhaps never—but I couldn't simply walk past him, not after what he'd done to Kenny Newhurst. As I passed him on his left side, I stopped and said, "You know, you left something behind at my flat the night you searched it—do you want it back?"

"What? What do you mean?"

I let my mind go blank and gave my body over to the training I'd received after I'd been assigned to O.N.I. We recruits had smirked at the training officer who had mastered what he called "the martial arts" during stints in the Philippines and China—until he gave us a demonstration. He hadn't taught us much, just a few basic skills, but we'd practiced them relentlessly.

With my right arm cocked, I pivoted on my left foot until my toes were turned in the opposite direction, swinging my right foot up and out. I put all the force of my momentum into a roundhouse kick straight into the Russian's face. His nose shattered, blood sprayed; he toppled over in his chair. When his partner jumped to his feet, I delivered a flat, swift chop to his throat. The blow wasn't hard enough to shatter his larynx, but he'd have to breathe through his nose for a while. As for Shovel-face, he'd have a new nickname by the time his nose healed: Flat-face. As the two Russians rolled on the floor, moaning and gurgling, I looked straight at the Professor, who hadn't budged from his chair.

"He didn't need to shoot the kid," I said.

"They will come after you," he said matter-of-factly. He didn't have to add: *And I won't stop them.*

I didn't respond—because I wanted them to come after me. The Metropolitan Police couldn't arrest them for attempted murder because the Soviets would, I was certain, produce diplomatic passports that would allow them to leave the country. And a kick to the face wasn't the full payback the two had earned for what they'd done to Kenny Newhurst. Without another word, I left.

CHAPTER 43

N THE MORNING, I CALLED PROVIDENCE HOSPITAL: KENNY NEWHURST
had been discharged to complete his recovery at home. I hailed a taxi
and gave the driver the Newhursts' address. *Should I have called first?* I
wondered. But what I had to say, I had to say in person.

Hard to believe less than two weeks had passed since my first visit to
the Newhursts' well-kept home. I didn't want to dwell on all that had happened, but it was impossible not to: the shooting of Kenny; my rescue of
him and frantic escape from the police; rushing to get Filbert Donniker
out of harm's way; going on the lam only to give myself up to the N.K.V.D.;
my torture; my encounters with Mara; the double mission to identify Brode
as the spy while convincing the Russians I had done their bidding. So far,
my wretched scheming was working—by delivering a false diagram of the
bomb, I'd begun to make amends for my past treason—but my conscience
was far from clear.

I paid the driver, straightened my hat, and walked briskly to the front door. Under my arm was the package I'd put together the previous night with Commander Paslett's help. The lawn was cut, the flower bed freshly watered. The storm door was open, so I knocked on the screen door frame.

"Coming," Georgette called from within. Walking from the kitchen, she didn't recognize me until she was a few steps away. "Oh my God, it's you!" Her welcoming expression recoiled into a mask of fear, of repulsion: eyes wide and blinking rapidly, mouth open, head tilted.

"Missus Newhurst, I'm here to ask for—"

Lyle's rush down the hall and his bellow of anger cut me off.

"Get off my property you sonofabitch!" he shouted. He yanked open the screen and shoved me in the chest. I didn't try to stop him, and the force of his blow sent me reeling—I almost toppled down the porch steps. Fortunately I didn't drop the package. Lyle raised his fist but didn't strike me when he saw I wasn't going to defend myself. His face was red, eyes bright with rage, his carefully parted hair mussed and his tie askew. Over his shoulder, I could see Kenny standing in the hall behind his mother. The Newhursts had probably been finishing breakfast, Lyle having a last cup of coffee before heading to work. I had no right to be there, no right to ask for their forgiveness; but no penitent ever does.

"Mister Newhurst, I'm here to ask for your forgiveness and for your son's. If you want me to leave, I'll go now and never return, I promise."

"Who the hell d'you think you are! You almost got my son killed!"

"It's the worst thing I've ever done in my life, sir, and the shame and remorse I feel for the harm I've done to you and your family will never go away."

My quiet tone placated him and he lowered his fist. Kenny was now standing next to his mother, who had her arm tight around his shoulder as they watched the scene from behind the screen.

"Everything okay, Lyle?" a man's voice carried loudly from the porch next door.

I kept my solemn expression fixed on Lyle, waiting for him to answer.

"Yeah, everything's fine, Pete, thanks," he said tersely.

"Lyle," Georgette called, "maybe you . . ." She trailed off when he held up his hand.

"Well, I suppose, if that's why you're here, then I guess you oughta come inside."

I nodded and followed him into the house, taking off my hat. Lyle ushered us into the living room where I'd lied to Georgette at the start of my misadventure. She and Lyle sat on the sofa with Kenny in the middle while I took one of the upholstered chairs facing them. I set my hat and the package on the coffee table. Kenny watched me with a mix of curiosity and anxiety. He was thinner than I remembered and had a bruise around his right eye but otherwise showed no signs of his trauma. He wore light brown trousers and a striped sport shirt. He'd just had a haircut, and there was a thin white stripe along the nape of his neck where the barber's razor had exposed the tan line. A good sign, that—meant he was spending time outside.

"How are you, Kenny?" I asked him. "Are you fully recovered?"

"I'm okay—I mean, I'm feeling pretty good, sir. The doctor says I can do anything I want now s'long as I still get lotsa rest."

"Please call me Ellis, Kenny. I never properly introduced myself." I stood and reached across the table to shake his hand. "Lieutenant junior grade Ellis Voigt, U.S. Navy."

"I'm Kenny Newhurst," he answered, bringing a smile to his mother's face.

"Do you remember me from that night at the Automat in May when I came into the kitchen?"

"A'course. You were with that old guy, and you had some sorta rig to secretly listen to two guys out in the dining room."

"Right. Kenny, I'm here to tell you I made a horrible mistake that night. I left the Automat believing the men we were dealing with—men who are trying to hurt our country—would only be concerned with me and the man who came with me. I didn't think they would go to the Automat to find out if anyone had helped us. But someone had—you. Because I asked you to. And without hesitating, you helped, and when I told you to tell no one about our visit, you kept that promise. And then I failed you, and your folks. I failed to protect you. I didn't come to check up on you until it was too late."

"But you came and got me from, from those men who were . . . hurting me."

"I should never have allowed them to find you in the first place, Kenny. It's my responsibility to make sure innocent people don't get hurt when they get involved in what I do, and I didn't meet my duty to you and your folks."

He didn't answer, his head bowed and hands folded in his lap. Was he remembering the pain and horror of being brutalized by the Russians?

"So I'm here to ask for your forgiveness, Kenny. I failed to protect you after you helped me. I came into your home and I lied to your mother when I was trying to find out where you were, all because I believed I had to keep my mission secret. And when I found you, and got you to safety, I fled like a coward instead of staying by your side." I almost added *I don't deserve your forgiveness* but caught myself. It was true, but to say it aloud would be inexcusably manipulative. And I was bone-weary tired of giving in to the instincts of deceit, deception, and manipulation.

Raising his head and looking me in the eye, Kenny said, "I forgive you, Ellis."

"Thank you, Kenny. I'm deeply grateful for your kindness."

He looked abashed and lowered his head again. Georgette squeezed his shoulder as Lyle watched me.

"Kenny, on behalf of the U.S. Navy, I'd like to present you with this." I picked up the package and extended it to him.

He tore the glossy blue wrapping from the box and lifted off the top. His eyes widened when he saw the cast bronze medal and blue ribbon fitted inside a velvet-lined case. His parents leaned in to look.

"What is it?" Kenny asked.

"The Distinguished Civilian Service Award. It's awarded to civilians who make an extraordinary sacrifice or contribution to the operations of the Navy, and you, Kenny, did both. Your efforts to help us at the Automat and the harm you suffered as a result showed exceptional loyalty to your country and personal bravery. I can't think of anyone more deserving of this honor."

"Oh my gosh," he whispered. "Can I take it out?"

"A'course," I said.

He cradled it in his palm and proudly showed it to his parents. His mother ran her finger along the bas relief of the Navy's insignia, an eagle spreading his wings across an anchor.

"Oh honey, it's beautiful," she said.

"It's really just for me?" he exclaimed. Lyle, Georgette, and I all smiled.

"You better believe it, Kenny," I said. "Now, I do have to take it back today because we want to confer it on you at a ceremony at the Navy Building in two weeks. The Chief of Naval Operations will be there, and a lotta other brass too, and you'll get to have your picture taken with them all after the medal is pinned on you. How's that sound?"

"That sounds great!"

"Here's the announcement with the details—this makes it official." I pulled the embossed envelope from my jacket pocket and handed it to Lyle, who carefully broke the seal and removed the embossed placard.

"Look at that," he murmured, handing the card to Kenny, who read it eagerly.

"Listen to this, Mom! It says I 'provided indispensable aid to a crucial intelligence mission, demonstrating valor, bravery, and devotion to the United States of America.' Wow!"

"We're proud of you, son," she answered as her husband nodded and patted him on the back.

Commander Paslett, knowing what had happened to Kenny, had eagerly agreed with me that Kenny deserved the award. Waking up the Chief of Naval Operations to get his immediate approval had caused quite a stir, especially since the commendation could only make vague reference to the mission, but Paslett had worked it all out the night before, even calling in a favor to get a temporary "loan" of one of the medals, which were stored in a safe.

"Can I tell my friends about this?" Kenny asked me.

"It's better to wait until after the ceremony, okay? But you can hang on to the medal til I have to go." His head bobbed excitedly as I caught Lyle's eye and asked, "May I speak to you and your wife for a moment?"

Lyle nodded and the three of us stood. I followed the Newhursts into the kitchen, where the breakfast plates were still on the table.

"I just have a few more things to tell you," I said. "First, it goes without saying that the Navy will pay all your son's medical expenses. Have the bills sent to me, Lieutenant junior grade Ellis Voigt, O.N.I., at the Navy Building, and I'll make sure they're promptly and fully paid."

"We will," Lyle said firmly.

Now I looked straight at Georgette. "Missus Newhurst, I again want to apologize for misrepresenting myself when I came to your home looking for your son. There's no excuse for my actions."

She didn't answer, and her return gaze was hard to read. Suspicion still in her eyes, yes, but was there also relief? Anxiety? Anger? Maybe all this and more—who was I to know or even try to guess what she was feeling? Lyle was right: I'd almost gotten their son killed and no medal, however distinguished, could erase the anguish, pain, and distress I'd caused them.

I cleared my throat. "Lastly, I want to say again how sorry I am for the trouble I've caused you and Kenny."

Georgette looked away, still silent.

Lyle paused. "We appreciate you coming here," he finally said.

"Thank you for hearing me out." I extended my hand and he shook it.

"What about the man who shot Kenny?" he blurted out. "When will he be arrested?"

I carefully considered my response. "Yes, he must be punished," I decided to say. "Would you like me to make sure this happens?"

"Yes, I would," Lyle answered immediately.

I looked at Georgette. She nodded firmly.

"Then I make this promise to you: The man who shot your son will pay for what he did."

They will come after you. So the Professor had warned me after I thrashed his goons. What would I do when Shovel-face came for his revenge? The N.K.V.D. wouldn't let me get away with killing him. Was there a way to make him suffer the pain he'd caused Kenny as well as me? At that moment, standing in the Newhursts' kitchen and studying their grim, resolute expressions, I had no answers to these questions. But this promise I would keep, somehow, I knew that.

TERRANCE WAS OUT WHEN I RETURNED TO THE NAVY BUILDING. I TOOK advantage of his absence from our shared office to surreptitiously draft and backdate a memorandum detailing how I knew what questions the N.K.V.D. asked its American espionage recruits, including the one Mason Adams Brode had challenged me with: *Are you ready to say good-bye to your family forever?* I kept the document simple, making sure the information provided was incomplete and couched in hearsay and conditional phrasing. *Suspect claimed Soviets asked . . . May also be the case Soviets ask . . . Suspect said he was told . . .* The "suspect" was a naval provost guard who had, in fact, clumsily entangled himself in a communist cell and was now serving ten years in the brig for letting his Red pals sneak into the Navy Yard one night to steal a prototype for a new periscope. I misfiled the forgery but made sure it wouldn't be too hard to find during a thorough search.

It was almost noon when I finished. Still no Terrance, so I wrote him a note before I went out for lunch: *Hey, what say you and me visit Margie's sometime soon? Your vacation from my winning charm and wit is now at an end and you can expect to see my mug every day now. Least I can do to soften the blow is to buy you a modestly priced dinner and some cold beers.*

Margie's was an ancient saloon that served superb breaded pork tender-loin sandwiches and never ran out of Schlitz. During better times together, Terrance and I had spent many hours there talking over cases. I hoped he'd see the invitation for what it really was, a peace offering. It was, though it was also something else: the second-to-last task I needed to complete to make my life normal again and see my wretched scheme to a close.

CHAPTER 44

EFORE MY LAST TASK, A VISIT TO A PAWNSHOP, I TOOK LUNCH AT A hash joint close to the Navy Building. I'd skipped breakfast, so I went with three eggs over hash with a stack of toast on the side and washed it down with too many cups of coffee. Scanning the headlines was like starting a novel—the names, places, and events seemed strange. TRUMAN, CHURCHILL TOUR BERLIN AFTER MEETING INFORMALLY AT POTSDAM CASTLE . . . EQUAL RIGHTS BATTLE FLARES IN CONGRESS . . . But not all of the headlines were unfamiliar: PACIFIC WAR TOUGHER, SAYS EUROPE VET. He wasn't exaggerating. After fighting in Italy and Germany, he was now serving in the Forty-first Infantry Division, which had the unenviable task of flushing Japs out of scattered bases in remote areas of the Philippines. The heat, jungle, and malaria were just as deadly as the Japs. *Hang on, buddy*, I thought. *Salvation is on its way.*

The counterman collected my dirty plates and topped off my coffee. I refolded the *Post* and lit up. How long would it take to deliver the bombs to a forward base? Figure a week or so to ready the weapons for delivery, then another week to ship them, probably on a light or heavy cruiser. Faster to fly, of course, but risky, too—what if the aircraft went down? Once the bombs arrived, a few days or more would be needed to finalize the mission and crew and wait for the right weather. I reopened the paper, found an events calendar, studied the days. If my estimates were accurate, the bombs would start falling in early August, unless the Japs surrendered first. But if the hard, bloody slog of the Forty-first Infantry was any measure, they weren't about to quit.

As I walked to the pawnshop, I marveled at the secret I carried with me. All passersby—men, women, and children; young and old; military and civilian; Negro and white—knew the war would soon end, but they had no idea how. And even when they learned what the bomb was, they'd never know, for real, what it could do. Yes, there would be lots of photographs of the leveled, blackened plains that had been cities, and there would be descriptions of the bomb's tremendously destructive power; but no account, however detailed, could even begin to capture what it felt like to witness the bomb's blossoming.

The pawnshop clerk, a middle-aged, paunchy man in an untucked shirt, took my stub without comment. He came back from the caged storage area and set my item down on the counter unceremoniously. It was a cheap mantel clock in need of refurbishment. The veneer was chipped, the face numbers tarnished. No one with sense would buy this clock. The key was missing, and I'd hammered the main spring to break the works. Better, more attractive clocks could be purchased for half the price of a repair. But what was hidden behind the works was priceless to the knowledge-able owner.

"Eight bucks," the clerk grunted.

I counted the cash, he swept it up, and the bills promptly disappeared into an unseen drawer.

"Got a box?" I asked.

"I don't got."

I shot him a look. "Eight bucks and you can't spare a box?"

"This ain't Safeway," he grumbled, but my glare wore him down. He shuffled into the back. I opened the hatch in the back of the clock, groped for the folded piece of paper, and slipped it into my pocket before he returned with a shallow fruit crate.

I spared him the trouble of responding to thanks, put the clock in the crate, and padded it with my newspaper. A clock and watch repair shop was just a few blocks away. The proprietor looked at me with pity when I asked him how much it would cost to repair my clock.

"Gee pal, hope you didn't pay much for this," he said. He was a thin man with a perfectly bald head, a crease around his right eye from clenching a loupe all day.

"Eight bucks, from A-Straight Pawn Brokers," I answered.

He snorted. "You got had, bad. See here"—he turned the clock over and pointed at the mangled works—"someone's pounded the hell outta it. You'd need a new works, and for something as run-of-the-mill as this, it's not worth it."

"Sonofabitch," I said. "So it's worthless?"

"Absolutely."

I checked my watch. "Dammit, I gotta get back. Think you could throw it away for me?"

"Sure. Now look," gesturing at the shelves of clocks around him, "we got lotsa nice pieces for sale here, if you're interested."

"Maybe another time. Thanks for the appraisal." I knocked twice on the counter, said good-bye, and left.

Had anyone tailed me? I hadn't noticed anything suspicious, but I wasn't taking any chances, not with the F.B.I. determined to nail me and the Russians likely watching me out of habit. If anyone traced my steps, the pawnbroker and the clock fixer would independently tell a true story: I was a guy with a broken clock.

As for the paper I'd removed from the clock, I took care of that on my walk back to the Navy Building. Hand in pocket, I slowly, tediously ripped it up, which was a lot harder than I thought it would be. When I had a handful of confetti, I paused to tie my shoe over a storm drain, dropped the shreds through the grate, and watched the dirty current carry them away.

And with that, the diagram of the bomb that Mason Adams Brode had delivered in May to Henry Himmel, the Soviet agent I'd killed, disappeared. The N.K.V.D. would keep looking for Himmel, but now that they had a replacement diagram, one they believed was authentic, the search would lose urgency. And the Soviets would soon commit untold resources and manpower to building the bomb the wrong way.

I knew they'd eventually succeed. My scheme would set them back, but they'd learn from their mistakes and find a way to their own gadget. I also reminded myself not to celebrate my double cross with abandon. The N.K.V.D. had agreed to let me go dormant, but they'd be back; I still needed to devise a way to permanently detach myself without ever exposing my past deeds. Agent Clayton Slater and the F.B.I. remained a pressing problem. How would I get them off my back? Finally, obstructing the Russians from getting the bomb wasn't complete absolution for my past treason. So how would I continue to make amends? Was being a loyal officer duty enough? Trouble still trailed me, even if I'd shed much of its weight. Still, I entered the Navy Building feeling better than I had in months. *Goddamn, I did it*, I allowed myself to think. I sure felt a lot more secure than I had in a long, long time.

Which is why I didn't think there was anything unusual about the summons from Paslett on my desk, ordering me to the conference room.

CHAPTER 45

HE WAS SEATED FACING THE DOOR. HER GINGER HAIR WAS PINNED
beneath an olive drab cap with a brass eagle badge that reflected the
overhead light. A mosaic of service ribbons brightened her tunic, and a
tan tie was perfectly knotted between the collar points of a matching shirt.
She looked right at me when I opened the door. Her expression was neutral,
uninterested, as if I was a delivery boy bringing in lunch. But I'd seen her
smile, many times; I'd caressed her smoothly planed cheeks; I'd thrilled at
the wet crush of her lips on mine; I'd gazed into her eyes studying me at my
flat and at a bar in Santa Fe. I clenched the doorknob to steady myself as
my legs went weak. I felt dizzy, stomach churning. I tried to set my face to
match her detached expression, let go of the knob, and entered.

The woman I knew as Mara—the beauty I'd bedded the very night we'd
met; who had tried to dope me for the N.K.V.D; who had traveled to New
Mexico to watch me for the Russians; who had endured and walked away
from a grueling interrogation after our encounter in Santa Fe—was not

a fellow traveler, not a Party member, not a Soviet spy: she was an Army captain.

I'd been played but good. All the cues I'd misread rushed back into my head. The setup at the bar the night we'd met, her ability to put on accents, the ease with which she'd found me in New Mexico, and the fact she'd weathered that interrogation were all evidence of her experience, training, and talent—not as a fellow traveler or Russian agent but as an officer in the U.S. armed services.

I felt sick but somehow snapped off a salute. Paslett put me at ease and motioned at an empty chair. I sat, now facing him and Mara. Next to her was a brigadier general, his stout frame swelling the buttons on his uniform, his fleshy neck edging over his collar. What remained of his hair was slicked and combed over a scalp that looked like worn leather, wrinkled and piebald. He watched me through heavily lidded eyes. To say he looked like a toad was an insult to toads. His cheeks bulged, his nose was crooked, and his lower lip drooped, exposing the dark recesses of mottled gums slick with saliva. But the features I took special note of were the black Mont Blanc pen lying on the table in front of him and the pinky ring with a nugget of a diamond. *Am I ugly? So what—I'm richer than you'll ever be*, the pen and ring said.

"Brigadier General Matthew Wilburton, Captain Gail Quincy," Paslett told me.

I nodded numbly. *Does she know . . .*

"General Wilburton is Deputy Director of the Strategic Services Operations for the O.S.S. He's been directing Captain Quincy in an undercover operation for some time." . . . *that I'm a double agent?*

Paslett paused, turned his head toward me. His look was an iceberg. "Captain Quincy infiltrated the same N.K.V.D. cell you did, Voigt. But you already knew that, didn't you?"

"Yessir," I said hoarsely. "I know Captain Quincy as Mara." *What has she told them? What if—*

"Just Mara?"

"And Elizabeth. In Santa Fe, she called herself Elizabeth."—*the Russians told her how long I've been on their string?* I swallowed bile, kept my lips pressed tight.

"Just so happens the captain was telling us about her time in New Mexico when you knocked."

Jesus, am I finished? For an instant, a torrent of dread images blackened my consciousness. Being arrested, in this very room; being dragged from the building in handcuffs; a windowless cell, tasteless food on a metal tray, endless hours of interrogation; the shame, shock, and humiliation on my parents' faces; the dangling straps on the chair in the chamber. But a vision of the bomb's brilliant, blinding light saved me. If Mara had suspicions, if she'd shared them, nothing I said or did now could save me. But if I went weak, if I squirmed and stammered like a man with something to hide, I'd sure as hell look suspicious. So what would an innocent man do?

Paslett started to say something, but I cut him off.

"Why the fuck didn't you tell me?" I shouted at her, jabbing a finger toward her. "Look what those bastards did," yelling now at the general. I yanked at my collar to expose the electrocution scar. "They tortured me, they shot a boy! He almost died, for fuck's sake!" I shot to my feet, my chair toppled over. "The front I put up to the Russians was hard enough without having to play her as a Red!"

Wilburton's surprise caused his mouth to sag further. Mara—Gail—didn't react at all to my outburst.

"Pick up your chair and sit down, Lieutenant," Paslett ordered me.

I complied and took a deep breath. "Look sir, I'm sorry—"

"Zip it, Lieutenant."

I shut up.

"She didn't know about you either, Voigt," Paslett said.

"What?" My eyes darted to Gail, who nodded slowly.

Wilburton cleared his throat. "When the O.N.I. operation came to our attention, I proposed to General Groves and Commander Paslett that we withhold your"—he gestured at Gail, then me—"true identities from one another in order to ensure the fidelity of our separate operations."

"You knew, sir?" I asked Paslett. He was part of the deception all along? All this time, I believed I was master of the maze, playing dual roles; and all this time, Paslett, Groves, and this Wilburton were running their own double game. Paslett's response to my question about the O.S.S. last night suddenly took on added meaning: *I'd forget about it if I were you, Voigt.* I also remembered what he had said the night before I gave myself over to the Russians: *I'll get Groves to say yes*. Was that how Paslett had clinched Groves's cooperation, by telling him about the O.S.S. operation, or had Groves been in on the fix from the get-go? Either way, Paslett's complaints about the O.S.S. had been feints all along.

"It was for your own good, the both of you," the commander said. "If the Russians noticed any change in your behavior toward one another, you both were finished, and I don't just mean for undercover work—I mean for good. As long as Captain Quincy thought you were on the Russians' string for real and you thought she was working for them too, you both behaved naturally."

How long had Paslett known? My decision not to tell him about any of my encounters with "Mara," starting with the night I'd met her, was now an enormous liability. As soon as we were alone, he'd demand to know why I'd neglected to tell him about "Mara" throughout the operation. For sure, Gail's briefings to Wilburton had detailed our encounters. Had the general already shared these briefings with Paslett?

"The very fact you are both sitting here, safe and sound, confirms the wisdom of our decision," Wilburton added. "Now we're well situated to merge our respective operations, or hunts, if you will, in pursuit of bigger quarry."

"'Merge our operations'?" I asked with a sinking feeling.

"They want us to work together," Gail said. It was the first time she'd spoken since I'd entered the room. Her voice sounded completely different: no trace of either a Southern or mid-Atlantic accent. Where was she from, for real? Who was she?

"To do what?" I managed to say. I barely heard Wilburton's needlessly wordy answer about how Commander Paslett would brief me, then we would all meet again. I hardly noticed the general and Gail take their leave, though I must have stood and saluted them. *Can't escape . . . can't escape . . .* The realization beat into my head like a metronome. My scheme hadn't failed—it had succeeded wildly! I'd so expertly posed as a Red agent that my superiors wanted me to keep doing it. Since May, when I'd made the decision to break with the Russians and make amends for my past treason, my greatest fear had been exposure. I had convinced myself, unshakably so, that fulfillment of my scheme would set me free, never suspecting that it might just keep me a prisoner.

"Voigt!"

Paslett's booming voice snapped me back.

"Sorry, sir, you were saying?"

"Why didn't you brief me about Captain Quincy?"

"Because I was sleeping with her, sir," I answered promptly. For all the risk such an admission carried, it was the only way to keep Paslett from getting suspicious.

"Starting when?"

"First time, the night I met her, sir. She played it like a one-night stand, but it felt like a setup. Sure enough, the night the Russians picked me up, she tried to dope my drink to make it easy for them. I Mickey-Finned her instead, left her passed out in my flat. When I got back from my interrogation by the Russians, she was still there. I decided to try and turn her, figuring she'd tell all to the Russians. It was kinda like life insurance: the Russians were more likely to accept me if they thought I still had some allegiances to our side and so I was trying to recruit her for us."

"Did you know she was coming to New Mexico?"

"Nosir. I figured there was no way anyone could get near me while I was on the base, but after Slater showed up, Colonel Latham sent me into town while he heard Slater out. Mara—I mean Captain Quincy—followed me to the bar where we had lunch. She was posing as a tourist. In order to keep the Russians happy, I had to tell her something, and the only way I could think of to do that without being overheard or recorded was, well, to go back to her hotel and whisper in her ear while we, uh, covered up our conversation by—"

"I get the picture, Lieutenant." He drummed his fingers on the table. "Hauling her ashes as part of your cover isn't a minor detail, is it?" A statement, not a question. He wasn't as yet satisfied with my explanation—I needed to give him more. Time for another risk, I realized.

"The thing is, sir, the way Mara—I mean Captain Quincy—found me, it was because the N.K.V.D. found me first." To appease the commander, I had to tell him about the first interrogation, at the empty factory, which so far I'd kept secret from him. I wished I knew how much he knew about the O.S.S. operation! Although Wilburton and Paslett had told each other about their undercover agents, that didn't mean they had shared full operational details with each other, so I had to be careful not to share more than I had to.

"Before they picked up Kenny Newhurst?"

"Yessir. It was the same two agents that I let pick me up later, after I'd been on the lam and we decided to let them find me."

"Why did you go with them?"

My fate rested on whether or not Paslett believed my answer. If it didn't ring true, he'd start to think harder about the F.B.I.'s suspicions, he might accept that the Bureau was on to something. He'd scrutinize all my previous operations, looking for irregularities. And he'd find them, including the forged document I'd just filed to cover my tracks regarding my knowledge of N.K.V.D. recruitment. The moment Paslett doubted me, I was finished. What I said next had to be the finest lie of a life already veined and ribbed with lies, falsehoods, and prevarication.

"Sir, I saw my opportunity and I took it. I was still serving out my spec, and we knew the Russians had made me when I posed as a Red during the last operation. I was sick to death I might never get another chance to do clandestine work again. So when they approached me, I thought I might plant a seed with them that I could be turned. And it worked, sir, that's why they sent Captain Quincy after me, not knowing she's an American agent. She was their bird dog."

"So you let Quincy think you'd turned even before we put together our operation to send you to New Mexico?"

"Yessir. And I didn't brief you because I wasn't supposed to be doing anything but taking calls on the nutter line til my spec was up. But I couldn't let a chance to front the N.K.V.D. as a turncoat pass us by."

"Jesus Christ, Voigt, how long do you think your leash is?" Paslett started. I bowed my head, the dutiful penitent, and happily took the brunt of the upbraiding that followed. The commander's anger meant he believed me. For Paslett, the ends justified the means—it was the same for all intelligence officers, whomever they served. The dressing-down was just to remind me who was in charge. Rank and office allowed him to keep me in the dark—not telling me that Quincy was an O.S.S. agent all this time!—but as his subordinate I didn't have that privilege.

"I'll never do it again, sir," I promised when he'd finished, seizing the opportunity to change the subject. "What did General Wilburton mean we're going to merge operations?"

Paslett sighed. "It's O.S.S.'s bid to keep Truman from axing them. The scientist you nailed in New Mexico, Brode? Wilburton is convinced Brode's father's the one who tumbled the Russians onto his son."

"Senator Brode's a Red, too?"

"They think so, but they haven't turned up anything on the old man yet. As soon as they found out Mason Adams Brode was the spy trying to give the bomb to the Russians, they went nuts. Lit up Groves's line, mine too. 'Merge, merge, we gotta merge,' they can't stop saying."

"What do you think, sir?"

"What choice do we have? It can't just be coincidence that a senator being secretly investigated for being a commie has a son who is a Red agent." He leaned across the table. "But here's the deal, Voigt—O.S.S. is finished, no matter what. They won't let go of this operation, but it's not going to save them, either, and you can take that to the bank." Translation: *We would work with O.S.S. so that we could take over the operation once Truman liquidated the O.S.S.* A brilliant move if we could pull it off—such a mission properly belonged to the F.B.I., but if O.N.I. could ice out the Bureau, we'd start the postwar era as shiny as a newly minted penny. And keeping the Bureau at bay was good for me, for sure.

"So Captain Quincy and I will stay undercover, then, posing as Reds, to see if we can find the Russian connection to Senator Brode?" I asked.

"Absolutely, and we need to set our terms pronto so O.S.S. doesn't shoehorn us out." He checked his watch. "I'm meeting with the director in ten minutes to do exactly that. Come to my office at sixteen-hundred and we'll get started."

"Yessir!"

I LEFT THE CONFERENCE ROOM FEELING BEWILDERED, CONFLICTED, AND scared. I'd told the Russians I was out because of the heat from the Bureau—now I had to persuade them I'd overreacted. Yet the Bureau really was after me. Paslett had bought my story about why I'd withheld so many details about my undercover work, but what about Captain Gail Quincy? Did she believe I was just posing as a Red, or did she have her own doubts? How would I string her along? How would we work together? To my shame, the thought our operational partnership might require us to "pose" as lovers aroused me. But would the Russians buy us as lovers or think something was amiss?

Gail was seated at my desk when I entered my office. Terrance hadn't returned—my note was still out.

"Quite a mess," she said, gesturing at the stacks of papers and folders.

"My partner's. I've been away, as you might recall."

She smiled faintly. "Quite a game they played on us, no?"

"Who are we to complain?"

"Our duty is just to follow orders?"

I sat down at Terrance's desk, facing her, and lit a cigarette. She out-ranked me, I should have been *sir*-ing or *ma'am*-ing her, but the two of us, we were way past the protocol of rank.

"More like play our part," I answered.

"Parts." She drew out the *s*.

"And you, you've earned an Oscar in my book. Mara, Elizabeth, Gail."

"You're a pretty good trouper yourself, Ellis."

"Are you always play-acting?"

"Are you asking if I faked my passion, Ellis?"

That wasn't my intention, but the directness of her challenge flustered me. "No, that's not—I'm not—"

She laughed and waved her hand. "Easy, kiddo, I was just joking."

Jesus, she was good—she'd effortlessly taken control of our back-and-forth.

"Why are you here?" I finally asked. Sitting in my chair, that was an obvious signal. *I know you, Voigt, inside out.* But what else did she want? Did she suspect me? How could I find out without tipping her off?

"Thought we might get a drink. I really do like highballs, and you look like you could use a Gibson."

"Little early, isn't it?"

She laughed again and took out the same gold cigarette case she'd been carrying the night I met her. She withdrew a cigarette, set it between her lips, and leaned across for me to light it. My match hissed, the flame shone on her lipstick. I looked straight at her as she inhaled, the tobacco crackling. Her eyes gave me nothing. She stood, exhaled smoke.

"It's never too early in my book."

I sank back into Terrance's chair and studied her, trying not to linger on her figure, trying not to remember her "passion" during the times we'd been together. Tried not to think about what might happen if I said yes to that drink. Tried not to think about how hard it would be to hide who I really was while running a risky undercover operation with her. And I tried, with all my power, to say no.

I failed.

"I know a quiet place this side of the Mall," I said.

She smiled. "Let's go."

ACKNOWLEDGMENTS

'M ETERNALLY GRATEFUL TO MY FAMILY FOR THEIR SUPPORT. MY WIFE, Amy, is first reader and dedicated listener—to give just one example of a thousand, her suggestions fixed a story line that had vexed me for months. The novel is much the better because of her help, her love, her inspiration. My parents, John and Dee, faithfully read drafts, and my sister Katie and her family made a long trip to cheer me on at a bookstore appearance in Milwaukee. I'm blessed to belong to a family of book lovers.

Lincoln Arbogast and Mike Zimmerman helped me plot a realistic gunshot wound (any medical errors are mine alone), and Matthew Gilmore, D.C. historian extraordinaire, assisted with historical facts about Washington. I always enjoy my conversations about writing with Edward Scholz. My agent William Callahan at Inkwell Management read the manuscript in record time; I'm deeply appreciative of his efforts to bring

ACKNOWLEDGMENTS

my fiction to the published page. It's a pleasure to work with Claiborne Hancock and his incredible team at Pegasus, especially Bowen Dunnan, whose editorial suggestions much improved the story.

I'm fortunate to be part of a wonderful community of writers in the Midwest Chapter of the Mystery Writers of America. I especially appreciate the support of Lori Rader-Day, Shaun Harris, Lili Wright, and Heather Ash.

I wrote much of *Rip the Angels from Heaven* while promoting the first novel in this series, *The Dead Don't Bleed*, and I want to heartily thank family and friends who came out to my public appearances and who encouraged me to keep working on *Rip the Angels*: in Minneapolis, the Ryan family (Dr. Agaloff will return!); in Chicago, Dorota and Zbigniew Kruczalak, Dawn Flood, Brian Sandberg, Heather Ahrenholz, Barbara Mirecki, and Paula and Stuart Barb; in Milwaukee, Eric Pullin, Tom and Pam Krugler, Bill and Christie Krugler, Jeff Krugler, Andy Krugler, Scott Lawson, Jeff Harrington, and Joe Adamak; in Washington, D.C., Don Litteau, Eric Christensen, Hannah Yoo, and Essie and Jamey Wagner; in East Lansing, Judith Rowell, Dan DeVaney, and Sara DeVaney; and in Platteville, Laurie Hamer, Kory Wein, Roy Shaver, George Smith, Mike Ira, Tracey Roberts, Winnie Redfearn, my colleagues in the History Department at the University of Wisconsin-Platteville, and Heidi Dyas-McBeth and Bill McBeth and everyone at the Driftless Market.